CANNON HILL

CANNON HILL

by Mary Deasy

An Atlantic Monthly Press Book

Little, Brown and Company · Boston

1949

Published June 1949

ATLANTIC—LITTLE, BROWN BOOKS
ARE PUBLISHED BY
LITTLE, BROWN AND COMPANY
IN ASSOCIATION WITH
THE ATLANTIC MONTHLY PRESS

*Published simultaneously
in Canada by McClelland and Stewart Limited*

PRINTED IN THE UNITED STATES OF AMERICA

To
Clara Woelfel Deasy

CANNON HILL

Chapter 1

IN THE YEARS JUST FOLLOWING THE CIVIL WAR, before Bard City had reached up to the hills above the river, people used to drive out for a Sunday excursion to a roadhouse or inn called the Cannon House, which stood seven miles away from the center of the city on Old Town Road, and had hitching posts fashioned of iron dolphins, and a garden with tables, and a little brass cannon standing in the front yard. It had been built by an Englishman named William Beauchamp, who had come west from New York to the valley of the Ohio shortly before the war, and bought up a good deal of the land on which the suburb of Cannon Hill was later to stand. William Beauchamp had been in the British Navy as a young man, and he claimed that he had served at Trafalgar and seen Lord Nelson die; but he was not quite old enough for that. It made a good story, though, for lazy summer afternoons, when babies were sprawling asleep on the grass, and small boys in Sunday jackets and knee pants stood listening open-mouthed to his tales of the *Victory* and the *Téméraire*. He grew to be something of a figure in the town.

If he had lived long enough, he might have become a rich man when the railroad came through to cross Old Town Road only a few hundred yards away from the Cannon House, and a pair of tool factories settled down across from it, and the fields and woods to the east were gradually transformed into the streets of modest brick and frame houses, the square with its little park, and the local business district of the suburb of Cannon Hill. But he was dead long before the value of his property began to rise, and his son Richard sold most of it to the first speculator who came along with an offer, so that he did not make a tenth of the money on it either that he could have made if he had waited a few years and handled the business with a little care. Later Richard Beauchamp went into politics, and spent what money he had received from his father's property on trying to get himself elected to Congress. He was a well-educated man, for William Beauchamp had sent him to Harvard to study law, but he had more good nature than good sense, and besides he belonged to the wrong party, so he never succeeded in getting elected to Congress. But he did hold a number of minor political posts, including one in the State Treasurer's office. Unfortunately there was a financial scandal in that office while he was there, and, though he was never involved in it directly, it put an end to his political career.

By that time, in the middle nineties, the Cannon House had long since stopped doing business as the jolly roadhouse of the sixties and seventies. For a while it had been leased to a pair of sisters, who had turned it into an academy for young ladies; but they had taken fright when the factories had begun to appear across the road, and had closed the school and gone away. Then an Irish couple, John and Maud Sorley, had opened it as a boardinghouse, chiefly for the men who worked in the factories opposite, but that venture had not been very successful either, and Sorley had simply disappeared one night, leaving his wife with their two small sons and their unpaid bills.

That was just after the scandal in the State Treasurer's office, when Richard Beauchamp's fortunes were at their lowest ebb. The Cannon House was the only piece of property he had left then of all that his father had once owned, and he would have sold that too, and lived very contentedly for a few years on what it brought him, if it had not been for his daughter Rhoda, who had common sense enough to ask herself what they would live on after that. She persuaded him that they should take over the management of the Cannon House themselves. With her to look after things, and a woman to do the heavy work and the cooking, she thought they would at least be able to manage well enough to keep a roof over their heads.

Rhoda Beauchamp was thirty-one when she and her father came to live at the Cannon House—a tall, handsome young woman, with her grandfather's piercing blue eyes and a vital, rather masculine nature. She had twice the energy and determination of her father. When she was seventeen she had been engaged to marry a man named Lefroy, a construction engineer, but on one of his trips west he had suddenly married a California girl and settled down out there. The marriage was not happy, and every now and then she received a sentimental letter from him. The letters kept alive a kind of irritated emotion in her. She had the sort of feeling for him that a woman has for a man who she knows is not worth her thinking of him, but with whom she has once been deeply in love. If he had come to see her she would have been jolly and indifferent with him, but she kept all his letters, even the maudlin ones which he wrote her after his marriage and which she had never answered.

It was hard for her to make a paying proposition of the Cannon House. Richard Beauchamp had shot his bolt; he spent most of his time, when he was not sitting in the little park in Cannon Square, or playing cards with his cronies, in plans to circulate a petition to have the name of the suburb of Cannon Hill changed to Beauchamp, in honor of his father. He was a nice little round man, rosy-cheeked and gray-haired, with an innocent, almost childishly enthusiastic nature. All his life people had been taking advantage of him, and they did it even now, when he had so little to give away. And his son Virgil was a great deal like him, so that it was always Rhoda who had to take him to task. The only thing that saved their relationship was their mutual sense of humor. Rhoda had her dead mother's sharp, Irish, magnificently tolerant relish of absurdity. If she could laugh at a situation or a person, her resentment against them disappeared.

She was very fond of her father; she treated him with an indulgence that had something almost maternal about it. Only when he had let himself be cheated, transparently and openly, by his own generosity or by a scheme that a child could have seen through, was she really angry with him. Then there was no mercy in her tongue. She was always sorry afterwards that she had given way to her temper, when she saw how crushed and miserable he was, but she could not help herself.

At the time that they came to live at the Cannon House she was still a young woman, and in spite of the failure of her own hopes and her father's ambitions, she still believed it was possible for them to make something of the future. But as the years went by, she began to realize that there was nothing better to look forward to, and the hot, restless temper gradually died down a little in her. She read a good deal, sitting in the big bare front parlor with her feet propped up on the fender, stopped worrying about the state of the house, and took the days as they came. It was a rather pleasant life, after all. When her brother Virgil's wife Mattie came to visit, she saw her looking disapprovingly at the beautiful marred broad-boarded floors, which had not been "done" since the days of the school for young ladies, and at the stained, old-fashioned wallpaper with its half-obliterated hunting scenes or dim greenish patterns of lilies and wheat sheaves; but she did not let it disturb her. She listened with an ironic tranquillity when Mattie dropped hints about how she might improve the appearance of the house.

"There's no use in my bothering with things like that," she would say to her, frankly. "The men don't care about it, and Father doesn't notice, and I can't see that it's worth such a fuss."

Mattie's own house on Sherman Street was full of cut glass, crocheted lace, and feathery Spanish grass in blue-and-gilt vases. It upset her to the depths of her orderly German soul to see anyone keep house less meticulously than she had been taught to do; it was a major issue with her. She gradually stopped coming out to the Cannon House; when she felt that she ought to see her father-in-law and Rhoda, she invited them to her own home. There she could sit in the midst of her own immaculate belongings and read her sister-in-law a silent lecture on her shortcomings as a housekeeper.

Rhoda was content enough with this arrangement. She and Virgil had been closer than most brothers and sisters when they were children, but since his marriage he had been so swallowed up by his wife and her relatives that she felt he had stopped belonging to her. And he was not of much more use to her than her father when it came to practical affairs. His father-in-law, Justus Kroener, who owned a surgical appliance store in the city, had helped him go into business and open a shoe store in Cannon Square when he married, but it was his personal popularity, rather than any business ability he possessed, that had kept the store going profitably since that time. He was a good deal like what Richard Beauchamp had been when he was younger, enthusiastic and sociable and rather naïve, the

wheelhorse on every local committee, and the favorite guest in every
home, since he was pleased with everything and could make any
gathering a success.

Richard Beauchamp had taken the idea into his head at last that
the only reason the Bard City Council would not act on his petition
to have the name of Cannon Hill changed to Beauchamp was that
they were afraid people would not know how to pronounce the new
name. One August afternoon in 1906, the hottest day of the summer,
he went downtown without saying anything to Rhoda and began to
make a speech on the steps of the City Hall. The people going in and
out of the building stopped to stare and laugh at the old man rambling on confusedly about his father, the sailor-pioneer, and about
his willingness to have the name of the suburb of Beauchamp spelled
Beecham. Finally someone who knew him came along, brought him
inside the building, and telephoned Rhoda. The old man was excited but docile; he had the idea that he had been called in to continue his speech before the City Council. When Rhoda arrived, he
told her about it happily.

"What do you think, ducky?" he asked her. "It's all turned out
just the way I always told you it would. People do the right thing
if you'll only give them time."

She got him home and called Dr. Greaves, but before the doctor
arrived her father had had a stroke, and early the following morning he died. She could not really believe that he was dead. She kept
remembering him as he had been on that last afternoon, calling her
"ducky," a name that he had had for her when she was small, and
saying to her, with that happy, faithful belief in human nature:
"People do the right thing if you'll only give them time." It was the
worst time of her life for her, worse even than the time when Lefroy
had thrown her over. She had been young then, and she had had
faith in life. Now she felt that she had nothing to look forward to.

One warm afternoon in early September, several weeks after her
father's death, Mattie Beauchamp came to see her. Ever since the
funeral, she and Virgil had been trying to persuade her to sell the
Cannon House and come to live with them. Mattie did not really
want her sister-in-law in her home, but she thought it was the right
thing to do, to have her, and she came from a sternly religious Ger-

man family who believed in being as unbending in their demands on themselves as they were in their demands on others. She was a woman who might have been called gentle-looking if she had not shut herself so rigidly behind the wall of her own moral judgments; she had a long, sallow face and large dark-brown eyes.

She sat in the parlor on that September afternoon, trying to bring Rhoda to a decision about the house.

"It's not the right kind of life for you, that's the whole song of it," she said, "living here alone in this old house with a flock of men. I was talking to Papa about it the other day. He thinks just as Virgil and I do—"

Rhoda smiled. She had a lovely, cruel, penetrant smile that lit up her whole face with serene intelligence.

"Oh, Virgil doesn't think," she said. "Somebody steers him, and he *sails*."

She felt that she ought to be grateful to her sister-in-law, but she disliked being made the object of a sense of duty, and, besides, she did not want to give up her independence by going to live in Mattie's house. She was rather weary of the whole subject; she wanted to be left alone, to decide for herself what she would do. But Mattie was incapable of surrendering any idea that she had clinched in her mind as right.

"And *that's* a nice thing to say," she remarked. "I don't understand you, Rhoda—everybody only thinking of your good, and you making a mock of it, as if we were all against you."

Rhoda shrugged up her shoulders. There was always this battle between her and Mattie. They were so much unlike that there was hardly any subject on which they could agree.

"And you know what people will say," Mattie continued. "They'll say we wouldn't have you, that you *have* to stay on here to keep a roof over your head and a stitch to your back."

"Well, then, let them say it," Rhoda said, with an obstinate laugh. "My mother used to tell me, 'If they're talking about me, at least they're not saying worse about somebody else.' You might remember that, Mattie."

She did not want to leave the Cannon House; it was the one place in the world that she loved. Still she did not feel sure that she could keep it up alone. And there was really nothing for her there. The men who lived in the house were like so many shadows flitting across her consciousness. She tolerated them, or laughed at them, or despised them. They were all a little afraid of her.

After Mattie had gone that afternoon, she still sat in the parlor, thinking about what she would do. The mood of depression that she had been in ever since her father's death returned again. She was forty-one years old, and for the first time she felt that her life was without direction. There was no one depending on her; she was alone. And she needed someone to work for, to plan for. The late summer sun beating heavily in through the bare windows seemed to weigh on her like a burden of emptiness. There was so much energy and determination in her. She wanted to make use of it.

After a time she went back to the kitchen, where Maud Sorley was going about, beginning preparations for dinner. When her husband had left her, she had gone with her two boys to live with her sister, and had supported herself ever since by working out by the day. Now for several years she had been working for Rhoda at the Cannon House. She was a small, plump, prominent-eyed Irish-woman, with something prim and disapproving in her appearance, as if she were a governess out of an English comedy; but the re-semblance faded as soon as she spoke. She could swear like a man in her shrill, richly accented voice, and she could work like a man, and she had a man's ideas about keeping house. Since she had come back to the Cannon House the curtains had disappeared from the windows and the carpets from the floors, but the house was clean and comfortable, and the meals plain and satisfying and delicious.

She looked up as Rhoda came into the kitchen.

"Has she talked you into it, then?" she asked directly. She did not miss much of what was going on in the house.

Rhoda shook her head indecisively. She went over and stood before the screen door, looking out past the paved kitchen yard, which was roofed over by the second-story porch that ran across the back of the house, to the garden beyond. She could remember herself, when she was a child, sitting in that garden, listening to her grand-father's stories about the sea. Even then it had been a favorite place with her; she loved the high white latticework walls that surrounded it, and the fruit trees that her grandfather had planted. And now, when the latticework was tumbling down, and the whole garden was overgrown with neglect, it was still the place where she could feel, inside the middle-aged, rather domineering woman that she was today, the little girl of thirty-five years before, happy and petted, in her curls and locket and sprigged muslin dress.

"Wisha," Mrs. Sorley was saying downrightly, "I should think you'd be glad enough to get out of this, now. It's a hard old life you have here, and your brother has enough for both. You wouldn't need to ask me twice, if I was standing in your shoes."

It irritated Rhoda, the blunt acceptance of hard fact that was in her words. She could not bear to stay and talk to her. And all this insistence upon the practical aspects of the matter seemed merely to crystallize the determination in her not to give up the house. There was so little else remaining to her that she cared about. She left the kitchen abruptly and went out to the front of the house again.

As she walked through the hall, the front doorbell rang. She went to answer it, rather impatient; she did not want to see anyone else that afternoon. On the doorstep there was standing a tall, powerfully built man of somewhere near thirty, dressed in a working-man's dark serge Sunday best, and a child, a girl, of seven.

"Is this Mrs. Beauchamp's?" he asked her. She noticed the voice, which had a peculiar reserved civility about it, in spite of the roughness of the accent.

"I'm Miss Beauchamp," she said. "There's no Mrs. Beauchamp here. Did you want to see me?"

He hesitated. "They told me at the factory across there that I might get a room here," he said, after a moment.

Rhoda looked again at the child standing beside him. She was a little perplexed about their relationship.

"Is this your little girl?" she asked him.

"Yes, it is."

"Oh, I'm sorry then," she said decisively. "I never take any but single men."

She could see the drop to disappointment in him, though the civil expression on his face did not change.

"Maybe you'd be able to tell me if there's somewhere else I could try then," he said to her. "I'm new in this place."

Rhoda thought for a little.

"There's Mrs. Mullins," she said finally. "She might have some room now. But she's half a mile away, at the other end of Cannon Hill." She looked down at the child, whose face was smudged with dirt, and pale beneath it with heat and fatigue. "You can bring the little girl inside while I telephone Mrs. Mullins and find out," she said. "She might like to have a glass of cold milk."

She held the door open, and the two followed her silently into the big cool parlor. She went back into the kitchen for a glass of milk, and when she came back again they were still standing in the center of the room.

"Sit down, sit down," she said, looking at the little girl.

She spoke brusquely; she had never learned how to talk to children; she treated them as if they were rather stupid adults. They were usually afraid of her. But this child looked at her with a certain self-composure, a reserve that was like her father's. There was a feeling of something kept back in both of them.

"What is your name?" Rhoda asked her, as she gave her the glass.

The child did not answer. She looked at her rather hostilely.

"Her name is Bronwen," the man said.

Rhoda looked at him. "That's an odd name," she said. "Is it Welsh?"

"Yes, it is."

He did not say any more. Rhoda went out into the hall to telephone. While she was talking to Mrs. Mullins she was aware of the perfect silence in the parlor. There was something about these people, she thought. The man looked as if he were in the grip of some fixed, painful idea. There was an air of terrific, obstinate power about him, and not only in a physical sense. He had the kind of shoulders that are never seen except in a man who has done the heaviest kind of manual work from the time he was a boy. She thought that he might have been a farm worker, or a construction laborer, but he was too pale to have been working in the open air. His head was interesting, well-shaped and bony beneath his dark cropped hair, with heavy, classically cut features: a true Celtic head. She went back into the living room. Mrs. Mullins had a room vacant, but she too had said that she would not consider taking a child. The man listened in silence as Rhoda told him.

"Then we'll have to look farther," he said, as she finished. She felt again the obstinate determination in his voice. "Thank you for your trouble."

"Isn't there someone you know here in town—?" she asked.

"We've just come in this morning."

She shook her head, rather angrily.

"You shouldn't have brought the child here if you had no place to take her," she told him.

She said that they could stay in the house temporarily, until he could make some better arrangement about the child. He had a letter of reference from his former employer; from it she learned that his name was Robert Brand, and that he was a coal miner, from a little mining town in the eastern part of the state. She looked at him in surprise.

"What are you going to do here?" she asked him.

He said he had already gotten a job in the Maitland tool factory across the road; that was how he had spent the earlier part of the day. She wondered where he had left the child while he had gone looking for work. He did not seem used to looking after her; there was no great air of intimacy between them. The little girl did not resemble him except for the eyes, which were dark blue like his, and very large in her face.

Rhoda called Maud Sorley and had her take the two upstairs. She was a little vexed over the whole incident; she did not know what she would do with a child in the house, even for a short time. When the man came downstairs again she called him into the parlor to suggest other places where he might look for rooms.

"I'll go right around," he said to her.

She knew he saw her unwillingness to have them in her house, and she felt a little ashamed of her own attitude.

"Couldn't you have left the little girl wherever it was she was staying, at least until you had a place to bring her here?" she asked brusquely, as if to defend herself.

He was silent for a moment.

"Her mother's just dead," he said after a little, bluntly. "I'm a bit unhandy about seeing after her yet."

"Oh," said Rhoda. She got up and began to walk about the room.

She was sentimental enough, under her cool, discerning manner, to relate her own recent loss to his. Without really wanting to, she told him about her father. He listened to her silently.

"Yes," he said, as she finished. "It's a hard thing."

After he had gone out again she was angry with herself for having spoken to him like that. She was not used to taking any of the men who lived in the house into her confidence. And he had not been responsive; she felt that there was something antagonistic behind that civil manner of his.

When he returned, he told her that one of the places to which she had sent him would have a room for him in a week or ten days. The woman had four children of her own, and had no objection to looking after another. Rhoda knew what sort the family was, and again she felt a little guilty about sending the child there. There was a certain refinement, a moody emotionalism about her that appealed to Rhoda. She liked the uncommon in children. Her brother Virgil's son, Sam, seemed such a quiet, ordinary boy that she had never been very much interested in him.

She gave Bronwen her dinner in the kitchen that evening, while Mrs. Sorley was setting the table in the dining room for the men. The child was not used to strange places and people, and she was so upset by the excitement of the day that she could hardly eat. Rhoda had no idea how to cope with the situation. She went into the dining room and said to Mrs. Sorley: "She'll be sick if she doesn't eat more than that."

"Oh Jay," Mrs. Sorley said, "it takes more than a missed meal to daunt them at that age. She'll make up for it in the morning."

She had her experience with her own two sons behind her, and Rhoda, who had always been rather impatient of her, felt with a somewhat humbled sense of reassurance that she could rely on her.

She went back into the kitchen again. The child had slid down from her chair at the table and was standing before the screen door, looking out at the garden. The sun was just setting, and the long

shadows of the pear and apple trees, and of the crooked grape arbor
with its broad leaves and globular fruit, were flung tangled and in-
tricate across the grass. The scents of the early autumn evening—
the winy scent of the ripening, sun-warmed fruit, and the cooler
smell of the coming darkness—were in the air. Rhoda saw the way
the child was absorbing what lay before her, the attention, perfectly
unconscious, almost rapt, with which she brooded over it. She was
so intent that she had not even heard Rhoda come back into the
room.

Rhoda went up behind her and put her hand on her shoulder.

"Do you like it?" she asked.

The child started at her touch, and looked around. She seemed to
withdraw into herself when anyone approached her.

"Yes," she said, bringing the word out almost reluctantly.

Rhoda felt helpless to reach her. She let Mrs. Sorley take her upstairs and put her to bed.

Robert Brand went to work the next day at the factory across the
road, and in the evening, as soon as dinner was over, he disappeared
from the house and did not come back till after ten. Rhoda had
only a few minutes' conversation with him, when they talked about
enrolling Bronwen in the Cannon Hill public school. The term was
just beginning, and she promised to have Mrs. Sorley take the child
around to the school the following day.

"I don't like putting you to so much trouble," he said. He seemed
unsure of himself with her, rather ungracious behind his polite, distant manner.

She looked at him irritably. "*Someone* has to see that it's done,"
she said.

The next morning, when Mrs. Sorley had gone to take Bronwen
to school and do the marketing, she was straightening up in the
rooms upstairs. In Brand's room she was surprised to see three or
four new books lying on the table. She looked curiously at the title
of the uppermost one: it was a beginner's textbook of algebra. Beneath were an elementary French grammar and a student's copy
of *The Merchant of Venice*. She stood there looking at them in
astonishment.

She made a point of seeing him that evening when he came back from work. The weather had clouded during the day, and it had begun to rain shortly before the factory whistles blew for closing. The men came in with their clothes smelling strongly from the damp. She called Brand into the parlor. He stood in the doorway, looking at her.

"Come in," she said impatiently. "I want to talk to you."

"You'd better wait till I've changed," he said, rather sulkily.

"I don't care how you look," she said, still more impatiently. *"Goodness!"* He came into the room, but did not sit down. "What are you going to do with those books in your room?" she asked him, point-blank.

He stared at her.

"I don't think that's your business," he said at last.

"Of course it isn't my business. But I want to know. I haven't wasted time being tactful about it; that's the only thing. I suppose you'd like it better if I had?"

He looked at her for a moment angrily, the dark color coming up in his face. Then his face closed again behind his reserve.

"Well, there's no secret about it," he said. "I'm starting at the free night school down on Walnut Street."

"Why?"

The quickness with which she pounced on him with her question put him off his guard a little.

"Well, you're a curious woman!" he exclaimed, surprised.

"I'm not only curious, I'm interested. I've been living in this house for ten years now, and in all that time I haven't had a man come into it who cared to trouble his head with anything deeper than the day's newspaper. I should think I *am* curious." She sat there looking straight up at him. "Well, are you going to tell me or aren't you?" she asked. "If you're not, you may as well say so, and be done with it; then we won't waste each other's time over it."

He looked at her rather defiantly, meeting her eyes directly.

"If you're so keen on knowing, it's a pity not to tell you," he said, with a slight irony that matched her own. "I'm going to study to be a doctor, and that's why I've got to go through the high school first."

She stared at him, controlling her astonishment, and knitting her brows slightly. She had a sudden sense of the importance of her not taking his announcement with too much show of surprise.

"A doctor," she said slowly. She nodded her head. "Well, you've cut out a piece of work for yourself, haven't you?"

"I have."

"How long has it been since you've been in a school?"

"Something like fifteen years," he said grudgingly.

"And you've worked in the mines during all that time?"

"Yes. I went down when I was thirteen." He gazed at her with a heavy look of challenge on his face. "You might as well come straight out and tell me you think I'm a fool," he said.

"I might," she agreed. She looked up at him with the same sharp composure. "Only it wouldn't be telling the truth. I *don't* think you're a fool. I think you've let yourself in for a terrible job, and I think you may get through with it and you may not; but I don't think any man is a fool who wants something and *does* something about getting it, instead of sitting back and complaining because he can't have it."

He stood there frowning at her, not quite certain of her sincerity. In return she looked at him, trying to imagine what it was that he reminded her of now, with his massively built, muscular body and heavy, classically cut features that might have been copied from some ancient coin. He would do for a Roman centurion, she thought; he would do for a miner; but he didn't look at all as if he would do for a doctor. His hands were as black and roughened from the coal he had dug as those of the other men in the house were from the grease of the factories where they worked. Still there was something about him. She believed in him, half against her will.

He seemed angry and a little embarrassed over their conversation. When Mrs. Sorley came to the door to ask Rhoda something about the dinner, he left the room and went upstairs. He came down a little later for dinner, and immediately after it was over went out again—to the school, Rhoda supposed. When he came back, shortly after ten, she was sitting in the parlor. She called him in again.

"Now listen to me," she said. She had gotten up and was standing in front of the mantel. It was still raining outside; the house was rather cold. "If you're really going through with this," she said, looking at him in her direct way, "you'll need help. I don't care what kind of mind you have; you can't have been fifteen years away from learning things out of books without having a hard time going back to it. I may be an interfering woman, but I'm not a stupid one. I can help you, and I will, if you like."

They stood there looking at each other across the room. She was right; even in the few hours that he had spent in the classroom he had had enough to realize the truth of what she said. Under his determination he was bewildered, almost panic-stricken, by the quickness with which the other students, all years younger than he, seemed to assimilate the lesson. But he did not know how to respond to her offer to help him. He looked across at her with a kind of angry uncertainty.

"Why should you help me?" he said at last. "I haven't asked you."

"I've asked *you*," she said. "Goodness, man, don't be such a baby! I wouldn't stand on pride if I were in your place. Or don't you think I know enough to give you your lessons?"

She came across the room, pulled the French grammar from his hand, and began to read rapidly the exercises at the end of the first lesson.

"Well?" she said when she had finished, looking up at him.

She walked across the room, carrying the book with her, to her father's big old-fashioned oak desk, which stood in one corner of the room. Brand did not follow her.

"Bring a chair," she said, without looking round at him.

He brought over a chair and sat down beside her. He was stiff and embarrassed and a little resentful. They were both quick-tempered—not a very auspicious augury for a pupil-teacher relationship. But he had learned to control his anger, and she forgot hers as soon as she had given way to it. She tried to be patient with him. She was cold with the fear at first that he would be stupid, and that *she* would be the one who was making a fool of herself; but he was not stupid, only slow, as she had said, at learning things out of books again. And he was intensely serious about it all.

They worked together over the lessons for an hour. Then he went upstairs to his room, while she stayed down and fixed herself a cup

of tea. As she sat drinking it in the parlor, with her feet propped up
in their old place on the fender, she laughed to herself, remembering
the way she had talked to him. She loved to be doing something, to
be managing and accomplishing. She was happier than she had been
since her father had died.

Chapter 2

AFTER THAT FIRST NIGHT IT WAS TACITLY understood between them that she was to go over the lessons with him when he came from the night school. She had had only the kind of half-useless education that had been given to young girls in the eighties, but she knew French rather well—she had gone to a school where the pupils had been required to speak it during certain hours of every day—and she had read a good deal during the past ten years. In mathematics she was not of much help to him; within a few weeks he knew as much as she.

They got along together much better than she had expected. He was really grateful to her for helping him, though he did not know how to speak about it to her. The second day they worked together, he asked her if there was anything he could do for her around the house.

"Goodness, no!" she said. "You're going to have your hands full enough, I should think, without looking for more work to do."

But he did not want to accept favors without a return. He went to Mrs. Sorley, who was ready enough to tell him about a screen door that needed mending, or a broken board in the cellar steps. He spent his Sunday on them, in spite of Rhoda's protests.

There was no more talk of his going somewhere else to live. Rhoda's determination not to sell the house was fixed in her now, and that Sunday she told him, as he was out in the kitchen yard repairing the back screen door, that she had changed her mind, and that he and Bronwen could stay on if they liked.

"It may not be the best place in the world to raise a child," she said, "but at least it will be better than throwing her into that nest of young Crumminses. There's never a clean stitch on any of them, and a new baby coming every year like clockwork, so she'd be doing nothing but drudging with the smaller ones in a couple of years."

He kept on working as they talked; when he had something to do with his hands he was more at his ease with her, less self-conscious and watchful. She liked to see him work; he had a way of handling his muscular bulk with a certain dexterity, a serious, almost disdainful ease. He was putting a new section of screen into the door, and did not look up at her as he said: "That's true enough. But what about the trouble she'll make for you?"

"She makes as remarkably little trouble as any child I've ever seen," Rhoda said. "Look at her now."

He turned around and glanced back toward the end of the garden, where Bronwen was sitting on her heels, watching Queenie, Rhoda's beagle bitch, and her new litter of puppies, lying in the sun outside the little tumble-down summerhouse. It was a warm afternoon, and perfectly still. After the rain of a few days before the leaves had begun to fall; they dropped slowly through the motionless air. The bees were thick around the fallen fruit that lay on the ground beneath the trees.

"Yes, it's a fine place for her," Brand said after a moment. He went back to his work again. "But I wouldn't have you keeping her if it makes too much trouble."

Rhoda was always surprised by the way in which he spoke about the child, rather indifferently, with only a kind of conscientious interest. It did not seem like him to be lukewarm in his personal relationships, any more than it was like him to be lukewarm about anything else that affected him. She was curious about his past life —what his relations with his family had been, what it was that had made him take this idea of being a doctor.

But it was not till weeks later that she learned anything of that. He had the Celtic reticence about his personal life; he seldom talked about himself. When she asked him questions about the mines, he answered them, but he did not go on to tell her what his own life had been like when he had worked in them.

One evening, when he came from the night school, Rhoda told him that Bronwen was ill; she had caught cold coming home from school in the rain the afternoon before, and now she was running a temperature, and had a rather bad cough. He went upstairs to see her, and when he came down again Rhoda was surprised at how upset he seemed. He sat down to his French lesson, but he could not concentrate on it; after a little he pushed the book away and shook his head.

"I'll be no good tonight," he said. "I'm worried about the way she is."

"Why," Rhoda said, "Dr. Greaves says it's nothing serious."

He looked over at her with a flash of anger that startled her.

"Yes, I've heard that before," he said.

He went upstairs again to Bronwen's room and sat with her most of the night. Rhoda heard him go downstairs once to the kitchen, and the rattle of pans as he warmed something for her on the stove. She was a little vexed with him; she was never really ill herself, and like most healthy people she found it hard to believe that everyone else was not just like her. If she had thought that Bronwen's illness was serious, she would have stayed with her herself during the night. Toward dawn she got up, put on her dressing gown, and went in to tell Brand rather crossly to go and get a little sleep while she sat with Bronwen. With her tall figure and her thick, graying chestnut hair in heavy braids, she looked in the faint dawn like some imperious Lady Macbeth.

In the morning Bronwen was better, and by the time Brand came from work in the evening she was sitting up in bed, eating oatmeal and milk. That night, when he came home from the school, he said something in an apologetic tone to Rhoda about the way he had been the night before.

"But I've lost two," he said. "It makes you go cold-worried sometimes for the one that's left."

"Two?" she said.

"My wife and my boy. And that began too," he said, with a sudden bitterness, "where the doctor said there was nothing to worry about."

She got most of the story from him that night. It was not the whole story, possibly because that went back too far and was too complicated for him to remember it himself, the way it usually is with the really important things that happen to people. And he might even have told it to her wrong, because he did not understand himself just what it was that had happened to him.

The way he told it was this: he had been married at twenty, and he was in love with his wife, who was one of those Irish girls one reads about, with blue eyes and red-bronze hair that reached to her knees. They were married for eight years, and they had two children, a girl and a boy, and if nothing had happened they would probably have gone on living in the little mining town, and being happy together, in spite of the thing that was inside Brand that made him want to get out of the mines. There had never seemed to be anything else for him to do but that work, and so he had done it: his father had been a miner too, a Welshman, who had come over to America shortly before Brand was born; and after he was crippled in a mine accident when Brand was thirteen, the son had had to go down to the pits to help out in the family. And then, just as things were getting easier at home, he met a girl and wanted to marry.

He told Rhoda that evening that it was only a few months ago, after his wife and son had both died of diphtheria—the two of them within three days of each other—that he had made up his mind to be a doctor. He was twenty-eight years old then, and he hadn't so much as been inside a high school, but that made no difference to him. Nothing made a difference. That was the great reason that Rhoda had for thinking he was telling it to her wrong. He was too sure of it. She thought he must have made up his mind a long time before that, before he had even met his wife; but then, after he had met her, he knew he could not do what he wanted with his life and marry her too, and what he wanted most at that time was to marry her. She thought that was the way it had happened because she knew that is the way things often do happen to a young man. He wants two things, and one of them is very far away and difficult, and the other is very near and easy. But when he has chosen the near one, it does not stop him from wanting the other too, and usually sooner or later he finds this out. Rhoda thought Brand found it out when his wife and son died, and that was the reason he was so sure of it, because it was what he had been wanting all along.

So he had made inquiries, and then had left his job at the mine to come to Bard City, where he could find the educational advantages that he needed. There was a sister with whom he might have left Bronwen, but she had her own family to think of, and Rhoda thought, though he did not say it, that he wanted the child where he could see for himself what was happening to her. She guessed as much as that he had cared so deeply for his wife that his feeling for his children had always been something secondary; it was that, probably, that was behind his ordinarily rather indifferent manner with Bronwen. But he could not bear the idea of losing her too; she was the only link that he had left between his old happiness and the present.

Rhoda watched him as he sat at the desk that night, writing out his French exercises, in shirt sleeves, his collar loosened and his sleeves rolled above his elbows: he always set about his studies as if he were going to do a piece of hard manual work. He wrote very slowly and seriously, like a child who is just learning to make his letters; it was one of the few things he did that made him look awkward. Rhoda thought of him sitting at the desks in the night school classrooms, which were made for the high school students who used them during the day. He would be much too big for them, and his powerful body would look cramped and ridiculous in its schoolboy's attitude. It made him seem simple and humble to think of him like that, but he was not a humble man, and even more he was not a simple man.

She knew that he did not get along well in his classes down there, in spite of the help she gave him. He had his own stubborn code about how much assistance he would take; he let her go over the lessons with him, explaining the French grammar and pronunciation, or helping him unravel the meaning of a passage from *Comus* or *The Merchant of Venice,* but he never brought his themes or exercises to her for correction; he did all of them alone. Only sometimes, when they had been handed back to him, with all his mistakes marked in red pencil, he took them to her for an explanation of some correction or other. Then he would sit there with the dark blood coming to his face, savage at his own incompetence, because he had not been able to find it out for himself.

He never went to any of his teachers to ask for explanations or help from them. One, the mathematics instructor, was several years younger than he, a pale, thin, serious young man just out of college, and Brand felt rather scornful of him, while at the same time it humiliated him to realize how far superior the other was to him in knowledge. In the French and the English literature classes the teachers were women, both elderly, who made him feel uncomfortable and clumsy, and whom he hated as if they were his enemies. His classmates were chiefly boys of eighteen or so, most of them ambitious young clerks with an eye out for future advancement. He made friends with only one of them, a slow young German who worked in a brewery, and who dropped out at the end of the first six weeks.

Rhoda had the feeling that things were going from bad to worse with him. The men had found out what he was doing, and there was a good deal of talk and laughing about it that went on among them. They could not understand what a grown man, who had had no more education than they had had themselves, was doing going to school like a boy half his age, and it made an outsider of him with them. Besides, he was putting away every penny he could against the time when he would have to be paying medical school fees, so he had neither the money nor the time to join them in any of their amusements. The only thing that kept them from making life miserable for him was the fact that they were afraid of him, of the great bunches of muscle they saw sloping down his arms from his shoulders, and the heavy cords of them going down his back, and knotted in front beneath his ribs. They did not want to get into any trouble with him, so they made most of their jokes about him when he was not around to hear them.

One evening in November, the night of the first snow of the season, he came back from the school in a savage mood. Instead of coming into the parlor, where Rhoda was sitting, as he usually did, he only muttered a "Good night" to her as he passed the door, and went straight on up to his room, treading heavily, with a kind of deliberate insolence, she thought, on the stairs. She sat there, rather angry, waiting for him to come down again; but the time passed and he did not appear.

She had half a mind to go upstairs and ask him for an explanation, but she was getting more and more offended every minute, and she knew that if she went up she would only quarrel with him. After a little she went out instead to the kitchen to make herself a cup of tea. His room was at the back of the house, directly above the kitchen, and as she waited for the kettle to boil she could hear him walking up and down above her. The house was quiet, with the particular soft quiet of a snowy night; everyone else had gone to bed, and all she could hear was those heavy footsteps, going back and forth, back and forth, above her.

She poured her tea and began to drink it. The walking still went on above; it began to be irritating to her. Then all at once she heard him fling up a window with so much force that the glass broke in one of the panes and came rattling down on the wooden floor of the second-story porch outside. She put her cup down in a temper, ran upstairs, and rapped at his door. He pulled it open, and they stood confronting each other. He was as furious as she.

"Now *what* is this?" she asked; she was a little afraid of him, but she would not let him see it. "Are you going to tear the house down with your bare hands?"

"Then you should have windows that'll open," he said, "so a man can get a breath of air when he wants it."

She looked at him in astonishment. The snow was blowing into the room, which was as cold as an ice-cellar already, but he was in his shirt sleeves, with a face as flushed as if he had been sitting before a fire. There were even drops of perspiration glistening on his forehead.

"Air?" she exclaimed. "Why, what's the matter with you? It's zero outside." She looked at him sharply. "Are you sick?" she asked.

He stared at her without answering. After a moment he said, in a thick, determined, furious voice: "I'm going to quit that school now."

"Oh, is that it?" She could feel all her blood coming up in her instantly; she felt as vengeful toward him as if he had cheated her of something of great value. But she kept her anger from showing; she spoke to him in a scornful tone. "Well, it's no more than I expected," she declared.

Her calmness seemed to inflame him even farther.

" 'It's no more than I expected,' " he repeated savagely. "Yes, and don't I know that—the lot of you, looking at me as if I was an ox trying to learn to read. I wonder if you'd be so quick at things yourselves if you'd spent fifteen years underground, with a pick haft in your hands."

"I wouldn't be so ready to give up something I'd set my mind on, I don't care if I'd spent fifteen years in the pit of hell," Rhoda declared. She made a contemptuous motion with her lips. "I suppose somebody's said something to wound your precious feelings. Well, if *they're* the greatest thing in the world to you, you can get your comfort out of them, for all I care about it."

She turned around and walked away from him, down the stairs. She was so angry that she was shivering. She went back to the kitchen, pulled on the old gray sweater that she wore in the garden, and sat down before her abandoned cup of tea. It was quiet now in the room upstairs. Her beagle bitch, Queenie, who had been asleep on the cellar landing, came padding up and put her head on Rhoda's knees. Rhoda reached her hand down and stroked her long ears, hardly conscious of what she was doing.

"And I shouldn't wonder if he'd get pneumonia on a night like this, in that room with that wind blowing in," she said angrily after a while, as if she were continuing a conversation with someone else. "The fool—oh, the great fool he is! Well, I'll be well rid of his foolishness now."

She got up a little stiffly, rinsed her cup and saucer at the sink, and went upstairs to her own room. The light was still on under his door. She went into her room, a little sick inside from reaction after her anger. She felt as she always had after she had quarreled with her father, upset and ashamed. She knew it was not an easy thing that Brand was trying to do, and that there was no one for him to talk to when things were bad. But she would not try to talk to him any more tonight, while her temper was still on edge; it would only be the same thing over again if she did.

The next morning he came downstairs with the money in his hand for her to have the broken pane replaced in the window. He looked as if he had not slept, but his manner was quiet and civil. She could not say anything to him in front of the other men. All day long, while he was at work across the road, she fretted about what had happened the night before. If she could have talked to him in the morning she would have been tactful and sympathetic with him, but by the time he came home in the evening she had had the opportunity to go over it all too often in her mind, and her irritation had come up again. She had the same bitter sense of futility in her that she had had so often over her father's repeated failures. She purposely avoided seeing him alone before dinner.

After dinner, when he left the house, she did not believe that he had gone back to the school. She imagined him out somewhere with the other men, drinking or playing cards, or over in the Polish settlement behind the Maitland factory, with the girls who worked in the shoe factory there. She told herself that it was no concern of hers what he did, but it *was;* she had put something of herself into his ambition, and she resented furiously seeing it lost. She sat in the parlor, trying to read, and growing grimmer and grimmer as the hours passed.

Then, at the usual time, she heard him come into the house. She waited, not raising her eyes from her book, expecting that he would go upstairs. But instead she heard him come down the hall to the parlor door. She looked up. He was standing in the doorway with his books under his arm, looking at her with the peculiar Welsh lack of expression on his face that he put on when he was in an uncertain situation. As she looked up he began to flush.

"Well," he said, "maybe you haven't the time for these things of mine tonight."

She took the words as they were meant, as an apology, and as an admission that he was asking her to go on helping him with his work. She knew that it was as hard for him as it was for her to ask someone's pardon in so many words.

"No," she answered him, simply. "I've only been reading a very dull book."

And without saying anything more she went over to the desk and drew out her chair. He brought his own and sat down beside her, and they began on his French lesson together.

She did not find out till months later what the incident had been that had caused the trouble. It had happened in the class in English literature: the teacher, an elderly widow who was related to Bard City's leading families, and who resented bitterly the fact that she had to teach school for a living, had criticized at length that evening, before the whole class, the theme that he had handed in to her the week before.

"It's not enough that there's hardly a sentence in it that's written correctly," she had said. "The paper is so filthy that I hesitated to touch it to correct it. I'd like you to remember that I wasn't sent here to teach pigs."

She was one of those thin immaculate old women who wear lace collars and amethysts, and she would not have understood, even if someone had told her, how it is almost impossible to get some kinds of factory grease off the hands. Brand did not try to tell her; he sat there looking straight ahead, with an air of almost brutal detachment. The only thing that changed about him was the color of his face. Whenever he was really angry he flushed dark red all over, neck, ears, forehead, and all. It was as if one could see the rage flooding him visibly, surging up in him and spreading till it almost suffocated him.

Rhoda was certain, when she saw that he had not left the school after all, that he would keep on with it, that he would not let anything turn him aside now. She began to feel pride in him; it was her battle as well as his, and she was exultant when he did well. But she was as keen and quiet with him as always. Sometimes, when they had finished their work, they sat talking together for a while in the parlor. He was always serious and respectful with her then, not so much at his ease as when they were working together. Their conversation was almost always impersonal; they talked about politics, or trade unions, or the world events of the day. It was a treat for her to have somebody to argue with who could stand up to her and give her back some of her own hard, straight thinking.

There was a certain amount of gossip caused by the interest she took in him. One Sunday evening in early December, when she was over at Virgil's house on Sherman Street, Mattie's relatives, her father and mother and her two sisters, were there. Mrs. Kronstadt, the older sister, a recent widow who had been left quite well off by her elderly husband's death, was teasing the younger, unmarried one, Bertie, about a young clerk who worked in their father's store, where Bertie also worked as bookkeeper. Bertie was the youngest of the three Kroener sisters, now just past thirty; she had a sallow face that resembled Mattie's, but she was still rather pretty in a smiling, timid way, with her big nearsighted brown eyes and curling black hair.

"You should see the way she dresses now for work," Sophie Kronstadt said, "her best embroidered shirtwaist—my word! A plain one's good enough for her now on Sunday. And have you noticed the new way she's doing her hair? *Mr. Fenway* likes a pompadour."

It always irritated Rhoda to see the way Sophie, who was a big, ruddy woman, with a vigorous, rather cruelly jolly manner, domineered over the rest of the family, except her father. She was especially ruthless with Bertie. Rhoda thought sometimes that she was unconsciously determined, having married without love herself, to see to it that her sister's life remained empty of love as well. A man could not cast an interested glance at Bertie, or she at him, without Sophie's turning all the force of her ridicule on them. The result was that Bertie was ashamed to act naturally with any man in her family's presence; she shrank into herself, was stiff and awkward with nervousness. Yet she could be lively and almost hoydenish when she was let alone, romping with Sam in the back yard when he was small, and coming in with her hairpins falling and her sallow cheeks flushed with color.

They were all sitting together in the living room that evening. Rhoda looked across the room to Sophie, who had begun now about the locket that Bertie was wearing.

"I wonder if it's still our father and mother's picture that's inside it," she was saying, "or is it somebody else's now? Let me just take a peek at it, Bert."

Bertie sat fingering the locket nervously, trying to smile as if it were all a joke to her too. Her defenselessness irritated Rhoda, but at the same time she was sorry for her too. She remembered how she had felt when she was a girl, just beginning to be in love with John Lefroy, and one of her aunts had dragged her feelings out to laugh at them before a family gathering.

"Can't you let her alone now?" she said to Sophie. "She's a right to her own feelings—*goodness!*—without everyone else's pawing over them."

Sophie instantly turned her clear, small, light-brown eyes on Rhoda. There was a certain animosity between the two women, though they had so little to do with each other; it was the inevitable clash of two strong, self-assertive natures.

"Oh dear," she said, "I suppose we ought to let the two of you sit in a corner by yourselves, and talk about your own true loves; it's not for old married people like the rest of us to meddle in such things."

Virgil Beauchamp, who had been talking to Justus Kroener, not paying much attention to what the women were saying, caught this remark and looked over innocently.

"What's this? What's this?" he asked. "Is it Rhoda?"

Sophie laughed. She did not quite dare to come out and say directly what she meant.

"Why, what are you so surprised at?" she countered. "Rhoda's a good-looking woman; there's no reason she shouldn't have an eye out for a good-looking young man if she likes, especially now that she's all alone."

"Well, it's the first I knew—!" Virgil began, in astonishment. He was always the last person in Cannon Hill to know that there was gossip going around about anyone; even if he heard it talked about, it made no impression on him. He was like his father; it went against the grain with him to believe evil of anyone. Now he turned to Rhoda. "What's this about, Rhode?" he asked her, smiling.

She did not answer him. She was so furious that she could not say anything for a moment. Sophie's words had come on her like a whiplash; she had realized, in a careless way, that the interest she was taking in Brand was causing some comment, but no one had ever ventured such a gross hint to her before.

"You don't mean to say you haven't heard what's been going on out there," Sophie went on, seeing that Rhoda said nothing. Mattie looked rather frightened; she was the one who had told her sister about Brand. "It seems you can be looking out one of these days to have a new brother-in-law in the family—that's all it is."

"Why, you're joking, aren't you?" Virgil asked, looking doubtfully from her to Rhoda.

"I hope she is," Rhoda said. She had got her self-control back, and fixed Sophie with her strong, piercing stare. There was something almost frighteningly intent about that look of hers, as if she were forcing the person on whom it rested to take the full weight of her nature behind it. "Because if she isn't," she said bluntly, "she's a busybody, *and* a fool—just as everyone else is who goes around repeating that sort of trash."

"Well, I never in the world meant—" Sophie began, trying to brazen it out, and laughing, with an indignant movement of her shoulders.

"You meant to say that I was taking an interest in Rob Brand because I had an idea he might marry me," Rhoda said, in the same uncompromising tone, "and that's exactly what you meant to say, Sophie. Well, I'm sorry to disappoint you, but not a word of it's true. I have no more intention of proposing to that young man than I have of proposing to the Pope of Rome."

She got up and said that it was time for her to leave. Virgil was upset and apologetic, Sophie rather disconcerted by her frankness. Still, as she left, she saw that they were not completely convinced by her words.

She walked home alone through the winter darkness. It was a bitter night, but she did not feel the cold. She walked fast, hardly thinking of where she was going. She felt shamed and furious. The thought had come to her that the same ideas that Sophie and the others had had might also have occurred to Brand. She tried to think back over his words and actions, to see if there had been indications of anything of that sort in them. Everything that had seemed so clear and satisfying in their relationship grew clouded and troubled in her mind.

She found herself walking along past the large empty field that separated the Cannon House from the cluster of small brick stores, saloons, and restaurants around the railroad tracks crossing Old Town Road. She stopped and looked out over the field. The night seemed very large in this open place. The field glittered faintly under the cold stars where the last of a light snow still clung upon the dead grass. She stood still, feeling her aloneness with a slight shudder. Since the end of her affair with Lefroy, she had never known a man whom she felt she could love, and she had grown used to the thought that she would live and die alone. Now she acknowledged something to herself. She acknowledged that the feeling that she had for Brand was the same that she had had for Lefroy long ago. She was more than a dozen years older than he was, she was a settled woman in middle age, but it was the same hot, possessive love rising in her now that she had felt as a girl of seventeen. And she knew now too, just as she had known on the day that she had received the news of Lefroy's marriage, that this feeling was on her side alone, and that pride, which was so strong an emotion in her, something clear and fierce and absolutely unbending, would keep her from ever admitting her feeling to him.

Someone came along the road behind her. She roused herself, and walked quickly on to the house. As she went inside, the warmth struck her and she shivered, realizing how long she had been standing in the cold. She could hear Mrs. Sorley in the kitchen, talking smartly to one of the men. She wanted a cup of tea to warm herself, but she could not face anybody just then. She went upstairs to her own room, lit the gaslight, and looked at herself in the mirror.

"Now, Rhoda Beauchamp," she said ironically, to her own image, "don't be any more of a fool than the Lord made you."

From that day on she put an end to talking to Brand more than to the other men, except for the time she spent in helping him with his work. She was deliberate and mocking and rather superior with him; it seemed to her at times as if he almost hated her. But he would not give up the work. And there was always a certain comradeship between them then. It was still the best time of the day for her, when he came in, late in the evening, from the school.

Chapter 3

Meanwhile, there was the child, Bronwen, living her own small, silent life in the house. During those first months she was like a lost creature, without the mother and brother who had been her nearest companions. The men tried to make up to her, but she did not want anything to do with them. And she did not make friends readily, either, with the other children in school. Living at the Cannon House, on the farthest fringe of Cannon Hill, with no neighbors but the open fields to the west, the factories across the road, and the forbidden cluster of shops and saloons around the railroad tracks to the east, she was something of a curiosity to them. Then, she had none of the things that the other girls had, and that were important to them—pretty clothes, dolls, possessions of any sort. She was self-contained and aloof with them, an outsider.

Yet she had strong affections, almost too strong. She had the deep Celtic instinct to cling to those of her own blood, and it drew her jealously to Brand, even though she seemed to sense the fact that she was more or less shut out of his life. He had very little time for her. Only occasionally, when he was doing something about the house and she came to watch him, they had a long talk together, or he told her stories about Wales, that he had heard years before from his own father. He had a serious, rather tender way of talking to her then.

"And what about school?" he would say to her.

"I don't like it"—very definitely.

"Why not, then?"

"It's sitting inside—and all the girls talk about is dolls, and tea parties, and playing house."

He laughed. "Well then, you ought to have been a boy. Is that how it is?"

She looked down at herself critically.

"No," she said. "I'm too small. I wouldn't want to be littler than the rest."

There was nothing about her that resembled her father. She was small, with the lovely, clear, rather rounded features that are seen in certain Celtic types, everything about her delicately but sturdily formed. Rhoda imagined her as looking like her mother, with her fair skin and blue eyes, and her soft, light-brown hair that might darken in time to bronze.

She was very proud of her tall, strong father; she judged all other masculinity by him. The other men in the house seemed dwarfed and pinched to her beside him. When he caught her up sometimes and set her on his knee while he sat working on a clock that had stopped running, or the broken hinge of a workbasket, she felt secure in the sense of his strength and largeness. She loved that feeling of security; it was the foundation on which her whole life seemed to rest.

But it was only rarely that they had times like these. More often, he was too occupied with his studies to have any time to give to her. Then she would spend hours with Queenie and her puppies, talking to them in a little, self-absorbed voice when she thought there was no one around to hear her. She did not understand about her father's going to school; it seemed to her that there was something vaguely disgraceful about it, because the men laughed at it, and the other children occasionally made remarks about it to her. It seemed to take him down from the pinnacle of strength and wisdom on which she would have liked to set him. And she resented, unconsciously, as children do, the fact that his studies seemed more important to him than she was herself.

There was a period of several months, in the late spring of the first year they spent at the Cannon House, when she was frightened with a recurring nightmare. A traveling carnival had visited the neighborhood then, and Mrs. Sorley had taken her to see it. While they were there, one of the gaudily decorated tents caught fire. The show that had been given inside was just over, and it was empty of spectators, but there was a good deal of excitement and some panic for a short time, when it was believed that one of the performers was trapped inside. It was just drawing on toward evening, and the flames stood out brilliantly against the shadowy sky and the gray indistinct shapes of things and people. Mrs. Sorley, who had a sharp curiosity and not a grain of fear in her, stood with Bronwen in the front rank of onlookers, watching till the flames had died down and there was only a blackened, glowing twist of wood and metal left.

Bronwen did not seem frightened at the time, but one night, a week or so later, she had a vivid dream that the house had caught fire and was burning down. She woke and, as she sat up tensely in bed in the darkness, the slight creaking noises that the old house made in the night-quiet became in her imagination the crackling of the fire. She got out of bed in panic and went into the hall. From downstairs in the parlor a light and the sound of voices came up to her. She ran down, in her bare feet and nightgown. Brand and Rhoda were sitting at the desk together; they were reviewing the year's work in preparation for the examinations that would begin the following week, and were working somewhat later than usual.

When she saw them sitting there so quietly, and everything in the house peaceful and safe, the reaction from her fear was so great that she began to cry. Brand and Rhoda looked up and saw her standing there in the doorway.

"Why, what's the matter?" Brand asked.

He thought she must be ill, as she hardly ever cried, and got up in alarm and went over and picked her up. She swallowed back her tears as she told him about the dream. She was still trembling, but she felt safe now while he held her.

Rhoda got up too from her chair before the desk.

"I'll go back and fix her a glass of warm milk," she said.

She went out to the kitchen, and Brand sat down again, holding Bronwen on his lap. He soothed her, and talked to her as she remembered his having done sometimes at home, when her mother had gone out for some reason in the evening and he had been left alone with the children. She lay with her head against his chest, holding to him tightly with one hand.

Rhoda came back with the milk for her.

"Now then," she said briskly, "drink this, and then it's back to bed for you, young lady."

Bronwen hid her face on Brand's shoulder. She was terrified of going upstairs into the darkness again.

"Let her stay a little while longer," Brand said to Rhoda. "She won't be in the way; she'll drop off to sleep in a few minutes."

Rhoda set the glass on the desk and sat down. She would have sent Bronwen upstairs if she had been her own child, but she did not want to interfere now. She took up the French grammar they had been going over and went on with the questions she was asking Brand. She looked at him a little ironically as he sat frowning at her over Bronwen's head, trying to remember the future tense of the verb *savoir*.

Bronwen fell into a drowse, hearing their voices as if from a distance. At last, when she was sound asleep, Brand carried her upstairs and put her into her bed again.

"Now she'll be down again the next time she wakes up in the night," Rhoda said practically, when he came back to the parlor. She was smiling a little. He looked at her rather angrily.

"It was the dream she had," he said. "She wouldn't have come down for nothing."

But a few nights later she had the dream again: the terror, the fire and smoke somewhere below in the darkness, the house that would twist and sink quickly into a blackened, glowing ruin. She got out of bed, and went to the head of the stairs. She was longing to go down, to have Brand take her up again and hold her until her fear had gone; but she knew that Rhoda had not liked her coming down the last time. At length the pressure of fear and loneliness was too great. She ran down the stairs and went to the parlor door.

Brand was working at his French again. It was the one of his studies that he had the least aptitude for, and this evening it had been coming particularly badly. He was struggling with the translation of one of the exercises in his textbook when Rhoda drew his attention to the doorway with a slight nod.

"Look what we have with us," she said to him.

He glanced up and saw Bronwen standing at the door. Rhoda's
calm, rather ironical words, which reminded him of the prediction
she had made a few nights before, and his own sense of frustration
at being interrupted in the middle of a lesson which he could not
seem to learn, made him burst out at her angrily.

"Here," he said, "this is getting to be too much of a good thing.
What are you doing out of your bed now?"

The look of appeal froze on Bronwen's face. She stared at him
with lost, terrified eyes.

"Well, can't you answer now?" he shouted at her.

Her face turned up to him dazedly. She stammered something
about the dream.

"That was a fine story the last time, but it won't do again," he
said, rather brutally. "Get back to your bed now, and no more
nonsense about it—do you hear?"

She turned around without a word and went upstairs to her
room. But in the darkness, as she lay in bed, a whole world seemed
to be tearing to pieces inside her. She lay on her back, crying blindly,
the tears drowning her face in a child's complete, unreasoning
misery. She could not have any emotions halfheartedly; it was
always as if she were caught up by a single overpowering mood that
used her body and mind as its physical outlet.

And afterwards, when the dream recurred, she lay clenched
against it, suffering the terror, rather than face Brand's anger again.
She watched him silently when she was with him; for days she was
torn between her longing to come close to him again and her
flinching remembrance of his rebuff. Then, as time went on, she
began to forget, and to be more indifferent to him. She seemed to
sense definitely from that time that the most important thing in his
life was something that she could not share. So she drew away from
him. She did not try any longer to make a place for herself in his life.

It was at about this time that her friendship with Rhoda's nephew,
Sam Beauchamp, began. He was in the same class with her in school,
but during those first months he had not noticed her much, sitting
in a corner of the schoolroom in her perpetual dark dresses. And
Mattie kept him away from the Cannon House; she and Virgil
hardly ever went there now.

Their friendship dated from one Saturday morning in early June, when Rhoda had sent Bronwen over to Sherman Street on an errand. The Beauchamps lived in one of the last of the big comfortable gray houses with wide scrolled porches and stained glass doors that faced each other under the double row of maples lining the street. As Bronwen came up the walk to the front steps, Sam was playing mumblety-peg on the Rogans' front lawn next door with Dick Rogan, whom Bronwen also knew, as he sat across the aisle from her in school. The boys called to her.

She stood in the middle of the walk, looking over at them silently.

"What are you doing over here?" Dick asked her. He was a lively, good-looking boy, with a rather superior manner.

"I've got to see Mrs. Beauchamp," Bronwen said.

"What for?"

She did not answer him. After a moment she started on up the walk again.

"Didn't you hear me?" Dick called after her. He was nettled because she did not pay more attention to him. "I said 'What for?' "

Bronwen looked around briefly over her shoulder, but did not stop. On an impulse, to frighten her, Dick picked up the open penknife he had been using to play mumblety-peg and flung it in her direction. He had not had the slightest idea of hurting her, but as she started quickly back it struck her on the right arm, making a deep gash a little below the elbow. The two boys jumped up instantly and came running over. Bronwen was standing without moving, holding her arm out a little from her side, and looking at the blood that was beginning to flow from it. Dick looked at the blood too, with a scared face.

"Look, I didn't mean to hurt you, Bron," he protested.

"My mother's in the kitchen," Sam said to Bronwen. He was a rather serious boy, dark-haired and blue-eyed, with a square, rough-featured face. "You'd better come on back and let her fix that."

He brought Bronwen around the side of the house to the back door. Dick followed them, but as they came around to the back of the house he stopped and asked Sam in a worried voice: "What are you going to tell your mother?"

Sam glanced around at him. "Go on home," he said. "I'll tell her it was an accident, while we were playing." He looked at Bronwen. "You won't tell, will you?"

She shook her head.

He brought her into the kitchen, where Mattie was doing her Saturday morning baking. She was rolling out pastry dough when the two children came in. At first she did not recognize Bronwen, and when Sam told her who she was the look of disapproval deepened on her face. She washed the flour off her hands and went upstairs to get the iodine from the medicine chest. Bronwen sat on a chair in the kitchen, holding her handkerchief over the cut. When Mattie came downstairs, she washed the wound out under the kitchen faucet and painted it with iodine. She was clumsy and rather unfeeling about treating other people's hurts. Bronwen could not help crying out when the iodine bit into the open cut.

"Now don't make a fuss; it's all over," Mattie said.

Bronwen kept back her tears. Her blue eyes turned dark as she looked at Mattie. She felt that the woman considered her a nuisance in her kitchen. And she saw the disapproving way that she looked at her, at her old dark dress and her dusty shoes.

Mattie tied the cut up with a piece of clean cloth torn from an old sheet. Then she went back to her baking again. She had just taken a pan of cinnamon rolls out of the oven, and she gave one to each of the children and sent them outside. They walked around together to the front of the house. Sam saw Bronwen looking at the big front porch, with its green swing, and its raffia mat, and its "elephant's-ears" on ornamental iron stands.

"Why don't you come on over after dinner this evening?" he asked her suddenly. "We're going to play hide-and-seek."

She shook her head, still hostile. "I can't. I wouldn't be allowed this far at night."

"You wouldn't have to stay till it got dark. It's light till past eight now."

But she refused again. He watched her go, a little puzzled, rather attracted by her aloofness.

The Monday following, he waited for her outside in the schoolyard when school was over.

"How's your arm?" he asked her.

"It's all right."

She pulled down the bandage to show him how it was healing. They walked along together away from the school.

"Did you tell at home what really happened?" he asked.

She shook her head.

"I told Dick you wouldn't," he said, with a nod of satisfaction.

When they came to Sherman Street he stopped, but did not turn off. She hesitated, looking at him.

"Do you want to come on home with me?" she asked, after a moment.

"All right."

"The strawberries are coming," she said, rather defensively, as if she had to explain her invitation. "We can pick some."

He walked out Old Town Road with her, past the end of the trolley line and across the railroad tracks, to the Cannon House. They spent the rest of the afternoon together, in the back garden, and Sam only got home in time for dinner. His mother asked him where he had been.

"Out to the Cannon House, with Bronwen Brand," he said.

She did not say anything more then, but after dinner, when he was doing his homework at the dining-room table and his mother and father were sitting together in the living room, he heard her talking about it again.

"I don't want Sam going out to the Cannon House," she said to his father. "I wish you'd tell him he's not to go without permission."

Virgil looked at her in surprise.

"Why, where's the harm in his going?" he asked.

Mattie's sallow face colored up slightly.

"None of those men living out there are Christians," she said rapidly. "Not one of them ever sets foot inside a church. I don't approve of Sam's going where he's apt to be under an influence like that."

Virgil looked uncomfortably at his newspaper. He knew that she included Rhoda in her disapproval, though she had not said so.

"Well, I don't see that it's going to do him any harm to spend a few hours there now and then," he said stubbornly, putting an end to the conversation.

But it was more than a few hours that Sam spent there that summer. He liked being with Bronwen, and there was something more; he liked the Cannon House itself. It seemed to him sometimes that it belonged to him more than the house on Sherman Street, which his mother made stiff and uncomfortable for him with her immaculate lace curtains and china ornaments and starched antimacassars. He liked the bare floors, and the old wallpaper, and the big rooms that were open all day to the warmth and light of the sun. And best of all he liked the garden, the crooked fruit trees, the currant bushes, and the grass that grew high, down at the end away from the house, so that it finally had to be cut with a scythe before a lawn mower could get through it. He remembered the stories that his father had told him about his great-grandfather's early youth on the sea, and about the time later on when he had come out to the valley and built the Cannon House, and they all seemed to come alive for him there in the garden. He was not an imaginative boy, but he had some of the same deep, stubborn sense of attachment to places and people that was in Rhoda Beauchamp.

He always had to come to the Cannon House if he wanted to see Bronwen; she would not go over to his home. She had an acute sensitivity to other people's feelings toward her, and she knew that Mattie did not care to have her around. Only, after a time, as Sam continued to make a close companion of her, Mattie felt that it was her duty to take something of an interest in her. She stopped and talked to her when she met her on the street, asking her questions, and pushing her hair back from her face with quick, nervous fingers.

"Does that hair ever see a brush?" she asked. "It's a pure shame— and look at those muddy shoes now; nice little girls clean the mud from their shoes."

The child stood stiff and silent under her hands, looking at her out of her blue eyes that seemed almost dazed with mistrust. Mattie asked her if Rhoda or her father ever talked to her about the Commandments of God, or about her Christian duty. Bronwen shook her head.

"Then you must come over to my house one afternoon, and I'll give you a little book to read for yourself," Mattie said.

But she did not go. She knew that the woman did not want her.

She listened to what the brown eyes said coldly to her, and not to the sound of the quick, civil words.

Another time there was a play given at the school, in which Bronwen had a part. The children's mothers were to make their costumes. There was a meeting of the women in the school hall over it, and Mattie offered to see to Bronwen's dress.

Bronwen had to go to Sherman Street and have the dress tried on. Mattie brought her upstairs, and in the shadowy bedroom, with its rosewood furniture and stiff flounced bedspread and pillow shams, she took off her everyday dress and put on the long white flowing costume that Mattie had made for her. She stood on a chair while Mattie knelt beside it, pinning in the hem. She felt the woman's antagonism, her rigid compelling of herself to the performance of a duty. When Mattie told her to turn, she moved obediently, like an automaton.

"There now," Mattie said to her at last. "Won't that be pretty?"

Bronwen stared at herself dumbly in the mirror. She felt helpless, given over to the woman's hard, clear benevolence.

Mattie took her downstairs and gave her a glass of lemonade and a cookie in the kitchen. A little later Virgil came in from his store, his round face ruddy with the heat of the June afternoon. Bronwen warmed to his friendly, rather boisterous manner and the eager enthusiasm of his speech, which made him stammer sometimes over certain words.

"And who might this be?" he asked, looking at her, smiling. "You've never traded our Sam in for a girl, Mattie?"

"This is Bronwen Brand," Mattie said. She smiled too; her husband's warmth called up a pale reflection even in her rigid quiet.

"Bronwen Brand? Oh, Sam's young friend, is it? Well, it seems to me we might have room for a girl in our house too. It's a hard life when a man comes home and hasn't a daughter to make over him a bit. What would you say to coming to live with me, Bronwen Brand?"

He loved children, and they responded instinctively to that love; there were no barriers between him and them. Bronwen lost her desperate stiffness and sat glowing with a shy, fugitive light under the warmth of being wanted, of being set at the very center of someone's attention. He was so different from Brand, who could never give her more than the outer edges of himself. The household suddenly took on a kind of glamour for her: she wondered what it would be like to live here, in this close family intimacy, with a father who would come home to play with her and adore her, and a mother to make her life simple and ordered, as the other girls' were.

But she had a deep loyalty to Brand, even to the life into which he had brought her; she would not have exchanged it for any other. And there was something in her that loved the freedom and the rather rough carelessness of her life at the Cannon House. As she grew older, left as always a great deal to herself as Brand continued to spend his days at the factory and his evenings at the night school, it was not Sam Beauchamp alone that she ran with, but a whole band of boys her own age or a little older, Dick Rogan, Francie Barr, the two Sorley boys, Gard and Ash, and others, changing from year to year. She liked to be with boys; they did not care what sort of clothes she wore, and they accepted her because she would do anything that they would do, even though she was smaller than they were. Still she was not really a tomboy. She was too quiet, and there was something about her that was hurt very easily, and that showed in her eyes. Sometimes, when they were all quarreling about something, Sam looked at her set, reserved face and thought how coldly she could place herself apart from them; but then he saw her eyes, with that expression of vulnerability in them, always that look of depth and stillness and childish vulnerability, as if what she saw struck farther into her than it ever did into anyone else. He usually sided with her in a quarrel; the two of them would go off by themselves if the others were all against them.

The big garden behind the Cannon House was a wonderful place for all their games, and through the long summers they gathered there almost every evening, waiting in the greening twilight till it was certain that no one else would come, and then choosing their leaders, taking sides, for the game they had decided on for the evening. Inside the house, Rhoda would hear the steady beat of the chant—

> One o'clock, the wolf's not here,
> Two o'clock, the wolf's not here—

or the shriek of triumph—"Home free, home free!"—bursting suddenly from a silence that had been alive with the stealthy sound of running feet and the quick breathing of the hunter and the hunted. She would look up from her book, alert, half-smiling: she liked the feeling of their intense young lives flowing round the house.

The Sorley boys were older than the rest. Gard, the elder, was a well-set, freckled boy who liked to lead, even to domineer, when the others would let him. Sometimes they rebelled, and then there would be a fight among them all, the two Sorleys always together, and able to take care of themselves even against superior numbers because they were larger and stronger than the rest. Bronwen hated it when these disputes arose. She never took part in them; she shrank into herself, away from the milling, thudding bodies and the angry cries. They made her world over into something brutal and ugly that she wanted to shut away from her. This was so even though there was seldom any lasting ill feeling among the boys. Only Dick Rogan, with his superior, studiedly careless air, really resented the Sorleys' domination. He was usually the one who challenged it, and started the chain of events that led to war among them.

One fall evening, when she and Brand had been living in Cannon Hill for four years, only Sam and the Sorley boys had come over to the Cannon House. It had rained during the day, and now, as the twilight came on, the garden was green and sodden under the heavy sky. The three boys felt rather aimless. They went down to the end of the garden, where a few summers before Brand had fixed up a swing for Bronwen under a big sycamore. The two Sorley boys got on it, the one sitting, the other standing facing him, with his feet spread on either side, and began to swing. Sam and Bronwen stood leaning against the white latticework fence, watching them. After a little, Dick Rogan came around the side of the house, and walked down to the end of the garden to join them.

"What do you want, Rogan?" Gard Sorley called out to him, as he came up.

He was ordinarily rather good-humoredly superior with the younger boys, but he recognized Dick as a rival, and he seldom had anything friendly to say to him.

Dick stood watching for a few moments as the two boys, seeming fused into a single flying figure, swooped out from the darkness beneath the tree and up toward the gray evening light of the sky.

"Sam and I made it higher than that the other day," he said, after a little. "Give us a turn and we'll show you how."

"Like fun," Gard jeered.

He and Ash kept up their swinging. Dick went over and stood beside the tree, waiting.

"Come on," he said, when several minutes had passed. "Give somebody else a chance."

Gard only laughed. The bodies of the two brothers sent the swing with fierce thrusts in a widening arc through the air. There was something impervious and mocking in their silence. They scooped their dark bodies from the darkness under the tree and flung them at the pale light of the sky.

"Are you going to stop?" Dick called, exasperated by that hypnotic, rushing motion.

Again there came the jeering laugh. The swing flew down swiftly to the darkness under the tree and, as it passed, Dick reached out suddenly and seized one of the ropes. The two bodies faltered; then the swing twisted, its wide arc broken, and careened sharply against the tree. In an instant the standing figure had swung loose and tumbled down into the mass of wet leaves that lay under the tree. He seized hold of Dick, and the two fell together, rolling over and over as they struggled. Then the seated figure too slipped off the wildly swaying swing, fell with the others, and there were three bodies fiercely tangled on the ground.

Bronwen shrank back against the fence. There was something intent and furious about the silence in which the boys were struggling. She knew that Sam had left her side and had gone to Dick's aid against the Sorleys, but everything seemed to be happening in the same swift, rushing movements that had been in the swoop of the swing a few moments before. The green wet darkness was coming, and the darkness, the deep, earthy odor of the sodden leaves, seemed thick with released antagonisms. There was a difference from the ordinary half-serious combats the boys were always having. They seemed caught up in a simple lust of hatred, all the mute animal antagonism between them released by the damp twilight and the sudden break in the fierce, thrusting rhythm of the swing.

She ran up to the house and called some of the men out to put an end to the fight. It made her feel sick to see their swollen lips and wet, torn clothes as they stood facing each other, panting and silent, with that blind animal hatred in their eyes. Then, slowly, it died out and they became ashamed and sullen; they changed again into awkward, half-grown boys, muttering excuses and worrying about going home to face their parents.

She kept aloof from them during that fall and winter. She did not want even to be with Sam; she walked home from school alone, then whistled for Queenie, and went out with her down the hill behind the Cannon House, to the big undeveloped tract of land between Cannon Hill and the neighboring suburb of Haddon. She had her favorite places, under the poplars at the bottom of the hollow where the creek twisted through, and a big flat stone at the top of the rise behind it, where she could sit and watch the trains, small and black and slow-moving in the distance, pass beneath her on their way in and out of the city. She liked to be alone now. It gave her a feeling of independence and strength. With the boys she had always been thrust into the background. Now, alone, there was something of herself that could emerge, be absolute, assert itself over her surroundings.

All this while, Brand continued to go to the school. He studied alone now; in most of his subjects he had passed the stage where Rhoda could be of much help to him. But she had begun to feel lately, though he did not speak of it to her, that there was a mounting restlessness in him, an almost unbearable irritation which he was carrying about inside himself. And, though it was easier for him to fasten his mind down to his studies now, he did not have the same obstinate patience, if he got into a difficulty with any of them, that he had had during the first years. Instead, she would see the rage and repulsion mounting in him like a flood; he looked as if he would have liked to tear the book, to destroy it, anything to escape from his bondage to it.

In a way, she understood what it was that he was feeling. The years were slipping away from him one by one; he was in his thirties, still caught in his boy's studies, while other men, younger than he, were already establishing themselves in their profession. There was a young doctor only a year or two out of medical school, Dr. Francis, who had recently opened an office in Cannon Hill, and she had seen Brand's eyes on him, bitter with silent envy. It was such a long road ahead of him. She saw him growing more reckless day after day, out of the sense of the futility of his struggles.

She did not question him, but she knew that there were more and more evenings when he stayed away from the school and went instead with the other men to one of the little saloons near the railroad tracks, or down to the Polish settlement behind the factory. He was spending a good deal of time there now with one of the factory girls, Anna Koszniewska. Rhoda, who heard all the Cannon House gossip, knew all about her. She had seen her passing on the streets on Sunday, in her holiday finery. She was dark and red-lipped and rather handsome, in a full-blown way.

And Brand was farther apart than ever from Bronwen. She had learned not to expect anything of him for herself. But she had the same deep loyalty to him. She would not bear to hear anyone speak slightingly of him; that was almost always the reason for her quarrels with the boys, and with Mrs. Sorley, who never spared the sharp edge of her tongue in speaking of him, any more than she did when she spoke of the other men.

One afternoon in the early spring of the following year Bronwen went out, with Sam and some of the other boys, to the old race-course half a mile west of the Cannon House, on Old Town Road. It had been abandoned now for years, since horse racing had been made illegal in the state, and they all liked to play in the old gray-roofed stadium, with its little tower and its tiers of wooden seats that were weatherbeaten and rotting with neglect.

This afternoon they began a game of baseball in the big oval field inside, but several of the boys had to go home early, and the game eventually broke up for want of enough players. The others hung around aimlessly, not able to decide on anything to do. Bronwen was with them; she had begun to take back her old place in the

band, though she was still rather reserved with them. And now that
they were all growing up, there were new relationships and antagonisms beginning to be felt among them. The Sorleys, for example,
who had always made something of a pet of her, as she was several
years younger than they were, began to resent something in her clear
aloofness. Ash, the younger, in particular, a quiet, sullen boy with
narrow features and his mother's prominent eyes, took pleasure in
tormenting her with his teasing.

After a while Gard Sorley suggested that they go down to Polishtown, as they called the Polish settlement behind the factories, and
see if they could find some excitement there. The others knew what
he meant; there was a feud between the Polishtown boys and the
Cannon Hill boys, and there was certain to be some sort of battle
if they invaded their territory.

Bronwen stood up. "Then I'm going home," she said.

The others, still seated on the grass, looked up at her.

"What's the matter, Bron?" Gard asked. "Afraid you'll get hurt?"

She did not answer him. Ash Sorley ran a spear of grass between
his teeth.

"She's afraid she'll get in trouble with her old man," he said.
"*He's* got nothing against Polishtown."

Bronwen turned back to him. "You leave my father out of it," she
said quickly.

She thought he was referring to the fact that Brand went down
there sometimes to drink with the other men; she knew nothing
about any other connection.

Ash stared at her. He had an old-looking face for a boy scarcely
fifteen, dry and calculating and discontented.

"Why don't he leave himself out of it then?" he said, provokingly.
"He goes down there often enough."

"That's none of *your* business," Bronwen flashed back.

The other boys were looking on, attentive and half-smiling. Gard
Sorley laughed, wanting to show his superior knowledge.

"You're darned right it isn't," he said to them. "It's Anna Koszniewska's business, and that's all, boys."

Bronwen looked down at him, stiff and uncomprehending.

"Anna who?"

"You'd better learn how to pronounce it," Ash said to her. "It'll be all in the family one of these days."

Gard laughed again. "Well he doesn't go down there to learn algebra; that's one sure thing."

Bronwen stood staring down at them a moment longer. Her face had gone white. Then she turned and walked away quickly across the grass. She only half understood what they meant. But she wanted it not to be so; with all her will she wanted it not to be so. She was afraid; she felt as if she were left alone in a strange, terrifying world.

She walked into the kitchen of the Cannon House. Mrs. Sorley and Rhoda were there together. She stood confronting them with her white face.

"I want to know about Anna," she said. "Is my da going to marry somebody called Anna?"

The two women stared at her.

"God between us and harm!" Mrs. Sorley cried. "Who's been talking to you now?"

"It was Gard—and Ash— All the boys knew—"

"The young blackguards!" Mrs. Sorley exclaimed. "Wait till I get my hands on the two of them now."

She was flustered, and bustled around the kitchen angrily, rattling the pans on the stove. Bronwen looked at Rhoda.

"Is he?"

Rhoda shook her head grimly.

"It would serve Rob Brand *exactly* right," she said, "if I sent you straight to him with that question. I'm sure I don't know why *I* should be the one to be worried with his nonsense."

"Eh, he's like all the men—bring a child into the world and then go his own way, like he hadn't a soul to think of but himself," Mrs. Sorley said shrilly.

"Be quiet, Maud!"

Rhoda spoke sharply. Mrs. Sorley shrugged up her shoulders angrily and went on with her work.

"There's nothing to get so excited about," Rhoda went on, to Bronwen, in the same peremptory tone. "Your father's not going to marry anyone—and you might just as well get all this business about Anna Koszniewska out of your head, because it's no concern of yours nor of those silly boys. If they have any more to say about it to you, you send them to me, and I'll give them something else to think about."

But she was upset, though she dismissed the subject as if it were of no importance, by the doubt and confusion she saw in the girl's eyes. Up to that time she had accepted the signs of Brand's restlessness with a kind of ironical quiet; she had refused to let it disturb her. She had seen her own father, after her mother's death, straying helplessly after the warmth and the intimacy that he had lost; there was something dark and rootless about a man's life then, and with Brand it was accentuated by the fact that it had been delayed in him, because he had deliberately put it away from him in order to absorb himself in his studies.

But her patience was coming to an end. If he did not settle down soon, he would fail in his year's work, and that might very well be the end of everything. And then there was Bronwen to think of; it was not being fair to the girl for him to go on as he had been during the past months.

He did not come home till late that night; it was after midnight when she heard him at the door. She knew that he had not been down to the school. He came past the door of the parlor on his way upstairs, and as he glanced inside and saw her sitting there, watching him silently, with a slight, ironical smile, he stopped, frowning at her.

"Well," she said. "This is a nice hour to be coming home."

"What difference does it make to you what hour I come home?" he returned, rather angrily.

She thought that he had been drinking; his exasperation was always very near the surface then. She continued to look at him calmly.

"I've been waiting all evening to talk to you about Bronwen; that's what difference it makes," she said.

She saw his face change.

"About Bronwen? What's the matter with her now?" he demanded.

"Nothing that you can't remedy. The boys have been talking to her about Anna Koszniewska."

The angry color came up in his face.

"I'll have something to say to those young thieves," he said threateningly, to hide his confusion.

She shook her head decisively. "No, don't blame the boys," she said. "They're only speaking the truth. *You're* the one who needs talking to, if you'd listen to a reasonable word from anyone. But it's no use trying to talk to you when you're in this state."

"This state? What state?" He stood there glowering at her.

She shrugged her shoulders quickly. "You know what state," she said to him.

"Because I've had a drink or two?" he asked, furious at her rather contemptuous calm.

"It's not quite that simple." She could feel herself growing tense inside with the stress of the battle between them. "You know very well what I'm talking about. *You're* going your own way, and let anyone try to stop you till you've landed yourself back in the dirt you tried to climb out of." She flushed up suddenly; all at once the fiery temper of her younger days boiled up irresistibly in her blood. "*You* a doctor!" she said quickly. "You'll never step inside the front door of a medical school. I don't know why I was ever fool enough to believe you would."

She could see the fury, like a dark cloud, gathering in his face. The blood swelled in the veins of his forehead. She got up quickly and walked across the room to stand facing him. She was not afraid of him; her anger carried her on so that she was hardly conscious of anything but it, burning inside her.

"I'll tell you what," she said, looking straight into his face, "you can just pack up and get out, if this is the way you intend to go on. I'm not *that* much of a fool, to stand for this kind of thing in my house."

She walked out of the room and up the stairs. But as soon as she was in her own room, with the door closed behind her, she knew that she had done exactly what she had not wanted to do; she had let her temper carry her away to say much more than she had had any intention of saying. She walked up and down for a few minutes in the room. Her anger had cooled; now she only felt desperately depressed.

She had not heard him come upstairs. After a quarter of an hour or so had passed, she suddenly made up her mind to go down again. At least she could not make matters any worse than they were.

She went down the stairs and to the parlor door. Brand was sitting in the chair before the desk, with both his hands clenched and resting on the desk top. He looked around as he heard her steps.

"What did you come back for?" he asked her bitterly. "Were you afraid you didn't make it plain enough?"

"I made it too plain." She came across and stood beside the desk, looking down at him and trying to smile. "I lost my temper," she said frankly. "And you needn't boast that you didn't lose yours, because the only reason you didn't was that I didn't give you a chance."

He stared at her stubbornly, not returning her smile.

"It isn't any joke," he said. "Not to me."

"It's not to me either." She stopped a minute. "Why don't you go to bed?" she said. "If you want to talk about it, we can talk about it tomorrow."

"I don't want to talk about it, tomorrow or any other time."

He got up and went over to the door.

"I want to help," she said. She had an extraordinary voice, harsh and inflexible, but capable of a compelling persuasiveness at moments like this. He turned around and looked at her. She was still standing by the desk. There was a little smile on her lips and in her eyes. "That was what I said in the beginning, wasn't it?" she asked. "It's still true."

He colored again. Her gentleness disturbed him more than her anger had done. Since he had first come to live in the house, she had never said that to him so clearly. There had always seemed to be a kind of impatience and antagonism in her manner toward him. And he had resented it, though he had rarely shown it. Now, in this instant, he saw deeper into her. She had always seemed so completely self-contained to him. And it hurt him, it seemed to shame him, to see that smile in her eyes now, which had an appeal and a kind of fear in it, behind its composure. He felt in an obscure way that it placed him under obligation to her. It made him less free. But it gave him too the thing for which he had been groping these past months—the sense of the absolute importance of his ambition to someone outside himself.

She saw him looking at her with that new perception. And all at once she felt tired. There was nowhere for them to proceed from that deep mutual recognition. Even friendship was beyond them; they struck against each other with the hard clash of natural antagonists. And yet they had need of each other. There were still things that she could do for him. And there were things that he had done and would continue to do for her, even if only unconsciously.

She put on her brusque manner again. His face changed; he said good night and went upstairs. The next day, when she saw him, he did not say anything to her about what had happened the night before. But she knew he went down to the school that evening. She felt a certain peace in herself. It was as if something had been said that made everything clear and simple between them. She had sacrificed some of her pride for him. But she was willing that it should be so. Now there was no more to be said. They had passed a certain milepost in their relationship.

Chapter 4

Brand graduated from the night school the following year. He had earned his high school diploma, and could enter medical school in the fall. It was the year 1912; six years had passed since he had begun his studies at the night school.

When the time came for his first term at the medical school to begin, he left the factory and got a job clerking in the evenings and on Saturday afternoons and Sundays at Symons's drugstore, on the corner of Beech Street and Old Town Road. The pay was small, but it would be enough for him to get along on, since he had already saved the money for his medical school fees. And he had to have a job that began when most jobs ended, and that would give him some free time for studying. There were never many customers in the store after ten o'clock, and then he would be alone there till closing time, at midnight.

It was Rhoda who, through Virgil, had found out about the job for him. She had spoken to Virgil about it one evening when she was over at Sherman Street. She knew that he was in touch with almost all of the businessmen in Cannon Hill, and would know of any openings that would suit Brand's needs.

Virgil, as always, was willing to help. He was interested in Brand's ambition; he admired him for going through with his plans.

"If I'd had some of that stuff in me a dozen years ago," he said, "I'd be doing something else now but fitting shoes and worrying about overhead and wages."

He regretted that his father had not sent him to college; he thought he would have liked to be a botanist. He was always going down in the hollow behind Cannon Hill on Sunday mornings in spring, and coming back with flowers which he carefully pressed between the pages of an old Webster's dictionary, down in his workroom in the basement. But, as in everything else he did, there was no method in his pursuit of his hobby. Nothing was ever put in place, or catalogued, and he had never really read a single book on botany from beginning to end.

But Mattie, like the rest of Cannon Hill, did not share in his approval of Brand's ambitions.

"I should think *you*, of all people, wouldn't encourage him in this medical school nonsense," she said outspokenly, to him and to Rhoda. "You know what too much ambition did to your own father."

"Oh Lord, that wasn't too much ambition; it was too little common sense," Rhoda said, answering her rather sharply, in resentment.

She hated the ugly, defensive feeling she had to have now with other people when they talked about Brand. Before he had begun at the medical school, few of them, outside the Cannon House, had paid much attention to his trying to get an education for himself; it was night school, after all, and it was his own affair if he wanted to waste his leisure time in scrawling exercises and reciting lessons like a schoolboy. But it was an unheard-of thing, to them, for a man like him to give up his regular work and make out to the world that he was going to be a doctor. They could not make up their minds whether it was more wicked or more ridiculous of him. Almost everyone had something to say about it.

The worst of them all was James Symons, who owned the drugstore where Brand worked. He was a man of about forty, something of a hypochondriac, with flat dark hair and restless dark eyes behind gold-rimmed spectacles. Although he had hired Brand, because he was willing to work for less than another clerk of equal usefulness and dependability would have cost him, it upset him terribly to have to think that he would ever be a doctor, in a position superior to his own.

"Night school," he would say to his customers, over the counter. "That's a different matter altogether. Algebra and history—" He moved his flat lips contemptuously. "But pathology, pharmacol-

ogy, anatomy— They'll have him out of medical college inside a
year."

He said as much to Rhoda one afternoon, when she was in the
store. He had a way of speaking very rapidly and emphatically,
enunciating each word as if he were in a pulpit, or on a speaker's
platform. She looked at him with her eyebrows raised and her cruelly
pleasant smile.

"Is that your opinion?" she asked, agreeably.

He was a little flustered by that cat-and-mouse smile.

"My opinion?" he repeated. "Why, what else could any sensible
man think, Miss Beauchamp?"

"He might think he was making a fool of himself by talking such
nonsense," Rhoda said, directly.

And she had her vindication when that year passed, and another,
and Brand was still going on with his class. He had changed in those
years; the restlessness had gone out of him almost entirely since he
had actually begun his medical studies. He was serious, almost heavy
in his seriousness, and in place of the furious temper that had rushed
out to meet disappointments and humiliations in the earlier years, he
was developing a rather brutal indifference to the circumstances of
his daily life. There was no energy to spare for anything but his
studies and the work of keeping himself and Bronwen fed and
housed and clothed. During the summers he went back to the factory
to work during the day, while he continued to come in to the drugstore in the evenings and on Sundays. And there were always the
heavy books under the counter, to be slipped out when he had a few
minutes' freedom.

Rhoda saw the change, the maturity of middle life settling upon
him. He did not need her now. He had gotten the work he wanted,
and he was doing it. Up to this time she had always seemed the
elder, the superior. Now they were on an equal footing. She knew
that he was farther away from her than he had ever been when he
had depended upon her, somehow, to keep him on the right road.
But she was glad for him. She had wanted him to find himself.

And she had something else to occupy her just then. She was beginning to be worried about Virgil's affairs; in the depression that
was being felt in the early months of 1914, his badly managed busi-

ness was having a hard time of it to keep going. There was a certain
tension now in the house on Sherman Street, particularly when the
Kroeners visited there.

On the Fourth of July of that year she went out to Ludlow Woods
with the Beauchamps and the Kroeners to spend the day. It was the
only outing of that kind that the elder Kroeners ever took. The German fraternal society to which Justus Kroener belonged sponsored
a picnic there every year, and it was a kind of family ritual for them
to attend.

It was a warm, placid day. A week before, Francis Ferdinand,
Archduke of Austria, had been assassinated at Sarajevo, but war
in Europe was still in the future. In a round pavilion overlooking
the river a German band lustily played waltzes for dancing. The
couples circled round. There were whole families on the floor, ample
mothers with graying husbands whose well-starched, well-brushed
neatness testified to their partners' housewifely care, young girls,
some really splendid, erect and long-limbed, and their young men,
even white-stockinged, black-shod, sober children.

"We ought to have a turn ourselves," Virgil said to his wife.

He loved dancing, particularly the energetic, rhythmic waltzes to
which his German connections had introduced him.

Mattie shook her head. "No, thanks," she said. "I've got a little
sense left. I'm getting too old to make a show of myself up there."

"Old!" Virgil said. "Well, *that's* nonsense, if I ever heard it." He
turned to Sophie Kronstadt, laughing. "What about you, Sophie?"
he asked. "Are you game?"

She laughed in return, narrowing her small, clear brown eyes.
She was full of life and energy, her stout, healthy body bursting into
heavy curves from beneath the white duck skirt and embroidered
shirtwaist that she wore.

"Of course I am," she said. "Come on, Virge. We'll give them a
look at what we can do."

They went up the steps to the dance floor together. She was a big
woman, as tall as he, but like many big women she danced lightly
and well, holding her shoulders proudly while her feet moved nimbly
in the steps of the dance. And Virgil was more than a match for her.
His ruddy face flushed with amusement and delight as he swung her

in great sweeping circles from one end of the floor to the other. They attracted a certain amount of attention: the two rather stout, middle-aged people dancing with such obvious zest and skill. It made Mattie fidget to see how people watched them. She hated to be made conspicuous in any way.

They danced two waltzes together, and then Sophie, out of breath from the vigorous exercise, said she was finished for the day. Virgil did not want to stop. He came down the steps of the pavilion with her, trying to persuade her to keep on.

"You're the best dancer on the floor," he coaxed her.

She laughed at him boldly, fanning herself with her handkerchief. "Listen to the man!" she said.

But she would not go back to the floor. He turned to Bertie, but she flushed up with nervous timidity, looking to Mattie for support in her refusal. She could not dance like Sophie, and she was ashamed to take the floor after her. Virgil looked at the group of women, shaking his head.

"Five young ladies," he said, including his mother-in-law with a droll glance, "and not a partner for me in the lot! That's hard luck now, if you like!"

The music came to an end. A master of ceremonies stepped to the center of the floor and made an announcement that brought laughter and applause. He was offering a prize to the couple who could dance best in wooden shoes. Virgil turned to Mrs. Kronstadt.

"Now, Sophie!" he said. "I won't let you off this time."

He was proud of his ability to dance in the clumsy wooden sabots. Once, at the wedding of one of Justus Kroener's nieces, he had danced in them the whole evening through—the only one of the company who had been able to keep it up. But Sophie still refused to go back to the floor. There was a streak of cruelty in her jollity; she liked to tease him, seeing him so excited.

Several couples had already gone up to put on the wooden shoes. The crowd was laughing at a white-haired old man, with limbs like the blades of a jackknife, who had persuaded his wife, a tiny brisk woman in a little black cap tied with ribbons under her chin, to go into the competition. Virgil was flushed with impatience and eagerness as he kept on arguing with Sophie. All at once, seeing that she was not going to yield, he glanced around determinedly over the crowd. His eye lit on a young girl whom he had met once or twice at the Kroeners'; she was standing with her family, frowning with excitement as her uncles urged her to go into the contest. She was only sixteen or seventeen, a splendidly built girl, tall, with dark eyes and dark-blonde hair, wearing a little flat straw sailor hat that seemed to give emphasis to the slight awkwardness of her movements.

Virgil went up to her directly.

"Now, Miss Frieda," he said coaxingly, "I'm sure you'll take pity on me; I need a partner."

The girl looked at him, startled. But there was something perfectly irresistible in his merry blue eyes and round, impetuous face. She let herself be led across to the pavilion and up the steps to the dance floor. Her uncles roared their approval behind her.

The music was beginning: French horn, trumpet, flute, and tuba, all running boisterously together in the vigorous, riant measures. The girl stood erect, flushed, facing Virgil. There was an amused, triumphant gleam in his eyes as he looked at her. She was so stiff, so determinedly proper, in her starched white dress and sailor hat, as if she had in her not a drop of the lusty peasant blood that had stamped out its gaiety for hundreds of years to the very tune that was frisking now about them. He slipped his arm about her waist. She stepped out decorously, propriety binding her limbs. He felt her, unpliant and self-conscious, in his arms.

But as the music surged heavily on to its rough, gay beat, he knew she would yield; already he felt her body beginning to follow that imperious rhythm, and her lips parted in her serious face, her feet moved more nimbly in their wooden shoes. The sound of dozens of heavy sabots clattering in rhythmic unison on the floor had an almost hypnotic effect, like the steady roll of drums. And the faces, as they swept past, were serious with the passionate sobriety and intentness of an emotion that frees itself in the movement of the body as a whole, rather than being required to express itself merely through the facial muscles.

The girl's face began to reflect that inner absorption. Her awkwardness vanished; she was strong limbs, young bending waist,

proudly set head, a body that leaped and swung and balanced,
caught up wholly by the music and the responding movements of
her partner. The spectators, looking up, saw her stern living radiance moving against the warm July sky. And one couple after another
dropped out of the dance, while still the old man with his jackknife
limbs wound jerkily round and round the floor with his tiny, black-
capped wife, and still Virgil and the girl swept in their lusty, stamp-
ing circles, she so serious, with her peasant's stern intentness, he
laughing and ruddy, the outlander, the stranger, alive from head to
heel with the pure joy of motion. The Kroeners stood watching in
silence, a kind of heaviness settling over them. Mattie's face was
flushed over the cheekbones in sharp nervous patches.

Then the music crashed to an end; the judges came to award the
prizes. Virgil and the girl were given second place. Their prize was
a pair of china pitchers, decorated with peaches and apples against
a background of blue. The girl grew stiff and uncertain again; she
flushed in embarrassment, not looking at Virgil as she accepted her
prize with a standoffish air. He brought her down the steps again to
her family.

"Well, you're a daisy, aren't you?" one of her uncles said to her.
"You're a high-stepper!"

She was ready to cry.

"Now," Virgil said. "Don't let them talk to you. It's not every girl
that can dance like that."

He was still rather out of breath, but splendid with life. The men
looked at him a little shyly. They stopped teasing the girl. They were
proud of her, and proud of the ugly pitcher, which they passed about
among themselves, examining it.

Virgil went back to his own family.

"Now, look what I've brought you," he said to Mattie.

She just glanced at the pitcher he held out to her.

"What am I going to do with that big ugly thing?" she said. She
was trying to seem noncommittal. "You should have let Frieda
Ziegler have them both."

"After I've danced myself out of breath to win it for you!" he
protested.

He felt their disapproval granitely ringing his bright enjoyment.

But he would not give in to it; with a kind of stubbornness he kept up his exuberant spirits.

They went over to the picnic tables to spread their supper. There was a vacant table a little apart, under a pair of elms. They settled on that one. The women began to unpack the hampers.

"Can I help?" Virgil asked.

"No, you can't," Mattie said, a little sharply. "You just go over and sit down with Papa."

It embarrassed her to have him offer to help her with any of her woman's work. In her family the women waited on the men; it would as soon have occurred to her father to make his own clothes as to pour his own coffee or to set his own plate upon the table. And it made Mattie uncomfortable to have her husband do such things for himself when her family was present, as if his willingness to do them made him less a man.

Virgil went over obediently and sat down beside Justus Kroener. His father-in-law, a tall, spare man in his early sixties, wore a beard of the long, patriarchal sort that had been common enough during the last century, but that was beginning to make him a conspicuous figure now. Virgil, in an irreverent moment, had once said that he looked exactly like Moses—"All the Kroeners act as if they invented the Ten Commandments, but only Justus Kroener looks as if he, personally, received them in a direct communication from the Lord." He was never very comfortable with his father-in-law. The older man was always so correct, so certain of the infallibility of his own judgments. And he had been the only man in the family for so many years; he was so accustomed to receiving the submissive respect and service not only of his wife, but of his three daughters as well.

He and Virgil began to talk about business. It made Virgil uncomfortable, took the glow off his good spirits, to have to think about how badly his own business was going, and to try to explain to his father-in-law how it was that he found himself in such a state. He broke off the conversation, and went over to his wife again.

"Haven't you finished yet?" he asked good-humoredly, putting his arm about her waist as she stood at the table, opening out the sandwiches from their wrappings. "We're nearly starved."

She drew away from him sharply, without looking round.

"Go on now," she said to him. "You haven't got one of your Frieda Zieglers now, that doesn't mind making a show of herself in public."

He realized that she was really angry about his dancing with the girl. All the pleasure went out of him. A combative, excited feeling began to come up in him. They were all against him then. He left her and went over to sit down again with Justus Kroener. His day was spoiled. He only wanted to be on good terms with everyone.

In a few minutes Sophie called them to the table. There had been a German thoroughness of preparation; nothing was missing. There were sandwiches of cold ham and sandwiches of hard sausage full of little round black spices; and deviled eggs, potato salad, the dill pickles that Mrs. Kroener made herself, in a big crock that stood in the Kroeners' cellar. Mattie was upset because the bees came round the sweet lemonade that she had made. They settled on the rims of the glasses. She was afraid of being stung. She never enjoyed a picnic; even with all her careful preparation, things did not go in such an orderly manner as they did in her own home.

When everyone had been helped, Justus Kroener went back to talking business again. He blamed the present situation on the Wilson administration—the lowering of the tariff and governmental interference with business. The women were not interested, but they sat listening submissively. Rhoda looked at Virgil with a rather ironical smile that kept him silent. She knew it was no use, their trying to argue with Justus Kroener. They could never touch the granite core of his self-belief. When they set themselves against the Kroeners, it was like flame playing about stone. There was a kind of heaviness about the family that was invincible, especially when they were all together.

"The weakest ones are being forced to the wall," Justus Kroener said. "They won't be able to keep up much longer at this rate."

Sophie wanted to liven the conversation. She turned to Virgil, teasing him.

"And which are you, Virge—one of the strong or one of the weak?" she asked him.

She was a little piqued with him too, because his dancing with Frieda Ziegler had put hers in the shade.

"Oh, I guess I can worry along a little longer," he said, rather stiffly.

Justus Kroener shook his head forebodingly. "You'll have to watch sharp," he said.

"Oh," Mattie said quickly, "you might almost as well tell a four-year-old child to 'watch sharp'; I don't think he has any more idea than that what goes into the business and what comes out of it."

She hardly ever criticized her husband before her family, but they had begun to terrify her lately with their gloomy predictions about his business. She could not bear the thought that he might fail. It was not the money loss that she particularly feared, but the loss in reputation, the loss of the right to hold up her head in Cannon Hill as the wife of an honest and respected man of business. She lay awake sometimes at night, praying that God would not call on her to give that up.

Virgil was hurt that she would talk about him in that way before the others.

"Well," he said, growing more excited as he felt them all against him, "it's a queer thing how I've managed to keep that store going for almost twenty years now, the kind of soft-brained baby you'd make me out to be. And done pretty well with it, too—"

In his excitement, as he made one of his emphatic gestures, he struck against the blue pitcher, which he had set carefully beside his place, and knocked it from the table. The ground below was stony, and the pitcher broke into several pieces.

"*Now* look what you've done, with your bragging," Mattie said, vexed.

He reached down and picked up the four large pieces into which the pitcher had broken. The blood came to his face as he stooped.

"There's no use picking them up; it couldn't be mended decently," Mattie said.

"What difference does it make? You didn't care for it anyway," he retorted, hurt and angry.

He sat looking at the fragments which he had laid on the table. His face was flushed and upset and joyless.

After the meal Rhoda walked down to the river with Sam. Sam was growing up; he was fifteen now, a well-set-up boy, dark-haired and blue-eyed, tall for his age. He was beginning to interest Rhoda; lately she had been looking for opportunities to talk to him when he came over to the Cannon House to see Bronwen. He was a Beauchamp, she thought, but with something of the solid Teutonic steadiness of his mother's family. It seemed a good combination to her. The Beauchamp men had all been headstrong, naïve, and rather unstable. She liked to feel that steady, dependable foundation in Sam's nature. Virgil wanted him to go to college and become a lawyer, as Richard Beauchamp had been. But she wondered sometimes if he was suited to that kind of life. He liked to be out of doors; he did not care for school, though he was conscientious enough about his work, and usually did well in it.

He was rather quiet as they walked along together to the river. He hated the sort of thing that had happened during the picnic supper. And he had just begun to realize that the kind of existence he had been used to all his life, in which money was always forthcoming for him to have any of the things the other boys he knew had, was not something changeless and inevitable.

He said to Rhoda after a little: "How bad is it about Dad's business? Is he really losing money?"

She liked his coming out with it so bluntly; it was characteristic of the Beauchamp men to shy away from any unpleasantness about money. They would give away their last penny, but they would *not* hear about debts and losses.

"I suppose it's bad enough," she said to him. "Not so bad as your grandfather thinks, and not so good as your father thinks—that's about the size of it."

They had stopped on a bank above the river, and he stood with his hands in his pockets, looking at the swiftly moving surface of the water, which was all gold and broken with the last light of the sunset on it.

"I wish I was a couple of years older," he said, after a while.

Rhoda smiled. *"That's* a wish that, at my age, has an uncomfortable habit of coming true before you can look around."

But he was lost in his own stubborn, serious thoughts.

"Just so I could get a job," he said.

"Your father wants you to go to college," she reminded him.

He did not answer. After a minute or two had gone by, he turned, and they began to walk back toward where they had left the others. The sky in the east was pale with the blue dusk. As they walked on, the first rocket mounted swiftly and burst in a shower of golden sparks.

They did not talk about that subject again. As the year went on, quietly enough against the background of war and turmoil in Europe, Rhoda knew there was mounting tension in the house on Sherman Street, but Sam did not bring it to her, at the Cannon House. He did not come there quite so often now with Bronwen. She did not go a great deal with the boys any longer; she seemed older, more mature than they were, while they were still full of nothing but their sports and games. She and Sam were still good friends, but they did not see quite so much of each other now.

Then, shortly before the new year, the blow fell on the Beauchamps. The news of Virgil's failure made the principal topic of conversation in Cannon Hill during the holiday season. It was a bitter Christmas for Mattie. Sam had hardly ever seen his mother cry before, but now she went about the house with her eyes red and swollen, and once he came on her in the kitchen, standing just inside the cupboard door, crying with her head down and her hands pressed in tight fists over her chest. She seemed to be trying to clench back the sobs inside her; she was as ashamed as a man of having her emotion seen.

She did not want to see anyone but her own family. And yet it was not really so bad. With Justus Kroener's help, Virgil had managed to avoid bankruptcy proceedings; he had been able to sell the business at a fair price, and, by taking a heavy mortgage on his home and disposing of one or two pieces of property that he had bought in his more prosperous times, he had scraped up enough to put his affairs with his creditors in order. But the results of almost twenty years of work had been swept away. Justus Kroener had offered him a position as clerk in his surgical appliance store, and there he would have to start all over again.

Sam had his sixteenth birthday just at that time. He still had another year and a half before he would finish high school, but he wanted to leave school at once and get a job. He spoke to his father

about it one January afternoon, when Virgil was down in the basement, puttering about at his worktable. He had not yet begun down
at the surgical appliance store, and meanwhile his own affairs
seemed to have been taken out of his hands; there was nothing for
him to do now but sign the legal papers that were put before him
by his father-in-law. When things came to the smash he had not
known what to do but stand helplessly aside and let others salvage
what they could for him. He was like his father in that, too: he
could not understand misfortune; it simply was something beyond
his grasp.

When Sam went down to the basement to talk to him, he was at
the worktable, trying to sort out some of his botanical specimens.
He looked up with a smile as Sam came down the steps. He had
grown interested in what he was doing, and had forgotten his
troubles.

"Look at this, Sam," he said, holding up a fragile dried stalk
bearing a single white flower.

"What is it?" Sam asked.

"*Trientalis americana*—the starflower. I found it last spring, back
of the old Longmill place."

Sam did not know how to begin talking about the job. He stood
with his hands in his pockets, looking at the pale winter sunlight
falling on the table from the small window set high in the rough
concrete wall. His father went on talking about the flower. Then
he noticed that Sam was not listening.

"What's the matter?" he asked, putting the flower down.

"Nothing's the matter." Sam was a little embarrassed. "I just
wanted to ask you if it was all right with you if I quit school and
got a job," he went on determinedly, after a moment.

He saw the hurt, worried look come into his father's face.

"No, it's not all right," Virgil said. He did not look at Sam; he
began to fumble with the papers on the table as if he were looking
for something among them. "You're going to finish high school next
year, and then you're going on to college," he said. "This doesn't
make any difference about that."

"I know it doesn't make any difference," Sam said. "I know I
can go to college if I want to."

"I'm not done for yet," Virgil went on. He was getting excited about it. It struck deeply at his pride that people did not think he was capable of looking after his own family. "Don't you ever believe it that I'm done for," he said. "A thing like this could happen to anybody. The big thing is not to let it discourage you. A man's never through as long as he believes in himself."

Sam knew that these were the things his father's friends had been saying to him during the past weeks, saying them awkwardly, not really believing them themselves, in the same way that they would say cheerful things to a person who was ill; but his father believed every word of it. There was so much eagerness and credulity in his nature. Even now, what had happened did not really seem to have come home to him. He could often forget all about it for hours at a time, especially when he was with his friends. It was only Mattie and her family who could make him feel genuinely miserable about it.

But Sam's leaving school would have been just such another constant mute reproach to him as Mattie's reddened eyes and altered manner were now. He was so hurt by the idea that Sam felt he had to give it up. He did not know whether he was glad or sorry that it had turned out that way. He was not sure yet what he wanted to do with his life. It had always been taken for granted that he would be a lawyer, and he had not thought about anything else. So that, on the whole, it was simpler for him, for the time, to go on at school.

He made up his mind, though, that he would get something to do in his spare time. A number of the boys he knew had jobs after school and on Saturdays, and through them he heard of a printing shop in the neighboring suburb of Warsaw Hill that needed a boy to deliver circulars. But when he went to apply for it, the job had already been filled. Then Dick Rogan, who had begun working a few months before at Symons's drugstore, decided that he had had enough of it there, and when he quit the job one Saturday afternoon Sam applied for it and was accepted.

He did not tell anyone at home that evening about what he had done. The Kroeners were coming the next day for Sunday dinner, and he wanted to wait till after they had gone before he said anything about the job. Since Virgil's troubles had begun, the family

seemed to have grown much more tightly knit; the Kroeners were
always over at Sherman Street now, or the Beauchamps were at
the Kroener home in Warsaw Hill, and every detail of the Beauchamps' financial situation was threshed over in endless, intimate
discussions. Sam did not want what he had done to come up for
that kind of discussion.

After church in the morning he went off down the hill with Dick
Rogan. The Rogans did not live next door to the Beauchamps any
longer, but the two boys were still close friends, in spite of the differ-
ences in their natures. Dick was a good-looking boy now, as tall as
Sam, but more slightly built, with a matter-of-fact, self-assured way
of looking straight at people that girls liked, but that his elders uni-
versally found irritating.

It was a gray, early February morning, and as they walked down
the hill it began to snow. The thin, falling flakes turned slowly in
the keen bluish air. There was a Sunday stillness over everything.

Sam told Dick about his getting the job at Symons's.

"You don't know what you're letting yourself in for," Dick said,
shaking his head.

"It won't be so bad, I guess."

"That's what you think. Just wait till you've been there a week.
Old Symons can think of more ways for you to spend a spare minute
than any other two people put together."

"You may be right," Sam said.

He had already had a lecture from Mr. Symons about dawdling
over deliveries, or stopping on the way to talk to anyone; and he
had been assured rather emphatically that he was expected to earn
the five dollars a week that he would make.

"I know I'm right," Dick said. "He's a fine case, if there ever was
one. And Bron's old man is almost as bad, in a different way. He's
never in there without a book under the counter. You can have a
fine time with him all right."

"You can't blame him," Sam said. "I guess that's about the only
time he has for studying."

Dick shrugged. "My dad says he'll never make a doctor anyway.
He says he'll end up as a vet."

"You can't tell," Sam said.

"Sure you can. Dad says he's heard of cases like that before."

Sam did not want to argue about it. He did not know Brand well; the older man was so seldom at the Cannon House when he went there with Bronwen. But there was something about him that he rather admired. He felt that he was different from the other men at the Cannon House, and from the businessmen who were his father's friends. And his loyalty to Bronwen made him defend Brand when the other boys repeated their elders' mockery or disapproval of his ambitions. But when he was actually in Brand's presence he was always rather uncomfortable. There was something so preoccupied and determined about him, it made Sam feel that he was of very little importance to him.

He and Dick went back home again around one o'clock. The snow was still falling thinly from a heavy, blue-gray sky, and the ground had a light covering now. Sam went into the house by the back door and took off his coat in the kitchen. His mother was there, with an apron over her Sunday dress, standing before the open door of the oven to look at something inside. She glanced at the sweater he was wearing under his coat.

"I don't want you to come to the table in that sweater, Sam," she said. "It doesn't look respectful to your grandparents."

"I'm going to change," he said.

He went on upstairs. While he was in his room he heard the doorbell ring, and a moment later the sound of voices in the hall downstairs. He could hear his aunt Sophie's voice above all the rest, strong and jolly and domineering: "Well, Mattie, for goodness' sake! You look like the man in the song—

> *Geld ist weg,*
> *Mäd'l ist weg,*
> *Alles weg, alles weg. . . ."*

They went into the living room, but when he came downstairs a few minutes later only his grandfather and his father were sitting there; his grandmother and his two aunts had gone out to the kitchen with his mother. His grandfather answered him when he greeted him, and then went back to talking to Virgil. He sat very erect in his chair, his heavily veined, old man's hands resting on the red plush arms and his feet set squarely on the Brussels carpet.

In a few minutes Sophie came into the room to tell them that dinner was almost ready. She said hello to Sam and joked with him because his tie was not quite straight.

"You're going to be one of those men just like your father, that needs a woman to look after him," she said. She went up to him and jerked his tie straight with her plump, capable hands. "Your aunt Bertie's in the dining room," she said. "Aren't you going to come out and say hello to her?"

She went out before him through the dining room into the kitchen, her black skirt rustling, stiff with braid. Sam went on into the dining room. His aunt Bertie was pouring water into the glasses on the table from a cut glass pitcher. She looked up as he came in.

"Hello, Sam," she said. "How is everything with you?"

She had a way of looking at people with a bright, timid smile, as if she wanted to be friendly but did not know how to begin. Sam had always liked her; she was his favorite aunt. He came over and leaned against the sideboard, watching her pour the water with her quick, deft movements, that always seemed to have something deprecatory about them.

"It's going all right," he said to her.

"Oh, that's fine, Sam." She put the pitcher down on the table, and he saw the color beginning to come up in her face. "I was afraid—" she started to say.

He knew she wanted to say something to him about what had happened to his father. She had not had a chance to talk to him about it alone before.

"No," he said. "It's all right, Aunt Bertie."

"I don't want it to make any difference to you, Sammy," she said, looking at him across the table. Her eyes were deep brown and earnest-looking without her glasses. "You oughtn't to have to worry about things at your age. Goodness knows, there's plenty of time for that when you're older."

She smiled, wanting to make a joke of it, because she was always a little embarrassed about talking seriously to him.

"You're the one who's worrying now," he said. He was a little embarrassed too.

"I don't want you to feel that you can't keep on having the same things the other boys have, or doing the things they do," she said. She picked up the empty pitcher again quickly. "You know I'd be glad to have you come to me if there's ever anything—I know how it can be when you're young."

She did not know how to go on, and stood there looking at him with her bright, anxious smile. It hurt him to think of her offering to help him like that. He knew that she did not have much money of her own; his grandfather paid her a salary for working at the store, but out of it she had to pay board at home and buy all her own things, and there could not be much left after that. And she had told him once, not long before, that she had been saving up so that she could go on a long trip sometime, to California, or to Europe, "to see the world," she had said. He could remember her when she was still young enough and pretty enough to have people talking about her getting married, but now they said that her mother and father could not do without Bertie, and he knew that she had given up hope herself that she would ever be married.

"Thanks, Aunt Bertie," he said to her. "But it'll be all right. I've got a job after school, beginning next week."

He wanted to warn her not to tell the others about it yet, but just then Sophie came into the room from the kitchen with a dish of celery to put on the table.

"What's this about a job?" she said.

"Oh," Bertie said, "it's Sam. He was just telling me."

"I don't believe it," Sophie said. She put the celery on the table and stood looking at them with her hands on her hips. "Does Virgil know about this?"

"It's only after school," Sam said. "It's at Symons's drugstore."

His mother and his grandmother were coming in from the kitchen too, carrying the hot dishes to put on the table.

"I thought it was too good to be true," Sophie said. "Virgil's still got that notion in his head that he's going to make a lawyer out of you."

"What is it? What is it?" Mattie asked.

She stood just inside the doorway, with a platter of sauerbraten in her hands, looking quickly from one to the other of them.

"Well, you don't mean to say you don't know?" Sophie said. She laughed and looked at Sam. "What's going on here?" she asked. "Is this some kind of secret?"

Sam wished that his mother had not found out about it like this, knowing that the others had heard of it before she had. While he told her about it she stood without moving, the platter still in her hands, looking across the room at him. When he had finished she went over, without saying anything for a minute, and set the platter down on the table, beside Virgil's place. Then she looked across the table again at Sam.

"I don't know that I altogether approve of that," she said.

Sophie laughed again. "For heaven's sake, Mattie," she said, "it's the first practical thing the boy's ever done. I was beginning to wonder if he had any Kroener in him at all."

"As long as his father is spending the money to keep him in school," Mattie said, "it seems to me he ought to concentrate on getting the most he can out of his studies." Her long face looked calm, but it was clear, from the flatness and rapidity of her voice, that she was displeased. "Goodness knows how long he'll be able to have the advantage of an education," she said. "He oughtn't to have the excuse of a job for not studying. And then there's the job too, the company he'd be keeping— He spends enough of his time as it is around the Cannon House, without learning any more wickedness from any of those men."

"He won't learn anything that'll do him any harm from Rob Brand," Virgil said.

He had come in from the living room with Justus Kroener while they had been talking. Sam glanced around at him, surprised. He had expected objections from his father, and none from his mother, and it was turning out in exactly the opposite manner. But he understood, in a way. It was all a part of the dumb, secret strife that had been going on between his father and his mother during the past weeks, she wanting him now to give in entirely, to merge his own identity, as it were, in that of her family, to become a Kroener in everything but name. He had failed her, and she had gone back in her own mind, for her pride's solace, to being a Kroener again, and if he wanted to be with her he must follow her. But Virgil was stubbornly resistant; he submitted outwardly, but he still kept within himself the belief in his own independence. So he would stand up suddenly for Sam's actions against her condemnation; it was a matter of the circumstances under which the disclosure had been made.

"As a matter of fact," he said, "he might learn a few things it'd be good for him to know—what it means to work for an idea—"

"I pray to God Sam never has any ideas like that—to try to make himself into something the Lord never intended him to be," Mattie interrupted him, firmly. She raised her head and looked straight across the table at him. "I've never approved of Sam's going out to that place," she said; "I've never approved of his friendship with the Brand girl; but what I have to say about such things has never seemed to count for very much."

She turned around without waiting for Virgil to say anything more, and went back to the kitchen again. Sophie said briskly: "That's just like Mattie—think first of the soul and let the belly go." She patted Sam on the shoulder. "Never mind, Sam," she said, "you've got the right idea. You can't put a dollar in your pocket without going down among the Philistines."

"What harm she thinks is going to come to him in that drugstore, with Jimmy Symons's eagle eye on him—!" Virgil said. He looked uncomfortable, though he was trying to pass it off as a joke. "He might as well be working for a bishop."

Then there was a new coldness between the mother on the one hand, and the husband and son on the other. Sam felt that his father was beginning to depend on him in a certain way; he was someone for him to go to for support against the Kroeners, someone who was intimately bound up with his vague, rather grandiose hopes for the future. Virgil had always been proud of his son, but now he began to understand that Sam was of a stronger fiber than he was himself. He began to solace himself with plans for his future, through the dull hours and the small annoyances of the surgical appliance shop. They seemed to promise him that *this* situation would not last forever.

It was a hard time for Sam. At home there was always the shadow of financial misfortune, and the silent breach between his mother and his father. There seemed to be nothing for him to look forward to as he sat in his classes in the high school. The work at the drugstore was not hard, but Mr. Symons made it onerous for him with his petty exercise of authority and his insistence that everything be done exactly according to the particular method that he preferred. Sam was rather easy-going, and he had always gotten along without much friction with his teachers at school, so that he had never before felt the pressure of authority very strongly. Now he developed a resentment that flared up at times to a boy's clear hatred against Symons's constant suspicions that he was doing his best to get out of the work, and against his unreasonable demands as to how the work was to be done. But he would not quit the job.

At school he heard the other boys talking of their plans in the corridors between classes. A fine spring was coming on, and every day after school and all day long on Saturday the crowd was out at the old racecourse, or down in the hollow, or bicycling off to the river. And because those had always been his places especially, because there had never been a time, as far back as he could remember, when he had not had them to look forward to at the end of the class hours that dragged slowly with the good weather and the wind and the damp spring earth outside, he knew day after day more about the feeling of being hemmed in by walls that he could not get outside of. The worst of all was that he understood that it was only his own sense of responsibility, pride, obligation—he hardly knew what to call it—that was keeping him inside those walls. He could go back to the old way any time; no one would lift a hand to stop him. And understanding that was the hardest thing of all. It was building the walls yourself, and locking the door yourself, and every day walking past the door and knowing that you could open it if you wanted to, and every day knowing that you would not do it.

Then he began to see that it was like that too with Brand. Watching him come into the drugstore every afternoon, seeing him moving about in the little dark shop that always seemed too small a place for him, caging him with jars and bottles, Sam realized that he was feeling the same things, only with all of them intensified and magnified, as they would be with someone older. Sam was only sixteen, and used to taking orders from older people, but he saw how it was different with Brand. In the factory and in the mines he had worked much harder, but once he knew the work he had not had to take orders often, and in the drugstore there were orders all the time, except when Mr. Symons was not there.

And there was a deep antagonism between the two men, the hidden, civil antagonism that comes only when the stronger must submit and the weaker, in all the knowledge of his weakness, rules. Only rarely it flared into the open. Symons had a hypochondriac's sudden nervous fits of temper, when he blustered shrilly and uncontrollably, like a woman. Then Sam saw the hot, living hatred in Brand's eyes, the brutal, personal animosity that dwells on every detail of its object's appearance with the desire to obliterate and destroy. He saw Symons falter and blench beneath the weight of that gaze. But it never went farther than that; it was like lightning flashing out, gone almost as soon as it had come. Then Symons would grow quieter, and the two men would resume their ordinary relations with each other.

Brand had a reserved, civil manner in the store. He did not talk much to anyone, and the customers usually preferred Mr. Symons to wait on them. When Sam first came to work at the drugstore, Brand did not seem to give him much attention. Then, gradually, a kind of bond grew up between them, a kind of loyalty. There was something in each of them that answered to a need in the other. Sam was at a period in his life when he was learning to bear the weight of a new responsibility. He saw his father's weakness now; he saw that he must depend on himself, and not on the child's image of the father as a tower of strength which he had relied on as long as he could remember. And he turned to Brand as a mentor and an example, without knowing that the very fact of his discipleship struck into the older man as the deep satisfaction of a need.

They did not talk much to each other, for Symons was usually in the store while Sam was there. When they were alone, Sam liked to ask Brand questions about the mines, what it had been like to work in the darkness, below the earth. It seemed to him that there was something glamorous about such an existence, and that it was much more suited to Brand than the life he led now, at school and in the drugstore. But Brand spoke of it bluntly, almost matter-of-factly.

"It's a job, like any other job," he said. "It's harder work than most—that's the only difference."

"But it's dangerous?" Sam said.

"You can get yourself killed without going to much trouble about it, if that's what you mean."

"Did you ever see anyone killed down there?"

Brand shrugged rather grimly.

"When?" Sam persisted.

"Well, the first time was the first day I ever went down. I was scared to death. I was only a kid—a couple of years younger than you are now. You get used to it, when you know there's nothing you can do about it."

There was something else that Sam wanted to talk to him about. He was beginning to think about the future. And he wanted to learn something from Brand, to find out why it was that a man felt he must do one thing above all others in his life. But he did not know how to begin. He did not believe, for himself, that he wanted to be a lawyer. Still there was nothing else, no other ambition, to put in its place.

One Saturday afternoon, late, when Mr. Symons had gone home for dinner, he and Brand were alone in the store. This was always the quietest time on Saturdays, and he knew that Brand liked it for study; but usually Mr. Symons saw to it before he left that there was something for him to do that would keep him busy over the dinner-hour.

This afternoon it was a shelf full of bottles, back in the prescription room, on which he was to put new labels. There were labels on them, but Mr. Symons had said that they were not perfectly clear any longer, and that someone might make a mistake, trying to read them in a hurry. Usually this sort of thing was Sam's job; he was a careful worker, and perfectly dependable; but Mr. Symons had given particular instructions before he left that Brand was to do the labels, and there would have been a great deal of trouble if he had come back and found them in Sam's handwriting instead.

There were no customers in the store, and Sam went back to the prescription room with Brand and helped him with the bottles. This part of the store was always overheated, and it was an uncomfortable place for everyone but Mr. Symons. Brand was in his shirt sleeves, with the sleeves rolled above the elbows. If anyone came into the store, he would have to put on his coat again before he went out to wait on them.

They worked for a while without talking much. Sam took the bottles down from the shelves while Brand wrote out the new labels to put on them. Sam noticed, just as Rhoda had done years before, how serious and awkward the act of writing made the other look. Yet he could work delicately and surely with his hands in other ways. It was only when he had a pen between his fingers that he looked clumsy and slow.

After they had been working for a short time, the telephone rang, and when Sam answered it, it was Mr. Symons on the wire, to say that he thought it would be better if Sam wrote out the labels instead of Brand, because his handwriting was more legible. Brand was to watch him, to see that he copied all the names correctly, and that afterwards the new labels were put on the proper bottles. Sam said all right, and hung up the phone.

"What does he want now?" Brand asked.

"He says I can do it if you keep an eye on me," Sam said.

He did not tell him the part about the handwriting. Brand looked up from the label that he was writing.

"What's the rest of it?" he asked.

"Nothing."

"What is it?"

Sam told him. He thought he might be angry, but he only got up and began rolling down his sleeves so that he could put on his coat and go back out to the store again.

"He's a crazy fool," Sam said after a minute. He watched Brand pull his tie straight and put on his coat. "You won't have to work for him much longer now, will you?" he asked.

"Not so long."

"He'll be plenty sorry when you're practicing, and you send all your patients to Hogarth's instead of here."

"He doesn't think I ever will be practicing," Brand said.

"You'll practice all right," Sam said.

"Yes," Brand said. He sounded sure of it.

Sam sat down at the table where Brand had been sitting, and looked at the last label that he had written.

"What is it about being a doctor?" he asked after a minute. He looked at the label and not at Brand; he was afraid that Brand would think he was asking him something that was none of his business. "Why do you want to be one?"

Brand did not say anything for a minute, and Sam looked at him. He was standing over beside the door. He did not look angry, only serious.

"It's because I know I can do it, Sam," he said. "You know how it is."

"Sure."

"It's the same as it is with anything that you know you can do. You don't want to waste it."

"Like tennis," Sam said. "Or baseball."

"Yes. You've got it, and you know you have, and you don't want to waste it."

Sam thought that it was a queer way to talk about something like that. Still, he understood in a way what Brand meant. Later he understood it better, because he found out how it was really that way inside everyone who had something good, only stronger or not so strong according to how much of it they had; but even then he understood it a little. He watched Brand go out into the drugstore. He had a book under the counter, and he got it out and began to read it. Sam liked him a good deal. He was glad he was doing the labels instead of Brand.

Chapter 5

SAM DID NOT GET OUT TO THE CANNON HOUSE
often now. He saw Bronwen at school, but she always seemed remote
from him there, separated from him in a girl's world. Even though
she had never made any close friends among the other girls, she had
to herd with them there, and not with the boys. He would see her
standing on the outer edges of a group in the corridor, with that
secret, hostile, indwelling expression in her blue eyes that he could
remember from the time when she had first come to Cannon Hill.
The other girls did not care for her; they thought of her as "proud
over nothing," and too reserved because she did not chatter her
secrets to them. But there was a gentleness, a peculiar Celtic civility
in her manner that made it difficult for them to dislike her.

One Sunday in April, a few months after he had begun to work
at the drugstore, Sam walked out to the Cannon House early in the
afternoon, just after dinner. It was a cold, fresh spring day; there
was a stiff wind, and the sky was blue and clear except for a few
big white clouds that were moving along fast, just over the horizon.
He cut across the vacant lot on the east side of the Cannon House
to the garden door, and pushed it open and went in.

Inside it was quiet and lonesome with the weed-grown grape
arbor and the blossoming fruit trees hiding the house. As he walked
up through the garden he saw only a couple of Leghorn chickens
scratching on the paved kitchen yard. He stood outside the back
door and whistled for Bronwen. In a few moments she came to the
door and opened it.

"Come on in," she said. "We're just finishing dinner."

She wore her invariable plain dark dress, and her hair was drawn
back from her face and hung down her back in a heavy brush. It

had remained rather more fair than brown, with bronze tints coming into it in certain lights. And, at sixteen, she was still rather small, with features as clearly and as delicately cut as they had been when she was a child.

Sam went into the house, and she closed the door behind him. She stood there smiling at him. He thought that she seemed excited about something, and happy.

"We're just keeping Robbie company," she said. "He was late coming from the store. You can have coffee if you want."

He shook his head for no. She often called Brand Robbie, as the men did; occasionally she still used the Celtic "my da."

"Come on in anyway," she said. "There's a new boarder; Frank Mallan brought him around. He's been all over the world, and Frank's asking him about it."

Sam knew Frank Mallan, a tall, thin young man who worked as a bookkeeper in the office at the Maitland factory. He was rather nice-looking, with a soft thatch of red-gold hair, and was very popular with the Cannon Hill girls.

"Where did Mallan meet him?" Sam asked.

He did not want very much to go into the dining room. It was too fine an afternoon to spend indoors.

"At one of those commercial language schools, down on Henry Street," Bronwen said. "Frank had a letter he wanted to have translated."

"I'll bet he did," Sam said. "I'll bet it was from one of those Polish girls of his."

Bronwen did not say anything. She did not talk to any of the boys about things of that sort. She had grown up in a house full of men, and she knew a great deal more about them than most girls of her age, but the knowledge had never really touched her. She stayed apart from it; it remained in its own world, and she in hers.

"Let's go on out somewhere," Sam said. "You don't have to stay, do you?"

"Not if you don't want to."

But she was disappointed. He could always tell by her eyes; they gave her away, in their childish vulnerability, even when she seemed to remain quite impassive.

"Well, it doesn't make any difference," he said. "We can go in for a while."

"You don't have to. We can go right out."

"No. I'd like to come in."

She smiled at him a little doubtfully, but, without saying anything else, turned and pushed open the kitchen door.

He followed her into the dining room. A dozen people had eaten at the table there, but only four of them were still in the room. His aunt Rhoda sat at one end of the table, with the sharp, subtle smile on her face that came whenever her interest had been aroused. A little way down the table Brand was finishing his dinner, and on the opposite side Frank Mallan was sitting beside a tall young man in his middle twenties, with an almost indifferently good-humored expression on his contradictorily keen and sharply chiseled face. Rhoda was talking to him when Sam and Bronwen came into the room.

"You ought to be ashamed to say it, then," she was remarking, with a jesting incisiveness. "How old were you when you ran off?"

"Sixteen."

"And broke your mother's heart, I'll swear."

"No. She died when I was ten."

The young man was smiling. He glanced over at Sam. He had the kind of smile, absolutely without self-consciousness or self-importance, that people naturally like. Sam thought that there was something curiously complete about him: the definitely chiseled features, the heavy sweep of straight, dark hair, the natural, offhand manner. The eyes were somewhat heavy-lidded, and the mouth curved and strong, rather small, like the mouth of a young man in an archaic statue.

"Well, I don't doubt you left some other poor woman grieving then," Rhoda said. "An aunt, or a grandmother." She was enjoying herself; Sam saw the quiet, satisfied smile on her face. "Did you ever go back?" she asked.

"Once. It didn't work out very well."

He looked at her with his self-possessed, smiling gaze, that gave her back something of her own hard brilliance.

"They weren't glad to see you? Or *you* weren't glad to see *them?*"

"A little of both, I suppose. My father had very definite ideas about my future."

"What business is he in himself?" Rhoda asked.

"God's business," the young man said, with a rather whimsical emphasis. "He's a minister."

"And *that's* what you were meant to be yourself?"

"No. There were two brothers before me, and they were both studying for the ministry when I left. I was slated to study medicine."

Rhoda glanced down the table at Brand.

"And rather than face *that*, you ran away from your home? How was it they didn't find you and bring you back?"

He laughed. "Why, do you want to hear all my sins?" he asked. "I joined the Army; I lied about my age, and said that my name was Nelson Langerhorne."

"That's the life," Frank Mallan said.

Bronwen had slipped into the chair beside Rhoda's, and she looked around for Sam to come and sit down beside her.

"Do you want coffee, Sam?" Rhoda asked, glancing over at him.

"No, thanks, Aunt Rhoda. We're going out in a minute."

"You'd better stay, Sam," Frank Mallan said. "You've never heard anything like this before."

Brand went on eating his dinner. He was not looking at the others. When Sam sat down he glanced down the table and nodded at him. Sam knew that he had to get back to the drugstore again. He would not have much time for talking now even if he felt like it.

Mallan was asking the stranger—his name, Sam learned, was really Neil Lamson—about the recent Mexican trouble, and the rest of them were all listening, but Brand did not seem to be interested in it. Sam had come in prepared not to be interested, but he found himself liking to listen in spite of that. He was glad now that he had come in. Bronwen glanced at him, saw that he was having a good time, and smiled. Then she went back to watching the strange young man again. She was pleating the skirt of her dress slowly between her fingers as she listened. Then she slowly smoothed it out again.

Lamson told them about Mexico, and then about Constantinople, where he had been during the Turco-Italian war. He did not talk

much about himself, but about the places where he had been and
the things that he had seen, and when he did talk about himself it
was always with a joke, as if it was not anything to be taken seriously.
Rhoda sat watching him. She thought that if she had been a man,
her life might have been like that. It would have satisfied something
in that keen, seeking, restless nature of hers to have gone from one
new excitement to another. And yet there was something in her that
was repelled by that very rootlessness, that need for the exotic and
the dangerous. She saw the two young people, Bronwen and Sam,
absorbing this new strange life. And she was glad that Sam stayed
aloof, and critical, not yielding entirely to his interest. Mallan's thin
face, almost girlish-looking under his red-gold hair, was flushed with
the warmth of his eagerness.

"Why, when I think of myself, tied to a desk six days out of a
week—!" he said, impetuously.

He wanted to be off and doing that very minute. There was a
little silence, that seemed to go running through the clear colorless
spring sunshine like a flame of new life. Then Brand got up deliberately. Mallan turned to look at him.

"What's the matter with *you?*" he asked. He was impatient because everyone did not share his enthusiasm. "There's the trouble
with us, now," he said quickly, to Brand. "Your father and my
father, they had the grit in them to start off life in a new country,
to come thousands of miles across the sea—and what do we do? We
coop ourselves up in a factory, or a shop—"

"You can get your head smashed in a factory as well as you can
in a war, if you go looking for it there," Brand said dryly.

He picked up his coat that was hanging over the back of the chair
and put it on. Mallan looked at him rather sulkily. There was nothing very romantic about an accident in a factory. He waited for
Brand to go out of the room.

But even after he had gone, the glamour did not return. Neil
Lamson, straightening up in his chair, began to talk to Rhoda in
a matter-of-fact way about Bard City, which he did not know very
well. He seemed unconscious of the flame of life that he cast into
the room, as if it were something apart from him. He took it for
granted that people would like him, and be drawn to him, but he

did not trouble to ask himself why. He lived his life as he liked, and if he drew others into it, it was without design, it seemed no more than a kind of accident to him. And he would not feel himself responsible for such accidents; he lived in himself, and he expected that others would do the same.

Sam remembered now about the afternoon that he did not want to waste. He turned to Bronwen.

"Do you want to go?" he asked her.

"All right," she said.

They got up.

"Where are you two off to now?" Rhoda asked.

"I don't know," Sam said. "We'll be around."

Bronwen stood waiting. There was something curiously silent about her, a quiet, absent tenseness, as if of expectancy.

Sam followed her out into the kitchen again. She stopped to take a heavy sweater from a hook behind the door, and pulled it on as she went outside. When they were in the yard she stood and looked at him.

"Where do you want to go?" she asked.

"I don't care. Some of the fellows were saying something about going out to the old racecourse this afternoon. Do you want to go on out?"

She shook her head. "I don't think so. You go if you want to."

"What do you want to do?"

"I just don't want to go out there this afternoon."

She whistled for Queenie, and she came walking slowly up from the back garden, where she had been sleeping in the sun. Bronwen reached down and stroked her ears.

"Let's go down the hill then," Sam said, after a minute. "Gee, it's a swell day. We ought to do something."

He did not know what was the matter with Bronwen. She had never been just like this before. He thought at first that she was upset about something, but when she looked up at him, crouched in front of him as she stroked Queenie's ears, her face was lighted and serious and happy.

"All right," she said.

She stood up again and put her hands in the pockets of her

sweater, and they walked down through the garden together to the door in back. Queenie trotted along beside them.

"Do you want her to come along?" Bronwen asked.

"Sure. She wants to come."

It was the middle of the afternoon, and the wind was still blowing, and the sunlight looked bright and fresh and uncertain on the grass under the moving branches of the trees. They did not talk much for a time. Sam was thinking about Neil Lamson, wondering what it would be like to have the kind of life he had, going wherever you wanted to, always plenty of excitement, and nothing to hold you when you were bored with it, thinking about how he must have been just his age when he had started it, then about how it would feel to do it yourself, to go away alone, hop a freight some evening, riding all night afterward, and waking up the next morning in a town you did not even know the name of. He and Dick Rogan had hopped a freight early one morning the summer before, but they knew it was the 6:10 that stopped half a dozen times between the Cannon Hill station and Port Lincoln, fifty miles down the river, and they had only gone as far as Melrose and then walked back. Nobody had ever found out about it, and they had talked about doing it again this summer, perhaps going as far as Louisville this time, saving up beforehand so they could stay there two or three days; but that was as much as they had ever planned. He did not think now that he would do even that, because as likely as not it would mean losing the job at the drugstore, and besides, with things the way they were at home, he did not want to do anything that would cause any more trouble there. Still he liked to think that it was all there if he ever really wanted it, the change, the excitement, all the new places and the new people.

They had cut through back lots, and then through the old Long-mill place, and were descending the hill now toward the winding dirt road that was the dividing line between Cannon Hill and Haddon.

"This Neil Lamson," Sam said to Bronwen, following his train of thought, "how did he happen to turn up here in Bard City?"

She had her head turned away from him, looking back for Queenie, who had dropped behind.

"I don't know," she said. "He just happened to, I guess. He's only been here about a week."

"He seems like a swell guy," Sam said. They came to the road, and he stopped for a minute while Bronwen turned around again and whistled for Queenie. "What does he do down at that school?" he asked. "Teach languages?"

"Yes. He must know so many, everywhere he's been."

She said it almost hostilely. Queenie came running up heavily, tired, and they crossed the road and went on through the trees in the direction of the creek.

"She's getting so old," Bronwen said, watching Queenie.

"Yes. But she still likes to come along."

He wondered if Bronwen did not want to talk about Neil Lamson. He did not know why she should not want to: she had seemed to like him well enough, back at the house. Everyone, except Brand, had seemed to like him. Brand had not looked as if he would have much use for him. But Sam could understand about that too. Lamson had been born with the chance to have for the asking everything that Brand had been sweating blood for years to get, and he had not cared enough about it to take it when it was right there, waiting for him. And Brand had, besides, the rather impatient contempt that most men who have done dangerous and disagreeable work for years, out of hard necessity, have for anyone who leads that sort of life for the mere love of excitement and change. There would not be anything so impressive about danger to someone who had lived with it because his livelihood and his family's had depended on it, knowing that he could not leave it whenever he wanted to, whenever he was too tired, or too bored, or too much afraid.

He walked along with Bronwen down the slope to the creek. The ground was still rather damp underfoot from the rain there had been the week before. When they reached the creek, they stood for a moment looking down at the water moving rapidly along its winding course. It was high, almost ready to overflow the narrow banks. The trees hung over it here, thrusting their roots from the bare crumbling earth that sloped down sharply to the creek. Bronwen sat down on the ground, with her back to one of the trees.

"Isn't it too wet?" Sam asked.

"No. It's nice."

He sat down beside her. She did not look at him; she hardly seemed to know that he was there. She was watching the water rushing by, with the absent, inward, curiously expectant look in her eyes that he had noticed back at the Cannon House. She did not say anything for a while. They could hear the wind clashing in the branches of the trees overhead, and there were the sudden lonesome flutelike calls of thrushes.

She said after a while: "Sam—"

He looked over at her. She was still sitting there looking at the water, her face half-serious and half-happy in the clear afternoon shadow.

"I want to ask you something," she said.

He waited. He had never seen her like this before. The usual quiet matter-of-factness of her manner seemed to have been shattered into a hundred different facets that came and disappeared swiftly in her face. It was like watching a clear, fast-moving stream to look at her. He could feel himself getting excited in an odd way, watching her.

"I want to ask you—" she said again. "Please, Sam, tell me the truth. Would anyone—would *anyone* think that I was nice-looking?"

He looked at her in surprise. He had never thought consciously of her appearance, as he had thought of the appearance of other girls whom he liked. He knew her so well that he did not even see her in detail when he looked at her, as a person does not see in detail a house he has lived in for many years. Now when he looked at her it was a strange feeling to see consciously the soft hair between fair and brown, the color of the eyes very deep and steady against the fair skin, and the clear curving lines of the features. He felt awkward and happy, cataloguing all this in his mind.

"Sure they would," he answered her. He did not know just how to say it to her. "You're all right, Bron."

"Am I? Am I really, Sam?" She stared ahead with a tense, happy frown between her brows. "You wouldn't say that if it wasn't true, would you?"

"No. It's on the level. I mean it."

She turned to him suddenly. "Nice-looking enough so they'd want to kiss me?"

He could feel his heart race quickly for a moment, then begin
to go in slow hard thuds. He saw her face, that was like the clear
fast water, turned to him with that strange lighted expectant look
on it. And he bent his head and kissed her, almost without knowing
the moment before that that was what he would do. Her lips were
soft and moist and clinging. He had kissed other girls, but it had
never been like this, and they had always laughed then, or kissed
back boldly, or run away; but Bronwen did none of these things. She
only sat there, leaning against him a little, with a faint smile on her
face and her eyes half-closed, as if she were trying to keep the feeling a little longer. Then all at once she drew away, coloring deeply,
and smiled at him in her ordinary way.

He had a sudden drop in feeling. It was as if she had taken herself
away from being with him the way she had been with him a moment
before, or it was even more than that; it was as if she had not been
with him even then, as if it had been someone else she had kissed
instead of him. He sat looking at her, feeling puzzled and half-
resentful, and after a moment she seemed to realize that he was
feeling like that, and the expression on her face changed again as
she withdrew herself behind the barriers of her reserve.

She jumped up and stared away from him, up the slope, into the
falling sun, where Queenie was running about now, snuffing the
ground.

"She's got something up there," she said, in her quiet, ordinary
voice. "Shall we go up?"

"No," he said.

He could feel himself getting stubborn inside, what his mother
called the Beauchamp disposition coming up in him. He had never
felt complicated like this inside about Bronwen before, and he did
not like it, and at the same time he was angry with her because
she was trying to make it seem simple between them again.

"What's this all about?" he asked her.

"It's not about anything."

She was closed against him, standing there with her face lifted,
staring into the sun. It gave him a queer feeling to be wondering
what was going on inside her. There had never seemed to be anything about her before that he could not understand. He did not

know still whether she had wanted him to kiss her or not. It was as if she had wanted him to, but as if she herself had been kissing someone else. That was a crazy thing to think. Still it was the way he felt about it. She had not been kissing him at all.

She said to him in that tense, quiet voice: "Let's *please* go and see what Queenie is doing."

And he got up, he followed her against his will. He was angry with her. Yet he did not really want to think any more about what had happened. There was something in it too complicated, too intense for him now. He wanted to throw it off; he wanted the simple outlines of the day to return. There was a new darkness in her, and a new light; for a moment he had touched them, and known them, but he could not keep it up. She was somewhere beyond him, brooding, waiting for something. And there were too many things for him to get clear in himself before he could follow her; there were too many other problems now that he had to solve.

So they went back to being boy-and-girl playmates for the afternoon. But she kept the tense expectancy in her manner. She did not know herself what it was that she waited for. Even in herself she did not know whether she had wanted Sam to kiss her or not. The whole afternoon was something that had happened to her without the necessity of her willing it.

But she continued to wait for something. When she went back to the Cannon House and saw Neil Lamson standing in the parlor doorway, the outline of his face half in brightness and half in shadow as the light fell on it from inside the room, a drenching warmth swept through her, and she turned and ran quickly to her room. She stood at the open window, looking out at the chill spring night gathering about the house. "I want—I *want*—" she said over and over, with a quivering, irritable impatience, inside herself. But she did not know what it was that she wanted. To go away, to touch impossible shores? The house was too small for her, the garden was too small; she wanted the whole night, the whole night, to take it, somehow, inside herself. And afterwards she went downstairs, and the lights dazed her, the voices were too loud; everything seemed clumsy and coarse; it lacerated her. She looked at Neil Lamson and saw his hands, blunt-fingered, with the dark hair springing on them,

and it was too real for her, it was not what she wanted. The reality
of him went through her sharply and harshly, piercing her as if it
had been a keen cold blade.

One evening after dinner, the week after he had come to live at
the Cannon House, she went out into the garden to look for her
black kitten, Timmie. It was not quite dark; there was still some of
the gray light of the spring evening. But it had rained during the
day, and now the air was misty with fog. The white blossoms of
the pear trees at the end of the garden seemed to surge and billow
through the gathering darkness. She could smell their scent, that
hung freshly in the cool wet air. The evening had the chill vital
pregnancy of early spring.

She went down through the wet garden, calling Timmie's name.
Then she saw someone moving through the trees. Neil Lamson
came up, throwing away the cigarette he had been smoking.

"Who's Timmie?" he asked. "Am I interrupting something?"

He stood above her, taller in the fog, and as if at a distance,
though they were standing near. She looked up at him.

"He's a black cat," she said. "Have you seen him?"

"A black cat? At night?" She could see his watching smile through
the thin watery grayness that separated them. He spoke to her rather
jestingly and tenderly, as if she were a child. "I didn't think anybody
but other cats could see *them*."

She smiled faintly. There was a curious quiet over her now, a
quiet that seemed to surround her like the slow billows of the fog.
She was aware of him as she had never been before, aware of him
now in his completeness, as an individual, a man, not as a congeries
of observed details. And she knew that he too was aware of her.
His voice was jesting and tender, as if to a child, but his eyes were
keen and remote and questing. She almost shuddered, feeling his
eyes on her through the fog, but she held herself in her quiet tenseness.

"I've got to find him," she said. "He's only small."

She made a move forward, tentatively. He seemed to loom in her
way for an instant. But he stood aside.

"We'll both look for him," he said to her.

They moved down through the garden together, walking separately, at a little distance from each other. As they advanced, trees came suddenly toward them out of the mist, and the wet branches dripped slowly as they passed beneath.

"You'll get yourself damp," he said to her.

"It's nice."

She shivered away from the cold brush of a bush against her face, but she loved it, the chill urgent night, the unreal silence of the garden in the fog. And she loved her awareness of him; it was as if she had suddenly developed a new sense, more subtle and more personal than sight or touch or hearing. She felt she would know he was walking there beside her if there were not a sound, not a glimmer of light. She had never yet touched him, never once. But she knew him now, without so much as turning her head to look at him. She felt the knowledge of him sinking deep inside her, into places where no one had ever penetrated before.

He asked her: "Have you always lived here?"

She knew his voice too, rather harsh and matter-of-fact, but full of a vivid, separate life. And she wanted to stand and hear it coming to her through the wet dusk; she wanted to hear the syllables for the sound of the new separate life that was pulsing through them, and not for the meaning that they expressed.

"Not always," she said. "Since I was small."

And she was sixteen now, she had cast the husk of childhood, swiftly, quietly, with no one to know except this stranger who looked at her with his calm, intent eyes. They stood silent beneath the white lifted dimness of the pear trees. She called rather plaintively, "Timmie—Timmie."

The kitten mewed almost under their feet. She stooped and lifted it in her hands. It was damp and soft, with curved clutching little needles for claws that caught at the cloth of her dress.

"Poor Timmie," she said. "Poor kitty."

She held it absently. They turned and went back silently to the house. They went into the kitchen. The light hurt her; she wanted to get away quickly, to be alone. She could not look at him in the light. She went upstairs to her own room and sat in the darkness with her head bowed, thinking dumbly of nothing, trying to keep the feeling of him as it had been in the garden. But it went away quickly.

She heard his voice as he talked to Rhoda downstairs. He seemed strange and removed from her; it seemed impossible that there should ever be the slightest connection between his life and hers.

But as the days went on, they came slowly closer to each other through the brief, accidental contacts of their daily lives. They seemed to share the knowledge of her maturity between them like a secret; it lay between them like an unexplored darkness. And all the while, as the others did, he treated her like a child. He brought chocolates home and offered her the choice of the box, teasing her as she hesitated among the pieces. Or he laughed at her coming in blown by the wind, her hair sticking wildly out from falling ribbons and hairpins. It made her furious, as if at a betrayal. The others, even Rhoda, thought she disliked him, when they saw her fiercely haughty manner with him.

One Sunday morning at the end of May, very early, before anyone else in the house was awake, she heard the door of his room open and his footsteps going quietly past her door to the stairs. She lay for a few moments, wondering. She could see the first light, pale and soft with the spring morning, coming into the room. She got out of bed and dressed quickly and went downstairs.

He was in the kitchen, making coffee. She stood in the doorway, looking at him, surprised. He seemed so full of a kind of quick, irritable life this morning. His gaze, when he looked over at her, came to her like a challenge.

"What are you doing up?" he asked her.

"I heard you come down." She looked at the coffeepot on the stove. "Are you making breakfast?"

"Only coffee. Do you want some?"

She laughed. A feeling of freedom and happiness came over her. It seemed entirely natural for the two of them to be there alone in the big silent kitchen, in the dawn.

"All right," she said.

She went over to the kitchen cabinet and got out cups and saucers and set them on the table. He had unbolted the back door and opened it wide. She went over and stood in the doorway, looking out. The air was soft and gray-blue, hardly touched with sunlight from the cloudy sky.

"What are you going to do, up so early on Sunday morning?" she asked him, standing in the doorway with her back to him.

"I'm going for a walk." He poured the coffee into the cups which she had set on the table. He seemed to hesitate for a moment. "Do you want to come along?" he asked.

She turned around. "Yes. I'd like to."

She sat down at the table and began to drink her coffee. His invitation had intimidated her a little, for some reason. But the happiness was still there, inside her; it beat its way back slowly in her blood. Lamson had not sat down; he had his cup in his hand and was lounging against the kitchen cabinet, looking out the open door. She watched him. There was something light and restless about his movements that she loved. She thought he had a look as if he were poised for flight. He seemed rather absent; she did not try to talk to him.

When they had finished their coffee, she stacked the cups in the sink. He stood watching her.

"Don't come if you don't want," he said, abruptly. "It looks as if it may rain."

"I don't mind."

She got her sweater from the hook behind the door. But she looked at him a little uncertainly. She was afraid now that he did not want her to come.

They went outside, and he pulled the back door to behind them. The action seemed somehow to shut them off in a world of their own. With the whole world of the outdoors around them, they were closer, shut in more closely together, than they had been when they were together in the kitchen. It was so still under the low sky. There was nobody about; the world was all their own. The gray air tasted soft, like rain.

They walked west on Old Town Road, away from Cannon Hill. Once they were past the factories the sidewalk ended, and they walked in the road, with empty fields on both sides. They passed the tall iron fence and the old brick buildings of the Protestant orphanage to the right, then the fields again, green and still in the Sunday morning quiet. She made a noncommittal remark to him now and then. The rather tense, irritable look began to clear from his face.

Once he laughed, and she looked at him suddenly, laughing too.

"What's the matter?" he asked her, smiling.

She hesitated a moment. "You laugh like a blackbird," she said, finally.

He laughed again.

"No, but you do," she protested, coloring.

They rounded a bend in the road. The gray domed slate roof of the old racecourse stadium came into sight, its little tower standing out against the sky.

"Have you ever been inside?" she asked him.

He shook his head. She looked at him interrogatively, and then, without asking him in words whether he wanted to go in or not, led the way through the long, weedy grass toward the gate. She felt a kind of proud possessiveness of him; for this morning at least he was hers.

They went inside the gate, and walked along before the tiers of wooden seats, some of them rotted and falling in, with the grass growing up to them so that one could not even see any more where the track had been on which the horses had used to run. It was quiet in here: they could hear the breeze moving with a whispering sound across the sweet coarse spring grass. Bronwen loved the feeling of aloneness she could get here, with the high rows of empty seats stretching all around, and the grass-grown track, and then remembering the way it must have been a long time ago, a band playing and flags flying and the crowds all cheering as the horses came thundering around under a blue spring sky.

They walked out slowly across the grass. The sky was growing heavier overhead; the occasional gleams of sunlight had disappeared. But there was a wonderfully clear, colorless light that seemed to come from all directions, not from the sky alone, but from the air about them and the earth under their feet as well. It was as if they were walking in some new element, bright and transparent and all-pervading.

Then the first thin drops of rain began to fall. They stopped walking. They were in the very center of the field. Lamson turned to her.

"Shall we go back?" he asked.

She did not answer. She glanced back at the silent tiers of seats rising around them. They were so much alone, standing there in the impersonal silence of this once-public place, in the gray veiling rain. She could not bear it that they should give themselves back to the rest of the world so quickly. She looked up at him, half-questioningly.

"It won't rain hard—will it?" she asked.

She saw him looking straight down at her. He seemed so remote, so sharply separate in the gray air, though they were standing near. She looked at him, asking, unsatisfied, her brows bent together. And suddenly, so quickly that it seemed to happen in a single moment of volition shared by both, she was in his arms, clinging close to him while he held her firm in a world that rocked and swung through the soft rain and the bright gray morning. And she did not want it to end; she wanted to remain fixed so, in the spring morning, in the rain, under the silent impersonal surveillance of those hundreds of empty seats, for as long a time as the earth should last.

But he became separate again; she felt him leave her while his arms were still about her, and she drew away, looking up at him. He was frowning slightly.

"This isn't any good," he said shortly.

"Isn't it?"

"No. And you've got to get home."

He turned and started across the grass toward the gate. She went beside him.

"*Why* isn't it any good?" she asked, rather childishly.

He stared down at her. "You know that as well as I do."

"Because I'm too young for you?" It was more a statement than a question, given rather heavily. She could have wept at having her moment spoiled by this prosaic cross-questioning.

"Because you're too young for anybody."

He put on his jesting air with her again. But it was an effort for him to keep it up. What there had been growing silently between them for weeks had shown itself, like a moment's lightning-glare, in the soft, unexplored darkness that had been between them. Now each of them knew what was in that darkness. And they could not go back altogether to pretending that they did not know.

They walked back to the Cannon House in the quietly falling

rain. Only Mrs. Sorley was in the kitchen when they came in, tying on her apron as she prepared to make breakfast. She looked at them with alert, startled eyes.

"And where might the two of you have been to, at this time of the morning?" she demanded.

"We took a walk," Bronwen said.

"Do you tell me so?" Mrs. Sorley said. "In the rain?"

Bronwen felt her clear sharp eyes on her. She laughed; a current of new, warm happiness began to flow through her veins.

"Yes, and we're starved to death," she said. "Won't you make wheatcakes for breakfast, now?"

She went into the cupboard to get the ingredients. She could hear Lamson coaxing Mrs. Sorley in the kitchen. His voice was like himself, alive and indifferent and good-humored. She stood in the cupboard, holding the molasses jug and listening to him. She felt full of a kind of brightness that had never been in her before; her whole life seemed to be running inside her in a swift, bright stream.

He was a little more withdrawn with her after that. But they were still growing closer every day, in the commonplace little intimacies of their daily lives. If they only passed each other on the stairs, there was a significance in it that made it the most vital happening of the day. They hardly ever saw each other alone. When they did, it was always in the house, where someone else might come in at any moment. And he seemed to have made up his mind that it was absurd for him to make love to her. She was nearly ten years younger than he was, and there was something still so childish about her. Even in her reserve there was something vulnerable and childish.

But they were growing too close; he could not keep up the pretense of distance. One afternoon, when she came home late from school, she met him just at the top of the steps as she ran upstairs to her room. She had her books in her arms, and her face was flushed with the heat and intent with haste. She did not see him till she almost ran against him at the head of the staircase. And before either of them quite realized what was happening, he had drawn her into the shadow of the high newel and was kissing her quickly and with a kind of bright, concentrated eagerness, her schoolbooks, still in

her arms, pressing sharply between them. Then there was the click
of a latch as a door opened behind them, and they parted as quickly
and as silently as they had come together. They did not need words
to help them to come always closer and closer to each other.

Yet all this time she did not really understand how she felt toward
him. There was something hard and complete about him that she
could not understand, that seemed to keep him separate from her,
no matter how close they came to each other. And there was none
of that gentleness in him that there was deep in Brand's nature, and
that she loved. But she needed someone, she needed a center for her
new universe. And sometimes what she loved best in him was that
clear hard elusiveness that she could never grasp; in her mind it
seemed to be one with all the other opening delights that she could
never have entirely—the maddening beauty of the night, the hoary
silver fall of the moon, the precise, delicate sound of a gentle rain
on leaves. So that, on those rare, sudden occasions when he held her
in his arms, she wanted to fling her own arms about him and press
him tightly to herself, as if in holding his body so she were holding
not only the bright, elusive core of his inner self, but also the night,
and the moon, and the sound of the rain.

The parts of his life that she could not share—his work, his
friends, all of his past—were like a dark shadow on her inner consciousness. He seemed to depart from her utterly when she stood in
a doorway and saw him laughing and talking, unconscious of her,
with the other men. He had become popular with them very quickly;
he had the ability to adapt himself without difficulty to any company. And sometimes, seeing how he had dropped so lightly, almost
at random, into the life he was living now, she felt a cold terror that
he would be able to leave it as suddenly and lightly.

She never dared to speak of this to him directly. But one July
afternoon, when he had come home from the school before the other
men had returned from their work, and had stretched himself out
on the old green hammock on the second-story porch to cool off, she
tried to find her way a little into all those other lives of his. She
stood with her back to the railing, facing him, affecting a superficial
calm.

"Do you like it, down at that school?" she asked.

He was lying lazily, with his eyes half-closed.

"It's all right," he said.

"But you don't like it—*really?*"

He considered. "No, I suppose not—really."

"Then what *do* you like?"

He opened his eyes, laughing a little at her determined, serious
face.

"I like you to swing the hammock for me," he said.

She flushed suddenly, almost offended.

"*Why* won't you ever talk seriously to me?" she demanded.

But she could not reach him. He only looked at her with his lazy,
tantalizing smile.

"I'll be as serious as you like if you'll swing the hammock," he
promised.

She reached out in silence and began with one hand to move the
hammock slowly back and forth.

"Now you're angry," he teased her.

"I'm *not* angry. I only want you to talk to me the way you talk
to other people."

"Other people don't mind it that I don't talk to them the way I
talk to *you,*" he said.

"Yes, but—" She broke off, irritated at her own inability to put
into words what she wanted to say. She looked at him with a tormented expression on her face.

"What do you want me to talk about, then?" he asked, relenting.

She shook her head quickly, still sensitive.

"Oh, about *you*—and what you like—and why you came to Bard
City—"

He turned his head to look at her, laughing again.

"I came to Bard City because I was out of funds, and because I
ran into an old friend in Chicago who said he had a berth for me
here."

She thought for a moment. "And were the reasons you went to
all those other places just like that too?" she asked.

"Some of them, I suppose."

"But you went to the others because you wanted to?"

"Yes."

She was silent again for a moment, while she continued to rock the hammock absently.

"And where do you want to go now?" she asked suddenly.

"Nowhere in particular. I'm very comfortable just as I am."

He was smiling at her, but behind his idle self-possession she sensed something taut, almost antagonistic to her.

"No," she said, feeling her face cold and stiff in the hot July afternoon. "But where *would* you like to go?"

He turned his head a little away from her.

"Well, there's always the war," he said.

She knew it was the answer she had been expecting. But she forced herself to speak as he had, without emotion.

"It's not our war," she said.

"A war is anybody's war." He turned his head again, staring up at the ceiling of the porch. "A war is like the earth," he said; "it's big enough for everybody who wants it."

She wanted to say—"Do *you* want it?"—but the words would not come to her lips. She stood swinging the hammock mechanically, with a blind, fixed face. She would not believe that he would ever leave her. He was a part of her life now, something as necessary to her existence as the sunlight.

But there were other times when she forgot the thousand threads of his life that she could not gather into her own hands, when they seemed of no importance, and she seemed to have the whole of him for herself, with the rest of the world existing only as a shadowy background. In the hot July nights he followed her sometimes back into the garden, and they stood under the deep blackness of the pear trees together. He made love to her only rarely, in sudden, almost unwilling instants, but there was the compulsion on each of them to be with the other. They lived in a state of laughing, dissatisfied tension that was only released when they were together. They were both intensely and unthinkingly happy.

The others gradually began to take notice of them. Mrs. Sorley, in particular, began to keep a watch on them. She noticed Lamson strolling back into the garden with his cigarette in the evening, when Bronwen was already out there. And, peasantlike, she was not blinded by the conventions of the time and place, which decreed that a girl hardly sixteen was still a child. She saw Bronwen's young breasts and the sturdy, delicate curves of her body. And she saw the eyes with the nascent, elusive light in them that had never, since the beginning of time, shone upon a child's world.

She spoke to Rhoda about it one evening, when she saw the two, Bronwen and Lamson, go back into the garden together.

"We'll be having a wedding on our hands before we know it," she said. "Have you been watching that pair of young jays walking out with each other?"

Rhoda looked at her incredulously.

"Bronwen?" she said, bringing out the automatic objection almost before she thought. "Why, she's only a child."

"A child, is it?" Mrs. Sorley said bluntly. "I've seen them at her age when they were married and had a child of their own. And that young Lamson's the one who'll be leading Bron that way if somebody doesn't keep an eye on him. They're both head over heels, or *I* never saw it before."

Rhoda wanted to argue with her, but she found herself cutting the ground from under her own objections. Once she had been brought to think of it consciously, she could remember half a dozen incidents that seemed to support Mrs. Sorley's contention. And she remembered too that, when she herself had been scarcely a year older than Bronwen, she had been engaged to marry John Lefroy, who had been almost as much older than she was then as Neil Lamson was older now than Bronwen.

She watched Bronwen when she came in from the garden that night. And then she wondered at herself, that she had been so blind. The girl's face was answer enough to all her doubts. The happiness in it was so intense, as if she had just been born into a magnificent new world. And she looked at Lamson radiantly and proudly, with the pride and the radiance of her love.

Rhoda could not sleep, thinking of it that night. She liked Lamson, but she knew that what was going on between him and Bronwen was dangerous. She knew his sort too well; she had seen it too often in her years of living among men. There was that curious completeness about him, the completeness of the wanderer, who carries his whole emotional life with him wherever he goes, as he carries his personal belongings. He would not leave anything behind when he went, no roots, nothing that could draw him back. And he *would* go; sooner or later she knew that he would go.

She blamed herself that she had not seen what was going on before. She had always felt that she was responsible for Bronwen, since Brand had so little time for her, but it had been a responsibility that she had been able to take lightly up to this time. Bronwen had always been so quiet and self-contained; there had not seemed to be much that she needed to do for her. And they had never grown particularly close to each other; since Bronwen had been crowded out of Brand's life, she had never been very close to anyone but Sam. Rhoda began to realize, as she lay awake thinking of it that night, why the girl had turned to Neil Lamson. She had arrived at a time of life at which the need for love was imperious in her. Then she had met Lamson, and whatever mutual attraction there had been between them had been developed and magnified by her loneliness. She had needed someone, and he had come. But Rhoda knew that it could never seem so logical and easily explicable as that to Bronwen. She had seen her eyes, blind with the radiance of her new happiness. She was living in miracle, not in fact.

Rhoda did not want to go to Brand with the matter. She knew he felt a kind of antagonism toward Lamson, though they had little to do with each other. And she knew he would be too angry to be reasonable or tactful. She wanted to speak to Lamson herself. She liked him, and they had become rather good friends.

She saw him walking up to the house from the end of the trolley line the next afternoon, while she was out working in the garden, and she went into the house to catch him before he could go upstairs. She brought him into the parlor. Her hands were still stained with earth, and her hair, that was growing gray quickly now, was wisped untidily about her face. She laughed as she saw herself in the mirror above the mantel.

"You might tell me to go and wash my face and hands before you'll talk to me," she said. "But you're a very polite young man."

He smiled at her from across the room, his head thrown back slightly, with his alert, watchful, indifferent air.

"Am I?" he said.

She nodded decisively. "Yes, you are. And, because you are, you're going to listen very politely to what I have to say to you, even though you may not like it one little bit."

He looked at her good-humoredly, without a sign of surprise.

"That sounds as if *you* were going to be very *im*polite," he said.

"I am." She stared straight at him with her keen blue eyes. "I'm going to ask you to go away."

He did not say anything for a moment. But she did not think that he was disconcerted, or even very much surprised, by what she had said.

"Why?" he asked presently.

"I think you know why. It's Bronwen. It'll be better for both of you if you put an end to that right now."

There was a slight, clear frown on his face. She thought that he looked hampered, somehow. But it was not her words that were troubling him, but something inside himself. She went on again.

"I don't know whether you've thought about where this is going to end," she said. "But *you're* not ready to settle down, and Bron's too young. It's no good for either of you. And you're the one who can do something about it."

He turned away with a sudden rather angry movement.

"How do you know what's no good and what's not?" he asked. "How do you know what I'm ready to do?"

But she insisted: "You don't want to stay. Not even for her. You've never believed you would. And it's not fair to her, to go on—"

He did not want to talk about it. He would have preferred to keep it all in the darkness of his own mind; he did not want to have to take it out into the light and examine it clearly and logically and disinterestedly. For so long now he had been accustomed to circumstances making his decisions for him. Something happened, something over which one had no control—a war, a chance meeting, a piece of good or bad luck—and one simply took the road that they predetermined. It was that sort of road that he had been following with Bronwen. He had never thought, really, of where it was leading. He had not even thought about how deep his feeling for her went. He was content to let it go on. And now there was this interruption, this interference. He was forced to think about it now, to make some decision.

He left the house after dinner that evening, and Rhoda did not see him again till the next day. It was late July now, a day of intense heat and color. The dark greens and browns of the trees in the garden blazed as if they had been fashioned of stained glass. Bronwen was sewing a new dress for herself that she wanted to have finished by Sunday, the day when she and Lamson saw the most of each other. But she could not settle down to it; she laid it down and went out into the garden, walking about restlessly under the trees. Rhoda wondered if she had guessed that something was wrong; she was extraordinarily sensitive to changes in the mental atmosphere about her. She knew that Lamson had not had an opportunity to speak to her yet.

The late afternoon came, and the men dragged home from work. They were tired and inclined to be short-tempered from the effect of the heat. When Lamson came, in his clean gray suit and white shirt, he looked clear and detached beside them. And he seemed in such a cool good humor. At dinner he joked with the others and brought them all to laughing. But to Rhoda there seemed to be a kind of tension in his good spirits. He did not look in Bronwen's direction. He seemed purposely to keep himself intact, away from her.

Someone began to talk about the war.

"Yes," Lamson said. "I happened to meet a friend of mine the other day, who's on leave from a Royal Flying Corps training camp in Canada. I've made up my mind to go up there and get into it too."

The others were immediately interested; they looked at him with the excitement of a group of schoolboys who would like to dare to follow a leader into some adventurous undertaking. Rhoda glanced over at Bronwen. The girl's face was as white as if someone had struck her. She did not say a word; she did not even look at Lamson. There was something stricken and fierce about her. Even beyond the fact that he was going away, the fact that he had not thought enough of their relationship to consider himself bound to tell her first of his decision struck at her harshly. She got up from the table as soon as the meal was over and went out to the garden.

She did not know whether or not she expected him to come to her there. With some instinct within her she knew that he did not want to come, that now that his decision had been made he wanted to keep everything in that clear and strenuous realm of action in which he was so splendidly at home. And she did not want to talk about it either, if it were really fixed in his mind that he was to go. Only she wanted to hear him say that things were not at an end between them; she wanted to hear him say that he loved her. If he would say that to her, she would forgive him anything; she would be able to live with the fact of their separation.

He came after a time. It was almost dark; the sky in the west was a pale clear green. Looking up at it from the darkness of the garden, they felt as if they were in some underwater world, seeing the pale light from above filtering through the green depths.

"I'm going on Wednesday," he said to her.

"Are you?"

She was surprised at herself that she could speak to him in such a natural tone. She felt as if the weight of the whole sky were pressing on her.

"Yes," he said.

He did not want to talk about it, to begin on reasons and explanations. And, after all, she understood. She had known all along, inside herself, that he would go. And he could not tell, himself, whether he would come back or not. He did not think about the future. Only he knew that he wanted her now. What had happened between him and her was something different from anything he had ever known before. But he wanted to keep it as it had been. When other people came into it, when it became burdened with prudential considerations and necessities, it would not be the same. So he was going away. But he felt that he would not forget.

He drew her to him in the darkness under the pear trees. But she was stiff and withdrawn. She wanted to be near him, but she could not bear it, knowing that it was coming to an end. She drew away and went silently into the house. She sat in her room, wondering how she could bear it. The world was being taken away from her. She wore herself out with her rebellion.

He was very tender and quiet with her during those last days before he left. He seemed to be going back, to protect himself, to the time that spring when they had first become aware of each other, and he had treated her as if she were still a child. She was quiet and unresponsive. A numbness had come over her; her emotions had worn themselves out. She knew that he was going away, and the knowledge made it seem to her as if he had already gone. He was insubstantial to her now.

He left the evening of the following Wednesday. His friend, the R.F.C. flier, came to the Cannon House for dinner. Bronwen saw them laughing and talking together. She felt as if he had already gone a great distance from her. She was shut out of his life completely.

She went upstairs to her room after dinner, not waiting to say good-by. There was a good deal of bustle and laughter below. Then she heard him running quickly up the stairs. He came down the hall to the door of her room and knocked.

She went to open the door. He was standing there, not smiling, but still flushed with the excitement that had been going on downstairs. There was a small square box in his hand.

"I want you to have this," he said, holding it out to her.

She took it from him mechanically and opened it. Inside there was a fine gold chain with a small, star-shaped locket hung on it. She looked up at him. The flush of excitement had died out of his face. There was a strained silence between them.

"I don't want it," she said to him suddenly. "I don't want to remember."

She pushed the box toward him blindly. His face was strained and puzzled. For a moment they seemed to hang poised on the brink of some decision. But someone called to him impatiently from below.

He took the chain from the box and fastened it around her neck. She stood stiffly, not moving to hinder him, her face turned a little away. He closed his arms around her.

"Say good-by," he commanded her.

She shook her head. She could not say it. And he kissed her and went downstairs. She heard him in the hall below, saying good-by to the others. There was so much talk and laughter. It hurt her, the words struck against her like weights, each one bruising her again.

Then a screen door slammed, the excitement fell, and she knew that he was gone. She stood at the door of her room, her face blind and wrinkled. But she could not cry. She felt empty and cold. And the house was empty, and the garden empty, and the night was coming with its empty stars. She felt that she was living alone in a world of ghosts. *He* was the only reality, and he was gone. She had only the narrow chain with the locket, lying as he had put it, about her neck. She took it off and hid it away in a drawer. She did not want to see it; she did not want to remember. She tried to make herself into something without feeling, something that had no need of love.

Chapter 6

THE SUMMER CAME TO AN END, AND ANOTHER school year began. Bronwen was farther than ever from the other girls. She stayed aloof; she did not want to join in the quick excitement of their talk, that always centered mysteriously now on the boys they knew. Now and then she had a letter from Lamson, friendly, hastily written notes that told of his new experiences and seldom referred to anything in the past. He was learning to fly; he expected to be sent overseas before very long. She suffered over having to answer his letters. In the end she always wrote to him rather formally. She could not put her real feelings into words; she felt as if she were writing to someone who was dead. And when she realized this consciously, she was terrified. She had never thought, before that, that he might be killed; the war had always seemed so far away, almost unreal, to her. But the feeling quickly disappeared again. She was too young, too living, to believe yet in the possibility of death.

She was very lonely just at this time. She did not run with the boys any longer, and Sam was still working at the drugstore after school and on Saturdays; he did not have much time for her. There had been a kind of reserve between them, besides, ever since the day that Neil Lamson had come to the Cannon House. She had stepped into a world where he was not ready to follow her, and he felt resentful, in a way, and rather impatient. He was not much interested in girls just then, and he wanted her as a companion or not at all. He had his own adjustments to make; he was finding life a complicated matter at the time. And the kind of companionship he really wanted he found in Brand. He made something of a hero of the older man. Brand's steadiness of purpose, his hidden, passionate belief in the work that he wanted to do, seemed to him so much more admirable than his father's impetuous instability. And he liked the hard sense of the realities of life that Brand combined with that hidden idealism of his.

So he went through the year, his last at high school. Only toward the end of the spring term he began to be attracted by a girl whom he saw in some of his classes. She was a slender, energetic girl, always very well-dressed, with ash-blonde hair and rather irregular features. He knew her name, Frances Hardy, but very little else about her, as she had just moved to Bard City at the beginning of the term, and lived not in Cannon Hill, but in Haddon. And as the school was a large one, and she had not become friendly with his particular group, he went on from day to day without ever coming to know her well. But there was something casual and decided about her that he liked. She did not mix particularly well with the other girls; she was inclined to lead, and they resented her self-assurance, and her clothes, which were so much more fashionable than theirs. But she quickly became popular with the boys.

At the senior dance, just before graduation, in the beginning of June, she came with Dick Rogan, wearing a clear lemon-yellow dress that made the other girls, in their graduation white, look uniformed and uninteresting. Sam was with Bronwen. She danced beautifully, but she was like something light and unreal, almost abstract, in his arms. He wished that he were dancing with Frances Hardy instead. But, though he knew Dick so well, he felt a kind of reluctance about going up to him and his partner. He was half-afraid that he would do or say something to make her laugh at him, or dislike him. Rather than risk that, he would let matters go on as before.

But after a time, between dances, Dick came up to him and Bronwen. He was alone, and there was a look between laughter and anxiety on his face.

"Say, Bron," he said, "we're in a spot. Fran's torn her dress, and I thought you might be able to help. She doesn't know one end of a needle from the other, and besides, she says she can't do anything herself while it's *on*."

Bronwen frowned slightly. Like most of the other girls, she was a little wary and ill at ease with Frances. But she wanted to help.

"I'll see what I can do," she said.

Dick linked his arms through hers and Sam's.

"Well, come on," he said. "What are we waiting for?"

Frances was standing in the vestibule outside the gymnasium where the dance was going on. She wrinkled up the corners of her eyes at the others as they came out.

"Hurrah," she said. "Reinforcements." She held up a wide flare of tulle that was drooping around her on the floor. "Look at me," she offered, whirling around.

Her dress was made in the fashionable tunic style, of yellow tulle, over a taffeta underskirt of the same color, and the tulle skirt, she explained, had been caught in the door behind her as she came out with Dick, and had been ripped almost half away beneath the tunic. Bronwen got down on her knees to examine the damage, while the two boys stood at the outer doorway, laughing and a little embarrassed. The transparent tulle was more ornamental than anything else, as it was the taffeta beneath that performed the real function of a dress, but they felt all the same as if there were something intimate about their being there.

"It's pretty bad, I'm afraid," Bronwen said, looking up at Frances after a few moments. "You've torn the skirt half off; a pin won't do any good, and it'll take a good while to sew it."

Frances looked down at the hanging tulle. She was not at all upset; there was a look of amusement in her eyes. Sam noticed the way her hair hung rather coltishly about her face, instead of being done up carefully in curls, like the other girls'. There was something unconventional and different about her, even in her features, the mobile mouth and the fine, slightly arched nose.

"Well, I can't go around *this* way," she declared, pulling impatiently at the tulle. She glanced over at Dick, her gray eyes lighting up suddenly. "I think I'll just pull the whole thing off and go *as is*," she said.

She was watching him to see how he took it. Dick was usually imperturbable, but he looked a little dismayed.

"Hey, don't—" he began.

She pulled decisively at the skirt, where it was still attached, beneath the tunic. It came away with a clear ripping noise.

"That's much better," she said, looking serenely and innocently at Dick. The tulle skirt fell about her feet, and she stepped out of it. "You'd better bundle it up in a corner somewhere, where nobody'll find it," she advised him. She whirled around again, with her arms out, admiring the effect of the taffeta underskirt. "Don't I look nice? The lastest style—"

Dick looked uncomfortably at the heap of flimsy yellow material on the floor. He did not know at all what to say to her. Even though he would never have imagined, if he had seen her at the beginning of the evening in the dress as it was now, that there was anything missing from it, he did not like to go back on the floor with her. He knew that someone would be sure to notice the change. She looked at him with her characteristic expression of amused challenge.

"What's the matter? Are you *afraid* to go back with me?" she demanded.

"No, of course not," Dick said, still uncomfortably. "But look here—don't you think if you went home and changed—?"

"You *are* afraid," she said. She was laughing. She turned suddenly to Sam. "Come on," she said. *"You* take me in. I don't embarrass *you,* do I?"

She linked her arm in his promptly. He was as incapable of resisting her as if she had been an army. He saw her hand, small and narrow and white, with its rather prominent bones, on his sleeve. There was nothing about her that was really beautifully formed and perfect, as there was about Bronwen, but it seemed as if her very imperfections had a glamour in them.

He went out into the gymnasium with her. The orchestra had just begun to play a one-step, and she turned, laughing, putting her arms up to him, and they began to dance. He had already forgotten all about the change in her dress.

"You live in Cannon Hill, don't you?" she asked him.

"Yes."

"Dick says you're going to the University with him in the fall."

"Yes, I suppose I am," he said.

He felt incapable of talking to her. It had all happened too suddenly. And in a few minutes it was over. Dick had come in and was dancing with Bronwen, and as soon as the music stopped he came over, a little sulkily, to where Sam and Frances were standing.

"What about this?" he said to Frances. "Walking out on me— You didn't give me a chance."

"You didn't look as if you wanted one very badly," she said.

He shrugged. "You can take off anything you want to—*I* don't care," he said to her. "Only give a fellow a minute to get his breath."

She went off with him, laughing, and glancing back for a moment over her shoulder at Sam. He stood looking after her.

"Do you like her?" Bronwen asked him.

"Yes—I guess I do," he said. He looked down at her. "Don't you?"

"No," she said, downrightly.

"I don't like her better than I like you," he protested.

He had thought for a moment, suddenly, that she might be jealous. But she only smiled at him with the indrawn, rather indifferent elusiveness that she seemed to have for him now. She was not really interested in what he felt.

He did not see Frances again till the night of the graduation exercises, two days later. She passed him in the corridor and stopped to tell him about the trouble she had had over the incident of the skirt. Mr. Dobyns, the principal, who had been at home ill on the night of the dance, had heard that one of the senior girls had taken off her skirt and danced half the evening in her petticoat.

"We had a big scene in the office," she said. "Mamma had to come, and Dick. Have you seen Dick? Didn't he tell you about it? Dobie didn't want me to graduate with the class, and Mamma was grand— She used to be on the stage once, you know, years ago. She told him we were related to all the best families in Chicago—"

The bits of information he knew about her family background were confusing and a little exotic; they added to the interest that he felt in her. She came from Chicago, and there was a rumor around the school that her father had been a broker, who had shot himself after he had swindled his clients out of a substantial sum of money. He knew that she and her mother lived now with her mother's sister and her husband, who was a building contractor, fairly well to do.

She told him that evening that she was going to study singing at the Bard City Institute of Music after her graduation, with a professional career in view. He felt as if she were going out of his reach. He wanted to talk to her longer, but it was time for the exercises to begin. Afterwards he saw her with her mother, a large, slow-moving, imposing-looking woman, talking to Mr. Dobyns. They were all laughing and talking together, on the best of terms. He could not go up to them. And he went home dissatisfied and restless. He thought over various ways in which he could manage to see her again.

A few days after the high school graduation had taken place, Brand graduated with his class from medical school. Sam went with Bronwen and Rhoda to the exercises, which were held in common with those of all the other colleges of the University. It was a hot blue June evening, and the big hall was crowded and stifling under the lights. For a time Sam could not pick Brand out from the long rows of figures, all alike in cap and gown, that were seated on the stage. Then at last he saw him at the end of a row, looking hot and uncomfortable in his unfamiliar costume. When he left his place and filed by the dean of the medical school with the others to receive his diploma, Sam saw that the gown he wore was too short for him, and tight through the shoulders. There seemed to be no dignity, no significance, in this moment for which he had worked so long. To Sam the whole ceremony—the speeches which the audience could only half-hear through the languid flap of fans, the long lines of graduates passing monotonously across the stage—seemed perfunctory and inadequate. Only the name in the list of graduates on the printed program—Robert Brand—had a certain serious finality about it.

When the exercises were over, he went back with the others to the Cannon House. They were all rather silent. So many things seemed to be coming to an end that night. Brand would be beginning his internship at the Bard City General Hospital; Sam was going to the University; and Bronwen was to take a business course that summer, so that she could begin to work in the fall.

They went into the parlor, the four of them, feeling like strangers with each other, at a loss. Mrs. Sorley came out from the kitchen and stood in the doorway with her arms folded, looking at them.

"Well," she said, "is it all over now?"

Rhoda nodded. "Yes," she said. "It's all over."

She sat down rather wearily. She had expected to feel so triumphant on this evening, but there seemed to be a kind of weight on her instead. She remembered the first day that Brand had stood in this room, ten years before. He had come into her life just at the time when she had most needed something to give it purpose and significance, and for ten years, in the daily routine of her living, her life had rooted itself in his. And now he would be leaving the Cannon House, going into a new world where she would not be able to follow him.

Mrs. Sorley was looking at Brand.

"Wisha, it's made no difference in the way you look, then," she said, shrugging decisively. "You look like a coal digger, Rob Brand, and that's the true fact. There isn't anything else gives a man shoulders like that. By the Lord, like a regular ox."

Brand looked over at her indifferently, rather abstractedly, without answering her. After a moment he walked out of the room and through the hall to the back of the house. They heard the screen door close behind him. Mrs. Sorley looked after him with a sharp little movement of curiosity.

"Mercy of God, what's on him now?" she said. "I never saw the like of him for the queer old ways he has."

Rhoda looked at her ironically.

"You might show a bit more respect now to a man with an M.D. after his name, Maud," she said.

Mrs. Sorley threw back her head with one of her martial movements.

"Well, he's the great one to be killed with grandeur now," she said tartly, "with two shirts to his name, and the cuffs of his trousers frayed out till you wouldn't find an old tramp wouldn't turn up his nose at them. It'll take more than a pair of letters after his name to make a fine gentleman out of Robbie Brand, or to make a doctor out of him either—and you won't find many folks in Cannon Hill that won't go as far as to agree with *that*."

She went back to the kitchen, satisfied to have had her say. Sam sat with the others a while longer, and then said that he had to be getting back home. He went out the back way, to see if he could find Brand before he left. As he crossed the kitchen yard, he saw him walking up and down in the garden. He looked over at the same time and saw Sam and came across to him.

"Are you going?" he asked.

"Yes. It's past eleven. I have to get home."

Brand stood there looking at him through the darkness.

"I'm glad you could come tonight," he said.

He had a grave, rather formal way of saying things like that, which Sam always thought of as being peculiarly Welsh. Sam looked at him, wondering what he had been thinking of, walking up and down out here alone in the garden. He did not seem excited, but Sam knew him well enough by this time to know that he was not quiet inside. There was an expression of energy and concentration on his face; it was as if the powerful inner compulsion that was ordinarily hidden behind the wall of his reserve was flaming out for the first time into the open.

"I wouldn't have missed it," Sam said, after a moment's silence. "It's a big night for you."

"You don't know how big, Sam."

Brand turned and began walking slowly down toward the end of the garden again. He was too restless to stay in any one place. Sam walked along with him.

"No," he said. "I'll bet it's a swell feeling, though."

"It's better than that." Brand was quiet for a moment, and then went on. "It's the best way there is to feel, Sam, the way you feel when you know you've made yourself into whatever it is you were meant to be." He did not look at Sam, a little embarrassed to be saying this, but wanting to say it, having to say it to someone tonight. "They talk about the miracle of birth," he said. "There's a kind of birth a man has to give to himself—finding out what he's good for, then learning how he can use it, how to go about becoming what he knows he has it in him to be."

He stopped talking, and Sam waited for him to go on again, but he walked ahead without saying anything more. They came to the end of the garden. Away to the right, across the dark empty fields beside the house, they could see the lights of Cannon Hill. Under the high, dark-blue summer sky they seemed small, and fraught with a kind of impersonal humanity. Brand stood looking at them.

"It's quite a feeling all right," he said slowly, after a time, "to think there are people out there who may be depending on you some day to make the difference for them between living and dying." He was not really talking to Sam any more. He was saying the things he had saved up to say until this night, until he had earned the right to say them to himself. Sam stood listening to him in the quiet darkness, watching his powerful figure looming there against the distant lights. "I want to do it well," Brand said; "I want to do it right. And, by the Lord, I can; I can do more than anyone else believes or knows. I can do it all now. I can do what I couldn't do for Maura and Rob, ten years ago. And I can say, 'I've done what I set out to do'—"

Under it all, Sam felt, watching him, there was a curious ambivalence in his feeling toward the people among whom he planned to do his work. He might have thought of beginning practice in some other place than Cannon Hill, when he had finished his internship, but that idea seemed hardly to have occurred to him. He wanted to stay here, to establish himself here, where he had had his hardest struggles. There was in him, on the one hand, the desire to use his knowledge in work that he had never considered as the means of bringing a merely personal success, only as the chance to use, for everything that it was worth to others, something very good that he knew he had. And there, at the same time, was the bitterness and the pride, the desire for acknowledgment. Both, to be fulfilled to their widest extent, had to be exercised here. Sam understood only a little of this now. It was not till years later, when he remembered this night, that he understood clearly what he only felt vaguely now.

He had his own difficulties facing him just at this time. There had been a family conclave on the subject of what he was to do, now that he had finished high school. His father was determined that he should go to college; he had not given up his dream of seeing his son a successful lawyer, able to take a higher place in the world than any of the Kroeners. And Mattie, though she was torn by her loyalty to her own family, finally agreed, and took his side. Sam was her only child; she wanted the best for him. She listened silently to

Sophie's heated arguments about money and her father's serious lectures on the value of hard work. Virgil had grandiose ideas about sending Sam to Harvard, where his own father had been educated. But even he realized that this was far out of the question. It was decided that Sam was to enter Bard City University, where there would be no high tuition fees or living expenses to meet.

Sam hardly cared what the decision was, one way or the other. He wanted to be able to help out at home. But things had settled down there during the past year; his father was making a decent salary at the surgical appliance store, and there was no longer such a sense of financial tension in the house. So he was satisfied to go on to the University. There was a good deal of war talk beginning to be heard during that summer of 1916, and he had a vague feeling that the whole problem of his future might be decided soon by something bigger than either his own wishes or those of his family.

He still thought of Frances Hardy during the summer. But he had not seen her since the night of their graduation. He heard from Dick Rogan that she had been away for a while, in Michigan, with friends of her mother's. But Dick was not on close terms with her either, since the night of the dance. In spite of the rather reckless manner that he liked to affect, he really had no desire to be different from the majority. He had quarreled with her because of the trouble she had made for him by her actions at the dance. Then they had made up again, but there was still a slight coolness remaining between them.

The University was at the other end of town from Cannon Hill. Sam had to change trolleys at Fenchurch Corner when he went back and forth to his classes. One afternoon early in October, a few weeks after he had entered the University, he was standing at the trolley stop, waiting for the Cannon Hill car, when he saw Frances Hardy get off a Ludlow trolley and come across the street toward him. She was wearing a black-and-white silk belted jacket and a small, close-fitting dark hat, and she was carrying a sheaf of music in her arms. She did not see him till she was quite near him. She smiled as she came up to him.

"Hello, Beauchamp," she said. "Are you going home?"

He said that he was. She examined the books he was carrying.

"Don't you look studious," she said. "Do you like it?"

"It's all right."

A Haddon car was coming up to the stop. She glanced at it and then over to Sam.

"Why don't you come on home with me?" she asked suddenly. "I haven't seen you for months. I've never had a chance to tell you how lovely you were the night of the dance."

She was so offhand about extending the invitation that he accepted it in the same way. He got on the trolley with her. It was crowded, and he stood before the seat he had found for her, looking down at her while they exchanged snatches of conversation. She took his books from him and held them on her lap. He was hardly conscious of all the people about them, the noise of the trolley, the bustle and movement of the streets. He saw her gray, cool, laughing eyes looking up at him, and her slender hands resting on his books. And he was ashamed and confused because the books, which were his, an extension of himself, looked so commonplace, and were marred already with inkstains and scuffed covers. He did not want her to look down at them, and at the same time, when he saw her hands touch them, he felt a strong surge of happiness that she was touching something belonging to him.

She lived on Duncan Street, in a rather odd-looking, new brick house with a blue roof and shutters. The neighborhood was newer and smarter than Sherman Street, though the lawns were smaller and the houses less substantially built. It was a neighborhood of young business and professional men and their families, the aspiring country-club set. Sam did not much like the houses, which were built in an imitation of Italian villas or Tudor cottages, instead of in the solid Victorian style of those on Sherman Street. But they had the glamour of strangeness for him.

Mrs. Hardy was in the living room, knitting, when he and Frances came into the house. Frances brought him in to meet her. Seeing her close at hand, he realized that she was not at all the sort of woman that her imposing presence made her appear from a distance. There was something helpless and good-natured and untidy about her. She laughed easily, a deep round chuckle, very infectious, and melted as easily into a ridiculously infantile pathos.

She looked at Sam with her round, friendly smile as Frances brought him into the living room.

"So you're Sam Beauchamp," she said to him, when Frances had mentioned his name. "Well, I used to know your grandfather once upon a time, and your great-grandfather too, if you'll believe it. I was brought up right over there in Cannon Hill, and it was the greatest treat in life for me, when I was just a little thing, to be taken out to the Cannon House on Sunday afternoons. *You* don't remember your great-grandfather, of course?"

Sam looked at her attentively, smiling a little. He rather liked her, immediately; there was something so genial and absurdly open about her.

"No," he said. "Hardly my grandfather, either; he died when I was only about seven."

"Well, he was a handsome man, your grandfather Beauchamp," Mrs. Hardy said (Sam knew that this was not strictly true, but she was so positive about it that it almost seemed as if it were). "But nothing to your great-grandfather," she continued, with an emphatic gesture. "He was an old man when I knew him, of course, but, my God, the handsomest creature—! He could have made his fortune in the theater."

Sam glanced at Frances, and she wrinkled her eyes at him, smiling.

"Don't let it puff you up, Beauchamp," she said. "All the men Mamma knew when she was young were *handsome creatures.*"

"Well, the men *were* handsomer in those days," Mrs. Hardy declared, placidly. "No offense to present company, of course."

She looked amiably at Sam. There was a box of chocolates on the table beside her, and Frances reached over and began looking inside it.

"Aren't you going to offer us a piece?" she said, peremptorily. "You *are* polite."

"You'll take what you want, I suppose," her mother said, equably.

She went on with her knitting. Frances took Sam's hand and drew him toward the door leading into the dining room.

"Where are you taking him now? You've just come in," the mother said.

"Well, we have to have *something*," Frances cried. "I'm going to make some lemonade."

Sam went back into the kitchen with her. He saw that her mother was rather an irritation to her; she was so quick herself, so sure and keen, and her mother was so obviously the kind who simply blundered happily through life. He thought that she must be like her father, since she was so different in every way from her mother, and he wanted to ask her about him, but he did not dare. The rumors he had heard about him might be true.

He watched her silently as she brought out the lemons and the glasses. The kitchen was somewhat untidy, and cheerful, not like his mother's, at home. She asked him to chip some ice from the big cake in the icebox.

"You know," she said suddenly, "you're very quiet, aren't you?"

He flushed up, surprised.

"I don't know. I've never thought about it. Maybe with you—"

She stopped squeezing the lemons and looked at him curiously, smiling.

"I like it," she said. "I always know just where I am with you."

He felt that she was older, more experienced, than he, not as he had felt during the spring of the previous year with Bronwen, that she was moving in a richer, deeper world than the one he was in, but rather that she had wider knowledge in that world which they both shared. Still he knew that she liked him, and sought him, and that gave him a feeling of inner comfort. And she simply took it for granted that he liked her. She was used to being liked, and admired; she had the aura of popularity about her.

They went out into the back yard to drink the lemonade. There were some garden chairs, and a small fishpond without any fish, the water greenish and full of bright-colored, freshly fallen leaves which drifted slowly on the surface. It was a warm day for October. There was the lazy, sensuous harvest warmth in the air.

She asked him with a rather negligent curiosity about his family. She wanted to talk about herself; there was something clear and definite and self-centered about her, that could not translate itself readily into other lives. She absorbed others; she herself was not absorbed.

"You've got such a lovely, healthy-sounding family," she said. "Everybody so nice and sane and normal."

He stared ahead, slightly embarrassed.

"What's the matter with yours?"

She laughed. "Well, you've met Mamma."

"I like her," he said.

"I know you do. That's one of the reasons why I like *you*."

"Well, then—" he began.

She reached over and took the glass of lemonade out of his hand. "It's too sweet, isn't it?" she said. "You don't have to drink it." He watched her pour it out upon the grass. "I can't do anything right," she said. "I suppose I *do* take after Mamma, after all."

"You don't look anything like her," Sam said.

"No. I look like my father." He could see her clinch herself a little against the words. "He was really a wonderful person," she said suddenly. "He died last year—I suppose you've heard about that. People love to talk about something that's none of their business."

He did not know what to say to her. Her face looked withdrawn and rather sullen. When she was like that, turned in on herself and without animation, the irregularities of her features became much more apparent. She could not really be called pretty then; there was something too hard and definite in the outlines of the narrow bones beneath the paper-white skin. But it was only in rare moments that one saw this. Ordinarily it was hidden behind the magic of her changing moods.

He stayed with her out in the yard till it began to grow cold and dusky. He suddenly realized that it was past six o'clock, and that he would be late for dinner at home. But still he did not want to leave. She looked so indolent and accessible, sitting in her garden chair, with her head lying against the back, turned so that she could look at him. He felt afraid that he could not get back again another time to this intimacy with her. He could ask her to go out with him, but even if she agreed it might not be the same.

"Will you come out with me Saturday night?" he said to her suddenly.

She shook her head a little against the back of the chair.

"Can't be done. Really."

His heart went down coldly. He got up rather stiffly from his chair.

"Ask me another time," she offered, looking up at him.

"Would you come?"

"Would I not."

And the cold went out of his heart again. He walked home quickly through the fall dusk, planning what they would do. But gradually the fear came back again, the fear of doing or saying something that might make her dislike him, or laugh at him. When he was with her he was carried along; it was a rather desperate, exhilarating feeling; but as soon as he left her everything that had happened became distant and incredible. He could not really believe that it had happened to him. And he felt that sooner or later she must find out about him, that he was really only an ordinary boy, living in an ordinary house, with ordinary parents and ordinary belongings, and that when she had discovered this, she would exclude him from her magical existence.

It was seven o'clock when he reached home. His mother had kept his dinner hot for him. She set a place for him at the kitchen table, and began to wash the dishes while he ate. He knew she was offended because he had not come home in time for the meal. But she rarely spoke sharply to him now; he was beginning to take his place in her eyes as a man, toward whom a certain submission on her part was due. She asked him after a little where he had been.

"Over in Haddon, at Fran Hardy's house," he said.

"And who is Fran Hardy?" she asked him.

He explained to her.

"She must be a mighty attraction, to make you forget your meal waiting for you at home," she said.

But she was not really displeased. He had always spent so much of his time with Bronwen Brand that she was glad when he took an interest in another girl.

But when he began to see Frances often, during the ensuing weeks, she wanted to know more about her. She felt that this was something important to him, and she could not go on with any satisfaction in the dark, not knowing whether to give or to withhold her approval.

She asked him to invite her one Sunday for dinner. Sam hardly wanted to; he did not want to risk Frances's perhaps not caring for his home, and his parents, and the way they lived. He felt that it was hard enough to try to keep himself up to a level of which she would approve, without being burdened with the responsibility for the actions of two other people and for a whole houseful of inanimate objects. The house, in spite of all his mother's care, was beginning to look a little shabby, now that there was no longer the money to keep it up as it had once been. It needed painting, and the parlor carpet was worn, the furniture was of a more old-fashioned style than that in the house on Duncan Street.

Still, at the same time, he wanted to ask her. It made her seem to belong more to him, having her to dinner in his home. She was not really *his* girl, though she went out with him frequently. He knew she still saw a good deal of Dick Rogan, and of two or three others as well.

She came on a Sunday just before Christmas. It was a cold bright day, that seemed cruelly to make the house look threadbare and ugly. His mother, as usual, was nervous at meeting someone new, and therefore rather abrupt. Sam knew at once, when he saw them together, that she and Frances would not get on. He saw his mother's eyes go over Frances's thin figure and coltish hair. She drew her whole self together in timidity and disapproval.

But his father redeemed the situation. He could still be as charming as ever when there was something to draw him out. And he liked Frances at once; a kind of confidential comradeship sprang up between them.

"Do they call you Fan?" he asked her, at the table.

"No. Fran, sometimes, or Francie. Why?"

He made an expansive gesture.

"It suits you. Gives you a Regency air. At least I think Regency is what I mean. High waists, narrow skirts, dashing ladies. You'd be surprised at how little I know about history, my dear."

She looked at him, amused.

"Now why doesn't Sam ever say anything like that to me?" she asked.

"Doesn't he make fine speeches to you?"

She shook her head. "You ought to give him lessons."

He laughed. "I'm all out of practice, my dear."

And in the parlor, after dinner, he monopolized her again. She sat beside him on the sofa, smiling at his plump, ruddy face that turned eagerly to hers.

"So you're from Chicago?" he asked her.

"Yes."

"And how do you like it down here, then?"

"Oh-h"—she had a way of drawing the word out with a curious, indifferent, reckless sound—"I like it anywhere, I suppose."

"It must have been hard for you, though, to leave all your young friends. A popular young lady like you—"

"Maybe I wasn't a 'popular young lady' there."

"Yes, you were, my dear. It's written all over you."

And she smiled, delighted with him. He shook hands with her when she left, and made her promise to come again. He was always eager and happy with new people; they had no demands to make on him, and his friendly, innocent nature was free to go out to them without fear of reproach.

Sam began to see even more of Frances as the turn of the winter came. He was over at Duncan Street several times a week now, coming out either after his classes at the University were over, in the afternoon, or later on, in the evening. He came to know her mother well, and the Baxters, her aunt and uncle. They all liked him, and there was a relaxed, easy tone in the house, so that he could go in and out as he pleased, without formality. Yet he knew that he was only one of several boys who were on these terms in the house.

And he could not seem to come closer to Frances. They knew each other so well now, and besides that, she let him make love to her, his rather clumsy, urgent, boy's love, that never dared more than an arm around her waist or a sudden kiss, and yet it made no difference: she was still utterly strange to him. He had no feeling of warmth and relaxation when he was with her; his whole being seemed screwed to a desperate pitch of endeavor, to make himself into what she wished him to be. And he could never tell what that would be: sometimes she seemed to like him simply for what he was, his seriousness, his blunt honesty, his quiet sense of humor, and again she mocked him and played with him, she wanted him to be something quick and hard and bright, like herself.

They used to go out now and then, even on the coldest nights of the winter, and sit on the front porch of her home, on the big wicker settee that stood at one end of the square concrete porch, and that, through Mr. Baxter's negligence, had not been taken inside at the end of the summer. She brought an auto robe that they wrapped themselves in, and, sitting huddled close against the cold, they watched the silent houses and the deserted street, talking almost in whispers, as if they were afraid of being overheard. She loved it when someone came down the street, hurrying by without an idea of their presence there in the darkness. And it was usually here that she let him make love to her, let him put his arms around her and kiss her, so that when he thought of her during that time she was always fresh and cold to him, her face cold and glowing and smooth in the biting night air, with only the mouth warm and moist.

But even in these moments there was no real security or happiness. He was always afraid that she would draw away from him with her brows raised impatiently and mockingly over her clear gray eyes. And then her uncle would perhaps fling open the house-door suddenly, standing there red and bulky and jolly in the doorway with the light streaming out behind him, peering closely into the darkness where they sat.

"Well, I'm damned!" he said. "You two young ones out here again? It must be warm work the pair of you are doing."

He made them come into the house and, after teasing them for a bit, began to talk to Sam about politics, or the war. Sam had so much hatred for him at these times that he felt himself go stiff and furious, hardly able to answer him, though ordinarily he rather liked him. And then the hatred would go out, too, to Frances, because she could laugh coolly at her uncle when he teased her, and would go and sit on the arm of his chair, twisting a lock of his hair about one of her fingers, and looking at Sam as if she had made an alliance with the other man against him.

So that, during that winter, he grew more and more confused and violent within himself; he was no longer the steady, good-humored boy that everyone had seen in him up to that time. And he was doing badly, too, at the University. He could not concentrate on his work; it suffocated him to sit listening to lectures, and when he was away from the University he had no time to think of studying; he wanted to spend every minute with Frances. Then, as he fell behind in his work, he was ashamed before his teachers and the other students, and began to cut classes to avoid the necessity of facing them with his ignorance. Some of his father's blind stubbornness came up in him. He would go his own way; he would do as he pleased, regardless of anyone. But it was no good, anywhere; there was no real satisfaction, even when he was with Frances.

Then, in the spring, in the midst of it all, came the war. And immediately, from the first moment, it was like a door opening for him out of darkness and confusion. There was the escape, the absolute, that he wanted. Only he could not acknowledge it to himself in those terms; he could not see it clearly enough in his own mind to know that that was what it was offering to him. He only knew that he wanted to go, to throw up everything and go immediately. But he knew what his mother would feel. He was only eighteen, too young for the draft, and she clung to that knowledge. She felt a bitter, silent, personal animosity against the war. She would not hear of it; she did not want it mentioned in the house.

For her, and for all the Kroeners, it was as if the whole world had suddenly been turned upside down. Justus Kroener had devoted his whole life to being irreproachable, as other men devote their lives to art, or to religion, or to making money; and now, in a moment, because of an accident of birth, which in itself meant nothing to him at all, he found that it had all gone for nothing; he was suspect, maligned, almost an outcast. He had not been born in Germany himself—his parents had arrived in America the year before his birth—but his wife had, and they had both been brought up to speak their parents' mother-tongue in the home. Later their three children had also been sent to the German-language schools that had still been kept up then in Bard City, so that even now it was not uncommon for them to speak German among themselves, and with their friends of German descent. And the fact that they had never associated themselves in any way with the militaristic spirit that was now dominant in Germany, even the fact that their parents had come to America to escape that very militarism, went for nothing before that damning evidence.

The Beauchamps went over to see them at their house in Warsaw Hill one Sunday early in May, several weeks after the declaration of war. They found the whole house full of dread and indignation. Justus Kroener sat in his big yellow plush chair in the parlor, looking gloomily before him and saying nothing. In the corner his wife, too agitated even to pick up the crocheting that she had always in her hands, sat huddled passively, listening to the talk of the others. She was such a small, meek, silent old woman, very stooped and round-shouldered, so that she seemed almost deformed. And the week before a group of children had shouted after her in the street, as she was coming home from her marketing with her little black string bag full of groceries, and one of them had thrown a stone at her, which had struck the bag and broken a bottle of vinegar in it. Now she was afraid to go out on the street. She sat huddled in her chair, not understanding, waiting passively, speaking only to tell the story of the broken bottle of vinegar—"and all down on my vegetables it went, the vinegar, and there was broken glass in my potatoes."

Sam had always been like the others, disregarding her, hardly conscious of her presence when she was in the room. But today she was terribly vivid to him. More than his grandfather's heavy gloom, more than his mother's bitter silence or his aunt Sophie's vehement indignation, she seemed to bring before him the strong, terrible light of war, which he wanted because it *was* strong, and terrible, and bright with a white impersonal light that could destroy the colors of his individual life. But it confused him in his wish, it hurt him to see her sitting there so passive and frightened, looking helplessly out of her faded eyes. He seemed to see the war for the first time, not as something that might affect him, but as something through which he, as a part of it, might affect others.

He heard his aunt Sophie ask his mother: "What is Sam going to do?"

"Sam?" his mother said. She spoke nervously and quickly. "Of course he's going to keep on at the University. Why, he's nothing but a boy—"

"Well, I wouldn't sit back if *I* were a man," Sophie said. She walked up and down in the room, her heavy body drawn up taut with fury. "I'd show them if I was as ready to go as the next one. Why, when I think—there was Papa's own brother that was killed in the Civil War; a *Kroener* was good enough for them then—"

"I *won't* have you putting ideas like that in Sam's head, Sophie," Mattie interrupted her, quiet and intense. Sophie stared around; she could not remember that her sister had ever spoken to her in that tone before. "He's only eighteen," Mattie said; "it's wicked nonsense to talk of his going." And then all at once, without warning, she began to cry. "It was all very well for Grandma Kroener, with her six boys," she said, in a strangled, whimpering voice, hardly like her own. "But we've only the one—"

Sam was horribly upset. He felt that he had to get away; he had to get free of that stifling atmosphere of fear and dread and clinging, possessive love. He muttered an excuse and left the house. He knew that Frances was spending the afternoon at home, as she and her mother were expecting some friends from Chicago. He did not really want to go to her, but he thought that if he could be with her he could forget for a while about the war, and about the question of his enlisting.

He walked all the way over to Haddon, almost five miles; the afternoon was coming to an end when he rang the bell at the Baxters'. It had been a bright-gray, sunless day, rather cold, hardly like spring. The light was beginning to fade now in the sky as he stood on the front porch, waiting for someone to answer.

After a few moments Frances came to the door.

"Why, what are you doing here?" she asked, in surprise. "You know I told you—"

"Yes, I know," he said. "But can you get away for a little while? I want to talk to you."

He looked so miserable and determined that she gave way, and slipped inside to get her coat. He heard her calling to her mother: "Sam's here. I'm going out for a minute. I won't be long." Then she joined him again.

"What's the matter with *you?*" she asked curiously, as they started off down the walk together. "You look positively grim."

"Oh—" he said. He did not want to talk to her about it. He wanted to go somewhere with her where they could be alone together, where he would be able to forget in her what had happened. But she would not be satisfied until she knew. "It's about the war," he said. "I've been thinking about getting in—and my mother goes all to pieces if anyone so much as mentions it—"

She looked down, interested.

"Do you really want to go?"

"Yes. I think so."

She gave him a sudden sidewise glance from under her falling hair.

"I wish I were a boy," she said. "I'd adore to go."

"It's not as simple as it looks."

"Is it not," she said. "Dick Rogan's going."

He walked along silently, furious with jealousy at her mention of Dick. He seemed to have so little of her, and she to have so much of him. He felt tied to her; there was nothing in him that she left free; and yet he did not really have her, she was not bound to him in the same manner. And he wanted to get away from that tie now too. He had to be let alone for a time to get his bearings in the world. He did not know what he wanted, whom he wanted, any more.

They walked out to the little park at the end of Duncan Street. It was still and deserted under the trees, with their small new leaves making a cold greenness in the dusk overhead. She walked close to him, slipping her arm through his.

"I've got to get back," she said.

"All right."

They stopped.

"I don't really want you to go, Sam," she said suddenly, looking up at him. "You won't pay any attention to what I said?"

"It doesn't make any difference," he said.

He went rather coldly with her back to the house. She became indifferent under his silence; when they reached the walk in front of the house she turned and slipped away from him, as if she did not expect him to come in with her.

"See you soon," she said, running up to the porch.

And the hatred came up in him again as he heard the cool tones of her voice floating back to him through the dusk. He walked away quickly. Yet he knew that this time, at least, it had been as much his fault as hers that their meeting had been so unsatisfactory. But she was a part now of the blackness and the violence inside him; he would have to get other things clear before he could see clearly his relationship with her.

The next afternoon, when he came from his University classes, he walked out to the Cannon House. He hardly ever went there now, since Frances had begun to take up so much of his time. Bronwen was still living there, going into town every day for her job as stenographer in a small religious publishing house, while Brand completed his internship at the General Hospital; but he had scarcely seen either her or Brand since the previous summer. His aunt Rhoda he saw occasionally, when she came to Sherman Street, and he had news of the others from her.

It gave him an odd feeling to cross the empty lot beside the Cannon House again, and go up through the garden to the back door. So much seemed to have happened inside him since the last time he had done that. He felt as if he were a different person from the Sam Beauchamp who had spent so many hours in that garden. He did not understand how he could ever have felt so quiet and whole, how he could have accepted life without seeing the terrifying, shameful possibilities it held within it.

Mrs. Sorley was in the kitchen when he came up to the open door. She stared around at him from the sink.

"Well, is it you now?" she said, rather pleased to see him, but hiding her satisfaction under her habitual half-sharp, half-scornful air. "It's been the deuce of a long time since you've been around here."

"Why, did you miss me?" he asked her, smiling.

She bridled. "Ah, as if I hadn't enough bothers of men underfoot as it is!" She turned full around, surveying him, with her hands on her hips. "Well, and 'tis a proper man you've turned into now, with the size of you—'tis, 'tis. I'll never see over the top of your head again. I suppose you'll have to be trotting off to the war now too, like *my* fine fellow, and the rest of them?"

"Gard?" Sam asked. "Has he enlisted?"

She nodded proudly. "Not that I won't say he didn't do it to get out of doing a decent day's work for his keep," she said, begrudging the emotion. "Eh, he put me all in a floosther, the blackguard, coming in on me with a piece of news like that. Well, there's Ash has more sense in him, anyway; he won't throw over a good job till they come after him with their summonses, or whatever they call them."

He felt awkward, talking to her about it, with his own decision still to make. He asked her if his aunt Rhoda was in.

"In the parlor, with his nibs," she said, tossing her head.

"Who?"

"*Doctor* Brand," she replied.

She could never be brought to accept the title; it seemed to rankle in her, as if Brand had assumed some absurd dignity which she was yet forced to take seriously.

Sam went on out through the hall to the parlor. He was glad that he had found Brand there. He knew he could talk to him. But then he wanted his aunt to go and leave them alone. He had come to see her, but it would be better to talk to Brand.

Rhoda and Brand were drinking coffee together in the parlor. There was a certain formality in their relationship, now that Brand was no longer living in the house. Sam thought that his aunt looked older than when he had seen her last, Brand much the same, except for a new sureness, a kind of calm that he had never seen in him before.

He sat down with them, and Rhoda poured him a cup of coffee. But he sat without drinking it. She saw how upset he was.

"It's the war, I suppose?" she said to him. "You're like the rest; you want to be off to it too."

There was something sad behind the sharp cheerful irony of her voice. She had come to be very fond of him, and because of that fondness she was afraid. She would not look at him with the same desperate, possessive silence that was in his mother's eyes, but he knew that she was afraid for him, and that she wanted to keep him.

She saw that he did not want to talk to her. After a few minutes more had passed, she made an excuse to go back to the kitchen and leave him with Brand. Sam sat looking down at the cup in his hand.

"What's the matter?" Brand said, after a little. "You look as if something was giving you a bad time."

Sam looked up. "It is, I guess." He wrinkled up his forehead, smiling a little.

"The war?"

"Yes. The war, and a lot of other things. I'm all mixed up, some-how."

Brand got up and walked over to the window. He stood there with his hands in his pockets, looking out.

"I guess that's a pretty chronic condition at your age, Sam," he said. "But going to war's not much of a cure for it."

Sam stiffened. "You don't think I ought to go either, then?"

"That's up to you. All I'm saying is that the things that you're mixed up about now are all going to be waiting for you when you come back. You're not going to get away from them as easy as that."

Sam stared stubbornly ahead. He felt the old confusion and violence coming up inside him. It was easy enough for Brand, he thought; he was almost forty; nobody would blame him if he stayed at home. And there was direction and purpose in his life; he knew what he wanted to do; he was not being pulled half a dozen ways at once by half a dozen different ideas and emotions.

Brand had turned around and was looking at him rather ironically.

"Unless you don't come back at all," he emended what he had been saying. "That would fix everything, all right. There's always that to say for a war."

"Well, if I didn't come back," Sam said obstinately, "it would be for a good cause."

He was embarrassed to be saying it; it sounded like the sort of meaningless talk he had heard so much of, from people whose sincerity he could not believe in, during the past few months. But it was true for him; he did believe it, though it embarrassed him to say it, to bring it out into the light.

He looked up quickly and saw Brand still standing there before the window, heavy and collected and silent. His anger flared out.

"You don't think much of this war, do you?" he asked.

"I don't think much of any war." Brand spoke deliberately, without apparent emotion. "You can't expect somebody who's just spent almost a dozen years trying to find out how to keep a few people alive and healthy to be very enthusiastic about it when several millions of them decide to do their level best to do just the opposite for several other millions."

Sam was silent. But the stubborn expression did not disappear from his face. He felt angry and sore before the clear, realistic certainty of Brand's words. This was not what he wanted, after all. He wanted someone to absolve him, to tell him that there was only one course of action for him to follow. He wanted to be like Neil Lamson, or like Gard Sorley, who could take the war as one more adventure, as if they lived absolutely to themselves, with no one else to consider.

He said to Brand, after a moment: "It's all right for you. You can make that kind of thing sound good, for you."

"How do you mean?" Brand asked.

Sam felt awkward. "About going," he said. "Nobody expects you to—"

"Oh, I'm going all right," Brand said. "That's all settled; I'll get in as soon as I finish up at the hospital."

He was perfectly matter-of-fact and decided about it. And his certainty, his tacit acceptance of the need for his service, gripped Sam with a kind of shame. The war was a sort of self-seeking for him, clouded about with the glamour of patriotism and adventure. And he knew that for Brand there was no self-seeking, no glamour, only the hard necessity for service. It made him ashamed and humble. He got up restlessly. He wanted to be alone now, to think things out.

He walked out through the garden and across the empty field beside the house. It was a windy spring afternoon, coming on toward dusk, the sky full of ragged clouds that were brightened with the last of the sunlight. The weeds he crushed underfoot as he walked smelled strong and fresh and full of a coarse, exultant life. He had never thought consciously before that it was good to live. But now it came to him, and with a kind of dread. He did not want to think about it. Those few words of Brand's seemed to have stripped the illusion from his thoughts of war. It was not what he had been thinking it—a boy's escape from reality into a boy's world of adventure.

He walked home slowly. Men were coming from work; the streets were full of movement and cheerful talk under the darkening spring sky. At the corner of Sherman Street, as he was about to turn off from Old Town Road, he saw his father get off a trolley that had come from town. He stopped and waited for him.

"Well, Sam!" Virgil said. He looked at him a little questioningly, almost with a kind of self-consciousness, as seemed to be his way lately. "You're coming from the wrong direction, aren't you?"

"I've been out to the Cannon House," Sam said.

They walked down Sherman Street together. Virgil began to talk about the happenings of the day down at the store. He was usually in a state of half-suppressed friction with Justus Kroener. But he did not think of leaving the store; his father-in-law was getting on toward seventy now, and he was hopeful that he would retire in a few years and leave the whole management of the business to him.

Sam found it hard to be attentive to his father's gossip about the store. And after a few minutes Virgil grew aware of this. He became silent and looked at Sam again with that questioning expression in his eyes. They had not been very close to each other lately. Virgil felt that things were going badly for Sam, and that he was the one to do something for him, but he did not know how to begin about it.

"I've been thinking," Sam said, after a little silence. He did not look at his father as he walked along. "And I've made up my mind now. I want to enlist."

Virgil said nothing. Sam looked over at him. His face was puckered up slightly, as if he were squinting against the sun.

"Yes," he said slowly, after a little. "I thought you might."

"You won't do anything against it?" Sam asked him.

"No." And he walked on again for a moment in silence. "We won't say anything to your mother till it's done," he said presently, rather heavily. "That'd be best, I think."

"Yes," Sam said.

He felt calmer, now that it was said. It was settled now. There was only this one thing for him to do. He looked over at his father, walking along slowly beside him.

"I'll be proud of you, Sam," Virgil said.

But his face was still puckered in its curious blind look of distress. Sam did not want to see it. He looked away. It was harder than he had thought it would be. But now it was done. He could not help being glad that it was so.

Chapter 7

HE LEFT FOR TRAINING CAMP SHORTLY AFTER-
wards. His father recovered himself and went about very proud of
him, stopping people he knew on the street to tell them about him.
But his mother withdrew farther than ever into herself, into the
rigid, bitter recesses of her religion. Once Virgil asked her if she
was not proud of her son.

"Proud of him?" she said, in her flat, rapid voice. "I'd like to
see what there is to be proud of when they send him back to us."

She could not even cry when he went away. Rhoda watched her
at the station. She looked like a woman to whom some bitter wrong
had been done, clenched and unforgiving. She held herself in too
tightly, and she suffered for it. And it turned her against Sam; she
could never really forgive him for what he had done. She could not
understand a man's reasoning about life; it bewildered her, and
drove her back to the hard certainties of her own inevitable judgments. For her there was right and wrong, with no other considerations beside them.

Rhoda put a good face on Sam's going. But inside herself, in a
different way from Mattie, she rebelled. She knew that Brand
would be going too, before very long. At home she was sharp-tongued
and exacting with the men; she envied them fiercely their freedom
of action. It irritated her almost beyond endurance to have to sit
passively, like a tame cat, while they went and did as they pleased.

She was sitting in the parlor one early June afternoon, reading
in her old way, with her feet on the fender before the empty fireplace, when she heard someone ringing at the front door. It was
going to storm; the windows of the parlor were all open to the heavy

blue air. Mrs. Sorley went to answer the door. In a few moments Rhoda heard her shriek of excitement.

"Ah, dear heart! Will you look at who's here now!"

Rhoda glanced around through the open door of the parlor. Neil Lamson was standing in the hall, laughing, and talking to Mrs. Sorley. He wore the uniform of a captain of the Royal Flying Corps. But he himself looked no different from the way he had when he had first come to the Cannon House, two years before. There was the same contradictorily keen and indifferent face, the same laughing eyes and strong, curved, self-possessed mouth. She felt a pang almost of dismay go through her. Still she was glad to see him; he seemed to bring life with him into the house.

She called him into the parlor, and he sat down with her there. Mrs. Sorley lingered in the doorway. Lamson explained that he was staying with the family of a friend of his in town, the same one with whom he had gone to Canada two years before. He was on leave before going overseas again; he had been shot down in France and later sent back to Canada as an instructor, but he had managed now to get himself transferred back to active service. Mrs. Sorley stood looking at him admiringly.

"Aren't you the bold boyo now?" she said. "Wouldn't you think you'd have had enough of that business, without going out of your way to get more of it?"

Rhoda sat listening with only half her attention while Mrs. Sorley told him about the men he had known in the house who had gone into the service. She was thinking of Bronwen. She did not want the girl upset again. And she would be upset. Rhoda remembered how she had been after Lamson had left, the almost terrifying remoteness that had come over her. She had simply wanted to separate herself from life; it was too hard to be forced to feel when there was nothing to feel but loss. And now lately, since she had started to work in town, she had begun to come alive again, to be happier and more at peace with herself. Rhoda did not want her to have to lose that again.

Lamson asked her about Bronwen after Mrs. Sorley had gone back to the kitchen.

"How is she?" he said.

"You'll see for yourself," Rhoda answered, brusquely. "She'll be home any minute now."

She was relieved to see that he spoke of her in such a friendly, indifferent way. But then she knew that it would hurt the girl more, just that matter-of-fact, pleasant interest. She wanted him to go away before Bronwen came. But he sat talking to her obliviously as the minutes ticked by. It was beginning to thunder outside. The air hung in the room very heavy and still.

She heard Bronwen after a time at the front door. Lamson was sitting facing the hall. He looked up. He was saying something to Rhoda about the war. She saw him draw himself together, with a peculiar kind of alertness. Then he stood up, with one of his light, swift movements.

Bronwen came slowly forward to the door of the room. She had recognized his voice the instant she had heard it, on first opening the door of the house. Her face was set rather stiffly. She stood in the doorway, waiting. She was in blue, and her eyes, of that same opaque, smoky blue, seemed pure color, set without life in her face.

"Well," Rhoda said, breaking in abruptly, "you see who's here."

Bronwen smiled a sudden, rather dazzled smile and came forward into the room.

"I recognized your voice," she said.

She put out her hand. Lamson held it warmly for a moment, laughing, in his own.

"I thought you'd have grown," he said. "You're exactly the same."

"Yes," she said. "I'm exactly the same."

He waited for her to sit down. But she remained standing there, in the center of the room, looking at him.

"What are you doing here in town?" she asked him.

He told her. She seemed to listen to him almost absently, as if she did not really understand what he was saying. A rush of wind came into the room suddenly from the open windows. The first big drops of the storm spattered down on the earth outside.

"Are you staying to dinner?" she asked him.

He smiled, looking at Rhoda. He seemed excited, beneath his composure. Rhoda met his gaze a little ironically, vexed.

"I hadn't asked him," she said. "But I suppose I'll have to now; I can't very well send him away in this storm."

"Thanks," he said, laughing.

He turned back again to Bronwen. But she wanted to escape. He had come too suddenly, without warning; she had to have time to put her emotions in some order. Now it was all a confusion inside her. She did not know why he had come. And she thought she must hate him, it hurt her so much to see him standing there, smiling and friendly and self-composed. She wanted to be like that too, to be able to face him calmly and good-temperedly, as if what there had been between them was no more to her now than a schoolgirl's folly.

She made an excuse, and went upstairs. But she could not shut herself in her room. She went out on the second-story porch. The trees were all bowing and whipping together savagely in the wind. Then the rain came driving in sudden white gusts across the porch. She stood back against the wall of the house. She was rather frightened of the storm, but it steadied her; it forced her attention outside herself. How could it be so important, that a man had come or that he had not come, when the whole garden surged furiously at her feet and the sky seemed to rush along, with the wind tearing at it and the thunder rolling against it in great shocks of sound?

She heard the men begin to come in downstairs. Dinner would be ready in a short time. She went to her room and waited; she did not want to see Lamson now except among others. When she went downstairs finally he was talking to Frank Mallan, who had been rejected by both the Army and the Navy because of a heart condition. He was full of envy and admiration for Lamson in his smart captain's uniform.

During dinner the talk was all of the war. Bronwen sat beside Rhoda; she would not look at Lamson. But she felt that he was watching her. And again she wanted to escape. She did not know what was happening to her; she felt as if she were waiting for a blow to strike her. She heard his voice talking to the other men. He belonged to them, to their world, not to her. She hardly knew that the rain was slackening and that the thunder was rolling away, leaving sudden blue vistas in the torn sky.

When dinner was over she did not stay with the others sitting

around the table. The rain had stopped; there were only the sudden
quick showers now as the wind shook the drops from the trees. She
went out into the garden. It was so much lighter now, under the
long mild sunlight of the June evening; it seemed almost as if
another day had begun. The garden was all wet and shining, as
fresh as in the early morning.

She sat down on an old whitewashed bench that stood in the
kitchen yard, under the porch. The robins were calling cheerfully
through the green, liquid glitter of the trees. She did not know what
she was waiting for. Queenie's successor, a young collie bitch called
Princess, came loping up to her through the garden. Her coat was
draggled and cool with wet. She sat down before Bronwen, pushing
her muzzle up under her hand to be petted.

The day's second twilight—the final, real one, after the false one
of the storm—began to come. Bronwen felt the grayness washing
over her. She became very quiet inside, almost passive. He would
go away without seeing her again. Then it did not matter. It would
be again as it had been before he had come.

The screen door opened behind her.

"Bron?" he asked.

She turned around swiftly, gathering herself together.

"Oh," she said. "Are you going?"

She stared at him, her eyes expanded, rather defiant. He seemed
puzzled, even a little ill at ease.

"Not quite yet." He smiled. "You don't seem very glad to have me
back."

"How long are you staying?"

"I have a couple of weeks' leave."

"Oh," she said mechanically. She did not want him to be near
so long; she needed to be left in peace. She got up and stood looking at him tensely, as if waiting for him to go back into the house.

He said good-by and left her. But it would not do; he knew even
while he said good-by to her that it would not do. The spark had
flamed up again in the darkness between them, the darkness that
only the two of them knew was there. And he went back unsatisfied
to the house where he was staying. All the while he was talking and
laughing with other people he was seeing her eyes, the stillness of

them watching him through the dusk. He wanted her; it was imperative in him now. He knew that he would go back to her. Something had been decided in him. He had always had a deep, almost fatalistic sense of the inevitability of life. A thing was meant to happen, or it was not meant to happen. So he did not think much about it. Only he knew that he would finish now what he had begun two years before. He knew that it was there still in her too.

He went back to the Cannon House the following evening, after dinner. It was cool and fresh after the previous day's rain. Clouds were blowing about in the sky. It might rain again before morning.

It was Brand's evening away from the hospital, and he was at the Cannon House when Lamson arrived. There was a coolness, almost imperceptible, but very definite, between the two men. Something in Lamson's clear, unself-conscious indifference exasperated Brand. He felt a kind of contempt for him, and yet he was always conscious of the other's life flowing so naturally, drawing people so simply and naturally to itself. It made his own isolation seem more intense.

Lamson asked him civilly about his plans for the future, and told him something of his own experience in a military hospital in France. But he was not thinking of what he was saying. Bronwen was sitting in a corner of the room, listening. He knew that she was waiting for something. And he wanted to get away at once, to be with her alone at once. There was too little time. He did not want to waste it in meaningless talk with other people.

He said, after a little, to Rhoda: "I haven't seen your garden. Is it still as nice as it was?"

She looked at him with her rather cruelly acute smile.

"You wouldn't see much in this dark," she said.

He was aware of the hostility in the room, shutting him off in the tight safe world of mere civility. He looked over at Bronwen. She would not meet his gaze. But she could feel him watching her brightly and humbly. And in spite of herself she flew to him against the others.

"We've got a new dog," she said. "Would you like to see her?"

"What does he care about that?" Rhoda mocked her.

But he got up, laughing, and stood waiting.

"We won't be long," the girl said, imperiously.

Rhoda thought that there was something really superb about her, flashing out only occasionally from behind her quiet, remote manner. There was a rich, deep source of vitality in her; she could be as stubborn and as passionate as her father. She walked out of the room with Lamson behind her.

They went out into the garden. It was almost dark, very cool and green. She whistled for Princess. The collie got up and came over from beside the bench where she had been lying, waving her plumed tail slowly.

"Isn't she nice?" Bronwen asked.

Lamson stooped and smoothed the collie's head.

"Yes," he said. "She's a fine bitch." He stood erect again, and looked a little vaguely out through the garden. "It's just the same, isn't it?" he asked.

"Yes."

They walked on slowly. They came under the darkness of the pear trees, where they had used to stand together, two years before. He stopped.

"Bron—" he said.

She looked up at him. He put his arms about her and drew her to him.

"Bron—?" he said again, questioningly, his voice heavy.

She wanted to hold back, to be sure of him. But he bent and kissed her, and she held him, suddenly alive with joy. It was inevitable, to her as well as to him. She put her hands to his face, wanting to know him through the darkness.

They walked on again, out of the shadow of the trees. He held her close against his side as he walked.

"We'll get married, Bron," he said to her. It did not even seem strange to him, that he should want to marry her. It was like a decision that had already been made for him. He wanted everything clear and complete between them. About the future he did not think; it would take care of itself, as it always did. "We'll get married tomorrow," he said to her. "We'll go away somewhere—"

And she accepted it simply; it seemed perfectly natural to her that instead of going to work the next morning she should meet him at the railroad station and go with him to be married. She walked beside him, listening to his voice more than to the words he used, intent on realizing him.

They went back into the house together. She saw Rhoda looking at her curiously. But she withdrew into herself again. She did not want anyone else to come near her now. She said good night to Lamson. They were both rather quiet, almost formal, with each other.

It rained during the night, and in the morning, when she started for town, the streets were wet and fresh. She had a little leatherette bag with her, in which she sometimes carried her lunch to work. It had been agreed that she was to meet Lamson at the information desk of the railroad station at half-past eight. She had thought she was perfectly quiet, perfectly decided. But as she rode into town on the streetcar her head hurt her; she wanted to cry. She looked at the familiar streets, clutching at them, wanting them back. She did not even know where she was going. And she was afraid; it was all fantastic, everything running swiftly, crowding her on, as in a nightmare.

She walked from the trolley stop to the railroad station. The streets were all full of strange people, crowding to work. She walked on beside them or past them, feeling dazed. She could not believe that she would really find Lamson waiting at the station.

But just as she entered the door she saw him, tense and alert, in his flier's uniform. He came toward her quickly.

"I thought you might not come," he said.

He laughed out of pure relief. He had been waiting almost an hour, afraid she might come before the time. Now he was very happy, very active. But then he looked at her standing there, her face clear and girlish and somehow terrible in its stillness.

"It'll be all right, Bron," he said to her, almost interrogatively, feeling a kind of tension, a sudden fear, like a sickness, inside him. He had not known it could be like this. He wanted it to be the way it had always been between them, absolutely without doubt of any sort.

She saw the slight frown between his eyes. And instantly her own fears vanished; she wanted to touch him, to let her own love flow into him with her touch. But there were people all about, the noise and business of the station.

"Yes," she said. "It'll be all right."

She slipped her hand into his. Her fingers were living and secret, touching his. And he smiled again, looking down at her. He had not realized that it could be like this. He had seemed simply set and intent to himself, following out an inevitable pattern. But there was an entire world more.

They had a half-hour's wait for their train. He had bought tickets for Port Lincoln, across the state line, on the other side of the river. For some reasons he did not want to go to a large city with her. He had been in the little river town once before, several years back. It would be quiet there, quite removed from the world.

The train was a slow one, that took several hours for the short trip. As they moved out of the city there was a sudden brief shower that dashed against the windows of the car, the drops flying gleaming and brilliant through the morning sunlight that continued to pour out from between the clouds. When they could look out again, they saw everything wet with summer rain.

She was delighted with the town when they arrived, shortly before noon. It was old, rather forgotten, with sleepy brick-paved streets lined with big elms and maples. They went directly to the City Hall. From the square they could look down to the river and see the water flowing broad and glittering under the midday sun. It was a very ordinary small town, with an ugly little business section that dated from Civil War days, and rather neglected homes, many of them set directly on the sidewalk, but quite nice with their white-washed brick and simple lines. She loved it all, the very signs that said *Main Street* and *Water Street,* the pigeons paddling on the damp bricks of the square, an old woman sitting in a rocking chair in a tiny front yard under an enormous lilac bush.

She did not know how it was managed, that they were married. She went with Lamson into a square brick building with a statue before it, and walked down dusty, wooden-floored corridors, and answered questions, and signed her name obediently as she was requested. But it was all an unreality, not so immediate to her as the old woman in her rocking chair or the pigeons walking sedately in the sun. It was unimportant; she was not even upset when it was discovered that there was no ring, the thought of one simply never having occurred to either of them. The ceremony was postponed while Lamson dashed across the street to a jeweler's and bought one. She stood looking out the window, remote and absorbed. Everyone was interested, anxious to be helpful. There was a kind of superb, quiet radiance about her. And she smiled at them faintly, only half hearing them. She did not really understand why they should be so upset and so helpful.

Then, when it was over, they went to the hotel. It was one of the big whitewashed brick houses that stood just off the town square. They had a room on the second floor, very large and high-ceilinged, with a huge mahogany bed and inside shutters at the windows. It was all green and silent, with the trees blowing outside and the sounds from the square very remote. In the evening the smell of the river came up cool and watery through the quiet summer darkness. She thought it was all quite perfect, exactly as it should be.

They stayed in the town for almost two weeks, till it was necessary for Lamson to leave. He had sent a wire for her, the first evening, to Rhoda, and another to Brand, letting them know where she was and what had happened. But they did not really exist for her now. When they wrote to her, she read their letters and then at once put them away and forgot them. She could not conceive that they were really upset and angry. And, at any rate, it did not matter. It was Lamson who had to urge her to write to them in return.

"What shall I write?" she asked him. "That I'm very happy?"

And she laughed, dissatisfied with the words. They were too small for what she felt; she thought that she would have to invent new words, a whole new language, to express it.

They had no desire to go anywhere outside the town. Wherever they went, they remained in their own world, a world which they had made for themselves and in which there was no room for anyone else. They asked for nothing but not to be intruded upon. The people in the town became used to seeing them walking down to the river together, or out to the little green park on the edge of the town, where there was an old Civil War monument, and a few white benches. Lamson was a somewhat conspicuous figure, in his unfamiliar uniform. But it was not for that alone that people noticed the pair. Their happiness was so superb; they seemed so completely removed from any of the petty conditions of living. It had an effect upon everybody with whom they came in contact. And they seemed quite unconscious of it; they were rather gentle, rather indulgent with outsiders, not really seeing them, not really caring what they felt about them.

The only person with whom they made friends was the old woman whom they had seen the first morning, rocking in her tiny yard in the shadow of the lilac bush. She was a widow with several sons, all on the river. She spoke to Bronwen one afternoon as she and Lamson were going by the house, and Bronwen, delighted with her, accepted her invitation to come inside for a cup of tea. She was so small and decided, yet a little afraid of them, and absolutely unable to sit still in her joy at having visitors. She wanted to know all about them, and told them she had known the moment she saw them, on the day they had first come into the town, that they were going to be married.

"You looked like two stone angels out of the church," she said.

Lamson, laughing, argued with her that angels were neither male nor female, while she shook her head, delighted to have him disagree with her.

"You'd better say saints," he told her, "if we *have* to be so ecclesiastical."

But she only shook her head more determinedly.

"I'm sure," she said, audaciously, "you haven't been spending your time now like a pair of saints."

He laughed again. "And what about angels?" he teased her. "Is that how *they* spend their time?"

"Oh, angels—!" she said, smartly. "They're up to all sorts of mischief—fighting, and such—"

She gave them tea with home-baked bread and some of her own raspberry preserves. The spoons she brought out were old silver-plate, worn and dull, but very pretty, with odd curved handles covered with twining leaves and flowers.

"I've had them since the day I was married, and that's fifty-five years ago next month," she said proudly, when Bronwen admired them. And she added, suddenly: "I'll give you one now; maybe it'd bring you good luck."

"No," Bronwen protested. "I won't break your set."

But she persisted; she went to fetch a bit of tissue paper to wrap it in.

"I've had my own share of good luck," she said when she returned, standing before Bronwen and beaming with the excitement of the gift. "Fifty years together, *and* five strapping sons, *and* a good roof over my head all the while. I was married during a war too; only it was a big wedding, with dancing, and all the neighbors in for miles around."

She wanted to gossip with Bronwen about husbands, innocently and confidentially, out of the naïve wisdom of her experience—men would do this, or that, and what was the best way to deal with the balky creatures they were. But Lamson sat there, clear and smiling and immovable. She was a little timid before him. He was so definite, so certain of himself. She became almost afraid for the girl. He had drawn her into the orbit of his own hard separateness, and she seemed to rest in it passively, like the full dark round of the moon within the arc of the shining crescent. The woman felt this vaguely, not understanding what she felt, and becoming a little confused. She was used to men of another sort.

They thanked her and left the house together. They did not really want her either; they wanted to return to their own world again. The town, and everyone in it, was more insubstantial to them than the slightest of their own emotions. There was a fire in the square one night, an entire block of buildings in danger, and the whole town seething with clamor and excitement. They saw it from their window, quite apart, watching the reddened sky as quietly as if it had been merely some artificial spectacle that was being staged in the town. If they must see loss, or suffering, they were compunctious and gentle, but it did not really touch them. They were like the stone angels to which the old woman had compared them, nonhuman, or extrahuman, because there was no answering unhappiness to be reached in them.

They spent a good deal of time in the little deserted park, with its Civil War memorial group, a cluster of young green-bronze figures

with guns in hand, staring quietly out across the river. There was
something reassuring to Bronwen in their young unchanging silence;
they made the reality of war seem very far away, something that had
no actual power to touch the living fiber of her and Lamson's existence. She did not think about the war; she had deliberately put it
away from her, as she had put away all the other events that had
formerly been a part of her life. Only at rare intervals she acknowledged it, she realized that it would take him away from her. Once,
as they passed the newspaper office, she saw a photograph of a burning plane on the bulletin board that stood outside it. And something
inside her twisted in horror; she felt sick, as she had when she was a
child, before the ruthless, alien, male lust for violence. She walked
on quickly; she wanted not to see, to return without seeing to the
simple happy world which they had built for themselves.

But that afternoon, as they walked out to the little park, she halted
for the first time in front of the monument and read the names in-
scribed beneath the young green-bronze figures staring out so quietly
across the river. And again she was shaken. There was something so
lost in the sound of the names as she said them aloud into the still
June afternoon. It had all happened so long ago, and there was only
this terrifying calm surrounding them now, where there had been
love and pain and fear and the million swarming sensations of life.
She could not bear it that anything that had once lived should be so
utterly lost. She ran her fingers over the raised letters of the names,
wanting to touch something, to feel that there was something tangible that remained.

Lamson watched her curiously.

"What are you doing?" he asked.

She turned round to him swiftly, her face anguished and stubborn.

"I can't make them real," she said. "They're only names."

She knew that he could not understand. He was male, entirely:
life to him was something personal, something complete in his own
self, not something he shared with a universal continuity of other
life, reaching blindly into the past and future. He took her arm and
drew her away.

"It's all so long ago," he said. "Don't think about it."

But she held herself stiff and stubborn, resisting him.

"I *have* to think about it," she cried. "I want to. I want to remember them."

With the whole force of her being she wanted to feel them alive and significant; she wanted to compel herself to believe that they were not completely lost. He stared at her, rather puzzled.

"What difference does it make?" he argued with her, patiently. "They all lived once; they had the same chance of life as anyone else. It's the same for everyone—"

She did not understand how he could accept it so calmly. There was something in her that could never accept defeat, that had to rebel and rebel till she was worn out with the struggle. But she let his fatalism cover her over now. She willed to forget the fact of death. She wanted to take the happiness that was offered her now, to feel how perfect it was in itself, unblurred by the past or by the future.

But somewhere deep in her mind the shadow remained. She could not really force herself to forget. The time that had seemed to stretch golden and ample about them began to contract to the dimensions of a few short days. On one of the last evenings before Lamson had to leave for the East, they walked together down along the river. And she saw with a kind of terror the dark water traveling smoothly by; it was as if she were watching time slipping tangibly away from her, the moments merging themselves insidiously in a smooth dark flow that she watched helplessly, unable to halt it, to hold it even for a single instant in her hands.

It was a warm night, heavily overcast, and very dark. She could scarcely see Lamson as he walked along beside her; she could only feel his arm about her, and the contact of his body all along her own. And she felt suddenly how strange he was to her, there unseen beside her in the blackness. She knew so little about him; there seemed to be nothing for her to keep of him beyond the mere personal facts of their relationship. She wanted to ask him about his parents, about the house he had lived in when he was a boy; she wanted him to give her something of his past.

He laughed at her insistent questions.

"Why do you want to know?" he asked her. "I was just like any other boy. I went to school, I got into mischief, I liked swimming and hunting—"

"But what was it like, the place where you lived?" she persisted.

She knew that his father was an Episcopalian minister, something of a scholar, and that he had two brothers, both a number of years older than he, who were also in the ministry now. But she could never really visualize to herself what his life with them had been like; when she thought of it, she had a vague sense of gloom, and that was all.

He was ready enough to talk about it, only a little indolent, as it did not really matter to him now, and so going on only as long as she urged him with her questions. He told her about the town in which he had been brought up, a small Massachusetts college town. She listened, strained and brooding.

"And were you happy, *then?*" she asked him, with the intensity that she put into everything that mattered to her.

"Yes, I think so," he said. "It was a little stiff—but I was the youngest, and I suppose they were easier on me than they were on the others."

"I don't even know your brothers' names," she murmured, upset.

"John and Frederick. John is the oldest."

But the names did not help her; she could not get into his past through them. She had to give it up. That part of him could never belong to her.

But she had the best now, the present, wholly and completely. And she gave herself again to that present; she went back to that world in which there were only the two of them, alone in the darkness that only they knew. Afterwards, as they were walking back to the hotel together, it was he who seemed thoughtful and rather disturbed.

"Has it been worth it, for *you,* Bron?" he asked her. "It's such a short time—"

She looked at him, startled. She could hardly see him through the darkness.

"But you'll come back," she said to him.

"Yes," he said. "Still one has to face it; there's the chance—"

She stopped, frightened. They were walking along one of the deserted streets, the night very close and dark and still about them, be-

neath the deep midsummer shadow of the trees. She turned to him.
And he was there, so alive and tangible, in the darkness beside her.
The knowledge that he would have to leave her in a few days was
absolutely unreal to her. So long as he was there, it did not touch
her; she could not really believe it.

The last day was bright, blazing with sun. They moved about in
their big, cool room, gathering their things together, in preparation
for their departure. He had wanted to leave a little earlier, so that
he could go back to Cannon Hill with her, but she had insisted on
staying till the last possible moment. Now they would take the noon
train to Bard City, and then he would have to go on to the East at
once, without stopping off. It seemed to her that it would be better
so; she did not want their last few hours together to be clouded with
the anger or coldness of others.

They were very quiet that last morning. They walked down to
the river for the last time. It looked dazzling, almost molten, broken
with flecks of absolutely golden light under the morning sun. He
took her in his arms. They were very close, but without happiness.
She wanted to cry; she felt as if something were dying inside her.

"When you come back," she said, "we'll come here again."

"Yes," he said.

But he did not want to talk about it. The old fatalistic attitude
toward life came up in him, hard and indifferent and serviceable.
If it was to be so, it would be, without their planning it. And if it was
not to be, they could not alter it. Still he too was driven almost mad
inside himself by the sense of the impending separation. He wanted
it to be over quickly now. He shut himself away from her, not wanting to feel, not wanting to see her face.

He paid the bill at the hotel and they left for the station. Everyone was very cordial, wishing them good luck and happiness. They
passed the City Hall, where they had been married not two weeks
before. But it seemed to them that they could hardly remember the
time when they had not been together. And when they got on the
train, it was amazing to them to find that nothing had altered, that
they passed the same fields and houses and towns, all quite un-
changed, that they had passed on their journey from Bard City.

Bronwen sat very still, beside the window. The presence of the other people in the car hurt her, and the noise, the monotonous, cheerful racket of the train. She wanted the quiet brick-paved square, and the pigeons, the river, the little park and the hotel with its big cool shuttered room. She could not have believed that one could want anything so passionately, and still go quietly and calmly and rationally about leaving it.

And the journey was so short. The fields and the little towns wheeled swiftly backward behind them, falling irrevocably into the past. The train drew into the Bard City station. She sat numb; she felt that she could not move. He asked the conductor a question which she did not understand.

"He says the train will stop at the Cannon Hill station," Lamson said, turning to her, explaining. "You can get off there."

It was another ten minutes. The train moved slowly forward, out of the station. He reached over and took her hand.

"Don't mind it," he said to her, in a low voice.

She looked at him desperately. She felt that there must be some-one to whom she could appeal. But there was no one. They were all caught in the huge machine of the war. She tried not to cry. He looked at her face.

"Don't mind it, Bron," he said again.

She thought that his voice sounded rather cold. But he only wanted it to be over. The train went too slowly for him. Since it had to end, he wanted it to end at once, that very instant.

The train stopped again, beside the familiar red-roofed Cannon Hill station. The conductor went through the car, calling the stop. Lamson picked up her bag.

"You haven't much time," he said.

She got up and walked to the door of the car with him. He stooped quickly and kissed her. She felt that it was all unreal; it was not really happening to her. But she was standing on the platform, alone, and the train was moving off again. She could not find his face at any of the windows. The strange faces looked down at her impersonally as they slipped past. She remembered that she had not even said good-by to him.

It was hot and still on the platform when the heavy rumble of the train had died away. There was a kind of lazy, everyday feeling. She felt as if she had been born again into a new, terrible, sterile world. The very air, the sky, were different. It was not the same world into which she had awakened that morning. And she wanted the other; she wanted the life, the richness. She could not bear it, this strange empty world.

She went mechanically to the street, and walked out to the Cannon House. It was all strange to her, more perfectly strange because of its familiarity. She had never really seen any of it before. It was so empty and terrible, under the burning afternoon sun. But she could not cry. The sterility had entered into her; her emotions seemed fixed and dead inside her.

She opened the front door of the Cannon House and went inside. Rhoda was in the parlor. She looked up, and then came over quickly to the door. She stared at Bronwen for a moment in silence, her blue, penetrating stare.

"Where is Lamson?" she asked.

Bronwen made an effort. "He had to go—" she said.

Her lips quivered downward. But she could not cry. Rhoda put her arm about her shoulders.

"Ah, you little *fool!*" she said. She was very much moved. She wanted to comfort the girl, but she did not know how to begin about it. "Your father's here," she said, after a moment. "Do you want to see him?"

Bronwen looked at her without answering. It made no difference to her whom she saw or whom she did not see. Only she did not want to have to answer questions.

Mrs. Sorley came running out from the kitchen at that moment, very much excited.

"The Lord save us!" she said. "Is that Bron? I thought I heard the door." She stood back, looking at her with her sharp little eyes. "Well," she said emphatically, "and I hope you're really married now?"

"Of course she's married; don't be an idiot, Maud," Rhoda said, fiercely.

Mrs. Sorley shrugged. "Eh, I'm saying nothing against the girl. But she wouldn't be the first to be led out of the way by a fine tale with no more truth in it than you'd put in your eye."

She spoke rather smartly; she was offended because Bronwen had left without confiding in her.

"Go and tell Rob she's here," Rhoda said to her. "And, for heaven's sake, don't go putting ideas like that in *his* head."

"Oh, is it me, now?" Mrs. Sorley said, bridling. "If she never has a worse friend than Maud Sorley, she'll be doing well indeed in this world."

She went out to find Brand; she was actually almost as upset as Rhoda, and the two of them found a certain relief for their emotions in speaking sharply to each other.

She went out to the garden, and in a few moments returned again with Brand, who had come out, as he often did, to spend his free hours away from the hospital at the Cannon House. During the past weeks he had been harsh-tempered and rather moody. Bronwen's marriage had come to him like a blow. He hated to think of her as Neil Lamson's wife; he did not trust Lamson; there was nothing about him that he liked or respected. But at the same time he felt guilty; he realized that he had left the girl more or less to her own resources. He felt that he had no right to interfere in her life. And at the bottom of it all there was a deep sense of loss, a feeling that the last link between him and the life he had had before his wife's death had been broken.

He came into the house to see Bronwen, but he did not know how to speak to her. He was miserable, seeing her so dumb and withdrawn. He knew she was suffering, and he would have liked to comfort her, as he had when she was a child. But she did not want him. She was not even really seeing him when she looked at him. He felt shut out of her life. He spoke to her almost brusquely, in his uncertainty.

She did not want to see anyone else now. She ate a little something in the kitchen before the men came home, and then went upstairs to her room. Mrs. Sorley came up and tried to talk to her.

"Well, you've got a fine piece of a man, agrah," she coaxed her, "let them say what they will. And he'll be coming back to you in no time at all now, with all the boys flocking into the Army to do their bit against the Germans."

Bronwen let her talk on. But she was not really listening, any more than she had listened to Rhoda or to Brand. She sat there silently, trying to realize inside herself that she had been with Lamson that very morning in Port Lincoln. But it was another world; she could not get back to it.

"You want a good night's sleep; that's what you want now," Mrs. Sorley continued to coax her. "Eh, I remember the day Robbie brought you here; you had the eyes in you just like you've got tonight—as deep as two wells; and not a word out of you, though I talked my arm off to you. Let's get you out of that hot dress, alannah, and then maybe you'll sleep a bit, and feel better in the morning."

She did as she was told, docilely; it made no difference to her if she sat up or went to bed. But after Mrs. Sorley had gone, she did not even try to sleep. She simply lay watching the gray summer dusk wash into the room, feeling slightly feverish in the hot, humid air.

After a time there was a knock at her door. Brand had come to say good night; he was going back to the hospital.

"I thought you might be asleep," he said, a little at a loss with her.

She shook her head, standing in the doorway silently. She was wearing a blue-patterned Japanese kimono that Lamson had bought her in Port Lincoln, and Mrs. Sorley had pinned her braids in a coil on the top of her head for coolness. She looked so small and young to Brand, not much older than she had been when she had come down to him more than ten years before, afraid of her dream of the fire. He wanted to help her. But it was not he that she wanted now.

She saw him standing there, looking at her rather helplessly. Somehow it eased her to have him caring about her unhappiness. She had felt for so long that she was a thing of indifference to him. She wanted to go to him and cry out her loneliness till she was better inside herself. But there had been a barrier between them for too long. Still she wished that he were not going away, into the Army. She wanted to feel that he was there, someone big and comforting, as he had been when she was a child.

"Will you be leaving soon?" she asked him, after a little.

"I don't know exactly. But you'll be all right. There'll be money coming in—my allotment, and Lamson's, I suppose."

She hated the way he said Lamson's name, coldly, dismissing him as if he were of no real account.

"I'll keep on working," she said to him.

"If you can," he remarked, dryly.

She stared at him rather defiantly. It was going to be this way then, whenever the subject of Lamson came up between them. And, as always, there was no question of a divided allegiance with her. Her loyalty was entirely for her husband now.

She went back to bed again after Brand had gone, and toward dawn fell asleep. The next morning, when she awoke, she seemed better, firmer, inside herself. But the emptiness remained. And the days before her seemed so endless. She felt that she had gotten into a state of suspended existence, which would last until Lamson returned. There was nothing that she could do but wait. She did not even think about what they would do when the war was over. When she thought of their being together, it was always in the past, at Port Lincoln, or at the Cannon House. The future was perfectly blind to her.

Chapter 8

SHE WENT BACK TO WORK THE FOLLOWING week. The war went on, into the winter, to another spring again. She had letters from Lamson, always quite cheerful ones, so that she could hardly visualize the realities of the war in connection with him. Brand was in France now too, attached to one of the evacuation hospitals. And through Rhoda she heard sometimes of Sam Beauchamp.

The war had brought Rhoda closer to Virgil again. He could not talk freely to Mattie or the Kroeners about Sam; they did not want to think about the war. When it was mentioned, they withdrew into the stiff, uneasy silence of the suspected. So Virgil went to Rhoda. He fell into the habit of walking over to the Cannon House almost every Sunday, when there had been a letter from Sam. There he could discuss the war to his heart's content, over a large colored map of the battle zone that he had bought.

One Sunday afternoon early in September, 1918, he walked over with Bertie Kroener, who had come with Sophie and the elder Kroeners to spend the day on Sherman Street. They had all been worried about Sam; they had not heard from him for some time, and then there had been word that he had been gassed, and was in the hospital with bronchopneumonia. But the day before, Saturday, a letter had come from Sam himself, saying that he was much better, and expected to be back with his outfit before many more weeks had passed. Virgil was so relieved that he went about spinning like a top with excitement. He had talked to Rhoda about the good news over the telephone the previous day, but he would not be satisfied till she had actually read the letter herself.

It was a fine Sunday afternoon, soft and blue and hazy. Rhoda was making peach preserves with Mrs. Sorley in the kitchen when Virgil and Bertie arrived at the Cannon House—"a heathen occupation for the Lord's Day," she said; "don't tell Mattie." She sat down to read Sam's letter, while Virgil perched on a corner of the table, pilfering fresh peach slices from a big bowl beside him and popping them into his mouth.

"Wisha, look at the man!" Mrs. Sorley cried. "Don't they feed you at home, now?"

He was one of her favorites; he always had a good-natured, bantering word for her when he came to see Rhoda. He laughed over at her now.

"Rhoda and I used to do this when we were about ten," he said; "do you remember, Rhode? I don't feel much older than that to-day."

He could not stay still for five minutes at a time; he insisted that Rhoda put on her hat and come walking with him and Bertie.

"In this state?" she scoffed. "I'd be a fine sight for Cannon Hill on a Sunday afternoon!"

"Oh Lord, what difference does it make?" he said impatiently. "We'll go down the hill; nobody'll see you. It's too fine a day to stay indoors."

She gave in, took off her apron, and went to get her hat. Virgil's excitement was infectious; he made her and Bertie feel almost as irresponsibly happy as he was himself. It was such a relief to all of them to be able to think of Sam lying safe and convalescent in a hospital far from the fighting, after the weeks they had spent in uncertainty. They walked down the hill together, laughing and talking. Virgil began to whistle. There was a kind of anxiety behind his happiness; he knew that Sam's safety was only temporary, and that once this burst of gaiety died down in him he would go back to worrying about him again. So he wanted to feel his high spirits to the fullest now.

It had been a long time since he had walked down here, where he had used to come quite often on his botanical rambles, and years before that, when he was a boy. He was delighted with everything, the hillsides yellow with goldenrod, the trees looking heavy under their dark-green, dusty, late summer leaves, the warm, lazy sunshine over it all.

"By George!" he said, "a person *does* give up something when he decides to grow up. If I was a boy, I'd have whole days to spend down here. Do you remember how we used to sail boats in this creek, Rhode? Lord, that's forty years ago now!"

"We *did* have good times," Rhoda said, smiling warmly.

Bertie had stopped to gather some asters that were growing in a beautiful blue surge up the hillside. She glanced up at them, her long, sallow face made rather cruelly unyouthful-looking by the proximity of the flowers, with their bright centers and pure blue-violet rays.

"That must have been nice," she said, in her colorless voice that was so much like Mattie's, flat and timid with reserve. She smiled "*We* were always such good little girls."

"Were you? Well then, you ought to just cut loose now," Virgil said, laughing. "*I* would, if I were in your shoes."

She colored up, rather pitifully. "Oh, at my age—!" she said.

"What's the matter with your age?" Virgil persisted. "You're a good seven or eight years younger than I am, and I don't intend to put myself on the shelf yet, not by a long chalk."

She looked down at the flowers, not knowing what to answer him.

"Virge is right," Rhoda said to her. "*Goodness*—it's bad enough, being under someone's thumb when you're a child, but letting it go on when you're old enough to put a stop to it is simply nonsense, and that's all there is to it."

They were both so energetic and full of assurance that it made Bertie feel for a moment that what they were suggesting was almost possible. She stood up, still bending over the flowers that she held in her hands.

"You know," she said quickly, "it's true, I've never really had a life of my own. But I *have* always thought that some day I'd go on a nice long trip, and see"—she laughed, with nervous gaiety—"and see if something wouldn't happen to me!"

"That's what I *would* do then; just wait till the war's over, and then off you go," Virgil said, enthusiastically. "Wouldn't I like to do that myself, though!"

"You!" Rhoda said, laughing. "We'd never have you back again, if you ever got off."

He laughed too, still enthusiastic.

"Oh, I suppose I'll have to wait till Sam comes home and makes a fortune for all of us; then I can go in style," he said.

They walked slowly on, up the hill toward Haddon. It was quiet and soft in the blue, late summer afternoon. Bertie said after a while, rather suddenly: "Doesn't it make you feel guilty, though—walking here, while boys like Sam are off somewhere in France, doing our fighting for us? *We've* had our chance at all this; *we've* had our own youth, whatever we've made of it, and now we're taking theirs— And it's something we can never give back; it doesn't seem right—"

She spoke disconnectedly, flushing up with the effort to say what was in her mind. She was very much in earnest. Rhoda stared at her, surprised.

"What can we do, though?" she said after a moment, shrugging. "We're caught in it, just as they are. I'd take Sam's place if I could. They'd take one look at me if I offered—'*Madam!*'—and send me off to a lunatic asylum. *We* were born at a luckier time; that's all there is to say about it."

She was almost fiercely overconscious herself of the truth of what Bertie had said, and so she chose to be rather cynical about it, because she did not want to get involved with her feelings. But her pleasure in the day was overcast. She felt it was true: they had no right to their happy ramble, since it was taken at the expense of others. She remembered how Sam loved this place. They walked back to the Cannon House silently.

The fall came on, full of hope for the end of the war. When Virgil came to the Cannon House now on Sunday afternoon, he was jubilant with the news of the Allied advances. Sometimes Bronwen came in to listen while he talked to Rhoda. She was overactive now, keeping every moment of time occupied, and growing rather thin. Her eyes looked enormous and full of an almost haunted gravity as she listened to them talk about the war.

"But aren't you interested?" Virgil demanded of her, insisting that everyone join in his enthusiasm. "Aren't you excited?"

"No," she said simply. "I'm afraid."

She had been looking for something in the future, straining forward toward it with all her strength, and now that it seemed almost within her grasp she felt only a kind of disbelief. She did not believe in herself; it seemed to her that because she wanted this to be so, it would not be so. There were times when she felt as if something must break inside her with this strain of waiting. Everyone assured her that it must soon be over now. But she remained tense and fixed in her disbelief.

One afternoon in early November she came home from work at her usual time. It had begun to snow, only a few light flakes; the air was pure and colorless and bright, just before dusk, with the few flakes of snow falling from the sky. She went inside the house. Mrs. Sorley was waiting for her, a little frightened, with an envelope in her hands.

"This came for you a half hour ago," she said.

Bronwen stood looking at the envelope. Something inside her became perfectly still, waiting.

"Aren't you going to open it?" Mrs. Sorley said. "You'd best read it now."

Bronwen took it from her automatically, opened it, and read the few lines which it contained.

"Oh, dear heart!" Mrs. Sorley cried. "Is it bad news, Bron?"

Bronwen looked at her, quite white, rather dazed. Without answering, she went upstairs and into her own room. Mrs. Sorley stood below in the hall, not knowing what to do, and muttering worriedly to herself. She was very much excited.

Rhoda came in from her afternoon at the Red Cross.

"You'd best go upstairs after Bron," Mrs. Sorley hastened to tell her. "She's had a telegram—oh dear, I think it's bad news for her."

Rhoda felt her heart go down. She took off her coat, shaking the few flakes of snow from it mechanically.

"Shall I go, then?" Mrs. Sorley offered.

"No. Let me alone. I'll go myself."

Rhoda went upstairs and knocked at Bronwen's door. There was no answer. She opened the door and went inside. Bronwen was sitting in a chair beside the window. Her face looked fixed and without expression. The envelope lay open on the dresser beside her.

"What it is, Bron?" Rhoda asked.

A quiver ran over the girl's face. Rhoda picked up the telegram from the dresser and read it. It was a brief, official communication of the death of Captain Neil Lamson. She put it down again carefully on the dresser. She felt absolutely helpless now, looking at Bronwen. There was nothing for her to say. Yet she *must* say something.

She went over and put her hand on the girl's shoulder.

"Ah, Bron," she said, "cry now, but don't sit there like that. The world's got to go on, whether we like it or not."

She felt very weary, rather old, as if she were done.

Bronwen pulled away from her and stood up, facing her. Her blue eyes stared at her blindly, full of passionate light.

"I want *him*," she cried out suddenly, in a high, hard voice. "I want *him*—now, here, this instant—"

Rhoda had never seen anything like it before: the tense, quivering will for the unattainable flung out implacably into the unliving darkness. She felt that the girl would never give in, never submit to the defeat of death. And she *must* give in, or be destroyed.

Bronwen went about silent, her will fixed, for several days. It made absolutely no difference to her when the Armistice was signed. Rhoda tried to talk to her. But she felt that she was speaking into a void. She wrote to Brand, hoping that when he came he would be able to reach the girl. But she knew it would probably be months before he would be able to get back to Cannon Hill again.

Then, after a week or so, Bronwen went back to work. But the first day she came home exhausted and feverish. She had hardly managed to get out from town by herself. Rhoda put her to bed and sent for Dr. Greaves. It was influenza; for over a week she was dangerously ill. Rhoda nursed her rather grimly; she *would* not have anything happen to her. She had never been very close to Bronwen; they were so completely different in almost every way. But she wanted her now intensely to live. Still the girl kept herself shut away from her. When she was growing better, Rhoda tried to talk to her about Lamson. But she did not want him mentioned; she wanted to keep him inside herself. She looked burned out now, very thin, and for the first time in her life rather fragile. There had always been a lovely, healthy sturdiness about her before that time.

The winter came on. One snowy Sunday afternoon, when Bronwen was well enough to sit up, Rhoda walked over to Sherman Street. It was a dark day; the snow was wet and heavy. She noticed a group of sparrows sitting huddled under the eaves as she came up the walk to the house, looking miserable under their draggled feathers.

Virgil came to the door when she rang, and let her in, obviously upset. She looked at him ironically.

"Oh Lord," she said, "what's the matter with *you?*"

She was tired of bad news and worries; she felt tempted to turn and walk out of the house.

"Well," Virgil said gloomily, "it's about Sam."

"Sam?" she repeated. "Why, what's happened to him?"

"He's not coming home," Virgil said. "That is, not just now—"

He brought her into the living room. The Kroeners were all there, in an atmosphere of solid disapproval. Mattie had Sam's last letter open on her lap. She looked pale, with reddened eyes and a tight, sallow face.

"Well," Sophie said to Rhoda directly, as she entered the room, "what do *you* think about this trick of Sam's?"

Rhoda looked around, and at once decided that, whatever it was, she was on Sam's side. Virgil, looking completely miserable, between his desire to defend his son and his wish to have him at home again, explained that Sam wanted to remain in Europe for six months or a year. As soon as he could get his discharge, he planned to go to that part of the Austro-Hungarian Empire which was now being made into the new state of Czechoslovakia, along with a friend he had made in the Army, George Korvas, whose family lived on a farm there.

"Did you ever hear anything to match that?" Sophie demanded. "Here the other boys are all falling over themselves to get home to their families as fast as they can, and our young man goes marching off in exactly the opposite direction with a stranger."

But it was not quite so simple as that. In his letter, Sam mentioned that the doctors at the hospital where he had been after he was gassed had advised him to live outdoors as much as possible for a time— "There's nothing to worry about," he wrote; "I'm as good as new now, but since an outdoor life is what's wanted for the time being, I can't think of a better place to get it than on a farm."

He went on to tell them about Korvas, who had been born in Slovakia but had lived in the States since he was fourteen; his parents, however, were still on the farm which the family had worked for two hundred years, and which, under the new government, they now hoped to be able to own.

"It will be a lot different from a farm at home, rather primitive, I expect, from what George says, and up near the mountains, where the land isn't too good," Sam wrote. "But it sounds like what I need now. And as I can't come back and settle down at the University again just now anyway—"

"He'd better forget about the University, after *this*," Sophie said bluntly, to Mattie. "How long does he expect you and Virgil to keep him in school? Good Lord, he'd be old enough to have a beard like a Cossack and a family of his own before he'd ever finish."

"Well, I suppose he couldn't help it that there was a war," Virgil said wrathfully. "That's the gratitude he gets, for giving a couple of the best years of his life to his country."

"His country's not asking him to go traipsing off to some outlandish corner of the world now," Sophie retorted smartly. "And if you ask my opinion, there's something more to this than the blind cat saw when it looked in at the window. It looks to me like our Uncle Henry all over again. *He* never wanted to do an honest day's work either, after he came back from the Civil War—thought being a hero once in his life was enough to get him into heaven, I suppose—"

Virgil was furious; even though he knew that at least the better part of what Sophie said, she said merely for the pleasure of seeing his temper rise, he could not prevent himself from flaring up in Sam's defense. Rhoda thought that she had seldom spent a more disagreeable afternoon. She did not know which she disliked more, Sophie's practical rudeness, or Mattie's silent, desperate conviction that Sam's health was completely gone, apparently as a direct visitation from Providence because of his having gone into the Army against her wishes. She went home at last in a really fierce temper.

"I don't blame Sam for not wanting to come back to *that*," she said, so upset she talked angrily to herself as she walked up and down in the empty parlor. "Lord! he couldn't satisfy all of them if he was Saint Michael and John D. Rockefeller rolled into one."

She felt as if things were piling up into a nasty state of confusion all about her. The end of the war, that had been going to solve so many problems, seemed to have left everything instead in a condition of upset. And she missed having Brand to talk things over with. He was trying to get home, but so were thousands of others, and he had to take his chances with the rest. But he wrote that he should certainly be in Cannon Hill before the spring was past. He had not given up his plans to open an office there as soon as he got out of the service.

When he did come, she saw at once that he had not changed. He had left off his captain's uniform and his D. S. C., and wore a cheap dark suit that he had bought in New York; he looked as if he had walked out of Symons's drugstore only the night before, with one of his thick medical textbooks under his arm. But it was not only in a physical sense that he had not altered. The war, that had come like a cataclysm into the lives of boys like Sam, had been to him only an intensification of experiences in which he had already served a hard, familiar apprenticeship. So it had caused no great revolution in his manner of thinking. Now that it was over, he was ready to go back and take up his old life at once at the point where it had been interrupted.

When he came to Cannon Hill, he brought with him an army friend, Dr. John Bart, who stopped over with him at the Cannon House for a few days on his way west to visit his parents. Bart was a research man, who had worked before the war in the laboratories of one of the large eastern medical schools, and was going back soon to continue his work there. He was a few years younger than Brand, and a head shorter, compactly built, determined, and rather blunt. He came from a family of scientists—his father taught physics at a western university—and he had the equable, practical approach to human relationships of his class. He and Brand had worked together during the greater part of their months overseas, and there was the kind of complete, unspoken understanding between them that Brand had found so seldom in his life. Perhaps it was the war that had brought it about this time. But the other man had the sort of nature with which Brand was most readily at home: very direct, absolutely uninfluenced by pretentiousness, and with a capacity for complete absorption in an idea.

Rhoda saw him curiously "sizing up" the Cannon House when he came. He was interested in Brand, and in finding out about the sort of world from which he had come. He and Rhoda were at first rather antagonistic, a little wary of each other. He had a way of looking at her out of his round, light-blue eyes with a kind of practical, cool speculativeness that irritated her.

"I suppose now you're the one who's packed Robbie so full of all this 'nobility of the medical profession' jargon, Miss Beauchamp?" he said to her abruptly one morning, when he came strolling out to the kitchen yard, where she was down on her knees before a big wooden tub, giving her collie bitch a bath.

She glanced up at him briefly, and then transferred her attention again to the collie, whom she held firmly by the nape of the neck while she scrubbed her unwilling face.

"What makes you suppose that?" she asked, satirically.

He stood leaning against the wall of the house, watching her, while he lit his pipe.

"Oh," he said, noncommittally, "it's usually women who run to ideas like that."

"Nice of you to say so! Meaning sentimentalism, of course—"

"Well"—he nodded—"if you want to put it that way—"

"If *you* want to put it that way, Dr. Bart. I've lived with men long enough to know that they can run a higher temperature of sentimentalism than any woman who ever breathed—*and*," she continued, rather grimly, "I've lived with Rob Brand long enough to know better than to try to put an idea into his head that he doesn't want there, or to try to get one out of it that he's made up his mind to keep."

"Do you need some help there?" he asked irrelevantly, watching her as she held the floundering collie determinedly in the tub.

"No, thanks. I'm about through."

She released Princess, who scrambled from the tub and stood to shake herself unhappily.

"Watch yourself," Rhoda warned him, "or you'll have a bath too." She dried her hands on her apron, and sat down on the wooden bench. "Well?" she asked, after a moment.

He looked back at her questioningly.

"Aren't you going to get on with the indictment?" she demanded. "What have I done to Rob that's so terrible? Made him want to be a doctor? And who made *you* want to be one, if it's a fair question?"

"Oh Lord, I'm not a doctor—not one of that sort, anyway," he denied, "the kind who thinks he's going to cure the ills of the human race out of a little black bag full of ipecac and paregoric and digitalis. *And* make a tidy little fortune out of it on the side—"

She shook her head. "No," she said, "you can't have it both ways, Dr. Bart. He's too idealistic, *or* he's too mercenary—"

"He's much too good a man to spend his life at a job that any reasonably intelligent human being with common sense and good manners can do as well as he can; that's what he is," Bart said, a little heatedly. "What you, and a great many other people, don't seem to realize, Miss Beauchamp, is that what happens to the human race, as far as medicine is concerned, is going to depend a lot more on the lab man who works at discovering the basic cause and cure for a disease than on the clinician who goes on happily doling out aspirin and clipping tonsils from one generation to another. Robbie's got all the makings of a good research man: he has the right kind of mind, he has the drive, and he hasn't parceled himself out to a lot of people in a lot of little obligations that he'll have to meet. I've been talking to him—but it seems his mind's made up—"

"And you lay that at *my* door?" Rhoda asked.

"Oh, not all of it, of course. But I thought you might have helped."

She shook her head. "I don't think so. He had all that in him before he ever came here. He always *has* taken the medical profession as a sacrament; if he hadn't, he'd never in the world have come this far." She looked at Bart with her cruelly pleasant smile. "I'm afraid you haven't the least idea what it *does* mean to him," she said, "or you wouldn't be trying now to disillusion him."

"I'm *not* trying to 'disillusion' him—damn it anyway, don't you see what I mean?" Bart said, impatiently. "You ought to know as well as I do that Robbie's never going to be a success in general practice anyway; the public doesn't give a curse how good a man is, if he hasn't got the qualifications they're interested in—the right manner, the right background, the ability to make himself look good, no matter how little he really knows. I wonder if you have any idea how much a doctor's reputation in a community depends on social and economic circumstances, and how little of it on sheer, downright ability—"

He was so obviously in earnest about what he said that she could not remain simply in a state of animosity toward him.

"Why don't you sit down?" she asked him abruptly, moving to make a place for him on the bench.

He came across, looking at her quizzically. She examined his hard-featured, sensible face and close-cropped, bullet-shaped head, and the round blue eyes that gave him a contradictory appearance of almost naïve candor.

"So you think he ought to give up the idea of practicing at all—is that it?" she said to him, after a moment.

"That's exactly what I mean. He ought to get right into research; of course it pays like the devil, but he doesn't care about that end of it, and anyway he's likely to be better off financially in the long run as a successful research man than he'd ever be as a complete failure in general practice. The big thing is that he'd have the chance to use the brains he has got instead of the social graces he hasn't." He pointed his pipe at her rather accusingly. "You talk about his taking the medical profession as a sacrament," he said. "Well, if it comes to that, where do you think he's going to be in the proper company —among the clinicians, who *have* to be commercial-minded, to make a success, and damned well *are*, the most of them, or with men who're doing their best, regardless of money or fame or public appreciation, to give the clinicians the tools to *cure* disease, instead of merely relieving its symptoms?"

She sat looking at him, a little bewildered and thoughtful; she had never considered the matter in this light before.

"Have you said all that to Rob?" she asked him.

"All that, and a lot more. I've jawed myself hoarse. But I might as well have been talking to a post."

"Well, you know," she said, slowly, "it's more complicated than it seems. I don't know how much you know about Rob's life. But a man doesn't go through all that for an idea, and then be willing to give it up just for someone's telling him that he ought to. If Rob had been willing to listen to good advice, he'd still be working across the road there in the Maitland factory—or he'd never have left the pits to come here in the first place. He has to work things out for himself."

"*You* might speak to him," Bart suggested. "I know he thinks a good deal of your opinion."

She smiled. "As long as it fits his own," she said. "And I'm not entirely certain that you're right about all this, either. Maybe he *would* be wiser to go into research, but as long as what he wants is something else—" She shook her head again; she looked rather wise and beautiful for a moment, in her wet apron and house dress, with her graying hair untidy around her face. "No," she said, "I want him to have what *he* wants, not what I want, or what you want, or even what is best for him. He's worked long enough for it—"

She had faith in him, she discounted Bart's sober predictions, and yet, when Bart had gone, she felt a kind of grayness coming over her, almost like fear. Ever since her father's death she had lived so much to herself, caring only for her own family and a few others, that she really knew very little about the rest of Cannon Hill. And when she looked around now she had misgivings. It was quite within the bounds of possibility that these people would not accept Brand as a physician. The two men practicing in Cannon Hill now, Dr. Greaves and Dr. Francis, both came from well-to-do families; they were friends of the president of the Cannon Hill Bank, of the leading clergymen, and of the factory owners, the Maitlands and the Brownes. So the people of Cannon Hill had grown used to the idea that their doctors should belong to a superior class. And they went to their offices, which in both cases were in their homes, with the pleasurable feeling that they were being received into houses which were finer than their own.

She wished now that Brand had at least not made up his mind to practice here, where people remembered so well the years when he had been working at the factory, and afterward at the drugstore.

But it was too late to alter anything. He had rented a flat over a bakery on Old Town Road, near the railroad tracks, and was already fitting the two front rooms up as a reception room and an office. Behind them were the living quarters, where he and Bronwen would live.

Rhoda went downtown with him to rummage the secondhand stores, looking for old dressers and commodes that could be enameled white and used as cabinets in the office, and for a few pieces of presentable furniture for the reception room. The living quarters themselves were furnished partly from the attic of the Cannon House. It hurt her bitterly to see how poor the place looked. But there was nothing to be done about it. As it was, almost everything had to be done on borrowed money. Bronwen had a little money of her own, from Lamson's insurance, but Brand would not touch that, though she was quite willing for him to use it. She came out of herself a little, helping with the flat and the office. But it did not really interest her. She and Brand had lived their separate lives too long; even in her intense need for someone, she could not turn to him now.

On the last evening before he moved to the new flat, Brand walked back to the Cannon House with Rhoda. They had been working late to get it ready, and both of them were tired and rather silent. It was only a short distance, hardly more than an ordinary city block away. Rhoda did not notice the fine spring night. She was turning over half a dozen problems about the new place in her mind.

"You'd better have your dinners at the Cannon House till Bron takes hold of things over there," she said abruptly, after a time. "It'll be a little hard for her at first."

"Yes," Brand said. "But I think she'll make out." He had hardly talked to Rhoda about Bronwen since the first day of his return. Still she knew he was worried about her. He could not rid himself of the feeling that he was a great deal to blame for the unhappiness in her life. "It's the best thing for her to keep busy just now," he said. "I'll see that she doesn't overdo it."

"She *has* been better since she's had something to do again," Rhoda admitted. She looked over at Brand's serious face. "I wouldn't worry about her too much, Rob," she said. "She's only twenty; she'll get over all this if you give her time."

They passed the empty field beside the Cannon House. The cool night smell of weeds and earth came out to them.

"It's a hell of a thing to say," Brand remarked, "but I can't help thinking it's the best thing for her in the long run that Lamson didn't come back. She never would have had anything with him; he wasn't the sort to be tied down with a wife and family—"

Rhoda shook her head soberly.

"I don't know. She *did* love him. And she's never had anything else, really—"

"Well, I'll see that she *has* something else, now. The worst is over; there ought to be some plain sailing ahead for both of us."

He was rather grimly confident, and happy in his impatience to begin his new work. She looked at him as he went into the house, into the light. He was so much older and wiser than the young miner who had come to her door almost thirteen years before. And still there was the same blindness of determination in him, which had been his strength then but might now turn to be his weakness. She was afraid for him. He would not bear to be disappointed, not after he had worked so long for fulfillment. And people could be so cruel in their prejudices, so indifferently cruel. She wanted to warn him. But it was as she had said: he would have to work it out for himself. It was the only way he could ever learn anything in life.

He went upstairs to his room, while she sat alone for a while in the dark parlor, with only the light from the hall shining in. She had opened the window: the night air came in, moving soft and black from the darkness outside. She had a sense of resting before the start of another struggle. It was beginning to tire her, this constant fight with life. She wanted to disengage herself, to be at peace now. Thirteen years before, she had thirsted for that struggle, to feel that she was coming to grips with life in any way. But now she had less energy, less faith in herself and in others. She wanted life now to be simple and easy. It made her wonder at herself. She hardly remembered that she had ever had such a feeling before.

Chapter 9

T<small>HE</small> <small>FOLLOWING DAY BRAND AND BRONWEN</small>
went to the new flat to live. The office was ready, and open. Rhoda
tried to feel that things would work out for them now. But John
Bart's realistic summing up of the matter had shaken her confidence.
She felt that she had been to blame, during all the years she had
known Brand, by tacitly encouraging him to ignore the immediate,
practical problems that would face him. She realized now how much
more profitable it would have been for him if he had spent more
time in making and cultivating the proper connections than in preparing himself simply to do the best work he could, to the absolute
limit of his abilities. He made friends so slowly that, except for Bart,
he had no intimates at all in his profession. And in Cannon Hill
there was no one of any influence to take him up. So she waited,
rather dreading the future.

It was not long before she was able to see which way the wind
was blowing. When she went to the flat, she could feel almost tangibly the tension that was gathering over it. The summer was coming on, and in the hot cooplike little rooms, with their green-painted
walls and makeshift furniture, Brand waited day after day, time
going by with the lonesome tick of the clock inside, the silent phone
waiting, and below, outside the open windows, the sunny street, busy
and indifferent from morning to night. She felt that it was unen-
durable to him, that endless waiting. However hard things had been
before, there had always been work for him to do; he had been able
to feel that he was doing something to pull himself out of the situation. Now it depended upon others. He had to wait, idle, for them
to come to him. And the idleness, in the stifling heat of the little

office, with the trains going by heavily beside the windows and the cheerful, indifferent traffic in the street below, made him tense and filled with violence. Still he kept a tight control over himself. Outwardly he was civil, rather grave, and silent. She had never seen him just like that before.

He had felt that he should be able to establish himself without great difficulty; Dr. Greaves was seventy, on the point of retiring, having already given up everything but office calls, and Dr. Francis had more than he could do in the growing community. But only a few of the poorer families called him in; even the Polishtown families preferred to go out to Warsaw Hill to Dr. Volling. There was not enough money coming in even to pay the rent on the flat. And the money he had borrowed, which he had counted on to see him through the first slow months, was melting away quickly, while he sat waiting.

Rhoda thought that if only a few of the well-established families in Cannon Hill would call him in, the others would soon follow. She had known them all well in the old days, when her father was alive —the Martins, the Banfords, the Considines. Toward the end of the summer she went to see Mrs. Considine, whose husband had been one of her father's greatest friends, and determinedly brought up the subject of Brand. Mrs. Considine was polite, and evasive. The Beauchamps had come down too far in the world for her to feel that it was worth her while to do anything she did not wish to do simply in order to please Rhoda. The Banfords Rhoda could not even bring herself to go to see: the old people were dead, and the son had made a good deal of money during the war; he and his wife found it more satisfactory now to measure their neighbors solely in terms of dollars and cents. The only person who was at all sympathetic was Miss Martin, a tiny, ancient spinster who had used to feed Rhoda cookies when she was a girl—"but of course," she said, "when Dr. Greaves retires this year, my sister and I will go to Dr. Francis. He's a married man, and I think—you see, my dear—"

Her tinkling delicacy jarred on Rhoda. She had lived too long among men; she had no patience any longer with feminine overrefinements and insincerities. She went home, feeling defeated. And all the while, through the solid center of Cannon Hill society, the

James Symonses and the Mattie Beauchamps who had from the first predicted failure for Brand, she sensed the satisfaction of a vindicated judgment. Those people would be the hardest of all to move, and they were the ones on whom, in the final analysis, Brand had chiefly to depend for a livelihood.

So the months dragged by. She felt in herself that, if there was a hell for a man like Brand, it would have this kind of rejection and this kind of disillusionment in it. And he was helpless against it; there was no way for him to fight it. She saw him closing a door in his mind against these people, the rage in him casting them out, furious to shame them and trample them as they had shamed and trampled him. He had brought them his best gifts, blindly and naïvely, and they had turned away from them and rejected them. He lived in a darkness inside himself, his will coiled blindly, waiting to strike. And all the while there was that curious civil gravity in his external manner. There was something horrible about it, to Rhoda. It was not like him; she would rather have had him burst out in one of his savage rages, as he had in the old days. But he would say nothing; he only went on, obstinately, from day to day.

Rhoda spent Christmas Day with him and Bronwen at the flat that year. Mrs. Sorley had dressed a chicken for her to bring over, and she and Bronwen spent the morning in the kitchen, preparing it for roasting and making a mince pie. Brand went out for a walk while they were busy over their baking. It was a cold dark day; toward the end of the morning it began to snow. The snow made Rhoda feel nostalgic and rather depressed. She remembered Christmases she had spent when she was a girl, and one in particular, when Virgil had been a fat little boy in a round starched collar, absolutely terrified of his grandfather Beauchamp as Santa Claus. She had been invited to spend Christmas at the Kroeners' with Virgil and Mattie this year, but she had not wanted to go. It would be a gloomy celebration there; Sam had not come home yet, and Bertie had been ill with bronchitis, and was still not very well.

When the chicken was in the oven, she sat at the kitchen table, watching Bronwen deftly rolling out pastry dough for the mince pie. Rhoda was a little surprised at times by her domesticity; she had become very expert in household matters during the months at the flat. It had been good for her, having this to do; but Brand's failure was a strain on her, with her own emotional life so upset too. And it had turned her farther away than ever from everyone outside her own little circle. Her sense of rejection was almost as keen as Brand's.

The pie was in the oven, and they were expecting Brand back at any minute, when the telephone rang out in the office. Bronwen went to answer it. When she returned, her face was flushed with excitement and anxiety.

"It was Mr. Banford," she said to Rhoda. "They've had a fire with their Christmas tree, and the littlest boy was burned on the hands and legs. I told them I'd send Robbie the instant he came in." She could not pretend to be quiet, knowing how important this might be to Brand. She stood for a moment looking at Rhoda, rather distressed and helpless. "If he would only come—!" she said.

She went out to the office again, to look out the front window at the street. A moment later Rhoda heard her running down the stairs to the door. When she came back she was out of breath and smiling.

"I saw him from the window," she said. "He was just coming down the street. I brought his bag down to him. Now goodness knows when he'll be back. We'll have to do something about the dinner."

The atmosphere in the little flat suddenly became cheerful. Rhoda went back to the kitchen and discussed with Bronwen what ought to be done about the chicken. They were both prepared with perfect equanimity to see the dinner ruined, if it was necessary. But they did what they could to prepare to keep it for a time. Then they went into the little living room to wait.

But before half an hour had passed, they heard Brand come in again. Bronwen looked at Rhoda in dismay. They both knew at once that something had gone wrong. He went into the office, and in a few moments came out to the living room in silence. Bronwen looked at him but said nothing, waiting. Rhoda was not so patient.

"Well, *goodness!*" she said to him. "What happened now?"

But he could not talk about it; he was too full of a dark fury that he could not release. He sat at the table with them, cold and dumb with rage. It was not till days later that Rhoda heard what had happened, from other sources. It seemed that the Banfords, who had been patients of Dr. Greaves's, had called both Dr. Francis and Dr. Cameron, in Haddon, and, when they had not been able to reach either of them at once, had turned as a last resort to Brand. But a few minutes after Brand arrived at the house, Dr. Francis had come, and Mrs. Banford had immediately insisted that she wanted him, and not Brand, to take the case. Francis, a little stiff and constrained with Brand, whom he did not like, had pointed out that as Brand had been the first to arrive, the case should be left in his hands, at least for the time being; but Mrs. Banford had been insistent, almost hysterical, and had made out of what should have been at worst a rather embarrassing situation an unpleasant scene. Of course Brand had turned the case over to Francis and had left the house. But he could not forget the woman's behavior toward him, or Francis's stiffness, or Banford's bungling attempt to smooth the matter over by offering him twice the amount of his regular fee. The darkness that had been gathering blindly inside him became fixed, rather terrifying. He continued to go on from day to day, seeing his few patients, walking obstinately as he fell deeper into debt. Rhoda gathered her resolution and spoke to him at last about writing to John Bart and asking his help in getting a position in a research laboratory, or a public health or government post of some sort.

"This *can't* go on much longer, Rob," she said to him. "It doesn't depend on you; nothing you can do will change things here. They've made up their minds about you—"

But he hung on, grimly. He was like Bronwen in that; neither of them could admit defeat. There was that passionate affirmation of their own will in them, something almost apart from reason, that was stronger and more compelling for them than considerations of prudence or common sense.

On the evenings that he had no office hours he went out and walked, away from Cannon Hill, sometimes going as far as downtown and back again. The long hours he spent in the little flat, penned up, waiting, drove him almost mad, and he felt sometimes that he had to get away entirely, go off to a place where no one knew him or noticed him in his idleness. So he walked down to the heart of town, where he could pass unnoticed in the crowds, or in the big municipal park, Cassilly's Grove, on the hill above it.

It was through this habit of his that he became acquainted with Philip Magnus. Rhoda read in the newspaper one afternoon a brief, guarded account of an "accident" that had occurred in Cassilly's Grove late the previous night, when Magnus and his wife had been driving there. According to this account, which was not very convincing even for a newspaper story, they had been held up by an unidentified man, and in the ensuing confusion Mrs. Magnus had accidentally been wounded by a revolver shot. The article went on to say that fortunately a physician, who had identified himself as Dr. Robert Brand, had happened to be walking nearby, and that as the result of his prompt assistance Mrs. Magnus's condition was not serious.

Rhoda, like almost everyone else in Bard City, had become familiar with the name of Magnus during the past few years. She knew that Philip Magnus had made a sudden fortune out of a patent medicine called *Nervi-San,* and that he had lately bought a large chain of drugstores in the city; she knew also that he had married Julia Maitland after her divorce from her first husband, Francis Maitland, the owner of the Maitland factory across the road. She asked Brand rather curiously about the incident when she saw him several days later. He had come over to the Cannon House, as he did occasionally in the evening, and she was making coffee for him in the kitchen.

"What sort of person is he, really?" she asked him. "No one seems to know quite where all that money of his comes from. It was all a little *too* sudden—"

Brand shrugged irritably.

"Oh, I suppose he comes by it honestly enough," he said. "You can't stop people from believing in miracles, especially where their health is concerned, and he was just shrewd enough to convince a good number of them that the particular miracle they wanted could be bought in bottles. As far as I can see, that's the whole story. Of course, he has a lot of other irons in the fire now—"

"One of which probably gives him a good deal of influence with our police department, or he'd be under arrest now for assault with a deadly weapon, or whatever they call it in legal terms," Rhoda said bluntly. "Is there any truth at all in that cock-and-bull story that was in the papers?"

Brand did not answer. She poured his coffee.

"Well, *goodness!*—you needn't say anything if you don't want to," she said, rather nettled. "But it won't stop other people from talking. I suppose the man was jealous—isn't that it? I remember Ella Considine's telling me that, before she divorced Maitland, that woman went down to Palm Beach as a sort of experiment, to see if she was still attractive enough to men to get the sort of husband that she wanted. She'd better have stayed with Maitland, the way it looks now."

She was not really interested in the matter, though in the old days she had known the Braces, Julia Magnus's family, rather well: they were the "poor relations" of a famous Bard City political clan that had furnished a Vice-President and any number of Senators to the United States during the past hundred years. So she dropped the subject now. She was only a little curious about Brand's irritation over the matter. It was hardly like him to let something of that sort disturb him. Still she thought that she had heard the end of it, as far as it concerned him.

But not half an hour later, while they were still sitting in the kitchen, the doorbell rang, and she discovered her mistake. When she went to answer it, a Negro chauffeur in uniform stood on the doorstep; he had a letter, he said, for Dr. Robert Brand, and he had been told at his office that he would find him here. She saw the long black limousine standing at the curb.

"Yes, he's here," she said to the man. "I'll give him the letter."

He said very politely that he would prefer to give the envelope directly to Dr. Brand. Rhoda stared at him.

"Oh, very well," she said.

She went back to call Brand.

"I suppose it's Magnus's car," she said. "It's half a mile long. Is he sending you some enormous fee in that envelope, that he doesn't trust it in my hands?"

She could not help being curious; there was something rather ridiculously solemn about the whole affair. Through the open door of the kitchen she could hear Brand's voice as he talked to the chauffeur in the hall: "No, there's no answer. Just tell him I'll get in touch with him later—"

He came back into the kitchen, with the envelope stuffed into his coat pocket.

"Well?" Rhoda asked.

He looked at her, frowning slightly, not really seeing her.

"What on earth is this all about?" she asked. "You *do* look off in the clouds!"

He roused himself. "It's nothing important," he said.

He crossed the room to the door, opened it, and went outside to the garden. It was a windy autumn night, rather cold. She could see him through the window, walking up and down out there. She was a little hurt, and irritated with him, because he had not wanted to take her into his confidence. She gathered up the cups and saucers, rattling them angrily in the sink.

He left after a time without coming back into the house to say good night. She had to go to bed with her curiosity unsatisfied. And she made up her mind, in vexation, that she would not be the first to bring the subject up again. She could be frankly curious, but she would not pry when a door had been closed against her.

She did not see him again for almost two weeks. And when she did, the explanation of what had happened that night was already public property. She heard of it first from Virgil, on a Saturday afternoon, late, when she had stopped in at Sherman Street. He had just come home with the news, which he had read in one of the evening papers: it was announced that Dr. Robert Brand had been appointed medical consultant in the latest Magnus project—a manufacturing drug company to supply certain standard items to the chain of drugstores that he owned.

She could not really believe it till she had seen the article herself. And when she had, she threw the paper aside grimly. Mattie was watching her with her calm curiosity.

"I should think you'd be pleased," she said. "It's quite a step up in the world for him."

"Oh, I'm sure the salary is very attractive!" Rhoda said, harshly. "But it's not exactly what he planned to do."

She could not help being bitter about it; she had been schooled too well in the field of politics not to recognize a sinecure, a respectable, gilt-edged *quid pro quo,* when she saw one. And she did not understand, knowing Brand as well as she did, how he could have brought himself to accept a connection like this, even under the pressure of the past year and a half. He had such a hatred of commercialism in medicine, such a contempt for patronage. She could not picture him in this new role.

"Well, he's put one over on Cannon Hill, all right," Virgil was saying, rather pleased. "There're going to be a lot of people changing their minds about him, now that he's tied up with a man like Magnus. I ran into Jimmy Symons on the way home, and he turned green around the gills when I broke it to him. I suppose Brand's not leaving private practice altogether. If he's not, he'll have more patients than he knows what to do with in a couple of months. Symons isn't the only one that's going to figure that if he's good enough for Magnus, he's good enough for him."

Rhoda knew it was true that there was a certain glamour about the Magnus name in Bard City, the magical aura of success. He was reputed to be one of the half-dozen genuine millionaires living in the town, and to many people, with the glitter of a new prosperity before them, he was a kind of living symbol of the realization of their own dreams. Since his marriage to Julia Maitland, a few years before, he moved in the best society in the town, but the story went, Virgil said, that his father had owned a pawnshop on lower Vine Street, and that he himself had begun life peddling *Nervi-San,* which was rumored to be an old herb remedy that his mother had brought over from Poland, from door to door down there.

"Now he's worth a million if he's worth a dime," Virgil said. He shook his head; he had grown quite red with excitement, thinking of it. "All it takes these days is a little initiative and vision," he declared. "This fellow Magnus is just one example of how a man with an idea can get ahead. Brand's mighty lucky to have gotten in with him. No telling how much there'll be in it for him, outside of his salary; a man like Magnus can give you plenty of inside tips if he's your friend."

Rhoda did not want to listen to any more. She felt that she had to get away, to have time to think. She made some excuse and left the house. But as she was walking home, through the quiet fall late afternoon, she felt the bitterness of her first disappointment and anger slipping away from her. Her old capacity for intolerant indignation was leaving her as she grew older; she had seen too much now, she understood too much. So she began to realize what it was that had made Brand act as he had in accepting the Magnus appointment—the characteristically violent, deep-blooded reaction against disillusionment and rejection. She knew that he could never do things halfway; either he must put his whole soul into them or he would not think of them at all. And she had been so close to the whole struggle; she realized how bitterly he had suffered during those long, shameful months of waiting. His strong, decent nature had been shut in by a wall of blind determination: he *would not* give in, he *would not* admit defeat before these people. So, when the opportunity had offered itself, he had accepted it, his brute will accepting it, no matter what the cost, suppressing every other consideration. And she knew the fierce satisfaction there would be for him now, in seeing himself vindicated before the people who had rejected him. He was not a humble man; he could not make himself into a humble man. She felt tired and tolerant and old, thinking about it all.

Still she did not want to see him just yet. But when she got back to the Cannon House, Mrs. Sorley came out to meet her at the door, to tell her that he was waiting for her, in the parlor.

"I told him you were over at Sherman Street," she said, "but he said he'd wait for you a while. Wisha, have you heard the news, now?"

"Yes, I've heard it," Rhoda said.

"The Lord help us," Mrs. Sorley whispered to her, "did you ever hear of a stroke of luck like that one? It was Ash came over here with that piece out of the paper: next thing you know, he says, there'll be our Robbie making his millions, along with Magnus. Is it the truth, now, that Mrs. Magnus would have been dead that night if it hadn't been for him?"

Rhoda went on into the parlor without answering her. Brand was standing before the window; he had heard her come into the house and was expecting her. She saw the heavy look of challenge on his face, so like the one she had used to see there when he had first come to live in the house, and had anticipated her anger over something that he had done. But she was not angry now, only empty and tired. She went over and took off her hat slowly before the mirror.

"Well, Rob?" she said, with a weary, ironical inflection.

He stood looking at her, not knowing quite how he was to take her toneless manner.

"I suppose you've heard," he said, after a moment, with a stubborn directness.

"Yes, I've heard." She put her hat down on the mantel and turned, without looking at him, to sit down in her favorite chair before the fireplace. "Did you come here to have me congratulate you?" she asked. And she glanced over at him suddenly, her keen blue glance clouded and impersonal. "Well then, I congratulate you."

"Thanks," he said. "I didn't come for that."

"Why *did* you come then?"

She began to see that, behind his calm manner, there was a cold, violent restlessness, a kind of self-lacerating fury that was only kept subdued by a positive, logical force of will. And she knew that she was exasperating him still further by her faint, stubborn irony. It was not what he had expected. He had come, apparently, to have it out with her, perhaps to convince himself, even more than to convince her, that he had been justified in acting as he had. And he felt defeated, seeing her accept the fact of his action so quietly.

"Well," he said after a moment, rather bitterly, "if that's all you have to say of it, I might as well be going."

"What did you expect me to say?" she asked him. In spite of herself, the anger rose a little in her too. "You know what you're doing, I suppose, and what you want," she said; "there's never been anything I could say that would change your mind when you'd made it up."

He colored up heavily, his face with the dark, spreading flush on it that she remembered so well from the old days.

"And what do *you* want me to do then?" he demanded. "Go back to waiting in that God-forsaken office for someone to come

around, or to call me because they can't get Francis or Volling, and
the women looking at me when I walk in the house as if they thought
I ought to use the back door?" He shook his head, furious. "No,
thanks; I've had enough of that. I had a lucky break, and I've got
sense enough to see it, and to hold on to it."

Rhoda looked over at him. It hurt her to see him so violent, the
furious *will* in him that tethered him to his decision in spite of himself. Her anger died out in her; she only felt helpless, rather wasted.

"I suppose you'll stay on here in Cannon Hill?" she asked, after
a moment.

"Yes." He spoke more calmly, growing fixed and stiff. "I'm going
to enjoy watching all the people who said I was a fool changing
their minds about me." The bitterness flared up in him again. "I
could have starved to death in that office, for all the use they had
for me," he said.

She knew it really was true; there had been that sort of battle
between him and them. And she knew too that it could have happened that they would have stood by, quiet and secure in their prejudice, till, out of disgust and anger and finally self-pity, he had lost
everything fine that he had in him, till he had turned into the thing
that they had said he would be from the beginning. Still she did not
want him to give himself over to his bitterness. So she tried to defend them against him.

"I suppose it was that they couldn't get used to the idea that you
were really a doctor," she said, rather wearily. "People are queer
about things like that. They want their doctors like their priests—
something a little mysterious about them, so that they can believe
in their God-given powers—"

"They want them rich," Brand said. He said it flatly, without
cynicism, stating it for her as a hard, accepted fact. "For them every
dollar a doctor has is like a written testimonial. Or like the crutches
that cripples leave at shrines. Every one a testimonial from a grateful patient."

She shook her head. "Well, you'll have the money now."

"You're good and right I will. Things will be a bit different from
now on."

There was nothing that she could say to him. She knew this, and waited for him to go. So at last he had to leave, defeated by her very refusal to cross wills with him. Her acquiescence had made an estrangement between them, deeper than any that had ever been caused by their quarrels.

Very shortly, she heard that he was thinking of leaving the flat over the bakery. And when Mrs. Considine, about that time, left Cannon Hill to go to California to live, no one was surprised that it was Brand who rented her square mansarded Victorian house on Old Town Road, near the Square. It was one of the oldest houses in Cannon Hill, and still one of the finest, very well kept up, with its big veranda almost hidden by vines, and its green lawn surrounded by a low stone wall. The furniture remained in the house, the dark, heavy, Victorian pieces that had stood there for over thirty years. And Rhoda thought, when she went to the house, that he took a certain satisfaction in its solid, old-fashioned appearance; it was a kind of symbol of his success to him, to live in the house and see it looking just as it had in the days when he had been struggling for his education, and would not have been asked beyond the front door.

He was not the only one to step out of Rhoda's life just then into a new prosperity. Mrs. Sorley was leaving her, after all the years she had been at the Cannon House; Gard and Ash had opened a garage together when they had come out of the Army, and things had been going so well for them that they felt it was not necessary for her to work any more. They bought one of the new bungalows that were going up in long identical rows on the other side of Cannon Hill, and made a down payment on a houseful of shiny oak furniture. Then, on the last day that Mrs. Sorley worked at the Cannon House, Gard came to call for her in his new automobile. He strode back through the hall to the kitchen, full of life, rather braggartly.

"Come on now, old lady," he shouted at her. "You've washed your last dish here. Pop on your hat and off you go."

He came up behind her and began to untie the strings of her apron.

"The divil choke your old gob," she said, pulling away from him, somewhat flustered. "Will you go on out now and wait till I finish up with my kitchen? I'll not be a minute, if you can keep your big paws out of the way."

He laughed, and went out to the car to wait for her.

"Go on now, Maud," Rhoda said to her. "Franciszka can finish that in the morning." She had a young Polish girl coming in to take Mrs. Sorley's place the next day.

Mrs. Sorley stood in the center of the kitchen, looking at her, rather upset.

"Ah, I don't like to leave you now, as true as heaven, I don't," she said, sentimentally. "How are you going to get on with that Polack of yours?—curse of God on the decent day's work you'll get out of *her*, and the men clamoring if their supper's five minutes behind. 'Tis a hard old life you'll have with her—'tis, 'tis."

"We'll make out somehow, I suppose," Rhoda said; she was always a little grim before sentimental displays. "And, Maud, remember, if things don't work out right and you should ever want to come back—"

"Ah, and why shouldn't they work out?" Mrs. Sorley interrupted her indignantly. "With my two fine boyos riding on the top of the world now?" She was a little offended, and jerked at her apron-strings, knotting them tighter in her haste. "For the love of the Lord, will you get me out of this thing now?" she said to Rhoda, peremptorily. "That boy'll be killed with waiting if I'm much longer."

She put on her hat and coat and rushed outside. Rhoda went to the front door to see her drive off with Gard, sitting proudly erect beside him in the front seat. She felt lonely, coming back into the house; it was the crumbling off of another of the edges of her life. And she could not help being a little irritated, and a little worried, about Mrs. Sorley's rather arrogant joy in her new prosperity. She did not miss much of what went on around the Cannon House, and she knew from hearing the men talk that the Sorley boys' success was not entirely due to the garage that they were running. It was Ash's dry, exasperated covetousness that had seen the profit there could be for them in the operation of the new Prohibition law.

A few months later, when she went to the Sorleys' to take a Christmas gift to Maud, she was received in a bright, littered little living room with a victrola in a mahogany console, a new player-piano, and a bookcase full of educational "sets" in gilt-stamped leather covers.

"Ah, you never had anything like this at the Cannon House, did you now?" Mrs. Sorley asked her triumphantly, seeing her looking around. "It's an old nuisance, with all this stuff, but the boys like it, and they're the ones that are paying for it."

Still Rhoda thought there was something pinched and frightened about her, almost pathetic, in spite of her new grandeur. They were rather cold with each other, feeling the barrier of their altered relationship between them. But when Maud began talking, in a fit of absolutely arrogant bravado, about the boys' wanting to send her on a trip to Florida that winter, Rhoda felt that a good shaking was what she needed; she was like a boastful child, with all the hard common sense she had gained in years of experience thrown to the winds.

Rhoda saw Brand only occasionally that winter, though she went fairly often to the new house, to give Bronwen advice and help with her housekeeping there. He was very busy now, with his own practice and his connection with Magnus. When Rhoda saw him, she sensed a new calm behind his reserve. Before this time, there had always been something angry and uncertain under the civility of his manner. She thought that she should have welcomed the change in him. He seemed more at peace than she had ever known him, in his relations with other people. Still she felt that it was only his pride that had been satisfied. He had been so bitterly humiliated that he could forget everything else now in his sense of vindication. But she believed that he could not go on permanently in that state of blind, unreasoning triumph.

She had hoped at first, however, that for Bronwen this new life, the sense of freedom from anxiety and pressure, would put an end finally to the emotional difficulties that Lamson's death had caused in her. But it was exactly the opposite that occurred. Rhoda began to realize that it was only the feeling that she was needed that had been keeping the girl up. During the winter she came down with grippe, and Brand engaged a regular housekeeper, in place of the Polish cleaning-woman they had had till that time, to look after things while she was ill. Then, even when she was better, he insisted

on keeping the housekeeper on; he was afraid that she had been
doing too much, and he wanted to make things easier for her. So he
took away her last reason for going on. There was no one who
needed her now. And she shut herself away again, as she had in the
months just after Lamson's death. Rhoda felt that she was living
merely mechanically and passively. She did not care about their
being better off, about their living in the new house, about the new
people that she met.

Brand, on the other hand, seemed on very good terms with both
the Magnuses. Rhoda met them together one afternoon at his house:
Magnus a man of middle height, still comparatively young, with a
face that in repose was a long oval, almost blank; his wife, whom she
had not seen since she was a young girl in her teens, a tall, still
handsome blonde at thirty-eight or forty. Rhoda knew that she was
living with Magnus on rather curious terms since the incident at
Cassilly's Grove; from her manner toward him that afternoon, she
gathered that she felt that now, after the terrible fright he had had,
when he thought he had killed her, she could have everything her
own way with him. But there was an almost tangible tension in their
relationship, in spite of their apparent agreement. Rhoda read in
Magnus's curiously solemn mask, which took on an almost automatic,
ingratiating mobility when he smiled, the signs of that intense, naïve
ego which seems so harmless under ordinary circumstances, but
which can burst out occasionally in violent action. There was something poorly balanced about him, some absolute dependence upon
others. And Rhoda saw how, in Brand's presence, he rested with a
certain complacency on the other's stronger nature. There was an
odd tendency on the part of both him and his wife, it seemed to her,
to place on Brand's shoulders the responsibility for their reconcilia-
tion, so that he was drawn at once, quite intimately, into their lives.

But Bronwen remained aloof, resisting any attempts to bring her
into this new world. Rhoda was with her one late spring afternoon
when Julia Magnus stopped by at the house to pick Brand up and
bring him home with her to dinner. Brand had just come in from a
call, and while he was upstairs, dressing, Mrs. Magnus sat down
with Bronwen and Rhoda in the living room. She had a blunt,
friendly manner when she wished to be agreeable, which she used

with Rhoda that afternoon, talking to her about Bronwen as if they had a common interest in her.

"I want her to come this evening too," she said. "I'll have some young people there; they won't all be of Phil's and Rob's vintage. I'm always asking her, and she always has some perfectly good excuse—"

Bronwen was rather obstinately silent. There was a silent flow of animosity between her and Julia Magnus, which the older woman refused to acknowledge. She was used to riding people down with her hard, clear will. But she could get no hold, not even this slight one of social obligation, on the girl.

Rhoda tried to smooth over the absolute refusal implicit in Bronwen's silence.

"Oh, Bron's still enough of a convalescent to like an old woman's pleasures best," she mocked: "tea, and early dinners, and her own bed at half-past nine. It takes so much energy to be young these days."

"Not more than she seemed to have yesterday when I saw her at the Wilton at lunch," Julia Magnus said, in her harsh voice, that gave every word she spoke a curiously naked, public sound. "She was with a very attractive young man, and she seemed to have quite enough energy for *him*."

Rhoda looked at Bronwen. But the other woman's words had not succeeded in drawing her out. She kept her shadowy distantness.

Brand came down.

"Are you ready?" Julia asked him.

"In a minute. Sorry to keep you waiting."

He went out to the office. Rhoda noticed that he looked at Julia Magnus with that completely civil Welsh lack of expression that he put on whenever he did not care to have people know what his real feelings were. She had a rather proprietary air with him that Rhoda would have guessed would irk him. Still it was agreeable for him, no doubt, to be on these terms of friendly intimacy with the woman who had once been Francis Maitland's wife. Like the house, she was a part of the pattern for him—the pattern of his own success.

When he came back he said to Rhoda: "Why don't you stay and have dinner with Bron? Hasn't she asked you?"

"No," Rhoda said. "But it doesn't matter. I have to get back."

She saw how Brand looked at Bronwen, with a kind of impatient energy. He could not understand her any longer; he did not know what it was that she wanted. Only he knew that she was against him, and that she did not want what he had given her. There was a new coldness between them, a kind of hostility, different from any that there had been before.

He and Julia Magnus left the house. Julia was wearing a bronze-colored costume, very chic under her light furs.

"Goodness! such elegance," Rhoda said, ironically. "I must say I'd have had a hard time, a few years ago, picturing Rob with *that*."

Bronwen lifted her shoulders.

"I should say *you* don't like her," Rhoda said to her.

Bronwen shook her head. "He doesn't either. He doesn't really want any of it. But he'll go on like this, just to be able to show people that he *can*—"

Rhoda looked at her rather helplessly. She wanted to talk to her about Brand, to make her understand better what it was that was taking place in him now. But she knew that Bronwen was too young to be able to compromise. She wanted Brand to be as he had seemed to her as a child—strong and sure in wisdom. And she judged him by that standard, feeling cheated when he did not meet it.

Rhoda asked her about the young man Julia Magnus had spoken of, the one who had been having lunch with her at the Wilton Hotel. She would have been glad if Bronwen had begun to be interested in someone again, but it turned out to be nothing of that sort. The young man she had been with was Neil Lamson's friend, the one with whom he had gone to Canada in 1915. She had found out that he was back in town, visiting his parents, for the first time since the end of the war, and had telephoned him, wanting to talk about Neil. He had seen him after his plane had been shot down, at the evacuation hospital where he had died.

Rhoda shook her head. "But what *good* does it do, to go over all that again?" she asked. "It's almost three years now."

"I don't care if it's a dozen," Bronwen said, coldly and fiercely. She stood at the window, pulling the cord of the blind between her fingers. Rhoda felt defeated. She knew how she had suffered herself, not for a few months, but for years after she had had the news of John Lefroy's marriage. But because the circumstances had been different, she had had her pride to keep her up. And it seemed so faraway now, almost unimportant, only one small part of a life that had gone on, in spite of itself, to other experiences and other emotions.

She wondered suddenly if it was something of this sort that had begun to happen to Bronwen, that she had begun to realize that the brief time she had had with Lamson was being overlaid, whether she wished it or not, by the life she was living now without him. During the months after Brand's return from overseas, when she had been living in the little flat, with something to occupy her, and take her out of herself, the normal processes of time had gone on in her without her noticing them; and now that she was free to go back, to remember, she was finding perhaps that the outlines were blurred, that the sharpness of emotion was no longer there for her to return to. So she had grasped at the chance to recall it by talking of Lamson to someone who could make his existence a vivid reality to her again. She did not want to forget; she wanted to keep it all there inside her, the richness and the life and even the suffering that she had once had.

Rhoda remembered what Bertie Kroener had said on the Sunday that she and Virgil and Rhoda had gone walking together down the hill behind the Cannon House—that they had had their own chance of youth and happiness, but that they had taken that chance away from this new generation for the sake of their own selfish safety and profit. She felt that she had to bear part of the weight of Bronwen's unhappiness. And there was Sam, too, for her to worry about. It was well over two years now since the end of the war, and he still seemed to have no inclination to come back to Cannon Hill. Mattie had given up expecting him. She went about hard and quiet, watching the house on Sherman Street growing older and shabbier in its strict German neatness, while her neighbors' homes were blossoming out with new overstuffed furniture and victrolas and beaded lampshades. Sophie had a theory that Sam was married, or had a girl at least, over in Czechoslovakia, and that that was the reason he was not coming home. All the Kroeners, except Bertie, were rather bitter about Sam, and Virgil had violent arguments with them because he insisted on defending him. Bertie wanted to say that she agreed with Virgil about Sam, but she was afraid of her father and sisters, and so she let him argue with them alone. She was growing more old-maidish than ever, with her clothes always timidly behind the new styles that were coming in, and she had never got up courage enough to go off on the long trip that she had been planning to take some-time after the war.

During the winter that followed, she came down with a bad cold, but they were in the midst of taking inventory down at the store, so that she felt she could not very well stay home from work. She kept on till the end of the week, but on Sunday her tempera-ture was so high and the pains in her chest and back so bad that they called Dr. Volling in to see her. He said it was pneumonia, and had her taken to the hospital at once. The Kroeners were all upset because none of them had ever been in a hospital before, and they felt that the prices were outrageous.

"She'd probably get well a lot quicker right here at home," Sophie said. "My word! I know what Grandma Kroener would have said about all this fuss. She'd put a mustard plaster on her chest and give her a whisky toddy, and have her up before Dr. Volling'd made up his mind what sort of fancy name he was going to call what ailed her."

Rhoda went down to see Bertie with Virgil one evening that week, after he had finished at the store. They said at the hospital that she was doing well, but she looked terribly thin and old, with her curly black hair braided tightly back from her patchily flushed face. Only her eyes looked so big and young and untouched by life. They did not want her to talk much, but she insisted on telling them how well she was getting along.

"Oh, I was all ready to give up when they brought me here," she said, "I was so scared! I couldn't think of anything but how Mamma was ever going to get along without me, and that I wouldn't be here to see Sam when he came home." She smiled rather quaintly, her old bright timid smile. "I even kept telling them that I wanted Mattie to have my amethyst set and Sophie my coral brooch, and that the money was to go to Sam. And Sophie kept saying it was all nonsense, and I was to go to sleep."

She was breathless from talking so much, but smiling, and happy to see them. She wanted them to promise to come back the next evening. But by the afternoon she was so much worse that they called the family in, and when Rhoda arrived in the evening she was already unconscious, and she had to go away without seeing her. Toward noon of the following day she died.

The funeral was a big German affair, very solemn and heavy, with relatives from all over the city coming to the services. It was raining when they arrived at the cemetery, and they would not let old Mrs. Kroener get out of the car. She sat on the edge of the seat, with the door open, watching while they lowered the casket into the ground. Sophie and Mattie were both crying, but Mrs. Kroener only sat huddled in her black coat, staring out helplessly through the rain.

"I can't see now—I can't see now," she kept saying to Virgil, in German.

He could not understand her, and called over one of the German relatives, a brisk, middle-aged woman, who chafed the old woman's black-gloved hands in her own and said in a hushed, businesslike way, "Now, now, it's all right, it's going to be all right."

After it was over, Mattie brought Sophie and her parents back to Sherman Street for dinner. Virgil asked Rhoda to come along too. She sat in the living room, trying to talk to the elder Kroeners. She had offered to help with the meal, but Mattie had never liked to have her in her kitchen, and she had Sophie there with her, so Rhoda had not pressed her offer.

After a while Virgil, who was in the restless, miserable state that he always fell into on an occasion like this, walked back to the kitchen too. Rhoda could hear him talking to Sophie and Mattie, but she could not understand what they were saying. Then all at once the voices were louder, and she heard Sophie say, in a determined, incredulous tone: "Well, I like that; I *do* like that!"

She did not know what sort of argument Virgil might be starting with her, in the mood he was in, and she got up and said to Justus Kroener that she thought she had better go back and see what was going on. When she got back to the kitchen, Sophie was standing against the sink, with a wooden-handled fork in her hand and the color high in her face, staring at Virgil, who was saying something about honoring Bertie's wishes, and about everyone's having heard her say that she wanted the money to go to Sam.

"*Quatsch!*" Sophie said to him rudely. "She was out of her head half the time; she never knew what she was saying. And besides, that money wasn't hers to dispose of; it's in a joint account with Mamma at the Warsaw Hill Building and Loan—Bertha Kroener and Mrs. Mathilda Kroener *or* survivor."

Virgil, who was even more flushed than Sophie, said that that was only a technicality.

"It was her own money, her own savings, every cent of it—can you deny that?" he said to her stubbornly. "She had every right to dispose of it the way she wanted to, and she wanted to leave it to Sam; there isn't anyone in the family who hasn't heard her say that, time and again, and especially those last few days—"

"Well, I can see we'd better get this settled right here and now," Sophie interrupted him.

She marched out, fork and all, into the living room. They all went in after her. Mattie was clutching at Virgil's arm, holding him back while she said something to him in her low, rapid voice.

"Why, I'd be ashamed!" she said. "Bertie not cold in the ground, and quarreling about money—"

"I wasn't the one who brought it up; remember that," Virgil cried angrily. "Good Lord, before I'd stoop low enough to do a boy out of a few thousand dollars—"

Sophie was talking to Justus Kroener. She wanted him to explain to Virgil how Bertie had only been able to save that much money because of everything that had been done for her at home, things that she would have had to pay for if she had lived anywhere else. She said that if Bertie were alive and in the room that minute, she wouldn't say anything but that the money belonged to her father and mother as much as it ever had to her, and that she, Sophie, didn't see what earthly claim Sam had to it, when he hadn't even cared enough about his own people to come home and see them when the war was over, and it looked as if he wanted to spend the rest of his life with strangers.

"How do you know what kind of reasons he's got for staying away?" Virgil interrupted her, firing up again at the way she spoke of Sam. "How do you know what that rotten gas did to his lungs during the war, and now he doesn't want to come home a sick boy, not able to make a living for himself?"

Justus Kroener began to talk to Virgil then in his dragging, granite voice, saying that he didn't see how there could be any legal question about the money's being his wife's now, and that he didn't think Virgil ought to bring a lawyer into a family matter like this; but, he added, if he thought it best to satisfy himself about it fully, he could always go to one and see what he had to say about it. He said that times might be good for other people, but things hadn't picked up for him after last year's slump, and he was going to have to put the money right back into the business, which was where Bertie had got it from, of course, in the first place. His wife sat in a corner, listening to him, and looking frightened when she heard her name mentioned. She did not understand what she had to do with it all, and she looked from Sophie to her husband as they talked, waiting to be enlightened. When Justus Kroener asked her if that wasn't what she wanted to do with the money, she said yes without understanding, because she knew that that was what she was expected to say.

Virgil stood in the big double doorway between the living room and the dining room, facing them, feeling them all against him, but stubbornly going on, stammering out his arguments.

"Oh, come *on*," Rhoda said to him at last. "Let's go out and take a little walk before dinner, the two of us."

She had not said anything all the while; she knew it would be of no possible use for her to get into it. She took Virgil's arm and succeeded in getting him out into the hall.

"It's still raining," he said, pulling away from her when they were alone out there. "Let me alone; why should I go?"

She pulled his coat down from where it was hanging on the hall-tree.

"Don't be such a baby," she said. "Here, put this on."

He obeyed her, still rather fiery. She found an umbrella and they went out under it. It was turning colder as the winter dusk came on; the rain was beginning to thicken to wet snow as it came down.

"This is a fool thing to do," he said. "We'll catch pneumonia ourselves."

He said that he was going to write to Sam and tell him to come home: "He's got a right to know what's going on here," he declared hotly. "Damn it all, Rhode, you know as well as I do that the last thing in the world Bertie wanted was for that money to go back in the business. You heard her say herself that she wanted Sam to have it."

"Well, Sam's not going to get it, so you may as well forget about it right now," Rhoda said to him. "He hasn't a chance. You'll only stir up trouble, and you won't have a thing to show for it anyway, in the end."

She did not want him to get so excited about it. He had begun to have too high a color lately, and to get short of breath easily; she had tried to persuade him to go to a doctor, but he said he was all right, he had never had a sick day in his life. She looked at him now as he walked along, and thought how much stouter and older he was looking these past few years. And yet she could still see in him the fat little boy in the round starched collar who was frightened of Santa Claus. It made her feel depressed to think of him going down every day to work in the surgical appliance store that he hated so much, with its fracture-beds and elastic stockings and wheel chairs that gave it such a grim and cheerless air.

"Don't you think that if I wrote to Sam and told him he ought to come home, he'd come?" he asked her, in a belligerent, uncertain tone, as if he wanted to be reassured in his belief. "His mother's always asking him in her letters why he doesn't come, but I've never said anything about it so far; I figured it's his life; he's got the right to do what he wants. But don't you think, if I wrote to him now—?"

Rhoda did not know what to say to him. It was hard to tell much from Sam's letters. He did not write very often, and when he did he seemed to like it where he was on the farm in Czechoslovakia. But from his last letters she had got the impression that he had made up his mind not to stay much longer, and so she thought it was safe to encourage Virgil now. She wished that Sam could come home and do something for him, but she knew it was going to be hard on Sam

too, to have the kind of burden put on him right away that his
mother and his father would want him to take.

She and Virgil walked around the block in the wet thin snow
that melted as soon as it struck the pavement, and when they got
back to the house again they were both feeling a little better. Mattie
and Sophie had the dinner almost ready, and after they had sat
down at the table old Mrs. Kroener sat there looking at the place
that had always been Bertie's with the tears beginning to roll down
her cheeks, and they all tried to be cheerful and take her mind off
Bertie. Nobody said anything more about the money.

Chapter 10

IT TOOK A LONG TIME FOR LETTERS TO GO BACK and forth between Bard City and Czechoslovakia, and it was nearly spring before Virgil had an answer to the letter in which he had told Sam about Bertie's death and asked him to come home. Sam wrote that he would leave as soon as he could, but that it might be a few months because there had been sickness on the farm, and he hardly liked to leave just when there was so much work to be done. When Mattie read this letter to the family, Sophie said to wait and see, and that it sounded like nothing but another excuse to her. No one except Virgil seemed to put much faith in the idea that Sam was really coming home.

But one morning in June, while Mattie was in the kitchen getting breakfast and Virgil was upstairs shaving, there was a ring at the front door, and when Mattie went out to answer it, there was Sam standing on the porch. She hardly knew him for a moment, he looked so much older and bigger than he had when he had gone away. She began to cry when she saw him, her face crumpling suddenly. Virgil came running down from the bathroom with the lather still on his face. He was almost crying too, he was so excited. Sam had to promise him not to tell anything important while he was upstairs before he would consent to go back and finish shaving and dressing. He was like a boy in his excitement; they could hear him upstairs, swearing impatiently at his own clumsiness as he fumbled hastily through the rest of his toilet.

"Taking the name of the Lord in vain, when he should be thanking God for your safe return," Mattie said.

She had gotten control of herself again, and only the way she went about with her lips pressed tightly together to keep them from trembling showed how upset she really was.

They all sat down to breakfast together in the dining room, and Sam had to tell them some of the things that had happened to him during the war, and listen while Virgil hastily poured out the family and the neighborhood news. They were all a little strange and awkward with each other; there was such a sense of unreality in their sitting there, just as they had used to do, as if the past five years had been erased in a moment. Sam had the same feeling that he had had all the while he had been walking over from the station: a feeling as if he had seen all this in a dream, and now for the first time was looking at it in the real world, awake. Everything seemed different, even the things that had not changed. He saw his mother looking at him across the table, with her lips pressed together as if she were trying not to cry again, and he knew that she was feeling the same way about how different he seemed to her.

She said to him: "I've prayed every night since you left home to have you back sitting at this table again. Every night for five years."

It embarrassed him to have her talk to him in that way. Before she had said that, they had all been talking and laughing together; but now all at once the excitement seemed to die down in them, and they sat there cold, not looking at each other.

"I can't understand," Mattie went on, in her clear, rigid voice, "why you didn't want to come home when the war was over, like the other boys. You know that we love you, and that we'd have been glad to take care of you while you were sick."

"But I wasn't sick," Sam tried to explain to her. "I was fine all the time, after the hospital. It was only what I wrote you about wanting to work outdoors for a while."

"You could have worked outdoors here," Mattie said. "Your grandfather says you could have gotten a job with the post office, delivering mail. There was no need for you to go to strangers."

She had never been able to understand that, his choosing deliberately to remain away from his own home, his own people. It had hurt her for years, like a humiliation. And now that he had returned, she could not prevent herself from reproaching him with it, though she knew that her words were taking the light out of his homecoming for both of them.

She got up from the table and went back to the kitchen, to begin cleaning up the breakfast things there. She did not want to cry any more, and she knew that she would not if she did something with her hands. When she had gone, Virgil got up and came around to take the chair beside Sam, where she had been sitting.

"Listen, Sam," he said, rather embarrassed. "You mustn't mind what your mother says now. It was a shock for her, you know, having you walk in like that after all those years. She'll get over it in a little while."

"I don't mind," Sam said. "I should have wired you from New York."

"When we got the letter saying you were coming home," Virgil explained, still a little anxious, "she showed it to Sophie, and Sophie got her to thinking there was something wrong about it, and that you weren't coming anyway. Sophie's always said you were married over there, or had a girl, and that was the reason you didn't come home."

"I'm not married," Sam said. "And there wasn't any girl. The devil with Aunt Sophie."

He was a little irritated, feeling the close, inquisitive family atmosphere beginning to envelop him already. But then he could not help laughing as Virgil repeated after him promptly and happily, "The devil with Aunt Sophie"—speaking in a low voice, so that Mattie could not hear him in the kitchen.

"You're going to be a big disappointment to her, Sam," he said. "No girl, no wife, and home on schedule."

"She doesn't necessarily have to believe it," Sam said. "Any of it except my being here. She'll figure it out some way so it adds up right."

"She can't add it up to anything that says you're not here." Virgil brought his chair a little closer. "Maybe we'll think up a few more surprises for her, now that you're here," he said. "I've got a lot of ideas. We'll talk about them in a day or two, when you've had a chance to get your breath." He gestured expansively. "You'd be surprised how things have changed around here while you've been away. You can clean up a million if you go about it right. All it needs is a little initiative and vision."

He began telling Sam about Magnus, and then about the automobile business, which he said was the coming thing in America. It surprised Sam to see how excited he was getting about it. All his life, since he could remember him, his father had been getting excited about one thing or another, but it had never before been about making money.

"But we'll talk about all that later," Virgil said hurriedly, hearing Mattie coming out from the kitchen again. "I tell you, Sam, I've got it all worked out. But we won't say anything yet to your mother."

Sam had already seen how the relationship between his father and his mother had changed during his absence. Before he had left, there had still been the open strife between them that had begun when Virgil had lost his business. But by this time his mother had won her battle; Virgil had *had* to give in under the quiet, never-ending pressure, and it was only on rare occasions now that his old independent spirit burst out in a flare of resentment or excitement. And Sam felt, with a sense of mixed oppression and loyalty, that his father was depending on him to alter matters now, that he had been looking forward to his homecoming as if to a deliverance.

Mattie came into the dining room.

"Virgil," she said, "it's eight o'clock. You'll be late at the store if you don't hurry."

"I don't care if I am late," Virgil said. He was still happy, and he did not want to leave.

"Yes, you do. Of course you do. You can talk to Sam this evening."

Virgil got up. "Come on down to the store with me, Sam," he said. "Come on down and be a disappointment to people."

"Later, maybe," Sam said. "I want to go over and see Aunt Rhoda."

He said good-by to his father and went upstairs to his old room. It was just the same as it had been when he had gone away, only there was a photograph of him in uniform standing on the chest of drawers. He went over to the window and looked out. The maple tree behind the house was gone, and there were two small boys that he did not know playing in the yard next door.

He walked over to the Cannon House later on that morning. His mother had telephoned Rhoda that he was coming, so that she was expecting him. He cut through the field beside the house, and came in at the garden door, just as he had used to do, to find her sitting out on the bench in the kitchen yard, waiting for him.

"I thought you'd come this way," she said, standing up and holding her cheek to be kissed. Then she put her arms around him and hugged him quickly. "Goodness, you *are* changed," she said. "I think you've actually frightened your mother a little. She seems to think you ought to have stayed eighteen all this time."

He laughed, and they sat down together on the bench. She was looking at him steadily, pleased with him, and showing her pleasure in her slight, keen smile.

"Europe seems to have agreed with you, Sam," she said. "You don't look like the same mixed-up boy who left here five years ago."

He shook his head, smiling at her also, but rather thoughtfully.

"I don't know, Aunt Rhoda. I've got a feeling that I'm starting in all over again."

"As bad as that?"

"Isn't it?"

He looked at her directly. She liked his way of coming straight to the difficulty.

"Yes, I suppose it is," she admitted. "You've simply jumped right into the middle of it again. They all *want* something of you—and I suppose you've already made up your mind that you want something altogether different for yourself." She was silent for a moment. "I hope it isn't that you want to go back there, ever, permanently?" she asked.

"No, nothing like that. I *did* like it there—the farm, the people, all of it. But I never thought of not coming home some day, for good." He looked down at the brick paving-stones at his feet. "It was just that I felt as if I *had* to have a chance to get things straightened out, after the war," he said. "And then, when I'd gotten the war out of my system, I still wanted to stay for a while, because things kept getting better, and clearer—" He broke off, a little embarrassed. "It's hard to explain," he said. "It was just as if I was beginning to see what was important for me, and what wasn't—"

"But that *is* the kind of life you really want?" Rhoda asked, after a moment. "The kind you had over there?"

He nodded. "Yes. When I started for home, I had it all settled that what I was going to do was to take the first job I could find and try to get enough money together to buy a small place of my own, somewhere in the valley, around here. But I can see already that Dad has been planning on something else."

"He thinks you and he are going to get rich together," Rhoda said dryly. "He's had some sort of bee in his bonnet ever since he heard you were coming home." She shook her head impatiently. "He's getting more like his own father every day. Because he sees a man like Philip Magnus grabbing a million dollars out of thin air, he thinks all he has to do is to reach out his own two hands and the manna will drop from heaven for him too."

She wanted to tell him to carry out his own plans, regardless of Virgil or Mattie, to warn him out of her own long, hopeless experience with Richard Beauchamp's fuzzy ambitions. But she knew that it would be useless; he would have to decide for himself how far he would compromise with his own wishes to satisfy theirs. Still she felt, as she watched him sitting there beside her, that at any rate there was something in him now, some inner balance, which would prevent him from doing anything drastically unwise.

He stayed to lunch with her at the Cannon House. When he finally went back home, in the middle of the afternoon, he found his mother in the kitchen, baking a cake. She looked at him rather nervously as he came in. It seemed to upset her, having him there alone.

"I don't want you to make any plans for this evening, Sam," she said. "I called your grandmother and your aunt Sophie, and told them you were here. They're coming over after dinner with your grandfather."

"All right," he said. "Fine."

She stood there before the table, looking at him with the expression of tension still on her face. He saw that she had something else to say.

"I called a few other people too," she went on, abruptly. "People I thought you might like to see." Her face, already reddened from the heat of the kitchen, colored up quickly. "I know your grandparents seem like very elderly people to you," she said, "and I didn't want you to feel dull. So I got in touch with Dick Rogan, and with Frances Hardy—"

He stopped still, in the middle of the kitchen, not saying anything.

"I suppose you know how well Frances is doing with her singing now," his mother went on again after a minute, speaking rapidly and not looking at him as she went back to mixing her cake batter again. "She has one of the big churches over in Haddon now, and these past two summers she's been singing in the operas out at Ludlow Woods."

"Isn't she married yet?" he asked.

He had had letters from Frances fairly regularly during the war, but after he had gone to Czechoslovakia she had stopped writing, and he had not heard anything from her since.

"Oh, no," his mother said quickly. "She isn't married."

He knew that she had not liked Frances when he had been going with her before the war, but he understood that now she would be glad if he would marry her, because it would mean his settling down in Cannon Hill, or at least somewhere in Bard City. He did not know how he felt about seeing Frances again. It had been a long time, and he knew that she must have changed as much as he had. But, thinking about her, he could feel the old vague, restless excitement coming up in him again. He wanted to see her; he remembered with a kind of urgency her thin, vital figure and her gray eyes that looked straight at him, laughing.

The Kroeners were the first to arrive that evening. Sam and Virgil were sitting on the front porch when they came up the walk, Sophie striding on a little in advance of her parents.

"Well, Sam," she said, "for goodness' sake! You don't look like a sick boy."

She came up the steps to the porch and put her hands on his shoulders and kissed him. Mattie came out of the house, hearing the voices.

"For heaven's sake, Mattie," Sophie said, "there's nothing the

matter with this boy. He's the picture of health." She said to Sam:
"Your mother's had you with one foot in the grave. She told me
only last week: 'If Sam's coming home, he's coming home to die.' "

Justus Kroener came up and shook hands with him, and his
grandmother kissed him, and they all went into the house together.
Sam thought of Bertie; it was strange not to have her there with the
rest of the Kroeners. It was one of the things that hurt him most,
that he had not come home in time to see her before she died. And
now, already, the others seemed almost to have forgotten her; it was
as if she had left nothing of herself behind her.

In the living room it was hot, and darker than it was outside, and
as soon as the lights were lit the June beetles began bumping against
the screens outside the open windows. They talked about the weather
for a little, and then Justus Kroener asked Sam what kind of trip
he had had coming across on the boat, and everyone stopped talking
and looked at him as if they expected him to begin telling them something. He said that he had worked his way over on a freighter out of
Marseilles, and that the trip hadn't been anything to talk about.
They waited for him to go on.

"It isn't very interesting about the trip," he said. "I'm afraid it
isn't very interesting about anything I did."

"Listen, Sam, you don't have to be modest with *us*," Virgil said.
Sam thought that he was like a different person, now that the
Kroeners were there: he wanted to talk, and the things he said were
not like the things that he would have said if they had not been in
the room. "What about the medals they gave you for the war?" he
asked. "They don't give you medals in the United States Army unless
you've done something interesting; I know that much about it."

Mattie was sitting on the sofa beside her father. She looked at him
quickly, and then across the room again at Virgil.

"I want to forget about the war," she said. "The war did no good
for anybody. I want to forget everything about the war."

"You ought to be proud of what Sam did," Virgil insisted. He was
not going to let it go. "All of us ought to be proud of what he did."

"He did his duty," Mattie said. "Now the war is over and he has
other duties."

Sophie laughed. "Don't be in such a hurry, Mattie," she said.

"Give the boy time. He doesn't look to me as if he's even made up his mind whether he's going to stay or not."

Her clear, light-brown eyes looked shrewdly from one to the other of them. The doorbell rang just then and Mattie, who had stiffened under Sophie's words as if beneath a blow, got up to answer it.

"Of course he's going to stay," she said.

She went out into the hall. In a few moments Sam heard voices talking and laughing out there. He recognized Frances's voice, cooler and huskier than he had remembered it. He could feel himself go rather cold and tense, waiting for her to walk into the room.

She came in a moment later, with his mother and Dick Rogan. He saw at once that she had had all her ash-blonde hair cut short, and that she looked very different, in her straight, pale-green dress, from the way he had been remembering her. He could not get used to the way the girls looked now. He got up, and she came across and shook hands with him, and then she looked at him and smiled, and reached up and kissed him quickly.

"For old times' sake," she said. "I'm terribly glad you're back, Sam."

"How's the boy, Sam?" Dick said.

He had not changed; he stood there looking at Sam with his old, self-assured smile, very thin and tall, with something of an air in his light summer suit. Sam shook hands with him.

"Sam," his mother said, nervously, "there aren't enough chairs. Will you bring one in from the dining room?"

She was always a little upset, on the defensive, when she had company in her house: she could not like people for themselves, or believe that they could like her for herself, and she felt consequently that she had perpetually to justify herself against their possible criticism. Sam went out into the dining room to bring the chair. When he came back, Dick was talking to his mother about the way he looked.

"I don't know," he was saying. "He just doesn't look like the Sam we knew. The minute I saw him I said to myself, that's not the boy we used to know."

"Yes," Mattie said. She looked up at him out of her calm, mistrustful brown eyes. "We feel that way too. It's hard to have him come back so changed. Of course it's what he's been through, but still it's hard."

Sam sat down in a chair beside Frances. She looked at him quickly. She was very strange to him. He thought that she was even better-looking than she had been when he had gone away.

"Isn't this marvelous for you?" she whispered.

He smiled. "I know now how the corpse feels at a wake."

"Poor Sam." She looked at him, wrinkling up her eyes at him in the old way. "I suppose I ought to have stayed away too. I was terribly curious to see you, though."

"That seems to be the general idea."

Dick said, leaning across Frances to speak to him, "We've missed you, Sam. Why the dickens did you want to stay over there so long?"

"I don't know. It just happened that way."

"Well, see that it doesn't happen that way again. You've got a lot of things to catch up on, fellow."

"What's that, Dick?" Virgil asked.

He moved over a little closer to the end of the sofa. He had been talking to Sophie, but he wanted to get away from his conversation with her.

"I was just telling Sam he has a lot of things to catch up on around here," Dick said.

"He'll have to work fast if he wants to catch up with you." Virgil turned to Sam. "Did you know that Dick is our rising young realtor here in Cannon Hill?"

"There's nothing to it," Dick said. "Anybody can sell real estate these days." He looked at Sam too. "What are you going to do, Sam, now that you're back?" he asked. "You aren't going on with the law?"

"No," Virgil interrupted hastily. "I'll bet Sam doesn't see himself spending four or five years more over books before he begins to get anywhere in the world." He was a little boisterous and guilty about it, not looking at Sam. "There's too much easy money floating around for you young fellows these days," he said.

"How right you are," Frances said. She looked at Sam, smiling. "Do you know that, Beauchamp?"

"I've been hearing about it."

"Look at the Sorley boys," she said. She was very bright, rather mocking. "They're making any amount of money now, and neither of them ever got past grammar school. Wouldn't you love to be a bootlegger, Sam?"

"Oh, come on, now," Dick said, grinning. "The Sorleys are running a garage, Fran."

"Or Magnus," she went on, not paying any attention to him. "Look at Magnus. I absolutely doubt that he could tell you the difference between a fraction and a surd. But that doesn't seem to have stopped him from doing awfully well with figures."

"Oh, Magnus," Dick said. "That's another thing now." He looked envious and respectful. "A man like that has financial genius; that's the only way to account for it."

He and Virgil began talking about the new factory that Magnus was putting up out in Covingdale.

"Maybe you don't know what that's setting him back," Dick said. "Listen, I've got it from a fellow who knows—a cool quarter of a million, that's all."

The conversation seemed to Sam to turn to money as inevitably as a weighted wheel brings up its recurrent, predetermined number. He sat listening for a time, feeling out of it, rather uncomfortable. He was conscious, with something of the old tension beginning to torment him, of Frances sitting beside him, of her voice running along, so cool and self-possessed, as she laughed with his father and with Dick. It was almost as it had been in the old days, when he had had to sit in the living room of her house on Duncan Street, wanting her alone, while her uncle or her mother talked to him. And he began to realize that there was something unfinished in their relationship, that the mere fact that an interval of time had elapsed since he had seen her last had not been a solution, but only a postponement.

He got up after a time, and went out to the porch. It was dark there now, with only a faint brightness from the lights inside. The dark and the quiet seemed simple and good after the close tension of the talk, the feel of all the half-remembered claims and relationships crowding in on him again, that there had been inside. He went over to the swing and sat down. The porch was just as it had always been, only a little older and shabbier: the big swing, the raffia mat, the "elephant's-ears" on their ornamental iron stands. Someone was playing a ukulele up the street. He could hear the ukulele, but not the words of the song that they were singing. It was not a song that he knew.

The screen door opened and he heard Frances's voice asking: "Are you out here, Sam?"

"Over here," he said.

"Oh. I was beginning to think you'd gotten lost."

She came over and stood before the swing, smiling. He got up.

"Don't get up," she said.

"I thought you were a searching party, to bring me back inside."

"No. Don't get up. I want to stay."

They were standing close to each other, and he kissed her then, as he had known he would, from the moment that he had heard her voice at the door. But she was like a stranger to him; there seemed to be no remembrance of the past between them, only this close present intimacy of the kiss. After a little she looked up at him. He could see her smiling in the dark.

"I told you not to get up," she said.

"I'm glad I did. It was a fine idea."

"Wasn't it though. Only now let's sit down."

"There'll be another searching party after us."

"Not for a little while."

She sat down on the swing, sitting in one corner with her legs tucked under her. He remembered her sitting that way on the wicker settee over on the porch of the house on Duncan Street, before the war. There was something confusing and tormenting to him in the waves of remembrance meeting the waves of strangeness. He stood there, looking down at her.

She asked him: "Are you really glad to see me?"

"Of course I am."

"You don't sound terribly convincing. Was there someone over there?"

He sat down on the swing. "Don't you begin on that too," he said.

She laughed. "All right. Tell me what it was like where you were."

"No. It would take too long."

He knew what it would be like if he began trying to put it into words. He could not tell about how the people he had known there really were, the things about them that were the same in people all over the world; and the things he could tell about—the houses with their peaked roofs and their fireplaces decorated with patterns of flowers and birds and hearts, the magnificent Sunday headdresses of the women, the thousands of tiny orange and crimson mushrooms growing at the edges of the forests—would come out like something in a guidebook, full of a false quaintness, and as if the whole thing were merely a pleasant spectacle staged for the benefit of the tourist. He had not been a tourist, and it had not been a pleasant spectacle to him; it had been something very good and very hard and at times disagreeable, and he would always be glad that he had been there to learn what people who had been working the same land for generations without ever possessing it, or being able to hope that they would possess it, could feel when it became their own. But it was not anything that he could tell about to many people. They would not want the clear, raw reality; they would always be better satisfied with the guidebooks.

"Why don't you tell me what's been happening with you?" he said to her. "What's everything like now?"

She reached up and took hold of the chains of the swing with one hand, still smiling at him.

"Hard to say," she said. "It's very exciting."

"About you and Dick, for instance?"

She wrinkled the corners of her eyes at him. "Aren't you observing, though." She sat for a moment without saying anything else, rocking the swing a little with her hand on the chains. "He's really very nice, you know," she said after a moment.

"He's crazy about you."

"Aren't you wonderful. All in half an hour too." She looked at him rather oddly, half-mocking, half-serious. "It's not as simple as it looks," she said.

"Nothing is ever as simple as it looks. Especially if it has people mixed up in it."

"I'm twenty-three," she said. He could feel her eyes on him, estimating him, as they had five years before, between mockery and the kind of odd inner sullenness with which she acknowledged the attraction between them. "I'm nice-looking," she said, "and I have a nice voice, but it's never going to make me famous. And I want a lot of things out of life."

He said nothing, watching her. He felt that her words were challenging him; there was the old challenge to him to fulfill the standards that she set for him, disregarding any others.

"I want all the things I had before my father died," she went on, still with that curious, cool appeal in her voice, as if she were a child demanding a gift. "I want to feel what it's like again to have everyone being nice to me because they know I have more money than they have. And I want to love somebody, and to have somebody love me."

"That's quite an order," he said. "But you ought to make it."

"Do you think so?"

"Yes."

"Do you really think so?" She looked straight at him, persisting.

"All you need," he said, "is a Magnus who looks like Douglas Fairbanks."

"Yes," she said. "Isn't it easy. You didn't happen to bring any old herb remedies back with you from Czechoslovakia, did you, Sam?"

"It wouldn't be any good if I had. I don't look like Douglas Fairbanks."

"No." She shook her head. "You look like an awfully nice boy that I used to know, only older—much older." She smiled again suddenly. "Do you want to know what you were like then?" she said. "You were really a very serious boy, in a happy sort of way."

"Was I?"

"Yes. Now you're not serious any more."

"I'm serious enough."

He felt that it was all not quite real, the sharp American speech, the strumming of the ukulele, the catch and strain of the old restlessness between them. And yet all the while he was with her he could feel himself going back inevitably to that past existence in which all these things had been commonplace, picking up the threads which he had dropped.

"I like you serious," she said to him. "Why can't you be serious again for me now?"

He laughed at the challenge in her voice, his blood coming up a little in him. But she glanced back over her shoulder, hearing someone at the door.

"Sam?" It was Mattie's voice. She sounded upset. "I wish you'd come in. Everybody's missing you."

"All right." He got up, looking down at Frances. "Are you coming?"

She smiled, jumping up, rather satisfied with herself. They went on into the house together.

When he came into the living room again, he saw at once that things had not been going well there. His father had been talking to Sophie again, and both of them were slightly aroused; there was an uncomfortable atmosphere in the room. When Mattie went back into the kitchen to get the refreshments ready, Virgil jumped up suddenly from his place too.

"I've got some prewar bourbon I've been saving for a time like tonight," he said. "We'll all have a drink on Sam's safe return."

He went out of the room at once. When he had gone, Justus Kroener and Sophie began to talk about Prohibition. Sophie said she had never been able to see the harm in anybody's having a glass of beer now and then, but she thought it was a good thing for the country to put a stop to all the hard drinking that was going on. Justus Kroener said he believed in abiding by the law. While they were talking, Virgil returned with the bottle and a tray with ice and soda and glasses, and at once Justus Kroener said no, thank you, nothing for him.

"Look here," Virgil said. "This is an occasion. We're all going to drink to Sam's future."

He began pouring the whisky. Mattie had come in behind him from the dining room. She said to him, rather tense: "Virgil, you know how Papa feels about the Prohibition law. Don't urge him now."

"Well, this once isn't going to hurt," Virgil said. He was getting stubborn about it. "We don't have Sam coming home to us every day in the year."

"It might be better if Sam understood right away that he was coming back to a country where liquor is prohibited," Mattie said, coldly. "If he has to see disrespect for the law, he doesn't have to see it in his own home."

Virgil went on pouring the whisky.

"What do they drink in Czechoslovakia, Sam?" Frances asked.

She was trying to make a joke out of it. Sam began to say something about the homemade plum wine.

"I'd like to know something about this future of Sam's, myself, that Virge is getting so excited about," Sophie broke in. Whatever it was that she and Virgil had been quarreling about, she had not finished with him yet; her small, clear eyes were narrowed a little in enjoyment of the battle. "What *is* he going to do, Virge?" she asked. "You haven't still got the idea of making another Dickie Beauchamp out of him, I hope?"

Virgil looked around at her, flaring up.

"Well, he might do worse," he said. He hated it when she spoke of his father as *Dickie Beauchamp*. "I'll tell you this much," he said, "my father was a kind husband and a good father and a generous friend, and it was no fault of his if he had his misfortunes in life—"

"Oh, he was generous all right," Sophie agreed. "A little too generous for his own good."

Dick began to say something to Mattie about the new Cannon Hill Bank building that was going up on Old Town Road. She answered him, but somewhat nervously; she was listening to what was going on between Virgil and Sophie.

"The Lord knows," Sophie was saying, broadly, "a man ought to be generous, but it's a good thing to know whose money he's being generous *with*."

Virgil set the bottle down on the tray.

"That's a fine thing for you to say," he said, his temper firing up at once. He would never bear it for her to refer to the old scandal in the State Treasurer's office. "*You've* got a right, haven't you, to say a thing like that?"

Sophie stared at him, self-composed and watchful, rather enjoying herself; she felt that she had the upper hand.

"I certainly have," she said, with emphasis. "I'd like you to give me one good reason why I haven't."

"Reason!" Virgil said hastily. "I'll give you reason enough."

Mattie stopped pretending to listen to Dick and said in a hurried voice, across the room: "Now we're not going to have any disagreements on Sam's first night."

"Sam's got a right to know what's going on," Virgil said. He had a bad color now, too high, a hard violent crimson that made him look as if he were suffocating. "If we're going to talk about generosity, he's got a right to hear about the fine generous relatives he has," he said. "He's got a right to know where the money of Bertie's went."

Sophie colored up too, at the mention of Bertie's name.

"We don't have to sit here and listen to that kind of talk from you, Virge," she said sharply. "You know as well as I do that Sam's never had any right to that money."

"All right. Legally, no." Virgil was speaking now in a loud voice, quite blind to the others, hurt and furious, like a child. "Legally, no. But if there was done with it what Bertie wanted done, what she told us on her deathbed that she wanted done, Sam would have that money today, and you know it, and I know it, and your father knows it, too."

"Virgil—" Mattie said.

Frances and Dick were doing the best they could at acting as if they were not there. They knew that they could not stop it now, and that the best thing they could do was to try to be as inconspicuous as possible. Mattie was still trying to stop it.

"Virgil," she said. "Papa is our guest. Sophie is our guest. Look what you are saying to them."

"I'm saying the truth," Virgil said. "I've said it before and I'll say it again—that money by rights belongs to Sam."

"We've been through all that and through all that. Nobody wants to hear any more about it. After all Papa has done for us, it's a nice return—"

"It's Sam's money," Virgil insisted. He brought his hand down on the table so that the glasses jumped in the tray. Sam could see him shaking and his face red with the cheeks shaking too. "You were all there when Bertie told us," he said. "It's Sam's money."

"I've never heard anything like this in all my life," Sophie said. "If this is the thanks a person gets—"

"The devil with it," Virgil interrupted her. "Is it that crummy little job? I never asked him for it. He can keep it."

Mattie and Sophie both began to say something to him at once. Sam could not watch it any longer. He got up and went over and took his father's arm.

"Come on," he said. "Let's get out of here."

"I'm not going," Virgil said. "This is still my house. The devil with all of them if they don't like it."

"Come on," Sam said.

Virgil came along with him. They went back through the kitchen and out on the back steps and sat down there.

"The devil with it," Virgil kept on saying. He was almost crying. "It's your money, Sam."

"I don't want it," Sam said. "I don't want any of their rotten money."

They sat there on the back steps, not talking: it was quiet and dark out there, and they could hear the crickets, and a tree toad from somewhere out in the back. Virgil was breathing hard, very much shaken.

"This is a fine homecoming for you," he said humbly, after a while.

His voice was still not quite under control. Sam looked over at him. He felt a little worried about him, he looked so bad.

"Forget it," he said. "It doesn't matter."

He did not want to talk about it any more that night. But he knew that he could not always dismiss it so. His father would not forget it; it was a rankling wound in him. The sense of his own impotence before the solid, rather superb indifference of his wife's family would continue to drive him almost to madness. Sam thought that his old eager enthusiasms seemed all to have been diverted now into the channel of a feverish dissatisfaction; his attitude toward life was a forlorn defiance, as if he were trying to convince himself by his own belligerence that he still had it in him to do as well as anyone else.

In the morning he came downstairs a little late, ate his breakfast hurriedly, and went off downtown to the store as usual. Mattie was cold and quiet with him. When he had gone, she came back to the dining room, where Sam was finishing his breakfast.

"I think you ought to go down and see your grandfather today, Sam," she said. "He's anxious to help you get a start in life, now that you're back, and I'm sure there's nowhere else you could get better advice. And I think," she added, coloring up a little nervously, "that you ought to tell him how sorry you are about what happened last night—"

He could not talk about it to her; she was too intent on him, too anxious to see him settled in his proper groove. It was like a reprieve to him when the telephone rang and she went out to answer it. She came back a moment later, saying that it was Dr. Brand; he had heard from Rhoda that Sam was home.

Sam went to the telephone. He knew of the changes that had come into Brand's life while he had been away. And it seemed to him, when he heard his name spoken as Mattie had just spoken it, and as some of the others had spoken it the night before, with respect, and almost with deference, that it was someone altogether different from the Brand he had known to whom they were referring. But when he lifted the receiver that feeling vanished. There was no change in the voice that came to him over the wire. Brand wanted to see him, and he promised to come that afternoon around four, when the other's office hours would be over.

But it was strange for him again to go up the walk that afternoon to the big, well-kept, comfortable-looking house that he had always known as the Considines', and think of finding Brand inside. He could not associate it with him; when he thought of him, or of Bronwen, it was always the Cannon House that he remembered with them. Almost deliberately, he realized, he had not thought of meeting Bronwen here this afternoon. He had never once seen her since her marriage. And he felt that the Bronwen whom he would see now, the Bronwen who had been Neil Lamson's wife, would be a stranger to him. So he was a little reluctant, but almost unconsciously, to see her now. He did not want to change the image of her that he had, and that was so closely associated with the best time of his life.

The front door was open when he came up the steps to the porch, and through the screen he could see Brand in the hall, talking to Julia Magnus, who was standing beside the door, about to leave the house. Sam had never met her, but he had seen her, years before, when she had been Francis Maitland's wife. He did not know that she had married Magnus since. She came out on the porch, still talking to Brand in her flat, brusque voice, which had something uncertain in it, in spite of its peremptoriness. Brand, following her, caught sight of Sam, and came up to shake hands with him, the expression of rather exasperated civility that had been on his face disappearing suddenly.

"Well, Sam," he said, smiling, "so you made it."

Julia Magnus stood waiting, a little irritated. She had not finished what she had to say. Brand introduced Sam to her, but she scarcely looked at him. She said to Brand, "Are you coming tonight, then?"

"I'll see if I can make it."

"You'll *have* to make it." Sam noticed the slight line between her eyes, which gave her a curiously tense, abstracted expression of unconscious inadequacy. "You know you're the only one who can talk to him when he's like this, Rob."

"He's all right," Brand said, impatiently. "Don't worry about it."

"I do worry about it." She spoke as if Sam were not present, absorbed in her own world, the line deepening between her brows. "I'm afraid of what he might do."

"He won't do anything."

"You wouldn't be so sure of that if you were standing where I am." She looked at him, insecure, rather terrified of her own insufficiency, in spite of her brusqueness. "*Are* you coming tonight?" she insisted.

Brand shrugged. "All right. I'll be there."

"Seven-thirty?"

"Whatever you say."

"Good!"

She went quickly down the walk to her car. Sam looked after her.

"So that's Magnus's wife," he said.

He was a little puzzled by her, not quite attracted, but acknowledging a certain charm.

"Yes."

"She's good-looking, all right."

"That's as good as you can make her," Brand said bluntly.

Sam knew that he had what people in the section of society that Julia Magnus belonged to would have called very simple and primitive ideas of morality, and he thought it was fortunate for him that his Welsh civility had prevented him from displaying them too obviously before people who did not agree with them.

"She used to be married to Francis Maitland, didn't she?" he asked.

"Yes, and she'll be married to someone else again whenever it suits her. *This* isn't going to last either."

But he did not want to talk about Julia Magnus. He stood there on the porch, measuring Sam with his eyes, and beginning to smile again.

"You're in fine shape, all right," he said. "Rhoda said you looked as if you were in training for the Olympics."

Sam laughed. "That was the farm work," he said. "There weren't any tractors or threshing machines where I was."

"How did it look to you?"

"Good. Very good."

"Better than the law?"

"Better for me, I think."

Brand nodded. They went into the house together, and Sam sat down in the living room while Brand went back to tell the housekeeper to bring the coffee she always had ready for him when his office hours were over. There was no one in the living room when they came in; it was dim and quiet, with the blinds drawn against the afternoon heat outside.

When Brand came back the housekeeper was with him, carrying a tray with a plate of sandwiches and the coffee. She was a tall, elderly woman, narrow-shouldered and straight, with a quiet, responsible manner.

"Where is Bron?" Sam said to Brand. He felt constrained, asking after her; there was that curious reluctance in him against seeing her. "Is she around? I'd like to see her."

"She'll be down," Brand said. "I told her you were coming."

He took off his coat and sat down, comfortable now, drinking the strong black scalding coffee that he liked, even in this hot weather. Sam looked at him, thinking how little he had changed; he looked somewhat older, that was all. And yet there was something, too—a new, rather impersonal sureness and ease. And behind that, again, he had a vague sense of there being still something else, some curious, ugly, fettered bitterness, different from any that there had been in him before.

Brand was asking him: "How does it look to you here, now that you're back?"

"I don't know yet," Sam answered. "I haven't had time to figure it out. Things have changed a lot since I was here."

"Too much."

"I wouldn't expect you to say that."

"I still say it."

Sam looked at him, surprised at the emphasis of his tone. He did not quite understand the whole matter of Brand's position with Magnus; only from Rhoda he had had some inkling of that.

"Why," he said, half-embarrassed, "I heard you were riding the top of the wave—"

Brand shrugged, the heavy gesture that he remembered. But there was a look on his face that he could not remember, an expression that seemed a mingling of irritation and a cold, forced logic.

"Yes," he said. "That's the way you hear it." But he did not want to talk about himself. He drew away from the subject, rather brusquely. "What about you, Sam?" he asked. "Rhoda said something about your wanting to farm a place of your own."

Sam shook his head. "Well, I guess that's something that'll have to wait a good while," he said. "Even if I had the money—I'll stay on at home for a while, anyway; I've been away long enough."

Brand frowned a little. "What's the use in that?" he asked. "If it's a question of money—"

"It is, but that's not it altogether. Things aren't going well at home; I don't want to walk out on it again."

"It'd be the best thing for you if you did. You'll get mixed up in that, and stuck somewhere at a job, and the next thing you know,

you'll be halfway through your life without having started at doing
what you want."

Brand spoke energetically, a little impatiently. Sam knew that
he was thinking about how it had been with him back in the days
when he had been working in the mines, with a family to support,
working every day at something he did not want, while the thing he
did want got farther away from him every year. He had never understood that so well before. But he knew that he would not accept the
offer of a means of escape that was tacit in Brand's words. He had
seen how his father had looked at him the morning before, as if he
were bringing deliverance. And he felt bound to do what he could
for him, not matter how little that might be. He remembered him
as he had been in the old days, and it seemed to him as if the changes
that he had seen in him were all a part, somehow, of a kind of illness
that was less physical than, in some odd, terrible manner, environ-
mental. He needed ease and simplicity and generosity, not this perpetual straining toward the fulfillment of ambitions that had no real
meaning for him.

He wanted to ask Brand about Virgil. He had heard from his
mother that he had been to see him, at Rhoda's insistence, but Mattie, with her usual blunt skepticism where illness was concerned, was
inclined to dismiss the whole matter as nonsense. Virgil had never
been ill, as long as she had known him, and she could not believe
that there was anything to worry about now.

Sam spoke about it after a little to Brand. "What's the matter
with him?" he asked.

The other looked at him bluntly.

"What's the matter with any man his age and weight who goes
at life as if it was a combination three-ring circus and Donnybrook
Fair?" he returned. "Hypertension. He ought to watch his diet and
keep his weight and his temper down."

"Is it serious?"

"It could be. He hasn't much respect for medical advice. You
know how he is. He's nice about it, but he forgets all about it as soon
as he's out of the office."

"He gets so excited about everything," Sam said.

It made him feel sick to think of anything's happening to his father. He sat there, upset, feeling that Brand was looking at him.

"I hate to see you get mixed up in it, Sam," Brand said, after a while. "All you'll do in the end is to make trouble for yourself too. If there's one thing I've learned from practicing medicine, it's that a couple of unhappy people in a house can make a happy one miserable a lot faster than the happy one can make them forget their troubles."

"Maybe so. But I can have a try."

"Well, if it doesn't work out, come around and see me—"

The housekeeper came in just then to bring fresh coffee. Brand broke off, looking over at her.

"Hasn't Bron come down yet?" he asked her.

"No, Doctor."

"Would you go up and tell her Sam Beauchamp is here?"

It was worse than ever for Sam now, thinking that perhaps Bronwen did not want to see him, and that if she came it would be only because she could not avoid it. He sat listening to the housekeeper's footsteps going away deliberately into the hall, the door closing, the footsteps slowly ascending the stairs, then listening for those other footsteps, for Bronwen to come, to open the door.

She came almost at once. When he heard the door open, he looked around and saw her standing there, just inside the room. She was wearing a thin dark-blue short-sleeved sweater and a white skirt, and for a moment he thought that she had not changed; she looked just the same, just as slender and small, with the eyes that seemed to be looking out from somewhere very deep and still, and the childish vulnerability of her face. It was only when she spoke that he realized the difference that there was in her. There was something about her voice that he could not even recognize. It was quick and low and almost toneless, so low that he had to concentrate to understand what she said. When she saw him looking at her, she went over quickly and sat down in a chair on the other side of the room.

"How are you?" she said, in that new voice of hers.

"I'm fine. It's good to see you, Bron."

"Do you want coffee?" Brand asked her. "Mrs. Markham just brought some fresh."

"No, thanks. I don't think I want any."

She sat in the chair with her hands lying along the arms, looking as if she had been cornered. Sam was quite certain now that she had not wanted to come down and see him. The telephone rang just then in the hall, and they all sat listening tensely while the housekeeper answered it, as if they had been expecting an important call. The housekeeper came to the door and said that it was Mrs. Magnus on the phone, for the doctor.

"Back in a minute," Brand said to them.

The door closed behind him. In the quiet living room the silence hung so thickly that Sam could almost feel its weight. He knew that he had to say something. But he could not talk to Bronwen as if they were strangers; he could not be merely civil to her. They had known each other too well for that. Yet he had the feeling that he was really seeing her for the first time now. When he had gone away he had been a boy, looking at her as a boy looks at a companion whom he knows well, without curiosity, almost impersonally. Except for that Sunday afternoon when Neil Lamson had first come to the Cannon House, he had never really seen her before. And there was something infinitely new to him now in her face, with its rather tense, exposed look, all her reticences revealing themselves, in spite of her, in her eyes. He saw that she was uncertain with him, as she might have been with a stranger. And it seemed to him that she was deliberately holding herself back from returning to their former intimacy.

But it was something more than a deliberate withholding of herself that was going on inside her. He could not know that for her, as well as for him, there was this sudden shock of the newness of their relationship, the shock of the necessity of recognizing him as a man when she had known him before only as a youth. And it was perhaps even more violent for her than it was for him, because it brought her, for the first time since Neil Lamson's death, a sense of close awareness of a man. She knew him so well, the rough-featured face, the blue eyes, the sturdy aloneness that always seemed to enclose him; and yet he was strange to her, too, a strange man, whom she had never seen before. It gave her a painful feeling of shock, as if she were being wrenched out of sleep, to look at him. She did not want that awareness, that awakening. So she shut herself away from him, speaking to him in civil, meaningless phrases, asking him about his life abroad.

They could hear Brand in the hall, speaking in impatient monosyllables over the telephone. In a few minutes he came into the room again, and began putting on his coat.

"I've got to go out," he said to them. He was angry about something. "I'm sorry, Sam."

"It's all right. I would have had to leave in a few minutes anyway."

"Will you be home for dinner?" Bronwen asked him. Her face was closed, without expression, as she looked at him.

"No. I've already told Mrs. Markham. I'll be out at Magnus's."

She did not say anything more. Brand said good-by and left the house. It was quiet again in the room. Bronwen was slowly drawing out one of the pleats in her white skirt between her fingers.

"I'd better be getting along too," Sam said.

She looked over at him suddenly. And she had a quick sense of panic; she wanted to prove to herself before he left that it had meant nothing to her, that sense of close, intimate awareness that she had never had before except in connection with Lamson. She wanted obstinately to stay in her own passive world; it was too painful to be wrenched out of it into any new life. She spoke to him quickly.

"No, please don't," she said. "Do you have to go right away?"

"Not right away. But I thought you didn't want to see me today."

She colored suddenly and deeply.

"I didn't say that."

"You didn't have to say it. I still know you *that* well, Bron."

She shook her head quickly, looking away from him again.

"It's not you, especially," she said. "It would be the same with anybody."

"But why?" he asked. "What's the good?"

"I don't know. I don't want people."

There was a silence between them. All at once she got up and walked across to the large victrola that stood in one corner of the room. She began to look through the pile of records on the stand beside it.

"What's it like for you, living here?" he asked her after a moment, rather gently. Her confusion made him more certain of himself, almost at ease. She glanced quickly around at him, not quite knowing what to answer.

"It's very nice," she said. "I suppose I ought to like it."

"But you don't?"

"No." She turned away from him again. "I don't like to live by someone else's bounty, by selling myself into someone else's world," she said abruptly.

He guessed that she was speaking of Brand's relationship with Philip Magnus. He knew that she was upset, or she would not have spoken so plainly. She was picking up the records one by one, not looking for any one in particular, and hardly glancing at the titles.

"I don't know what you *like*," she said, turning to him suddenly, a little desperately.

"It doesn't make much difference," he said. "Anything will sound good to me, I've been away so long."

She put on one of the records, and a voice sang "Japanese Sandman" to them in a throaty whisper. She sat on the arm of the sofa beside the victrola, watching the black disk revolve and the needle trace its slow circles toward the center.

"You oughtn't to feel that way about it," Sam said presently, through the music. "What is it about Magnus? He's straight enough, isn't he?"

She looked over at him hostilely, as he remembered her looking when she had been a child.

"No, he's not *right*," she insisted, in an almost angry, downright manner. "I don't know anything about him, I don't want to know; but everything about him is wrong— And it's especially wrong for Robbie," she continued suddenly, after a moment's pause. "He has to be *all* right, or he's nowhere at all."

"He's learned to compromise," Sam suggested.

She stared over at him, her blue eyes very determined.

"Well, *that's* not right," she said.

"Everyone has to, to some extent, anyway. I'm finding that out."

"*I* won't find it out."

There was something defiant in the way she said it. And yet, really, she was afraid. She was so conscious of him, there in the room with her. She felt suddenly that she had to insist on the fact of Lamson's existence, both to herself and to him. She asked him abruptly, without any preparation, whether he had ever had any contact with Lamson while he had been overseas.

"No," he said. "None at all." The music came to an end and he watched her bend over the victrola, removing the record. Her hands were so familiar to him, not brown as they had been when she was a child, but with the same narrow span and quick fingers. It seemed incredible to him that the man of whom they were talking had been her husband. "I didn't even know, till months later—" he said. "I'm sorry about it, Bron."

She put on another record and switched on the victrola. It was a flippant, rather vulgar tune. Her whole face came alive suddenly in a passion of dislike; she had not even known what it was that she had put on the machine. She turned it off quickly.

"Do you know I didn't know myself for a long time what it was really like—I mean, how it was when he died?" she asked him suddenly, as if she were forcing herself to speak about it to him. She began looking through the records again, having to occupy herself while she talked. "It all sounds as if it were something that had happened a long time ago, somehow, the way they notify you—you can't *realize* anything about it, the details, any more than you realize them when you read about someone's dying in a newspaper. But last year I met a friend of Neil's, Comyn, who saw him, just a day or so before he died, in the hospital, and I asked him questions—"

"You oughtn't to have, Bron."

"Why not?" She turned to him, her face passionate. "It all happened to *him;* it was real for *him.* I wanted it to be real for me too."

"But what good did it do?" Sam asked. "You couldn't help it any more. And it's different, really, when it happens to you, from the way it sounds—"

"His plane crashed and burned, you know," Bronwen went on, ignoring him, with her strange, suffering, obstinate face. "Comyn saw him in the hospital: his face was covered with strips of gauze, but Comyn could see his lips, so puffed out and swollen that he couldn't understand what he said when he tried to talk. And the doctor told him that his hands were burned to mere stumps—"

She was trying to hold herself calm, but he could see her shoulders shuddering under the thin sweater.

"He shouldn't have told you," he said, rather angrily. "It doesn't do any good. And, remember, it was all over for him in a few days. *You'll* have to go on thinking of it."

She put a record of Caruso's on the victrola, quickly and mechanically, hardly knowing what she was doing. The golden voice soared and hung in the quiet room, with the drawn blinds moving lazily against the sun and the warm air outside.

"You can't realize how *apart* you can be from suffering like that, your own suffering, till you've gone through something like it yourself," Sam said. "It's as if you developed a whole new self inside you to meet it; the ordinary, everyday *you* isn't in it at all. And you know you've got to take it all, and that you'll get through it somehow—"

She looked at him without seeing him, reliving something inside herself.

"I used to dream about it, for months," she said. "I'd see the plane burning— It was like the nightmare I used to have when I was small, about the house being on fire. Did I ever tell you?"

"No," Sam said.

He was a little surprised at her sudden reference to their childhood. She had seemed to want to ignore all that, to put it behind her. But she had looked at him for a moment with sudden warmth, almost appealingly.

"You've got to think of it as if it was only a bad dream, Bron," he said. "That's the only way."

"No," she said. "How can I?" She shut herself away again, rather antagonistic. "It's not a bad dream; it's real, perfectly real, and he's dead—"

But she had to force herself to feel it; the fact that she had spoken of it to him seemed to take it outside herself, to make it somehow inevitable and final, separate from the need for her emotions. And it gave her a sense of loss, to have it taken away from her. There had been nothing else in her life for so long. She wanted to have it back again.

Sam got up to go away.

"I want to see you again, Bron," he said to her.

But she would not look at him, trying to make herself indifferent.

"I suppose we will," she said, not committing herself.

She did not want to feel that she wished him to come. But the wish was there. She could deny it, but it was there all the same. She was a little dazed, waiting for something, half in dread.

Chapter 11

At the beginning of the following week Mattie spoke to Sam again about what it was that he intended to do. She always went out to Warsaw Hill to church with the Kroeners on Sunday morning now, and she had taken the opportunity this week to talk to her father about Sam. Justus Kroener was on close terms with so many of the older, conservative generation of businessmen in the city that she knew he would have little difficulty in finding a place for Sam with one of them.

Sam was willing to have the matter settled now. He had made up his mind what he would do, and one job at a desk seemed much the same to him as any other. On Justus Kroener's advice, he went to see an old acquaintance of his, John Ziegler, who owned a shoe factory in the basin of the city. Ziegler was willing to take him on as shipping clerk. He came home that evening to tell Mattie and Virgil that he would begin work there on the following Monday.

Mattie was quite satisfied, a little relieved to have it settled so easily. But Virgil could not finish his dinner, he was so upset. Instead of going into the living room to read his newspaper when the meal was over, he went off downstairs to the basement. When Sam came down the steps a few minutes later, he found him over at his worktable, fussing about rather forlornly with his botanical specimens. But as soon as he saw Sam, he left off and came over quickly to meet him.

"I'm glad you came down, Sam," he said. "I want to talk to you."

He sat down on one of the basement steps, and Sam sat down beside him.

"What's the matter?" he asked.

"Well, it's about that job." Sam could see the excitement coming up in him as he talked. "I don't like to see you getting stuck in a place like that, Sam. John Ziegler's like your grandfather; if he sees a modern idea coming, he'll run a mile to get out of the way. There's no future for you there." He hesitated for a moment. "What I had in mind," he went on suddenly, "was for the two of us to go in business together."

Sam looked at his excited, earnest face.

"In business?" he asked. "What kind of business?"

"The automobile business, Sam. Selling automobiles. I've had that in mind for quite a while now." Virgil got up from the steps and stood looking down at him expectantly and eagerly. "How would you like to go into it with me?"

Sam hardly knew how to answer him.

"Why," he said, after a moment, "I hadn't thought of it—"

"I know, I know," Virgil interrupted him. "But listen, Sam, you've been away a long time; you don't know the way things are going here. There's a gold mine in automobiles these days. I've gone into it all; I've got the figures—" He hunted hurriedly through his pockets and found a pencil and a small paper-bound notebook. "I've had the idea for quite a while that we might go into this together when you came home," he said, "but I've been waiting to talk to you about it till I had it all worked out. We could have gotten the Ford agency in Cannon Hill if you'd been here six months ago, and I had a talk just yesterday with Fred Messner—you must have seen that new place of his, up on the Square—and *he's* thinking of selling out and going to California in a couple of months—"

He sat down again on the steps so that he could show Sam the figures in his notebook, scribbled there in his hasty, earnest handwriting. There were computations of all sorts—profits, costs, a naïvely optimistic calculation of the number of families in Cannon Hill, Haddon, and Warsaw Hill that would be in the market for new cars during the next three years. The only thing he did not seem to have thought of was where he was going to get the capital in the first place for a venture like that. But when Sam brought that up he was quite prepared: it was Justus Kroener who was to let them have the money.

"As a loan, if he has to have it that way," he said. "But, morally,

the best part of what we'd need is yours, Sam; it belongs to you.
Bertie never had a thought in her head but that you'd get that
money when she died. If she'd had the slightest idea of how your
grandfather was going to behave, she'd have made a will; I know
that much about it."

It was incredible, Sam thought, but it was true: even after what
had happened on the night that he had come home, his father still
believed that he could somehow argue, or persuade, or shame Justus
Kroener into giving up that money. It was a part of his dream, an
essential part, and so he could not afford to let it go. Sam did not
want to be the one to make him see the reality of the situation. But
he felt that it would be crueler to let it go on, to encourage him.

"Suppose he doesn't see it that way," he suggested. "That could
happen—"

"It won't happen." Virgil was positive, happy over his figures.
"Good Lord, this is a sure thing, Sam. We'll be able to pay that
money back in a couple of years and never miss it. All we need is a
start, and we'll be on Easy Street before we know it."

But he had to stop, hearing Mattie calling from the head of the
stairs. He put his notebook and pencil away hurriedly, looking rather
guilty; it was obvious that he did not want her to know anything
about his plans. She would have no faith in his ability to carry out an
undertaking of this sort. And Sam could not bring himself to tell him
that he felt the same way. He saw how his father had fixed on this
plan as an escape from the inevitable conclusion that there was
nothing for him to do but to go on in the old, trammeled way in
Justus Kroener's shop. He wanted so much to be independent again,
and lavish, happy, as in the old days. So he would not allow ideas
of practicality to stand in his way.

Sam could not talk to his mother about it. But the next day he
went over to the Cannon House to see Rhoda. He knew that she
understood Virgil better than anyone else in the family did, and that
she could be sympathetic and sensible about him at the same time.
She knew a little already of Virgil's plans, and listened attentively
while Sam told her about the conversation he had had with him
the evening before. But her response, when she spoke, took him a
little by surprise.

"It's all nonsense, of course," she said, brusquely. "But you'd never get him to believe that. So why don't you tell him straight out that it's not what *you* want?—and then it's just possible that he'll forget it."

He shook his head. He felt that that was exactly what he could not do. And, after a moment, Rhoda relented too. She knew what it would do to Virgil if Sam came to him bluntly with such a statement as that. Yet she was sure, in herself, that it would be the best thing in the end. She remembered her own father's cherished plan of getting the name of Cannon Hill changed to Beauchamp, and how she had humored him over it, out of the wish not to hurt him, till it had become an obsession with him that she could not break. She did not want Sam to be involved in a situation like that.

But she realized that he must go his own road. He had come to her, as he had gone to Brand, because he liked and trusted her, but in the end he reserved the right to make his own decision, whether or not it agreed with their advice. And she felt that there was a certain sureness about him now on which she could rely.

For himself, he felt as if his whole life were flowing about him during this time, dark and fluid, waiting for him to grasp it in decision. He knew that the place in the Ziegler factory was nothing final, that his relations with his parents, with Frances, with Bronwen, as he had taken them up on his return, were none of them final. But he had learned something of the inevitability of events during the war, and afterwards, working on the land. There were things that would happen, in spite of all probability, and things that would not happen, in spite of all probability. He had learned not to force a decision when the time was not ready.

So he went on for a few weeks, learning the work at the factory, and going occasionally to Duncan Street to see Frances, or to take her out for the evening. She was a little piqued with him because he had taken the job at Ziegler's; she felt that he could have done better than that. She wanted him to make use of his friendship with such people as Brand, or the Rogans. So there was a kind of battle between them. But she was drawn to him, just as she had been before the war; there was an undeniable attraction between them. And he went on with her, feeling as he had on the night of his return, that they had not finished with each other, that there was something still to be resolved between them.

One July evening, when he went over to Duncan Street after dinner, she had to leave almost immediately for an unexpected rehearsal at the church where she sang. He walked over with her through the heavy summer dusk. There was a feeling of slight tension between them always now, which neither of them liked to admit. She wanted to cover it over with an air of absolute frankness. It gave her a heady sense of recklessness to feel the strain of a definite antagonism between them, beneath the attraction that they felt for each other.

When they reached the church, she stopped at the foot of the steps leading to the door and turned to face him.

"I'm sorry about tonight," she said. "What about tomorrow instead? I'm singing out at the Woods, but we can go somewhere afterwards."

"Fine," he said.

"You can come to the opera or I can meet you after it."

"I'll come. I'd like to hear you sing."

He had never heard her in a public performance; he was a little curious.

"It's not much of a part," she said, shrugging. "The local talent never gets the good ones."

"I'll bet you're darned good," he said.

She laughed. "Aren't you polite. But I'm not. I'm really not. I'm not being modest. I haven't the voice and I haven't the appetite. A really good diva can swallow life whole."

"I never thought about it that way."

"It's true. Opera is a very primitive business. The Italians have the right idea about it. And, good heavens, the singing they can do. They enjoy every minute of it."

She was always rather mocking about her career; she did not take it very seriously. He was curious about this part of her life. It seemed quite outside their relationship, something foreign. He promised to meet her at the Woods shortly after eight; the opera was *Carmen* and, as she was singing Mercedes, she did not have to be on stage till the second act.

When he arrived at Ludlow Woods the following evening, he saw that they had enlarged the pavilion since he had been away, but one thing was still as he remembered it: the big canvas tents behind the pavilion which the minor singers used as dressing rooms. The members of the chorus, looking hot and garish in make-up and Spanish peasant costumes, were already standing about outside the tents, waiting for the first act to begin. He asked one of them where he could find Frances, and the man pointed out the open flap of a tent just behind where they were standing. He looked around and saw her, still in street clothes, a white dress and a tight-fitting white hat made entirely of feathers, standing just inside, talking to a woman wearing a dark wig and a short red skirt and peasant blouse.

She looked up and saw him at once as he came over. They walked along together past the waiting groups in peasant costume. It gave Sam a queer sense of unreality to see them, with their made-up faces and tawdrily brilliant costumes, under the bare electric lights which were strung above the walks; it was such a short time since he had been living among people to whom a not dissimilar type of costume was ordinary daily dress that there was something offensive and false to him in these representations of it. He said something like that to Frances as they walked on together, and she looked up at him curiously.

"I can't imagine your really living for years in a place like that," she said. "There's something a little fantastic about it."

"Why should there be? They're just the same as people over here."

"I'm sure they are. Only now you're over here again, you don't want to go back, do you?"

They passed under a tree, and she stopped, looking up and laughing, rather malicious, lifting her face for him to kiss her.

"This sort of thing, now," she said, as she drew away from him again and went on. "I suppose you don't have anything like that in Czechoslovakia."

They could hear the applause from the pavilion as the conductor came out before the audience, and then the bright, insistent march rhythm of the overture.

"Do you want to go out front and listen?" she asked. "I'll have to go and change in a little while. It takes me ages to make up."

"When you have to go," he said.

He sat on a green bench with her while the chorus distantly vocif-
erated—

Drôles de gens que ces gens là,

and Micaela's voice wavered pathetically through the hot blue night.

"I've got to go," she said to him, after a time. "I really must." She
had taken off her hat, and her short blonde hair looked rough and
shining in the dark. "Imagine wearing a wig on a night like this?"

She liked to make herself important, laughing, but wanting to
feel that she impressed him. She rather paraded her intimacy with
this different world.

He walked back with her to her dressing room, and then went
around to the front of the pavilion to hear the opera. As he went
down the aisle to his seat, he saw Brand sitting with the Magnuses
and a dark, bulky man whom he did not know. He had never seen
Magnus before, but he had heard him described, and he was not
difficult to identify. There was a certain air of tenseness about the
whole group; Julia Magnus was rather too intent on the music,
while her husband, with his mechanical smile very much in evidence,
leafed rapidly through the pages of his program. Beside his wife's
still rather magnificent blondeness, he looked ordinary and almost
insignificant. The stranger, who was a new Russian basso, quite
handsome in an obvious, overgrown, middle-aged way, was between
him and Julia, and shifted his heavy shoulders occasionally as if he
found his place somewhat uncomfortable, while he blinked nervously
at the stage.

When the first act was over, Sam walked around to the rear of the
pavilion again. Frances was made up and in costume; with her brows
darkened and her eyes emphasized with mascara, her face looked
small and delicate and precisely defined, like that of a girl in a
Japanese print. He had never seen her made up like that before. It
was very becoming. She asked him if he liked her that way.

"Any way at all," he said.

"I wonder. You probably prefer some magnificent Slav, with a
figure that belongs on the prow of a ship."

She turned to speak to a pair of women from the audience who

had come up and greeted her. Sam glanced down the lighted walk
between the pavilion and the line of tents; it was crowded with
singers in costume, members of the orchestra, and people from the
audience. He saw Magnus and his wife talking to the conductor.
Frances, turning from her conversation, caught sight of them at
almost the same time.

"You mustn't miss this," she said. "Come on over with me. These
are people you have to meet."

They went over together, and she introduced him to the Magnuses
and to the conductor, Dr. Gorza. Julia Magnus looked at him with
her irritably friendly stare.

"You know Dr. Brand," she said to him.

"Yes."

"I haven't any idea how I know that. Have I ever seen you before?"

"At his home, several weeks ago," Sam explained.

She did not seem to think it necessary to agree to remember. Her
eyes moved away from him to the stocky, elderly figure of Dr. Gorza,
who was telling Frances that he had invited a few people to come out
to his house after the performance, and asking her to come too.

"I'd love to," she said. "But I'm with Sam tonight."

"Bring him, bring him too," Gorza said. He leaned forward and
whispered in her ear: "We haven't enough young ladies, you know.
What kind of a party can we have without young ladies?"

Sam gathered that the Magnuses were going to the Gorzas' too.
When the three of them had gone off again, Frances looked up at
him, smiling, her darkened eyebrows raised.

"Don't you want to go?" she asked him.

"Not particularly."

"Neither do I. But you can't turn people like that down."

"We might try it and see."

"Don't be silly. You might make an important connection. There's
always the chance."

She was smiling, but he saw that she did not want to argue about
it. She was slightly flushed, brilliant with satisfaction.

She had to leave him then to go on stage, and he started back to
his place again. As he walked around beside the pavilion he ran into

Brand. They had not seen each other since the day after Sam's return home. Brand looked at Sam, a little surprised, and smiling slightly.

"Isn't this out of your line?" he asked.

"And yours!" Sam laughed. But he knew that Brand had the Welshman's natural instinct for music. It was only the external atmosphere surrounding the opera that did not suit him. "I came with Frances," he explained. "She's singing tonight."

"Then if you're in a hurry to get back—" Brand began.

"I'm not."

Brand looked at him a little curiously. He knew something of the way things had been between him and Frances. But he asked no questions.

They began to walk along one of the gravel paths leading away from the pavilion. The music of the second act was just beginning. Sam noticed that Brand seemed in an abstracted, thwarted humor. There was that curious, tethered restlessness about him that he had noticed the last time he had seen him.

"You're with the Magnuses, aren't you?" Sam asked, after a little. "I've just met them; they were back talking to Fran and the others."

Brand looked over at him with a slight frown.

"Listen, Sam," he said emphatically, "don't *you* start thinking of getting in with that crowd now."

Sam stared at him, surprised.

"It's not very likely, is it?" he said after a moment, laughing. "I'm not much their style."

"No more am I, but I've gotten there just the same," Brand said. He looked at Sam almost angrily. "Why do you think I didn't offer to put you in touch with Magnus myself, if I thought it would do you any good?" he asked.

Sam was silent. He did not quite understand the other's sudden anger. They were walking down toward the little artificial lake, where a few ducks were quacking and rustling sleepily in the reeds along the edge.

"I suppose it looks good to you," Brand went on after a time, still roughly, "what you see I've got now?"

Sam did not know how to answer. He shook his head.

"I don't know. I hadn't thought about it," he said.

"Well, you *ought* to think about it, before you start out to make the same sort of fool of yourself," Brand remarked. He had stopped beside the lake, looking out over it with a rather fixed, ugly expression on his face. "You don't want to go rushing at it the way I did. I couldn't wait to get out of one kind of trouble and into a worse."

Listening to him, Sam thought for some reason of the night that he had graduated from medical school, when he had talked about his plans for the future. Sam was beginning to understand it all: the blind will that had driven the other to accept his position with Magnus rather than admit defeat at the hands of the people to whom he had come with that curiously ambivalent offering of his work, and the cold, fettered irritation that was galling him now. He watched him standing there, looking clenched and heavy, imprisoned somehow.

"Why," he said after a moment, awkwardly, "I didn't know it was that bad with you—"

Brand shrugged. "What do you think it's like, then, playing nursemaid to a pair like that?" he asked, jerking his head contemptuously in the direction of the pavilion. "I didn't give a dozen years of work to learn enough to do *that*."

"Well, there's your practice—" Sam said.

"And that's all there *is* going to be, after this fall," Brand interrupted him, with an almost brutal definiteness. "If I can't make a living at it then, without Magnus's name behind me, I'll go back to digging coal before I'll crawl back in this hole again. I've had some rotten jobs in my life, but I'd trade this for any one of them."

He began to walk along again beside the lake. The anger died down in him; he was a little ashamed of his outburst.

"I'm sorry, Sam," he said. "I just don't like to see you starting something that you may not like having to finish. I'll be out of this in a few months now, and I don't want to be responsible for dragging you in."

They walked back to the pavilion together. Brand began to return to the civil, rather indifferent reserve of his ordinary manner as they approached it. He said to Sam: "Why don't you come out to the house for dinner some evening? Bron was saying the other day that I had a right to ask you."

"Was she?" Sam was a little surprised; he felt a sudden flame of pleasure kindle in him. "I thought the last time I was there, she wasn't particular about having me come back."

"Well, she's like that now," Brand said. "Will you come Wednesday?"

"Yes, then, if it's all right with Bron."

"I'll tell her."

They separated, going to their seats. The second act was well begun; Frances, in a bright yellow flounced dress and a deep blue shawl, was on the stage, in the scene at Lillas Pastial's inn. Sam settled down to watch and listen. She looked different to him again beneath the lights of the stage, rather artificially pretty, like a false flower, and quite composed, perfectly conscious of her own identity in the midst of her acting. And he could not help comparing her with the Carmen, who was an Italian, aging, somewhat stout, and coarse, but who threw herself into her role with a magnificent completeness, so that the audience was caught up and borne along with her into the final illusion of the music. He watched her now, rather avoiding looking at Frances. She was so separate from him up there beneath the lights; he had never been able to see her with quite so much detachment before. It gave him a feeling of release, somehow, as if the physical separateness cut some mental bond between them, too.

Between the acts, when she asked him what he thought of her, of her voice and her acting, he evaded telling her what he really thought. She did not mind it that he was not enthusiastic; it was not something that mattered seriously to her. But she did not want him to admire the Carmen, either. She slipped into a series of amusing, slightly scandalous anecdotes about her, all somewhat patronizing of her because, in spite of her splendid voice, she was hardly more than a peasant, and dressed ridiculously, and spoke in ridiculous, broken English.

When the opera was over she changed into her street clothes quickly, not bothering to remove her make-up, so that she could go out to the Gorzas' at once. Gorza had taken a house near Ludlow Woods for the summer, a rambling Victorian place, all red plush and

grand pianos. When Sam and Frances arrived, there were already
thirty or forty people in the big double parlor. The windows and
doors were all open, but it was furiously hot, the air hanging like a
heavy curtain of heat in the rooms. Frances introduced him quickly
to three or four people, and then Gorza came up and took her away,
whispering and giggling something to her about Julia Magnus and
the new Russian basso. Sam found himself standing beside the
Carmen, who was wearing a deep purple dress with fringed sleeves,
and eating with appetite from a plate piled high with little sandwiches. She smiled at him.

"We get hungry—you see?" she said to him, nodding down at the
plate, unperturbed to find that she was being watched.

"They ought to have killed the fatted calf for you, after that performance tonight," Sam said, laughing. "You deserve it."

Looking at her off the stage, he wondered how she had ever
managed to create the illusion of vibrant, passionate youth—this
plump, overdressed, middle-aged woman. But there was the voice
still, strong and thrilling, rather wonderful even when she was only
talking about food and the weather. And there was something direct
and earthy about her that he liked. He stood talking to her for a
while, until someone came up to take her away.

A girl in an ice-blue beaded dress was singing a popular song in
the midst of all the racket of conversation, leaning on the piano and
smiling down at her accompanist. Sam looked around for Brand,
but he could not see him in the shifting, crowded rooms: he wondered whether or not he had come. He saw Frances over in a corner,
very animated, in a group centering around Gorza. There was
nobody else that he knew, and after a little he went out through a
pair of open French doors to the big porch that ran around three
sides of the house. The night air was damp and hot, but fresher at
any rate than it had been inside. He leaned against the porch railing
and lit a cigarette. He could hear the voice of the girl in blue still
chanting throatily inside over the rise and fall of the talk.

When he came back into the house again, the room was several
degrees noisier and hazier with smoke and heat than it had been
when he had left it. The girl in blue had stopped singing, and the
Russian basso was amiably thundering out some of his native folk

songs: the deep-throated words, interspersed with sudden *Hoja's* and shrill, irrelevant whistles, flew heavily about, dominating the confused noises of the room. Sam looked around for Frances. After a little he found her in the back parlor, talking to Gorza and three or four others at the buffet table that was set out there, and eating cucumber sandwiches and smoked sturgeon. She looked over at him as he came up, and smiled at him brightly.

"Oh—Sam," she said. "There you are. Have you had anything to eat?" She turned to Gorza: "Sam's just back from Czechoslovakia. You'll have to get him to talk to you about Polish food—or is there a difference?"

Sam knew that she wanted to make capital of his experiences with Gorza. And he was somewhat unresponsive with the older man, who had been drinking a little and was in a happy, expansive mood. When he finally moved away, Frances turned to Sam with her brilliantly made-up face rather sullen and offended.

"*Why* did you have to be like that with him?" she asked. "And when he was being so charming to you?"

"He's a little high; he'd be 'charming' to anybody," Sam said.

She stared at him for a moment. "Oh," she said, "it's all right for *you;* he's nothing to *you;* but you might think of what he can do for *me.*"

He wanted to leave, but she said they could not possibly go just yet, not when Gorza had made such a point of asking them. And, when some of her friends came up, she suddenly grew cheerful again, and introduced him to the round, blonde Micaela of the night's performance, who she said had been begging to meet him. The Micaela was very pretty, very empty-headed, but quite unaffected and nice, and he sat on the stairs with her for half an hour and talked to her about dogs. She said she was very fond of dogs, but she asked him some amazing questions about them. He could see Magnus smiling his curly smile at a pair of elderly women in diamonds and black, at the buffet table, and Julia Magnus sitting in a corner with the Russian basso, who had left off singing; but Brand was nowhere in sight. Sam guessed that he had gone home after the opera; it was not the sort of party that would appeal to him.

After a while he and the Micaela ran out of dogs, and he turned her over to a young man in flannels and a bow tie and went out to find Frances again. She was in Magnus's orbit, and very reluctant to leave it, but she saw that he had made up his mind this time about leaving. Gorza kissed her resoundingly on the forehead when she said good night.

"My little Sally," he declaimed. "The prettiest girl at the party, and she's leaving."

"I'm not Sally, I'm Frances," she said to him, laughing.

But when she was in the taxi with Sam, driving out to Haddon, she drew back into her rather hard sullenness again. She sat close to him, but withholding herself from him, looking straight ahead out of her bright gray eyes.

"Are you angry now?" he asked her, watching her white-powdered profile, the slight, fine arch of her nose, in the darkness. And he felt again for a moment tormented and unsure, sitting there beside her, as he had felt years ago, before the war.

She shrugged her thin shoulders, sulkily.

"Oh, I don't know. *Why* did we have to go? I've never been asked there before."

They were both silent for a time. He looked over at her. And he wanted suddenly to force the issue between them, as he had never been able to do before; he wanted to clear the confusion once and for all out of his mind, so that he could see their relationship sharply and simply for what it was.

"It hasn't been much good, has it?" he asked her, abruptly.

She looked over at him, startled.

"What do you mean?" He felt her soften suddenly, almost in alarm; the taxi made her lean nearer to him as it turned a corner. "It doesn't have to be like this," she denied. "You *know* that."

"What could it be like, then?"

She smiled. "Can't say, really. That's up to you."

"I think it's up to both of us."

"Aren't you serious now," she said.

She smiled at him still; he could see her gray eyes very brilliant, laughing and waiting in the darkness.

"I thought that was what you wanted."

"So I did."

She leaned against him again, and he kissed her, but it was as it had been the night of his homecoming: there was nothing between them but the mere physical sensation; they remained apart, rather antagonistic, and watchful of each other. But he saw that it pleased her because she held him even with that. She drew away, looking at him.

"You see how it can be," she said.

"Yes," he said.

And he suddenly knew that he wanted to be free of her: now, in a moment, the realization of it crystallized in him quite hard and sure. There was something barren and repellent about her desire to hold him even in the face of their mutual recognition of hostility; she was like a magpie, bright-eyed and predatory, carrying its cold, useless treasures to its nest. The taxi stopped before her house and he got out. She was all definite and shining in the darkness, in her white dress and her feathered hat. She stood watching as he paid the driver and the cab drove off.

"You're awfully sure you're coming in, aren't you?" she asked him, a little malicious, but wary, startled. She had begun to sense the crisis between them.

He went up the walk beside her.

"Why don't we stay out here for a while?" he asked deliberately, as they reached the porch.

"Like the old days?" She laughed. "But I *am* tired, Beauchamp."

She stood watching him a little uncertainly; she did not know what was coming. Only she saw him standing there looking at her, quiet and detached, really apart from her, as he had never seemed before.

"Don't you want to stay a while?" he asked her.

"Oh, I don't think so—tonight," she said, with apparent unconcern. But she was a little afraid of him, and angry, feeling set down, though she would not admit it either to him or to herself. "You'll come around again," she said, once more rather mockingly, wanting to assert herself.

He did not answer her. But there was something in his continued detachment that warned her. She looked for her key in her bag, wanting something to do to cover her uncertainty.

He took the key from her and opened the door.

"You'll call me, I suppose?" she said to him, the desire to make sure of him flaming up in her again, conquering her pride.

"Do you want me to?"

She did not answer him. And he saw that she knew as well as he, as they stood facing each other before the door, that there was no real satisfaction to be looked for in their relationship. If they had met that moment, there could not have been less between them. Still she looked at him with her clear, reckless eyes, waiting for him to speak again.

"I don't think it will be much good," he said at last. "Do you?"

"Oh," she said quickly, offended, but with an excited, cold laugh, "if *you* don't think so, that's enough!"

She held out her hand for him to give the key back to her. And as her fingers closed over it, brushing his own, he felt how she snatched it from him, really furious with him, under her air of good-natured, contemptuous calm.

"You used to be just like this before the war, when something didn't go exactly the way you'd expected it to," she mocked. "Do you remember? You'd go storming off; I never knew whether I was going to see you again or not."

Yet she knew it was not at all the same; she knew he had never been able to look at her in those days as he was looking at her now, not confused and resentful, but certain of himself, with a quiet, logical detachment.

It ended with her going off abruptly, as if by way of asserting herself once more, into the house, and leaving him standing there alone on the porch. He went off slowly down the steps. While he was walking home he put her completely out of his mind. It did not seem necessary to him to think about what had happened between them. There was a feeling of finality about it, as if they had reached a dead end together. And he knew that it was not really important to him now. He did not want to think of it any more.

Chapter 12

DURING THE DAYS THAT FOLLOWED HE WAS calmer, quite at peace with himself. He settled down to his work at the factory. He did not care for it, and the confinement was irksome to him after the years he had spent outdoors, but there was a certain satisfaction in having something definite to do. His mother was relieved and surprised, seeing him accept it so quietly. Only Virgil, of all the family, was dissatisfied with him, almost indignant. He spoke to him again about his plan of their going into business together.

"But, as long as that's not possible, I have to have something to do," Sam explained, patiently. "And this seems as good as anything else."

He thought that his father would gradually forget about the idea as time went on, as long as no one flatly opposed it. And he did not believe that he would actually go to Justus Kroener with it. But there he was mistaken. On the Saturday after he had been out to Ludlow Woods with Frances, his father came home from the store red and furious. He had laid his whole scheme before his father-in-law that morning, and the older man had refused absolutely to give him any assistance in the venture, or to hear anything more about his claims on Sam's behalf for Bertie's money. And the worst of it was, that now it would be all over the family about his plans, and he would have Mattie's disapproval to face, and Sophie's, as well as Justus Kroener's. He was completely dejected, talking to Sam about it that evening.

There was not much that Sam could say to him to make things better. But he promised himself that he would do what he could, at

any rate, to put a stop to the family's persecuting his father with
endless discussions of the matter. The next day, when he went over
to Warsaw Hill, he had a short conversation with Sophie that both
astonished and affronted her.

"*Well*," she said, at the conclusion of it, "your mother swears
you're a Kroener, and I've always said you took after your father,
but after this I think I've changed my mind. I've never heard anything like *this* before except from your aunt Rhoda."

But she looked at him with a new, rather wary respect, and she
did not bring up the subject of Virgil's plan that day. Mattie too was
surprised and a little intimidated by Sam's direct determination on
the matter. She was beginning to realize that she had to take him
into account. And it upset her; for so many years now she had been
growing used to the idea that hers was the dominant will in the
house. She could not help resenting it that he could stand out against
her, and against the whole weight of the Kroener opinion.

On Wednesday of that week, he went to Brand's for dinner, as
he had promised. It was in the midst of the fine, calm, hot midsummer weather that sometimes brooded for weeks over the river
valley. There was an inevitability in the movement of time, a deliberate, simple procedure from morning to darkness, and from darkness to still another warm, clear, full-hanging day.

Bronwen had been waiting all week for him to come, since Brand
had told her of the invitation. She felt suspended in this simple,
pregnant rhythm of time; the intense calm of the days, with its slow
pulse beating in strong life through the recurring dark and light, was
like something she held within herself, mastering the rhythm of her
own existence as well. She went about as always, self-contained and
rather vague, withholding herself. Only when she went out to the
Cannon House something hurt her, some memory that she was
forced to recognize. She remembered the time when Brand had first
brought her there, when she had been a child. She had been living
for so long now in a shut circle of memory: the few years of her
knowledge of Neil Lamson. And there was something now that was
sending her back, beyond that time, something that was forcing her
to recognize the fact that her life had not begun then nor ended then,
that there had been other years for her, and other names.

She had not spoken of Sam to anyone—not even to Rhoda, who
wanted to talk of him—except when she had said suddenly to her
father one evening that he ought to ask him to come to the house for
dinner. And after she had said it, she was astonished at herself, as if
it had been someone else who had spoken, and then had foisted the
responsibility for the words upon her. She did not want to see him;
she wanted to remain in her passivity, out of the way of life. And
when he came, she was still and remote with him, as if she had nothing to do with him.

Sam felt a little cheated, watching her, almost angry. He did not
know yet what he wanted of her. But it was not this silent, fixed
withdrawal. He watched her as she sat at the table in her white
dress, her head bent, looking away from him vaguely at the cloth.
He wanted to fasten her attention somehow, to make her realize him.
But she would not look at him. He talked to Brand, trying to seem
calm, and interested in the conversation. But there was the quick,
impatient blood beating inside him. He was almost pleased when
Brand was called out as they were finishing the meal. He knew she
would have to speak now, to enter into some sort of relationship with
him. She could not send him away at once.

When they left the table she asked him hesitatingly if he would
like to go outside, as it would be cooler there. He agreed promptly.

"I'd like to see what it looks like back there in the garden now,"
he said. "I used to come here with Aunt Rhoda when I was about
six. I remember Mrs. Considine had some late roses she was very
proud of."

He stood looking at her, smiling a little, quite certain of himself
in his slight inner exasperation. She had meant to take him out to
the big, vine-hidden front porch, not to the garden behind the house,
but she did not know how to oppose him now. She felt a little helpless, invaded, before his quiet determination.

They went out by the back door, through the kitchen. She saw
the housekeeper, who was clearing up the dishes there, look up and
smile at the pair of them, curious and rather pleased, as they came
through. And it reminded her suddenly, in an instantaneous evoca-
tion of the past, of the glances that had been cast at her and Lamson
as they had walked together through the streets of Port Lincoln. She

could not bear it, the present to come blurring her sharp vision of the past. She walked on quickly, not to see the woman's face.

Behind the house there was a slope of grass, with a pair of round flowerbeds laid out in it, and shrubs set along the low stone wall that separated it from the houses on either side. It was rather too neat, and commonplace enough. But even here, in the warm, heavy dusk, it was possible to feel the great brooding body of the earth lying in its midsummer stillness under the calmly darkening sky. Bronwen stood looking up, feeling a little dazed, as if she could sense herself swinging slowly through space with the passive earth on which she stood.

They began to walk on, away from the house. Along the wall, at the back, a tangle of climbing roses, their deep crimson almost black in the dusk, stood quite motionless, like a pattern of flowers on a frieze. Sam stopped before them.

"They're the same," he said. "Nothing has changed."

He looked at her. She felt that he was demanding her acknowledgment of something. He wanted to take his old place with her, to have back the intimacy between them. His insistence was like a weight upon her. The scent of the roses came to her, very still and fresh. She stood tense, gathered into herself, in her resistance.

"There's no place to sit out here," she said in a little, objectingly. "We can go out to the porch."

"What's the matter with the wall?"

He reached out and took her hand, quite matter-of-factly, to draw her over to the low wall. She went with him. But as he sat down she stood before him, unyieldingly.

"I'll spoil my dress," she said.

He laughed, looking down at the smooth flat stones.

"No, you won't. They're as nice as any garden chair."

He was quite determined, and good-humored in his confidence. She moved slowly and sat down beside him.

"Don't you like it here?" he asked her.

She gave a fine thin shiver of irritation, glancing over her shoulder.

"It's so—on display," she said.

There were neighbors out in the yard next door. She knew they would be watching them, gossiping and smiling. She had become like a person who is without some outer, protecting skin in her sensitiveness to the presence of other people. Sam saw that she was suffering. And he gave in suddenly, with a feeling of grayness coming over him, as if it were all no use.

"All right," he said. "We'll go in."

They went into the house again. As they came through the hall, they heard Brand at the front door. He had returned early; the call had been close by, and had turned out not to be anything important. They all went out to the porch together. But in a few minutes Bronwen said that she had a headache, and went inside. They heard her go upstairs to her room. Sam was silent, feeling defeated, his determination in abeyance. He saw Brand looking at him.

"I suppose she didn't make it too pleasant for you," Brand said, rather ironically. He was a little exasperated that she should have wanted to ask Sam to the house, and then behaved in this way with him.

"No," Sam said. "But it's all right. I know how it is with her."

He did not want to talk about her to anyone, not even to Brand. There was nothing that he could put into words, only this feeling that he knew her as the others did not, and that he wanted to insist to her that she acknowledge this too.

He did not see her again for a few weeks. The fine weather broke, and there was a period of showery days, rather like the first approach of autumn, though it was so early, still in August. Then, between the cool rains, the sky would clear and the world appear again, fresh and new, in the summer sunlight.

He started out to walk over to the Cannon House on one of these afternoons, a Sunday, around four o'clock. But as he passed by the empty field beside it, he saw Bronwen come out of the door of the house and turn to walk east, in the direction from which he was coming. She was wearing a thin, pale-green dress. She did not see him till he had come quite near, and then suddenly she looked up, recognizing him, a little at bay because he had startled her. He stopped her on the walk.

"Have you been to see Aunt Rhoda?" he asked. He stood looking down at her, a little unprepared himself, arrested, by the meeting. "I was just on the way there myself."

"Yes," she said.

She was relieved, thinking that he would leave her. But he continued to stand before her, barring her way.

"Where are you going now?" he asked her suddenly. "Somewhere in particular? Or are you only going home?"

"Yes, I'm going home," she said.

She spoke almost reluctantly, and rather quickly, in her effort to seem impersonal. But he would not let her pass.

"Why don't you walk along with me for a little, then?" he asked. "It's early still."

He stood waiting. She wanted to say that she could not, that she must get back at once. But he was so definite, so full of his hard, insistent determination, over against her. She could not defend herself against it. She turned, and they started off together, out Old Town Road, past the Cannon House.

The sun, that had been out brilliantly most of the day, was beginning to be overcast with soft, fine, dark vapor as they walked along. There was a stillness in the air, which seemed heavy and soft, almost tangible. They were both rather silent. She walked a little apart from him, with her head bent, as if in a vague obstinacy. But she was simply absorbed in her own sensations, the strange hurt of life quickening in her veins. She could not be with him without feeling that. And she did not understand how it could be so; she dreaded it. She wanted to be left alone. She hardly saw where she was going.

The gray domed roof of the old stadium came into sight as they rounded a turn in the road.

"Let's go in, shall we?" Sam said to her. "I haven't been out here since I've been back."

She stopped short in the road, looking up, suddenly startled out of herself into consciousness. The morning she had walked out here with Lamson, when she was hardly sixteen, came back to her intensely.

"No," she cried. "No. I don't *want* to."

"But why not?"

He stood looking at her, surprised. She did not answer him.

"Why not?" he repeated, patiently.

"Because I *don't* want; that's all," she said, forced to answer him.

"It's *not* all. Is it because you were ever out here with Lamson?"

"Yes."

She saw all at once that his face was tense with irritation, almost violent.

"Damn it, Bron, you were here with me before you ever heard of him," he said quickly.

He turned away from her and walked in through the gate, not looking back. She stood watching him. A kind of darkness came over her; everything inside her seemed dissolving in a swift, fluid shock of feeling, warm and painful. She could not bear him to go away, to separate himself from her in anger. And she did not understand it, that it should make this difference to her.

While she stood there, the sky, that had been darkening quietly, dropped spots of rain; one of the cool, sudden showers of the past few weeks was coming on. She saw him turn and begin to come back. He looked at her, not seeming to see her. He was tense and quiet, rather detached.

"We'd better get under some shelter," he said. "What about the stadium?"

She followed him without speaking. The rain was slanting down more quickly now, driving against the wooden tiers of seats. He saw that it was next to useless, looking for shelter there. But under the stadium, beneath some of the still comparatively whole rows of seats, it would be protected and dry. They had used it often as a lair, or a hiding-place, when they were children. He went inside, stooping to avoid the broken supports.

"Are you coming?" he asked, turning.

She came forward, glancing about her, a little dazed. There were ravels of grass growing; it smelled cool and damp, with the rain beginning to drip through from above. He looked around for the dryest place.

"It's nothing but a shower," he said. "It will be over soon."

She came over to the place to which he beckoned her. He saw her thin dress splashed and darkened with the rain.

"Are you very wet?" he asked her.

She shook her head. She felt as if she were moving in darkness; she could not quite realize herself or him as individuals; there was only this new, utterly still consciousness of feeling flowing between them. He came and stood before her.

"We'll sit down," he said, "shall we?"

"Yes."

The ground was a little higher here, sloping up slightly from the old track outside, so that the grass was quite dry, and safe from the rain. She sat curled with her feet under her, looking away from him, suspended, as if she were waiting.

"What are you thinking?" he asked her suddenly.

She shook her head, turning to look at him. He saw her eyes, wide open and questioning.

"I don't want you to be angry," she said after a moment, simply.

"I'm not, Bron."

She bent toward him slightly, and he put his arm about her, drawing her to him so that her head rested against his breast. It seemed quite natural to them both, quite simple. A curious stillness came over them. She felt lapped in darkness, hearing the steady beat of the rain above her, and feeling the slow, regular pulsation of his breathing as if it were the movement of the earth on which she rested. And she was wholly at peace, her tension exhausted, hardly conscious of herself except as she was a part of the heavy thundering of the rain and the quiet rise and fall of his breathing. Everything else had lapsed; it was as if, in an utter, moveless quiet, she were leaving everything of herself but this single knowledge that she was a part of him, and, through him, of the living universe.

The rain began to slacken overhead. And at last she raised her head; she gathered herself out of the darkness, looking at him with dazzled eyes, as if she had just awakened from sleep.

"Has it stopped raining?" she asked.

"We'll see."

He withdrew his arm, getting to his feet. She watched him, seeing the stillness on him too. But it terrified her a little, returning to the old world of reality in which he was distinct from her, someone with a distinct, unknown will and thoughts. She got up quickly and followed him into the open. A few bright drops were still falling from the sky, which was all scattered and ragged, with the blue beginning to come through. He turned around, hearing her behind him.

"It's all right," he said to her. "We'll go."

They walked out through the gate and turned back along the road in the direction of Cannon Hill. They were very quiet, with a warm feeling of closeness between them. Neither of them wanted to talk about it. The rain still fell a little, fitfully and brightly. There were busy robins out on the wet fields, and cardinals flashing through the trees. She felt fresh and new, like the washed earth. She turned to him, smiling. He loved her smile, running so quickly, elusive and swift, that he had almost forgotten.

As they went up the walk to her home Brand was coming out on the porch. He looked at the two of them, surprised.

"I thought you went out to the Cannon House," he said to Bronwen.

The old protective, shadowy quiet descended on her again. She answered him quickly and went into the house. And as soon as she was alone a depression came over her; it hurt her mind to think; she did not understand what had happened to her. As if in defense, she turned back to her memory of Lamson, but she could not find it; the sharp reality of it was utterly gone. She felt as if she had been holding tightly to a mere shell of life which, at the touch of reality, had suddenly crumpled in her hands and shown her the emptiness within. She felt the blood running in her now, hot and young and strong. And it hurt her; it hurt her to breathe, to see, to feel the life wakening in her again.

Still she had her times of sheer happiness, moments when the world was as incredibly wonderful to her as if she had suddenly been born into it afresh. She loved the mornings, when she awoke and looked from her window at the silent early world flooded in the first sunshine, the houses all sleeping, and only the birds flitting suddenly from tree to tree. She loved the hot fierce August noons, and the long breathless sunsets that quivered and subsided beneath the slow dark inevitable coming of the night. And there was a wholeness in her with the world, a sense that she fulfilled herself in it and it in her. Then she grew depressed again, and shrank away, halfdazed, a little afraid, wanting her old passivity.

She saw Sam often now. Sometimes he came to the house in the
evening, after work, and while he talked to Brand she sat silent,
listening to the sound of his voice, which was so strong and matter-
of-fact, reassuring to her for some reason. Or she saw him at Rhoda's,
where she went often on Sundays, and they walked home together
afterwards. He stayed apart from her, waiting, but she had an odd
feeling that their lives were knitting themselves together. It was not
as it had been with Lamson, when she had been tormented always
by a sense of separateness, a feeling that they were living their lives
in different worlds, and that they reached each other, really, only
when they shut themselves away from everything else in a world
in which there was no one but themselves. She could touch Sam in
the smallest happenings of her daily existence; they moved in the
same world, with no strangeness between them.

No one who knew them believed otherwise than that they had
simply taken up their old friendship with each other. Brand was in
a rather tense, thwarted, unobservant mood; he had made up his
mind, as he had told Sam, to leave Magnus's employment when the
agreement between them terminated, in the fall, but in the meantime he felt more than ever imprisoned in the ugly mesh of his position; he was not likely to look deeply enough into Bronwen to notice
the change in her. And Mattie, seeing Sam going so often to Brand's
house, thought only that he went to talk to Brand. She knew that
he had broken off with Frances, but it had never occurred to her
that there was something happening between him and Bronwen of
immeasurably more importance to him.

Besides that, there were other things on her mind. Virgil had been
depressed and irritable since Justus Kroener's final refusal to have
any more to say to him on the subject of Bertie's money; he came
home from the store and strayed about the house, dejected and restless, not like himself. Sam spent a good deal of time with him, but
he was stubborn in keeping to his peevish misery. And in September,
when the Cannon Hill Businessmen's Association held its annual
harvest festival, the committee, which was made up this year chiefly
of younger men, for the first time did not invite him, out of courtesy,
to help in making the arrangements. He was left out completely, and
it wounded him deeply, more than he cared to admit. He pretended

that he did not mind, and put on a scoffing air toward the whole idea
of the festival. But his real feelings were perfectly clear for anyone
to read.

On the Saturday evening that the festival was to begin, he came
home from town somewhat excited and upset. He said he had had
a bout of dizziness in the store that afternoon after lunch, and had
had to leave the floor and go off to rest for a while. Sam wanted to
call Brand, but Mattie was certain it was nothing but the heat and
something he had eaten at lunch that had disagreed with him. It had
been a hot, humid day, the intense, heavy, river heat that was at its
worst sometimes at the very end of the summer. She gave him a light
dinner and afterwards, as it was so warm in the house, he went out
to the porch to lie down on the swing and rest.

Sam had planned to see Bronwen that evening. He went out to the
porch shortly after dinner, undecided whether to go or not. There
had been no definite engagement made between them for the evening, and he knew that she would not be expecting him more than
on any other night.

Virgil looked around when the screen door opened. He was
propped up comfortably on the swing with a cushion at his back,
reading the evening newspaper in the early dusk.

"Going out?" he asked.

"I thought I would." Sam came over and stood leaning against
the porch railing, looking at him. He thought that he still looked
rather flushed and uneasy, though he seemed quite cheerful. "That
is, if you're all right," he added.

"Why, what are you trying to make out of a bit of dizziness?"
Virgil asked. "I'll be right again in the morning." He was a little
boisterous about it, almost as if he was frightened, like a boy, and
was trying to hide it. "You won't be putting me underground with
a little upset like this."

"No," Sam said, smiling. "I don't think we will."

Virgil looked at him, reassured, his eyes lighting up suddenly.

"I've got more *go* in me still than a lot of these young fellows
who think I'm ready to be put on the shelf," he said, emphatically.
"You remember that, Sam. I'll get my chance yet, to make them all
sit up and take notice."

Sam did not want him getting excited over that again. He felt that it might be better after all if he left him alone. Then he would go back to his newspaper and after a little, when it grew too dark to read, would perhaps doze off there in the swing. He broke off the conversation, saying that if he intended to go out he would have to be starting.

He walked up Sherman Street to Old Town Road. But he was still rather disturbed about Virgil; he could not quite shake it off. He wanted to speak to Brand about what had happened. When he got to the house, though, only Bronwen was at home; Brand was out on a call. She saw that he was upset about something. He could feel her eyes watching him, very still and deep, waiting, wanting to help.

"What is it?" she asked.

He told her.

"We'll go out for a while, shall we, Bron?" he said.

"Yes."

They went down the porch steps together. It was growing dark. The streetlights came on, yellow and peaceful under the high, dark-blue sky. The groups they passed were all on their way to the festival, out at the other end of Old Town Road. They walked down Beech Street, away from the excitement.

"Shall we go down the hill?" he asked her.

"Yes," she said. "Wherever you like."

She was very immediate to him that evening, not lost in vagueness, holding herself aloof, as sometimes even now she was. He felt that she was there for him, that if he reached out to her she would be whole and perfect in her response. And it was so white-hot and clear in him now, his love for her. He wanted her to know it, to acknowledge it. He knew he could not do without that much longer.

And she, walking close beside him, was simply content, quiet, but with a warm flame of life flowing through her veins. She felt as if she were a part of the tranquil, throbbing, harvest dusk, as if what happened to her happened as simply and as inevitably as the night happened to the land around her. They crossed the road at the foot of the hill and climbed the long slope toward Haddon. Then, at the summit, under the tall sycamores that stood singly, like sentinels, their white bark glistening slightly in the thin darkness, they stood looking down at the small lights shining brightly below them. He took her in his arms and she looked up at him, her eyes blazing with a light he had never seen before. Then, as he put his mouth on hers, she cleaved to him, and he held her close and deep and still, while the faint night-sounds chirred and creaked on quietly about them.

She drew away at last, looking up at him once more. Her face was dim and white in the darkness. But she was all new and whole, filled with the assurance of love. And she wanted to feel it radiating and blazing all about her, out of the present, into the future and even the past. She could not bear it that there had ever been anything different in her life. She was puzzled, suffering from it, remembering the day that he had kissed her first, when they were both sixteen. She had a moment of perfect anguish, when she struggled to understand the pattern of their lives. But then it died away, and she accepted it, she accepted that things had had to be so. And, after all, it did not matter; the past was over and dead for her.

They walked back quietly toward Cannon Hill again. They walked like lovers now, very close, without words. And at the foot of the hill, where the creek ran quick and dark under the poplars, he stopped and kissed her again, softly and repeatedly, as if he were reassuring himself of her, and her of him. He wanted to say it to her: "I love you, Bron. I love you." And when he had said it, there was nothing else necessary; it was sufficient and perfect, all of his needs in the compass of the words.

As they came up the slope again toward Cannon Hill, there was a flare of light over the horizon. They had walked west, and now they were coming out on Old Town Road near the large open field where the harvest festival was being held. As they approached, they could see the turning, lighted circle of the Ferris wheel against the sky, and hear the bright, mechanical music of the carrousel. It was nearly ten o'clock, and the place was thronged. They looked at it curiously as they passed by, the rather artificial excitement of it failing to touch them in their close, quiet world. It was as if they bent from another planet to watch it, seeing it turn in the night distantly with its twinkling lights and its dimly moving figures.

But as they passed the dark shapes of parked automobiles in the field beyond it, a bulky figure, just opening the door of the one nearest them, turned suddenly to call to them.

"Sam— Is that you, Sam Beauchamp?"

Sam stopped and turned. He recognized John Vanderdonck, who owned the leading Cannon Hill dry-goods store, on the Square. The older man came toward him, heavily.

"You haven't heard what's happened, Sam?" he said.

Sam felt a wrench of dismay go through him. He thought instantly of Virgil.

"Why, what is it?" he asked.

He saw the florid, excited face of the other peering at him through the darkness.

"I thought you wouldn't have heard," he said. "It was about half an hour ago—your father was out here, acting a bit queer, and then he was taken bad—a stroke, they say. I saw him myself—"

He was distressed, breathing heavily as he spoke; he had known Virgil well for many years. Sam stood perfectly still, listening to him.

"Where did they take him?" he asked.

"Why, Frank Rogan had that big car of his here, and they brought him home."

"You don't know how bad he was?"

Sam bit his lip. He could not quite believe it yet. It had come on him too suddenly. He saw Vanderdonck looking rather curiously from him to Bronwen.

"No," he said. "Somebody said he hit his head when he fell— He was still unconscious when they took him home."

Sam nodded. He could not wait for any more. He glanced quickly at Bronwen.

"I'll go with you," she said, anticipating him.

"I can drive you over," Vanderdonck put in. "It'll be quicker."

They got into the car. Sam could feel Bronwen's fingers just touching his own as she sat beside him. They were at the house in a few minutes. He saw the lights blazing upstairs and downstairs as he ran up the steps to the porch.

The front door was open, and he went directly into the living room. There was no one there, but through the open doorway he saw his mother and his aunt Sophie standing together in the dining room. They both turned, hearing his step. He went in to them, while Bronwen remained standing in the living room.

"Where is he?" he asked his mother, quickly.

She nodded her head slightly to indicate the upstairs. She was white and rigid, with an odd, corrosive bitterness about her. Her eyes quickly took in Bronwen in the living room, and then returned to rest again on his face.

"And how—?" he asked.

"Dr. Brand is up with him now," she interrupted him. "He hasn't said yet."

He was startled by the fixed, deliberate emotionlessness of her tone.

"But what happened?" he insisted. "And what was he doing, out at the festival—?"

The bitterness flamed up in her then; she stood confronting him with the blood mounting to her face, showing in sharp patches beneath the sallow skin.

"Yes," she said quickly, "it's a nice time for you to come walking in with your questions, when it's too late to do any good to anyone. You might have stopped him if you'd been at home, instead of going out after your own pleasure—"

He thought that she was upset at his bringing Bronwen home with him at a time like this, with the intimacy that it implied between them; but that was scarcely enough to account for her coldness and anger with him. He looked over at Sophie, seeking an explanation from her. She too was heavy and grim, unlike her ordinary self.

"Do you mean to say," she asked, interpreting his questioning glance, "that you don't know *all* that's happened tonight? Well, take a look at that, if you please."

She moved aside and he saw, lying on the table, a thick roll of bills, wadded and crumpled. He looked at the two women, perfectly bewildered.

"Yes," Sophie said, nodding sharply, as if in confirmation. "There's almost two thousand dollars there—and where on earth he got it from is something that all of us would like to know."

She went on to tell him the rest of what she and Mattie knew of what had happened that evening. Shortly after Sam had left the house, Mattie had come out on the porch to find that Virgil had disappeared; he was not in the house, and the only clue she had to his whereabouts was a neighbor's statement that he had seen him walking up the street toward Old Town Road. It was quite unlike him to go off like that without saying anything to anyone, but she thought he might perhaps have walked up to the drugstore for tobacco, or something of that sort, and so she had stayed waiting for him for an hour or more. Then, as he did not come, she had tried to reach Sam at Brand's, and finally, really uneasy, had telephoned the Kroeners, who had come out at once from Warsaw Hill.

But they had hardly arrived when Mr. Rogan and two or three others had brought Virgil home from the festival. They said that he had been there only a short time before he had been taken ill, but that everyone who had seen him had noticed that he was acting strangely. He had been very much excited, almost incoherent, and had in his pocket a thick wad of bills, which he pulled out to show rather recklessly, saying that he was as well off as the next one, and that he was going into business soon with Sam. Then, just as people were beginning to wonder at him, and to stop and stare, he had suddenly said that he felt ill and wanted to sit down, and he was walking over to the picnic tables when he staggered and fell. No one had any idea where he had been up to the time that he had appeared at the festival, or where he had gotten the money that was in his possession there. The roll of bills had slipped out of his pocket when he fell, and the men who brought him home had been uneasy and embarrassed as they turned it over to Mattie, aware that something was wrong about it, and afraid that some of it might have been lost.

It infuriated Sam, seeing that to Sophie, and perhaps even to Mattie, the question of the money loomed more important than Virgil's illness. They were shocked and terrified at the thought that he might have done something to disgrace them and himself. The first idea that had occurred to them had been that he might have gone down to Justus Kroener's store, to which he had a key, and taken the money from the safe. There was always a large sum there at the end of the month, as Kroener still clung to his old-fashioned business habits, which included a dislike of frequent banking. And, in the family anxiety to prove this comparatively saving theory, Justus Kroener had gone into town at once to see if this was what had actually occurred. But, even if it should turn out to be so, and the whole matter hushed up inside the family, Mattie still felt that Virgil had dealt her self-respect a blow which she could never forgive. And both she and Sophie were inclined to put a part of the blame for the whole affair on Sam, since he had refused to let them make it perfectly clear to his father how impossible it was for him to carry out his idea of going into business again.

Sam did not want to stay to hear any more of it. He left the dining room and started up the stairs to the second floor. As he reached the head of the stairs, Brand came out of Virgil's room. He saw Sam and came toward him.

"How is he?" Sam asked quickly.

Brand shook his head. "There isn't anything I can do, Sam." There was always something rather angry, defeated, about him when he was faced with the fact of death, as if it were the result of some personal failure on his part. "He can't possibly last for twenty-four hours," he said. "You may as well know."

"Yes," Sam said. He felt as if a great weight had come down on him. "What is it?" he asked.

"Cerebral hemorrhage. The right side is paralyzed. He's not conscious; he'll go off like this, without ever knowing—"

Sam tried to take it in, to realize it. He had faced the reality of death often enough, in the war. And yet, somewhere deep inside him, there were the agonized tears of a small boy deprived of his father. He felt that he could not bear it. He went past Brand abruptly and into the bedroom.

Virgil was lying on the far side of the big double bed, with his head turned a little away, so that Sam could see at first only the stout bulk of his figure under the bedclothes and his thin, slightly tousled, graying hair. Then, as he came around the bed, he saw the face drawn down, quite unnatural, and the mouth opened in the heavy, labored breathing that seemed to go on like the hoarse, regular panting of a machine. He sat down by the bed and took his father's hand. It was oddly limp and nerveless, and lay in his with an inertness quite unlike that even of an unconscious person. He realized suddenly that it was the paralysis: it was the right hand that he held in his. And he had a moment of horror; it was not his father who lay there, but something utterly removed from him, an inert bulk, grotesque and heedless of his love.

He heard Sophie come into the room behind him. She walked across to the bed, and with a few dexterous jerks and pats straightened the covers which Brand had disarranged during his examination.

"You'd better go downstairs," she said, glancing at Sam as she finished. "Dr. Brand is talking to your mother."

It made the blood flame in his veins to see her matter-of-fact acceptance of illness and death. There was this hard, accepting practicality somewhere deep inside every woman when she was confronted with dissolution, he thought: where a man stood helpless and terrified before the blank end of the individual, she busied herself with the last needs of the body, as if that alone were at stake, as if she could accept the needs of the dying as she accepted the needs of the infant, secure in an unconscious knowledge of the larger flow of life embracing them both. But he could not endure to see it now. He went out of the room and down the stairs.

Bronwen was in the hall, waiting for him, when he came down. She stood looking at him without speaking. He could hear Brand in the living room, talking to Mattie.

"Come in with me," he said to her, in a low voice.

She shook her head in silence. After a moment he went on into the living room alone. Brand turned around, hearing him.

"I've told your mother, Sam," he said.

Mattie was sitting at the end of the sofa, leaning forward, with her hands tightly clasped on her knees. She looked up at Sam. He went over and put his arm about her shoulders. But she was quite tense, unyielding.

"I'll stop around the first thing in the morning, Mrs. Beauchamp," Brand said to her. "And you'll call me if there's any change."

He went out into the hall. Bronwen stood beside the stairs. He gave her an odd, penetrating glance.

"Are you coming with me?" he asked.

She looked at Sam, who had come out into the hall behind Brand. "You'd better go, Bron," he said. "There's nothing you can do."

He saw the way that Brand looked at Bronwen, his sudden, rather deeply startled comprehension of the fact that she and Sam had come into a new and complete relationship with each other. But there was nothing to be said now. He turned to Sam.

"This business about that money," he said to him. "For God's sake, don't worry about it. If there's anything I can do about it—"

"Thanks. But I think it's nothing, except that he thought he was taking what belonged to him—or rather to me—by rights."

Sam could not help speaking bitterly about it; he could not help feeling that his grandfather was to some extent responsible for what had happened. Brand shrugged a little, heavily.

"Yes, I know about that," he said. He had heard it before, from Rhoda. It was incomprehensible to him, and rather mean, this close family bickering over money. "Has anyone thought to tell Rhoda about what's happened tonight?" he asked, after a moment.

"No, I suppose not," Sam said. "I'd better phone her."

"Don't bother. I'll drive out there myself. She'll probably want to come right over, and I can bring her."

Sam knew that he wanted to be there when she was told. It would be one of the bitterest things for her to bear, to lose Virgil. She had always felt so protective toward him, as if she could somehow be responsible for him against the great, battering shock of life. And now, like the rest of them, she would be helpless.

Brand and Bronwen left the house, and Sam went back upstairs to the room where his father lay. But he could not stay there long; the pressure of his own helplessness was too great on him. He went into the upper hall and stood there, leaning against the wall, in the darkness.

He heard Rhoda come in downstairs. She spoke to Mattie and then came upstairs, quickly. Her mouth was set in a straight, harsh, ugly line. She had been crying. She came up to Sam and grasped his two hands hard, one in each of hers.

"May God punish them, Sam," she whispered, fiercely.

She was even less able than he to evaluate justly the extent to which the Kroeners had been responsible for what had happened that night. She was like a mother who can see no fault in her child, but only in those who have thwarted and injured it. She went inside the bedroom to see Virgil. But when she came out again, her anger had already faded under her consciousness of the inevitable approach of death. She felt empty, used up. She had been through all this so exactly before with her father. It gave her a feeling almost of horror to see how closely the son's death was paralleling that of the father.

She went downstairs with Sam. Justus Kroener had come into the house a few minutes before and was in the living room, talking to Mattie, when they came down.

"Do you want to stay here tonight?" Sam asked, as they reached the foot of the stairs.

Rhoda shook her head. "No," she said. "I'm better off going home. It isn't as if I could do anything. And I *don't* want to quarrel, Sam—not while he's dying; I couldn't bear it."

She spoke harshly, looking toward the living-room door. But there was something subdued about her, unlike her ordinary self.

Sam wanted to walk home with her; it was late, past midnight now. But she preferred to go alone. She was the kind of woman who is easier bearing her emotions where no one else can see. He knew that she would go home and do something grotesquely commonplace, in the middle of the night—wash her hair, or put her dresser drawers to rights.

When she had gone, he went back into the living room, to his mother and his grandfather. Mattie looked up as he came in. There was something less bitterly frightened about her now. Justus Kroener had found, when he went down to his store, that it actually had happened as they had suspected: it had been from the safe there that Virgil had gotten the money that he had had that night. And her relief was so great that for the moment she was almost appeased; she could accept the approaching death of her husband as if it were some hard, inevitable, impersonal fact, which had no direct bearing, really, upon her own life. It went through Sam like a cold fire, the realization of her essential inner indifference. And he acknowledged suddenly to himself something that he had always sensed, from the time that he had been old enough to understand the meaning of love—that she had never loved Virgil, that she had married him without love, as prudent, dutiful, and unimaginative young girls often do marry, to please convention rather than themselves, and that the whole history of their life together had been the history of a bitter, unyielding struggle on her part to make him over into the image of her own wish.

And it all seemed so useless now, so paltry. He went out and sat alone on the porch, thinking of it. What did it matter that his father had failed in his life? It was only the *humanness* of him that mattered, the terrible human individuality which they were losing and which would never come again. And it was this impersonality of death that maddened him, this great, primal, irresistible weight which had already descended on his father, and was slowly and methodically stripping him of every vestige of that individuality, forcing him into the blank universality of death.

His mother and Sophie had made plans to divide the night between them in Virgil's room. Sam went to his own room after a while, and lay down on the bed without undressing. And, contrary to his expectations, he fell asleep almost at once. But in an hour he was awake again; it was only three o'clock by his watch. From the room across the hall he could hear the great, dragging breaths, which seemed to fill the dead silence of the house now. He stood at the window, looking out. It was dark and still, with a little autumn coolness coming into the air, the sky clear and high.

He went across the hall to his father's bedroom. Mattie was sitting beside the bed, wearing a dark printed wrapper. She looked up as he came in and shook her head. There was nothing, no change. She was quite calm, somewhat strained-looking from lack of sleep.

"Will you let me watch?" he asked her, in a low voice. "I'll call you if there's anything."

But she did not want it. She could endure it all so long as there was the consciousness in her that she was doing her duty. He left her alone again and went back to his own room. He thought of Bronwen, wanting her badly.

He sat on the bed and watched the sky fading toward dawn, and then the sun rising, the early breeze springing up, moving brightly over the fresh, silent world. But it was all apart from him; he was shut away from it, in the clayey room of death.

Around six-thirty he heard Sophie moving about in the adjacent room. She went downstairs, and a few moments later Mattie came to the door of his room.

"Sophie's making breakfast," she said to him. "You'd better fix up and go on down." She looked at his bed, rather disapproving. "What need was there for *you* to sit up all night?" she asked. "You'd better have gone to bed properly and got a decent sleep."

She went back to Virgil's room again. When he went downstairs a little later, there was the smell of coffee and bacon in the kitchen, and Sophie, wearing one of Mattie's aprons, was moving about briskly. It was very commonplace and normal, with only a slight element of strangeness because it was Sophie, and not his mother, who was moving about in the kitchen.

He had breakfast with her: Mattie was to come down when Sophie had finished, and could go upstairs to take her place. There was a silent antagonism between the two in the kitchen. Sophie wanted to draw Sam out, to know exactly how he felt about what had happened the previous night. She was a little on the defensive, insinuating and hard.

"Are you hungry?" she asked him, setting his plate before him on the table.

"Yes."

"Well, there are people who'd think you were unfeeling to admit it. *I* don't see it that way."

"Why should you?" he asked.

He would not quarrel with her; he was perfectly civil, only rather silent.

As they were finishing breakfast, Brand arrived at the house. It was not quite eight o'clock. Mattie and Sophie were both put out because he had come so early, before they had had time to put themselves and the house into the perfect German order that they considered the only proper face to show to the world.

Sam went upstairs with Brand. As they were going up the stairs he heard how the hoarse, stertorous breathing that came from the bedroom had changed since he had been downstairs. There were deep, frightening pauses in it now—then it would resume again, a little less regularly than before. They went into the room. Again the heavy pause came in the breathing.

"What is it?" Sam asked.

Brand went over to the bed. And, in a moment, with an odd, gurgling sigh, the deep, exhausted pumping of breath ceased altogether; the form on the bed lay inert, finished with life. Mattie crouched over the bed, wiping the spittle that had flowed from the open mouth. And the morning sun was beating so warm and simple against the blinds that had been drawn to shut it out. Sam turned away. He went out of the room and down the stairs.

Now that it was over, it became removed from him; the ritual of arrangements in which he was immediately involved had nothing whatever to do with the reality of his emotions. He could not understand how the others could sit solemnly in decision over the details of the burial; all that filled him with a kind of bewildered repulsion. His father was dead: it remained simply to commit him back to the earth. For him, that was all. He did not want to make it into a social occasion, to which it was necessary that the corpse, as well as the mourners, come attired in the proper clothes.

But there was nothing that he could do against it. And he went through it all as best he could. He was rather still and abrupt, living in himself. He went the next day to see Bronwen, but they both felt as if they were divided, somehow, by what had happened. The weather had turned wet, and they could not go outdoors. Brand was at home; he sat watching them in his steady, uncritical way. He began to talk to Sam about what he would do now. But it was too early. He wanted to leave his own affairs deliberately in the background for now.

The funeral took place on a rather dismal day, when the brown and yellow and scarlet leaves hung heavily from the trees. There had been a battle between Rhoda and the Kroeners over where Virgil was to be buried, on the Kroener lot in the Lutheran cemetery in Warsaw Hill, or in the old Cannon Hill cemetery where all the Beauchamps were buried. And Rhoda, as usual when she had really set her mind on something, had had her way. She felt a kind of clear, deep satisfaction in her victory. She loved the little, almost neglected cemetery, with the square white Beauchamp stone set so massively in the center of it. It was so lost, so secure in the white serenity of the past. She had rebelled fiercely at Virgil's death. But here there was no tragedy, only the sense of inevitability that is in life as much as it is in death.

She watched the coffin disappear slowly into the dark, moist earth. And she could not cry; it seemed to her at that moment that it was they, the living, standing huddled so forlornly under the gray arch of the sky, who had need of her compassion. They were so vulnerable, they clung with such hidden terror to the small importances of their daily lives. And to each of them there came these moments of confusion, when the wrappings of their own man-made dignity and security fell from them suddenly and left them naked and single, face to face with their terror, confronting the mystery. It was too hard for them; they were too frightened of their own souls. So they clung to each other, and hid themselves beneath a heaped-up mass of trivialities, creeping about beneath them to be protected from the mystery that shone too darkly about them.

Rhoda looked at Mattie's rigid face, at Justus Kroener, shut behind the shaky barrier of his own irreproachability, at Sam's rather tense, stoic pose, at the decent, ordinary faces of the Kroener relatives, full of a vague uneasiness before a situation in which ordinariness was not sufficient. And she felt a hot passion of human feeling for them flow through her; she was one with them all; they were all walking so blindly under the naked sky. She was shaken, full of love. Then the mood broke; they struck at her with irritating voices, irritating gestures. She could not bear to be with them; she went home to the Cannon House, where the walls remembered what she remembered, where the garden had not forgotten a fat little boy in his Sunday knee pants and jacket, listening to his grandfather's stories of the sea.

Chapter 13

THE DAYS PASSED AFTER THE FUNERAL. THERE was a good deal to do, decisions to be made. Justus Kroener took on himself the chief business of settling Virgil's affairs. He was so used to managing the family affairs that he simply took it for granted that he should be left in charge of anything of that sort. And Sam let him take his own way; it did not matter to him what was done. He felt quite alone now in the midst of the family. They were all rather wary of him, somewhat resentful of his reserve with them. When they were together they wanted to talk to him of his father's death, secure in the confidence of their united strength. They wanted to overwhelm him with the granite weight of their opinion. But he was unresponsive, keeping himself intact against them. He would go his own way. They could make no progress against him.

Justus Kroener asked him to come over to Warsaw Hill one evening after dinner. Sam believed that it was because of some business connected with the settling of his father's estate that he wanted to see him. But when he arrived, his grandfather did not begin on that subject. Instead, he brought out an old passbook of the Warsaw Hill Building and Loan Association, one that bore the names of Bertha and Mathilda Kroener.

"I intend to turn over the money that was in Bertie's name when she died to you," he said without preliminary, in his heavy, dragging voice. "I want you to verify the amount."

He handed the book across to Sam. They were alone in the living room; Sophie was out, and Mrs. Kroener had gone back to the kitchen when Sam had arrived, to leave the two men to talk business together. Sam looked at the open passbook that his grandfather had given him. He was taken by surprise, and was silent for a moment. Then the resentment came up in him. The older man dealt his decisions so finally, he seemed so completely certain of himself. And Sam realized what it was that he wanted to do with this gesture. He wanted to stand free of the possibility of reproach, before Sam and before the rest of the world, to place himself beyond the shadow of culpability or of criticism. And it infuriated Sam that he should believe he could do that merely by the sacrifice of a sum of money.

He pushed the passbook back across the table.

"I don't want any of that," he said, definitely. He felt a certain angry satisfaction in his refusal. "You've always said I didn't have any right to that money. Why should you want to give it to me now?"

The thin blood came up in the older man's face. He was not used to being thwarted in his own house.

"Why I'm doing it is my own business," he said. "It's nothing to do with your having a right to it. As far as that's concerned, you haven't any. But I'll do what I like with my own money."

"And I'll do what I like about taking it," Sam said bluntly.

He met his grandfather's gaze, the blue eyes sunken but still clear, with the expression of coldly humble self-esteem in them that he had always disliked. He had always felt at a disadvantage before that gaze. But there was something different between them now, some new realization which they shared. He saw his grandfather's life now as a rather miserable, insufficient creation, always being pieced out to a semblance of adequacy at the cost of actions that could never really cover the smaller man inside. Yet he was a godly man, living uprightly, according to his lights. Only, there was not enough inside. And he knew, unconsciously, of his insufficiency; he worked constantly and rather desperately to cover it.

"You do as you like," he said now, stiffly. "But I intend to put that much money in the bank, to your account. It makes no difference to me what you do about it then."

Sam knew that it was useless to say any more. He would do as he had planned, whatever was said. But it was worse between them than if nothing at all had been done about the money. Sam could not help being bitter when he thought of how much it would have meant to his father if this had been done before his death. He was tired of it all now, a little hard.

His mother learned of what her father had done. She did not approve; she stood firmly on the principles by which she had made her old decision. There was a constant, wearying tension now between her and Sam. She wanted them to give up the house on Sherman Street at once, either for a smaller place in Warsaw Hill, or to go and live with the Kroeners there. Since Bertie's death, old Mrs. Kroener had been growing increasingly feeble, and now there must be someone with her constantly. It was irksome to Sophie, who was always going somewhere, and hated to be tied down. She would have liked to have Mattie come and live with them, so that most of the burden would be taken from her shoulders. And the elder Kroeners were both willing to have this arrangement made.

Sam had not made up his mind yet what he would do. He went one evening, a day or two after his talk with his grandfather, to see Bronwen. He wanted to talk to her, to put the situation between them into words. He could not act without her; she was too closely bound up with his future. Since Virgil's death there had been a kind of shadow between them. There had been so much for him to do that he had hardly seen her. And he wanted badly to be with her, to go back to the closeness with her that he had had on the night of Virgil's illness.

But when he arrived at the house, only Brand was at home. He asked him in, and they went into the living room together.

"Where *is* Bron?" Sam asked.

"At the Cannon House. She went over to see Rhoda." Brand looked at Sam in his direct way. "She won't be late, I suppose."

"I'll walk over after a while. I want to see her."

Brand stood by the mantel, filling his pipe from a round tobacco jar.

"What is it about you and Bron?" he asked after a moment, without turning around. "Are you in love with her?"

"Yes." Sam did not know quite what was coming. Brand had the Welsh reticence in speaking about anything like this, an odd, grave respect for the privacies of others. But he had brought the subject up himself. "I want to marry her," Sam went on after a moment, deliberately. "I haven't said anything to her yet, so I don't know—"

He watched Brand light his pipe and draw on it slowly.

"She's been different since you came back," he said, after a little. "I think she wants you."

"Yes," Sam said. "I think she does."

Brand nodded. He looked at Sam directly.

"You'd be good for her," he said. "She hasn't anything here."

"Most people would say she has a lot more than she'd have if she married me," Sam said.

But he felt, really, that that did not matter, not to the essential thing between them. They wanted the whole life that belonged to the other, whatever it was. Only they did not want to be separate: that was the important thing.

Brand did not carry the subject any farther. Sam noticed a difference in him this evening from the way he had been, a curious brightness, rather tense, but satisfied. He put it down to the fact that he was nearing the end of the term of his contract with Magnus. He would be free of that very shortly now.

But he said nothing about that to Sam. They talked instead about what Sam would do now. Sam told him what Justus Kroener had done with the money that had been in dispute so long between him and Virgil.

"What's stopping you from using that to make a start at getting a place of your own?" Brand asked. "If you need any help—it still goes, what I told you when you first came back: I'd like to be in on it—"

"Thanks," Sam said. "But I can't tell yet. I'll have to wait a little."

He wanted to talk to Bronwen first. And it gave him an odd feeling, as if there were something burdensome and terrifying laid on him, to think that he wanted to bind himself for his whole life to the wishes and feelings of someone alien to himself. Yet he did want it; without it, there was nothing. And until it was decided he was unsettled, without purpose.

When he left Brand half an hour later, he went straight to the Cannon House. It was nearly nine o'clock on a clear, chill autumn night, dazzling with moonlight. He found Bronwen in the kitchen with Rhoda. She was ready to leave, but first they were going out to the garden to gather some of the pears that were ripening now on the trees there, so that Bronwen could take them home with her. Every year the old trees still bore so many that Rhoda was plagued with the problem of what to do with them.

Sam said that he would go out and gather the pears. He went outside with the basket that Rhoda gave him. The garden was clear and sharp in the moonlight. Rhoda's collie bitch, Princess, came slowly across to him from the other side of the kitchen yard and nuzzled at his hand. He talked to her for a moment in a low voice. When he went on down the garden to the pear trees, she stood for a little watching him, indecisive, her plumed tail moving slowly, and then settled down again on the paving-stones.

Sam stood looking up at the heavily weighted trees. It was so bright that he could see the fruit distinctly, almost the color of the ripened ones, like a smudge of rosy shadow laid along them. He saw that he could fill the basket easily from the lower branches. But he did not hurry. He wanted Bronwen to come out to him. He was almost sure that she would come.

The kitchen door opened and closed, the sound very clear in the crisp air, and he turned around and saw her walking from the house. She came up slowly and stood at a little distance, looking at him.

"Will you have to climb the tree?" she asked.

"No," he said. "The lower branches are still full."

She came under the trees and reached up, beginning to help him fill the basket. He worked on, stopping now and then for a moment to watch her quick, slender figure in its lovely, almost reverential poses as she stood with arms raised to the tree, or stooped with her burden to the basket. He felt the happiness striking through him, bright and keen as the moonlight.

"Bron—" he said.

She stopped and looked at him. And she came straight to him; he held her, standing with his back to the tree.

"Bron, do you want me?" he asked her, after a little.

She drew away, to look at him.

"Yes," she said. "Don't you know?"

"I want to be sure. I want you to say it."

"But why does it make a difference then, if you know—?"

She looked at him curiously and rather heavily, withdrawing herself a little. She had an unconscious and almost superstitious fear of bringing their relationship into the open; it seemed to her as if they could keep it as it was only if they went on as they had been doing, without admitting it in words even to themselves. It was her fear of entering wholly into life again, of being hurt again.

She looked at him standing there in the shadow of the tree, rather terrified of him in his steady determination.

"I want it to be settled between us, Bron," he said. "I want us to be married—I told Rob that tonight."

She could not bear it, that he should have spoken of it to anyone. "No," she said, quickly. "Why did you do that?"

"Are you angry?" he asked, looking at her attentively.

She moved away a little, out from under the trees, into the bright hard moonlight.

"Why need you have done it?" she repeated.

He was silent. She knew that she had hurt him. And it was an anguish to her, suddenly. She came back to him quickly, and reached her hands up to his face.

"No," she said. "No—"

She wanted to cry. He kissed her very gently, not understanding what it was that she felt. He felt again the burden and terror of what he was doing, trying to fuse their lives into one. Yet at the same time he was so full of happiness, fulfilled and contented as he had never been before. Her grief seemed to bring them very close; he was shaken and softened, holding her quietly.

"It doesn't matter," he said, comfortingly. "It doesn't matter."

But she became clear and bright now, won away from her fear.

"Yes," she said. "It does matter. Why shouldn't you tell him? It's so, it's true."

She wanted to hear him plan for their future; she had to convince herself wholly now that it was not only the small moment of the present that they shared, but the long blaze of the future as well. She listened while he told her about what he had wanted to do ever since he had lived those three years on the Korvas farm, about the farm of his own that he wanted to have. But she could not make it real to herself, the thought of sharing a house with him, of being an integral part of his daily life, not for a few days or weeks, but for the round of years. She felt insufficient, a little frightened.

"Wouldn't you care for that?" he asked, sensing her withdrawal.

She looked up at him, putting her hands quickly along his sides, under his arms. She had to touch him, to make sure of him, that he was there for her, in the future as well as in the present.

"Yes," she said. "I'd love a farm. But I'm afraid—"

He looked at her questioningly, not understanding.

"But why?" he asked. "That it will be too hard?"

She shook her head without answering.

"It *will* be hard, Bron," he said, soberly.

"No, it's not that at all. I'm only afraid—*you* won't be there."

She looked at him tensely, wanting to see if he understood. He returned her gaze steadily.

"Yes," he said. "I'll be there."

And her tenseness broke suddenly; she believed him utterly, like a child. She smiled at him, almost joyfully.

"What a long time Miss Rhoda will think we're taking to pick a basket of pears," she cried. "Is it full now? Had we better go in?"

He picked up the basket and they walked up toward the house together. He thought that she looked quite insubstantial in the white moonlight. It was in a light like this that one saw best the really lovely lines of her face and body, running so simply and so delicately.

She went up to the house, walking quickly beside him.

"Are you going to stay?" she asked.

"No. I'll walk home with you."

They went into the house, to say good night to Rhoda. She was in the parlor; she heard them come into the house, and then they stood together in the doorway, looking at her with the dazzle of their happiness still on them. She had known there was something on foot between them. But tonight it had come into the open; they were quite certain of it, and rather superb. She looked at them with her penetrant smile.

"Well," she said, "didn't it take you long enough out there?"

"Yes," Bronwen said, laughing.

But she did not try to explain; she was a little confused, with her happiness like pure flame about her.

Rhoda sat thinking about it when they had gone. It gave her an odd sense of satisfaction, quite apart from her feeling for either of them, to think that they would marry, that there would perhaps be children who would be of her blood and of Brand's. Since Virgil's death she seemed to herself to have been living as if she were standing face to face with a blank wall. And now, suddenly, there was this new door opening before her. It was very touching and wonderful to her.

She wanted to speak to Brand about it. But she did not often see him now. It was just at the time that he intended to break off his connection with Magnus. Then, a week or two later, she heard from Bronwen that he had gone out of town for a few days, to a medical convention in the East. It was rather odd, she thought; he had not much use for meetings of that sort.

She felt a return of her old, wearying apprehension for him. He had said very little to her about his decision to break off with Magnus. They had never quite been able to get over the distance between them that had begun when he had first accepted the position; there was an awkwardness, what seemed a resentment on his part, and a coldness on hers. And even when he had made up his mind to put an end to the situation that had caused the division between them, he still had not come to tell her of it himself. She had had to hear of it indirectly, through Bronwen and Sam. And it was from Bronwen too that she had learned that there had been some difficulty with Magnus; he was reluctant to have Brand go, his curious, naïve vanity exacerbated because the other wanted to be free of the connection. She was half-afraid that there would be trouble ahead for Brand; Magnus's influence in the city was very wide, and he might make it difficult for him if he chose to. She was not even certain in herself that Brand would keep to his resolution of leaving Magnus if it was made perfectly plain to him that there *would* be those difficulties. She thought that he had based his decision on the certainty that he would be able to retain the

practice he had built **up** during the past few years. And if he saw
that this was impossible, she did not know what he would do. Only
she believed she understood how hard it would be for him to give
up all that he had gained by his association with Magnus.

On the evening that he was expected back, she was sitting in the
parlor of the Cannon House, reading before the fire. It was a clear,
dark-blue autumn night, very hard and still, holding the house
strongly in its stillness. She heard someone come in at the front
door, which was seldom locked. She looked up. Brand had come in,
and was standing in the hall.

"Why, what are you doing here?" she called out.

He came to the doorway. And for some reason she was reminded
of the evening, years before, the day after they had quarreled about
his decision to leave the night school, when he had come into the
house and stood just there, as he was doing now, looking as though
he were not certain of his welcome.

"What is it?" she asked again, putting aside her book and looking
at him. "Why don't you come in and sit down?"

"Thanks. I will."

He took off his coat and came into the room. She saw that he
was deliberate and reserved, as he was when he had something on
his mind.

"When did you get back?" she asked him, seeing that he would
not begin of himself.

"Just now. I haven't been home."

She understood that he had something important to tell her. She
sat looking at him, waiting.

"Well," he said bluntly, after a few moments had passed, "I may
as well tell you. I'm going to leave Cannon Hill. I didn't want to
say anything till I saw whether I could work things out. But it's all
settled now—"

She could not really believe it, what he was saying. She sat staring
at him with her brows bent, arrested, leaning forward a little in her
chair. Then an idea came to her, an explanation. She raised her
head slightly.

"You've been to John Bart?" she asked him. "You're taking a
laboratory position?"

But he shook his head. "No, it's nothing like that." He looked at her rather challengingly, waiting for her response. "I'm going back to practice where I came from," he said, "to a little mining town you'll never have heard of—Spartacus—about twenty miles from where I used to live."

She was too unprepared; there was only the shock of surprise for her for the moment. As she tried to gather herself, she saw his face change, the heavy obstinacy coming into it.

"Well," he said shortly, "that's all there is about it." He could not wait for her understanding; he wanted it whole and clear, or not at all. "I thought I'd tell you," he said, flatly.

She knew his disappointment as well as if he had put it into words. And it was a kind of fierce joy to her, that he had come to her for understanding when there had been no one else to whom he could bring this decision that had sprung from the deepest roots of himself. It had been so long now since he had turned to her for anything. She understood suddenly that it was with him almost as it had been in the old days, when there had been no one but her to understand what it was that he saw when he looked at himself in the world. So he had come to her, hoping for that understanding again. And because he was not sure even of her response, he could not wait for it; he wanted it at once, without question or cavil.

He would have gone now, straight out of the house, in his hot disappointment. After all, he was sore and sensitive about this; he knew what a fool he would be called to throw away the position that he had built up here with such effort. But she stopped him; she spoke to him emphatically, in her haste.

"Sit down," she said. "*Goodness!* you come in here with a piece of news like this, and you expect a person to take it all in a single swallow. I want to know *all* about it."

She sat watching him demandingly, holding him with her keen, deep gaze. And after a moment the defeated expression disappeared from his face. He understood her; he understood that she was offering him her pride in him, her readiness to approve of what he had done. He needed few people in his life, but there were these moments of blind, almost instinctive action when the need was imperative in him to feel that he was not standing utterly alone, a single grain of defiance beneath the whole crushing weight of prudence and logic. And it was she who could best give him that hard, practical faith, that understanding that did not need to be put into words.

He did not sit down again, but he stood before the mantel, talking to her. It was very simple, what he had to tell her. Ever since he had begun to examine his position with Magnus, when the first stubborn satisfaction in his success had begun to die down in him, he had been tormented by a contempt for himself that had in it all the black Celtic fury before disillusionment. Very well: he had his comfortable world, his success; he was Doctor Brand; he had done the thing that he had set out to do. And yet all the while he knew that it was not enough; it was not what he wanted. He had to be *all* right with himself, as Bronwen had said; compromise was a kind of death to him, a wall of blankness to beat against. And it was not of this that he had thought during those years at the Cannon House, of this careful, comfortable existence in which he served people who would have been served as well even though he had disappeared from the face of the earth. He wanted something more, the sense of his absolute necessity to a group of people, as a lover demands the sense of his absolute necessity to his beloved. He could not put it into words, but he wanted it. When he thought of spending the rest of his life in Cannon Hill, even though he would be free of his connection with Magnus, he felt as if he were being shut in, imprisoned away from his proper air.

And at last, very suddenly, one night when he had not been able to sleep with the irritation of thinking of it, and had gone out for a walk, he had simply made up his mind to throw it all up, to go back to a place where he knew he would be in contact with what to him were the essentials of his profession—human beings in need of help which he alone was willing to give them. It was a night of full moonlight; there was an exaggerated brilliance drenching the earth. And he felt suddenly that all his powers of being had come alive again, as it had not happened to him since he was a young man. He did not *make* his plan; it was simply there for him, quite plain and familiar, as if he had been living with it for a long time and had now only consciously looked at it. The very next day he had begun his inquiries. And now he had settled everything; he would leave for Spartacus as soon as he could wind up his affairs in Cannon Hill.

Listening to him, Rhoda thought with a kind of despair of the difficulties that he was plunging into again—the indifference, prejudice, and distrust that would rise up against him in the old weary human pattern, different in outward form but not in inner meaning. She knew that for thousands of years men had worn their lives out in the simple wish to *give* instead of take from their fellow men, and that oftener than not their reward had been no more than the mistrust or contempt of those whom they had come to serve. Still one could not give up because of that. And she realized that this at last was right for him, that it was something he must do for himself as well as for others. So she acquiesced. He would do what he could: that was enough. There were few men who would do as much. And she gave him the full weight of her approval. Only the sense of loss rose in her when she thought of his going away.

They sat talking for a long while in the bare living room, with the hard quiet autumn night outside. She looked at him, still in mid-forties the same rude, powerful figure, with the old slouch of the mines still on his shoulders, as it had been when he had first come to her door. He would not be out of place in Spartacus. She saw that there was a kind of wholeness in his life, as there is only in those existences which center inevitably about a single large idea. There would be deviations and irregularities, but the pattern would be there, broadly outlined, as if by so many simple strokes of a pen. She knew so many people whose lives seemed mere pastiches, made up of the incongruous tags and ends of other peoples' existences. It was good to find one that set down its own design boldly and surely, without regard for the prejudices or the preferences of others. And she knew that she had helped to form that design. It was what she had always wanted: a strong clear impress made on life.

Brand left for Spartacus late in November. For the first week Bronwen was with him; she wanted to see for herself that he was settled comfortably there. She and Sam were to be married in a month or so, when he had carried out his plans for the farm he was buying in the valley. Meantime she would stay with Rhoda, at the Cannon House.

Mattie was going to live with the Kroeners. Bronwen had been to see her, when Sam had told her that they were to be married, but there was the old gulf between them that had been there ever since Bronwen had been a child. The older woman could never bring herself to live under the same roof with her, to feel that she was not the mistress in her son's home. But she would not confess that it was her own dislike of this that was preventing her from being with Sam. She made his life very bitter for him with her attitude that she was not wanted in his home. And then one evening, just when she had driven him to the point where he had turned on her in Bronwen's defense, she left him and walked straight out of the living room, where they had been talking; he found her in the kitchen, sitting in a chair with her mending basket on her lap, her head bent, crying, as she tried to fit a sock over her darning egg. He could not bear to see her cry; he wanted to make it up to her. But she stifled herself, she drew away from him again. Her love was so touching and wearisome to him, with its perpetual measurings of right and wrong, its rigid sentimentality. Yet he could not make himself over to be as she wished. He realized that they were better apart.

He wanted it all to be settled now, for the last ends of this old life to be cut off sharply, so that he and Bronwen could begin the new. During the week that she was in Spartacus with Brand, he made the final arrangements for selling the house on Sherman Street. It was a wrench for him to give it up; it seemed to him that he was losing the only part of his father, of his own past, that still remained to him. But he had to break clean. The house was the last symbol of his minority. He stood free and solitary, waiting for the new creation of existence between himself and Bronwen.

On the Sunday of her return, he went to the Cannon Hill station to meet her. For two days past it had been raining, but that afternoon it had begun to clear, and when he walked out to the station, shortly after five o'clock, it was wet and fresh, the buildings and the bare trees drenched with damp, and the low sky trailing still with mist. The train was late, and he stood outside on the platform, waiting. There was a feeling of oppression on him from the events of the past few days. He wanted the train to come quickly. He walked up and down restlessly on the platform.

But when the train came at last he stood back, waiting still, rather obstinate in his mood of emptiness. A group of people crowded past him on their way to the train. Then he saw her behind them, just coming down the steps, in a coat of strong blue color, with a round, turned-back collar, like a schoolgirl's. And for a moment he could not move; he was struck through with such a flood of happiness, as if the whole world, everything about him, had suddenly fallen into place, become whole and ordered once more. He saw her looking about for him, standing just where she had gotten off the train. He went toward her quickly. There was something so lost and unyielding about her, standing there alone. It made his heart turn to look at her.

He stopped before her. "Was it a bad trip?" he asked.

She shook her head, looking up at him with a faint, withheld smile before all these others.

"No," she said. "It's really not far, you know." She glanced about, wanting to get away.

"Do you want to go right on over to the Cannon House?" he asked.

"Must we?"

"No." He wanted them, too, to be by themselves for a while first. "We can leave your suitcase here," he said; "I'll pick it up later. Where do you want to go?"

But it made no difference to her; she only wanted to be alone with him. They walked away from the station, without purpose, past the Cannon House, along the wet road beyond.

"How is it going to be there for Rob?" he asked her, after they had walked on for a little in silence.

"I don't know." She had not talked much to him about Brand's decision; he felt that it seemed something rather strange and alien to her. She did not quite understand how people could take their lives in their hands so, with a kind of deliberate violence. "It's such a hopeless, ugly place," she said. "I don't think I could bear it, to live there."

He felt a heaviness in her, the strain of her wanting to understand, to share something that was out of her world.

"Don't worry about it, Bron," he said to her. "It's what he wants."

"Yes," she said, agreeing, but still broodingly, "it's what he wants."

They had walked out past the factories to where the road strode past the open fields beyond. They were all bare and flooded now under the clearing sky, with gleams of light from the setting sun reflected from each little depression where the water was still standing. And all at once Bronwen stood still, looking at it, the drenched fields, the falling sun burning through the mist, the trees standing bare and powerful overhead. It came to her how good it was, how good, and how powerful with life. She saw it as if for the first time, new-created for them, and thrusting life on her, whether she fought it or accepted it, as it thrust life on each blade and root that would quicken in the spring. It gave her a kind of peace to feel this, to feel herself passive as the earth under the clearing skies. What did it matter, after all, so long as one could be a part of this universal life? And as she stood there the exultance came up in her; she turned quickly to Sam, wanting him to see this too, to look on the fields and the trees and the setting sun with the same wide love that was opening in her.

"And this," she cried, in her quick, joyous wonder, "this is what *we* want—isn't it?"

He looked at her, understanding. The sun was going down slowly, in its red simplicity, over the earth. They stood together on the wet, glowing road.